POCKETS OF DARKNESS

POCKETS OF DARKNESS

JEAN RABE

Boone Street Press

POCKETS *of* DARKNESS

Businesswoman…antiques expert…and cursed
by a demon!

Jean Rabe

Boone Street Press

Boone Street Press
Illinois

POCKETS OF DARKNESS
Copyright © 2015, 2021 Jean Rabe

First Boone Street Press Edition: 2021

Name: Rabe, Jean, author

Title: Pockets of Darkness / Jean Rabe

Description: First Edition. Boone Street Press

Identifiers: ISBN 13: 978-1-7325267-3-0

LCCN:

Printed in the United States of America

✾ Created with Vellum

For Donna Thomsen,
who breathed life into my city

1

Elijah rocked back on the heels of his Brunello Cucinelli wingtips. He drew his collar up and fixed his gaze on the weathered sign hanging slightly askew above the door: DON'T JUDGE A BOOK ...

By what? By its cover, the saying went.

His mind replaced the ellipsis with something more fitting: by the neighborhood it's sold in. This was an abysmal borough, and the buildings—this one in particular—ought to be condemned. The structures were grimy shades of gray, separated here and there by darker charcoal smudges of alleys. Despite the cold wind that deadened his senses he smelled grease and dirt and the biting odor of piss.

Elijah couldn't remember when, if ever, he'd been in a part of the city so beat down.

A siren's wail sliced through the air. Always he could hear sirens in the city. It just seemed a little louder here, more desperate. There were other traffic sounds, too, but from beyond his line of sight—the constant shush of tires against pavement oddly snowless for the middle of January, the blat of horns. There'd been only a couple of cars trundling along in this block, more rust than paint, their occupants eyeing him, necks craning as they drifted past. Not a single cab.

He'd taken one from Hudson Street, but it dropped him off five blocks to the south. He'd written the address of this bookseller wrong, transposing the first two numbers, and so he'd had to hoof it for a stretch.

Don't judge a book by the absolute utter dump it sits in, he mused. After several minutes he had made no move to step inside.

Elijah shuddered when three teenagers swaggered past, one purposefully elbowing him to set him off balance.

"'Scuse me," the youth laughed.

The trio stopped a few doors down and huddled in conversation; the one who'd bumped him had a flat, angry face and gave him a serious up and down. Elijah knew they were talking about him.

With any luck they'd mug him. His appearance practically screamed: *Come and get me!* Middle-aged white man in a sheepskin-lined overcoat, designer shoes, thick leather briefcase at his side that looked a few decades out of date, but by its bulk promising something interesting inside. He looked down at the briefcase and sneered.

Elijah wore a Rolex. He worked his arm so the coat sleeve came up to show the watch. It was 5:45. According to a placard nailed to the door, the bookseller closed in fifteen minutes.

Please come and get me! he silently begged. *Dear, God, let them come and get me.*

He'd been mugged a few times this month and emerged with only a handful of stitches and bruises that he'd hid beneath his expensive clothes and that had cleared up quickly. Just last week he tarried at a Brownsville subway stop in the early morning hours when some homeless man took the bait and beat him up. Didn't take the watch, or the briefcase, only his wallet and the virgin wool Armani jacket he'd been wearing at the time.

He didn't file a report with the police, not then or the times before. The hoods were only after his cash on all those occasions, and he never carried more than a few hundred. No serious damage done, no lingering wounds or scars. *Didn't muggers recognize a Rolex?*

He'd tried the ploy again just two nights ago, this time braving one of the subway stops in Washington Heights. Two muscle-bound gang members with matching tats had been intent on taking him up on his unspoken offer: *Come and get me.* But a cop appeared on the steps, and they veered away. Tired, Elijah had called it a night.

This trio? They might prove his salvation and negate the need to enter the bookseller and shell out a considerable amount of cash. He could weather one more beating, couldn't he?

"Come and get me you sons of bitches," he whispered. "Come and fuckin' get me. Come and take it all, assholes."

The one who'd bumped him had a gun. Elijah saw the grip of it when the kid adjusted his hoodie. His stomach twisted. He just wanted them to mug him, to rob him blind. Take everything and thereby save his soul. But the gun had escalated the threat; he did not want to die.

The tallest said something loudly in Spanish: *something something idioto rico something else.*

Elijah recognized "idiot" and figured they were talking about him.

"*El necio se quede parado alli,*" the tall one said. "*Idioto.*" A pause. "*Ahora!*"

They all faced Elijah. The gun he'd spotted was drawn, along with a second that was waved proudly like a flag. More Spanish was uttered; they rushed at him, and …

Elijah propelled himself forward and into the bookshop, closing the door behind him and exhaling loudly.

"*Más tarde!*" The tall one called through the glass. He tapped on the door with the gun for effect. "*Vamos a esperar para usted.*"

Elijah didn't know a lick of Spanish, but the threat was clear enough. He expected them to follow him inside, but that didn't happen.

"Come and get me. Yeah, right," he mumbled. "Come and fuckin' get me."

3

2

The three youths walked past the bookseller twice more, peering in through the window and tapping on it. They crossed the street and disappeared from view.

Elijah relaxed.

"Los hombres se quedará fuera. The *cholos* won't come in here, no."

Though narrow, the shop was deep, and Elijah had to walk in farther to see the speaker: a woman in the back corner. She sat behind a pitted wood counter that had an old-time cash register on it.

"The *cholos* are afraid of me." Her accent was thick, and Elijah had to concentrate to pick through it. "But they might wait for you, dressed the way you are, fancy man. Call a cab when you're done shopping, yes." A pause: "And you better shop fast, *hombre muy blanco.* I close in a few and I'm thirsty. *Qué chamaco más lindo.*"

She was Latin, he assumed, like everyone else he'd seen since hitting this section of the city. Small, almost tiny, certainly not even five feet. Her hands and fingers fluttered like bird wings. At first glance he guessed her to be about twenty, but she was maybe twice that; she had little age crinkles at the corners of her eyes.

"Excuse me, I—" He continued to stare. The woman's sweater was a stark white cable knit, thick and without any indication of nubs from wear. Elijah knew clothes; it wasn't cheap. "I'm not here for books." He looked down and to his right. "I'm here for ... I'm looking for—"

"We don't carry those dirty magazines."

"No. I'm—"

She drew her lower lip under her teeth, and her eyes narrowed as she studied him. She had a nametag, a little plastic one: ADIELLA. It was Hebrew; his own name came from Hebrew and meant the Lord is my God. He didn't know what hers meant, and it didn't matter; a Hebrew name certainly didn't fit her.

"You Elijah Stone? The *güey* who called yesterday?" She wore lots of makeup, silvery blue shadow and long eyelashes that were probably false. Her manicured nails were painted peach and tipped in glitter. "You called and—"

"Yes. I called yesterday. I—" Elijah noticed two customers in the shop, an elderly woman and a teenage boy who carried a plastic shopping bag that advertised DOLLAR GENERAL. Maybe grandson and grandmother. Both Latino. Elijah figured he was the only white man in the neighborhood. The pair stood in front of a shelf of books with Spanish titles. "I called yesterday afternoon. It was about—"

Adiella shook her head, her bird-fingers fluttering faster. Huge silver hoop earrings bumped against her shoulders. A wooden necklace with colorful beads carved in the shapes of wild animals dangled from her neck, and a silk scarf with more animals on it was wrapped tight around her head, hiding whatever hair she had. "This business we will conduct is for after hours. Like I told you yesterday, yes. The Corona will wait for me a little while." She looked to her customers. "And you'll have to wait too, Elijah Stone ... for a few."

Elijah shifted his weight to the balls of his feet and set the briefcase down, scowling. The floor was a dark hardwood, deeply scuffed and with no trace of wax, gently dipping in places. He unbuttoned his coat. It was warm in here; or maybe it was just his nerves causing him to sweat. It smelled fusty, the air heavy with old paper.

He glanced at the shelves. Some sections were clearly marked: mystery, science fiction, romance, textbooks. Everything looked used

5

and had colored dots on the spines—red, yellow, blue, green, likely price codes. The covers had been stripped from many of them. The sale rack had no rhyme or reason. William Shakespeare's *Romeo and Juliet* was shelved between a dictionary of word origins and a volume titled *Aviation Awards of Imperial Germany in World War I.*

Don't judge a book by the company it's shelved with, Elijah thought, or by its price. He stepped forward and picked up the Shakespeare. No sticker on its side, but a price was penciled inside: $230, with a line drawn through it and remarked to $90.

Elijah would pay good money for clothes, but for a half-inch thick volume with flea-sized type and dated 1918.... he wouldn't shell out a quarter. He didn't have much time for reading, and when he did it was usually the *Wall Street Journal* on his iPad. Who read real bound books anymore? He only owned a half-dozen—these passed down from his father and kept because he thought they would look good on a shelf. He replaced the Shakespeare.

On the only empty space of wall hung a poster of a border collie leaping into the sky after a toy. The slogan beneath it: *Frisbee-tarianism is the belief that when you die your soul goes up on the roof and gets stuck.*

Elijah suspected his soul was going to be stuck in a very bad place if the bookseller didn't help him. Again he glanced down and to his right.

"*Necesito chamba. Tú sabes de algo.*" The teenager and the old woman were at the counter making their purchases.

"No job here, kid," Adiella said. "I'm the owner and the sole employee. But try El Burrito Loco on the corner. He's looking for a dishwasher."

The teen mumbled a thanks and left with the old woman in tow.

Adiella walked around the counter and to the front of the shop, turned the sign to "closed," and deadbolted the door. Elijah noticed there were no bars to pull across the window like in the other storefronts in the block. He guessed she either wasn't worried the shop would be targeted—her merchandise not appealing to the neighborhood thieves, or she had some security not readily noticeable.

It was growing darker outside. Night rushed at the city during winter. Streetlights popped on as he watched, the ones not broken. Neon flickered from Mo's Tap across the way. A big tan and rust-colored car chugged past, slowed, and a man got out and headed into the bar. Faintly, Elijah heard sirens again.

Adiella had been saying something, but he'd missed the first part.

"... find me, eh?"

He turned from the window and looked at her. She'd taken off her nametag and was smoothing her bird-fingers against her sweater. Her pants were forest green linen, well-tailored and pressed, creased in the front and ending above a pair of khaki tennis shoes that were scuffed on the toes. Elijah gritted his teeth at her fashion faux pas. She was overly dark, had to have some black in her, he decided.

"I said, Elijah Stone, how did such a fancy white man find me?"

He reached into the pocket of his coat and pulled out a business card. Lady Lakshmi was in block letters. Beneath it in italics: fortunes told, séances hosted, exorcisms performed.

"She told me about you. I mentioned that yesterday when I called."

"Because Lakshmi, she couldn't help you." Adiella folded her arms. "Strong in the arts, that woman. And she did nothing? Other than to send you here?" She didn't wait for an answer. "More to the point, how did you find her?"

He didn't answer. A client from a few years ago knew about these places, and Elijah had called in a favor to get a referral. That took him from one shop to the next to the next, most of them in the Village. Finally to Lady Lakshmi in Manhattan, and now here to this dump in the Bronx.

"Ah, secrets, confidences you don't want to reveal, eh?" Adiella shrugged. "No matter then, Elijah Stone. Did Lakshmi tell you I am expensive?"

"I have money." Elijah had a lot of money, and he was willing to give her all of it. Every last one of his more than considerable cents. I don't care what it costs, he almost said. Could she read the anxiety in his voice?

"I charge by the hour," she said. "Three thousand."

"How long will it—"

7

"More, depending."

"Depending on—" In truth he didn't care. "Just … can you just—"

Adiella stepped past him and slipped behind the counter again. He caught a whiff of her: she had on something by Estée Lauder. Probably White Linen, running about $80 a bottle. His secretary only wore Estée fragrances, and after half a dozen years he was intimately familiar with her and them. Another whiff: definitely White Linen. The floor had creaked with every step he took in this shop, but Adiella moved soundless across it, graceful like a cat. Keeping her eyes on him, she reached low and brought out two thick red candles, reached again and retrieved a heavy-looking book.

"You're going to do this here? In a bookstore?"

"From the street, no one can see into this corner," she said.

"Excuse me," Elijah said. "Don't you want to know what the problem is? Why I've—"

A wave of her bird-fingers, and he shut up. She lit the candles and flicked the light switch behind her, dropping the shop into shadows.

The candles smelled of something exotic that Elijah couldn't place; it blended well with her perfume. He stared at the flames, straight and tall as if they'd been painted in place.

He padded closer and felt a heady rush of dizziness, like he'd just done a line of the purest coke and was floating from the effects. Adiella's lips worked, but no words came out, her thin fingers twitching rapidly. In fact, Elijah could no longer hear anything: no sirens, no shush from cars, no music from the bar that had its door wide open despite the cold. He swallowed and tapped his foot and couldn't hear that either. Her bird-fingers fluttered, and he saw a pattern to the movements, like a woman knitting.

Dizzier still, he watched her open the book and turn to the center. It was written in a foreign language, looking like Japanese or Chinese Kanji. He couldn't see it clearly. Her fingers floated across the characters as if she was reading Braille. He noticed wrinkles on the backs of her hands and studied her more closely. No lines on her face save around her eyes. Those eyes had a rheumy look, the brown of them washed out. Perhaps she was quite a bit older than he'd first placed her. A strand of white hair came free from beneath her scarf to tease her ear. There was roundness to her shoulders that hadn't been there before and that also spoke of age. Her mouth continued to work.

Still no noise.

She was attractive, no matter her years. Her face heart-shaped, cheekbones prominent, nose flared a little, eyebrows high and thin, expertly shaped. Her lips were a fleshy-brown. They'd been red when he first entered the shop; he remembered that. Elijah was good at catching details. She'd been sucking her lower lip under her teeth, rubbing away the shade of lipstick she'd had on. He spotted a fleck of red on a front tooth. Lipstick?

Blood?

What made him think it might be blood?

His knees started to buckle and he reached forward and grabbed the edge of the counter. In that instant sounds rushed at him: her voice, husky and melodic, like a spoken song that he couldn't understand; a faint police siren; music, a bluesy piece that probably came from the bar; laughter from some dive apartment directly overhead; a car door slamming; someone yelling in Spanish. *Cojones*, he made out that word. *"Estás barracho,"* he heard following something shattering upstairs.

Elijah heard his heart, too. It pounded and threatened to ride up into his throat. Was it nerves, or the result of a spell she was working? A handful of weeks ago he would've laughed at the notion of magical spells, witches, and the like. But not now ... now he knew they existed in the city's dark heart, hidden and almost impossible for the Average Joe to find.

Expensive to find.

Three thousand by the hour, she'd said.

He'd already dropped thirty grand just getting to this point.

The bar music changed. Something old and gravelly like a Louis Armstrong rip-off. More cars went by. The siren faded. Adiella talked louder, her words sing-song now, and still nothing familiar, though certainly not Spanish. Lady Lakshmi said this woman was the very

9

best.... if only she could be persuaded to help. And apparently he had persuaded her with his promise of money.

Three thousand an hour.

She hadn't even asked him what he needed. Did she know? Could she see it? He looked down and to his right. Was she just filling time with her mumbo-jumbo to bilk him out of money? Or maybe Lady Lakshmi had told her about the ... thing. Maybe traffickers in magic gossiped.

The ceiling creaked. Someone walking overhead, something else shattering—a plate maybe. A second set of footsteps, heavier. A shrill cry, then laughter, a hush, and moments later rhythmic banging; a headboard against a wall, he guessed.

Adiella's voice grew louder still.

Time passed and the banging overhead stopped. An angry car horn blatted out on the street. He heard shouts from an argument and then the horn barking again, but he didn't step away or turn his head to glance out the window. Elijah intently watched Adiella.

Her fingers drifted off the page and gestured like a conductor might to an orchestra. Finally the candle flames moved and smoke trailed up from them—diaphanous serpents rising to join the patterns on the painted tin ceiling. She trembled and her face practically glowed with a fine sheen of sweat. He watched her gulp in the fusty air. Her chest heaved.

Another tune came on across the street; he recognized Wynton Marsalis' *Root Groove*. Another siren wailed. The couple upstairs giggled and turned on a television.

Adiella coughed and slumped forward, hands splayed across the spread in the book and small body quivering.

Is she all right, he wondered, or is this a part of some elaborate act? He opened his mouth, then thought better and waited quietly.

After a few moments she righted herself and reached to the wall behind her, flicked on the lights and blew out the candles. She closed her eyes and let a silence settle between them. In it he listened to an argument out on the street and what he thought was either a gunshot or a car backfiring. Theme music from an old sitcom trickled down from upstairs.

"You have acquired a demon," she pronounced.

Elijah pushed away from the counter. "A demon? You know for certain that's what it is? It's a demon? A real demon? Fire-and-brimstone from hell?"

"An old demon, a soul beast." She shook her head, more wisps of white hair coming loose from her scarf. Definitely some age to her. Maybe sixty, shrunken from the decades. Maybe she could appear whatever age she wanted.

"Can you see it? This demon?" He didn't bother to hide the incredulity in his voice. "Did your ... spell ... whatever it was you did ... let you *really* see it?"

"See it? The beast is here? In my shop?" Her eyes went wide, a mix of surprise and anger. "You brought a demon into my shop? You dare?"

"Of course it's in your shop."

"You dare! You brought it with you?" Her face drew forward into a point. "You dare!" She shouted at him and made the sign of the cross.

"I can't help but bring it with me! It goes where I go. I could have explained that if you'd—"

She dismissed him with a snarl, closed her eyes, and whispered, rolled her head like she was working out a kink in her neck. Her voice sounded like wind seeping in under a door, a gentle and persistent susurrus that went on at length. When she opened her eyes again her expression was calm, and her voice was even.

"I cannot see the demon, no, Elijah Stone. "Where is it?"

"Right next to me. *It's always right next to me.* It's staring at you." He pointed to a spot near the briefcase.

"Ah, that is what I feel. I feel its eyes on me."

"So get rid of it!" Elijah ground his foot against the floorboards. "That's what I'm paying you three thousand an hour for, right? Get rid of it. That's what I came here for, what Lady Lakshmi sent me here for. Just get rid of the damn thing." *Please, dear God, get rid of it.*

Adiella turned a page in the book and read silently while Elijah continued to fume and worry. She reached below the counter and brought out a second book, and later a third.

A car with a busted muffler clunked by. Another revved its engine. He heard shouts in Spanish, then things settled down and the bar music caught his attention: Kanye West's *Coldest Winter*. Appropriate for the weather, he thought. More time passed, and Elijah's legs grew sore from standing. The couple upstairs turned off the television. He looked at his Rolex: 9:15. Had three hours really passed? No wonder his legs felt like wood and his feet were numb. He needed a restroom.

A fourth book came out, this one about the size of the Shakespeare tome he'd glanced at earlier. She relit the candles, turned off the lights, and started chanting more erratically than before. The animal beads clacked as she twisted this way and that, her shoulders jerking.

"Is it gone?" she asked, finishing undeterminable minutes later. She looked even older to Elijah now, eighty, ninety, brittle and frail like she might break with any breath, like casting the spell had added decades to her small frame.

"No. It's not gone. It's still watching you, and it's babbling in some language I can't understand. It's always babbling." He rubbed the side of his head. "It only shuts up when I'm sleeping."

"This demon," she said, squaring her shoulders and again blowing out the candles. She waited a beat before turning the lights on. It looked like a few of those decades had melted from her, and she stood a little taller. She made the sign of the cross once more. "This demon, describe it to me, yes."

"It's fuckin' ugly."

"In detail, please."

When Elijah finished his account he crossed his arms. "Shouldn't you have asked me about this, oh, say nine thousand dollars ago? Tell you what it looks like? Sounds like? It smells, too. In fact—"

"It is not a demon I am familiar with, Elijah Stone." She tucked the errant hairs back under her scarf. "And I have faced many demons. I have exhausted my magic in an effort to sever this parti-cular beast from you. It should have worked. My magic is strong."

He would have called her a charlatan, the word churned in his mouth, ready to spring out. But he held his tongue and merely thought it. *Rip-off. Fraud. Con artist.* He wasn't about to write her a check. He'd bring out his cell phone, call a cab, maybe call the police while he was at it, and—

"It should have worked, but it is a dominant demon that has attached itself to your soul. As I said, old. Very, very old. It defies me. And that it can hide from my sight ... its power is great. You say it babbles?"

"Well ... it makes noises. I figured it was talking."

"I hear nothing."

"I've gathered pretty quick that only I can see it, and only I can hear it."

"But you can't understand it?"

"Hell no."

"Powerful," she repeated.

"Powerful? Horrible is what it is. And it's caused me nothing but grief. It's ruined my life, ruined everything. It's killed. Because of that ... that ... *thing* I have no one left in my life. My girlfriend, gone. My mother, sister. It's never hurt me, just the women in my life I cared about. It's just me now and that ... that ... damnable demon."

"Lakshmi could do nothing, not exorcise it. And I cannot sever it—"

"So why the hell am I here? Why—"

"But unlike Lakshmi, I can save you, perhaps save your soul. I cannot sever it, but—" She waited a moment. "—I can provide a remedy. And it is not such a difficult one, Elijah Stone."

His bladder threatened to spill over, but he stayed put. "You can't get rid of it, but you know—"

"—someone who can."

Great, Elijah thought. Another business card to send him to another hole-in-the-wall and another fakir. More money tossed away. But any amount of money would be worth it if only—

"You came by this demon, Elijah Stone, by stealing it, yes?"

Elijah swallowed hard.

"That is correct, yes? You stole the demon?"

He shook his head. "I didn't know it was a demon. I didn't see it then. Only after—"

"But you stole it."

"Sort of."

"Yes or—"

"Yes, I stole it. Damn it all to hell, I stole it! But how ... how did you know that?"

"That is how the demon's previous *socio ... marido ... compañaro ... dueño*—" She tried out one word after the next, settling on "—attendant. That is how the previous attendant rid himself of it, had it stolen. My magic told me that much, that greed is probably the trigger to the horrible curse. The covetous pockets of darkness in your soul stirred the demon and attached it to you." She put the candles and books back under the counter. "That man, the previous attendant, he lured you—perhaps not intending you specifically, but lured someone, you—to steal the demon. He must have divined the nature of his curse ... and the remedy. You solved his ugly problem by willingly ... eagerly, in fact ... taking it on yourself. It is how the curse and the beast pass from one to the next. Greed, desire, ambition, those dark pockets, all of those things wrapped in the trigger. The demon cannot be given away."

"Curse." Elijah's jaw clenched. "I am cursed. I stole the briefcase," he admitted.

"Thou shalt not steal," she whispered in her wind-under-the-door voice.

"Two months ago I took it."

"Thinking you had stolen some great corporate secret. That is what you do, yes? Steal secrets from one company and sell them to another?"

Elijah didn't answer.

"It was a secret you stole, but not what you were looking for."

"The briefcase was filled with useless paper. It looked interesting, important at first glance. Looked like what I was after, so I took the case. But I got it home and went through it and found it incomplete, useless."

"And—" she prompted.

His story came out. "I tried to throw it away, but the briefcase reappeared in my office an hour later. The creature showed up with it. I tried to burn the briefcase, but it won't burn. Run over it with a car, it's unscathed. Throw it in the river, and it comes back. I left the briefcase at work, and the damn thing was at home waiting for me, along with the—" He searched for the word and spit it out like a piece of rotten meat. "—demon. I left the briefcase at a park bench, but it appeared in my hand when I called for a cab. I left it behind in the cab, but that didn't work either. I can't lose it, and, you're right, I can't give it away. I've been daring people to mug me. Subways, bus stops, in front of your shop. I wanted someone to steal the damn briefcase just like I'd stolen it. So it seems without any spell or old musty book I'd already hit on the way to get rid of it. The demon is clearly attached to the briefcase. Except no one wants to steal the damn briefcase. My money. My coat. My shoes. Italian hand-stitched, they pried off my feet. They'll take those things. Not the briefcase. Never ever the briefcase."

"That briefcase, Elijah Stone, it looks like something you'd get at Goodwill. Who would want to steal that? And it stinks."

The briefcase did have a rather foul odor to it, Elijah admitted, like banana peels that had blackened in the trash. But the demon itself smelled worse.

"I don't know why I'm the only one who can see it. Only fucked up me." Tears welled in Elijah's eyes. He had taken the briefcase because of what he thought was inside.... what was *supposed* to be inside, what he was going to be paid an ungodly sum of money for. "It's driving me mad."

"I know someone who will steal it from you, Elijah Stone. I know an individual who will unwittingly take your soul beast and your curse and thereby save you."

"You do? How? When?"

15

"Your address," she said. "I will need that."

He fumbled in his wallet and pulled out one of his business cards, smoothing a crinkle in it, and turning it over, retrieving a pen and scrawling an address. "That's where I live."

"Eighty-Fifth and West End. Expensive." She took the card and placed it in a little box next to the cash register.

"How much will all of this—"

She glanced at a clock above the Frisbeetarianism poster. "You owe me twenty-seven thousand, five hundred—"

"Wait a minute, I thought you said three thousand an hour—"

"I thought you did not care what it costs."

Had she read his mind?

"It will take time," she said, "for me to contact this thief. I have included that in my bill."

He pulled out his checkbook and willed his bladder to keep holding. He laid the checkbook on the counter and started writing.

"I prefer a bank check, Elijah Stone. Or cash."

"It won't bounce. My word."

"On your soul, it will not bounce, yes." Her voice had an edge to it. "On your soul which hovers on the brink of damnation because a demon accompanies you."

"And this thief—"

"Is very good."

"I'd have to be in my place when he comes. Because wherever I go, the damned thing goes with me. I'd have to be there and—"

"The thief will come when you're sleeping."

"I sleep like a rock. That's the only time I'm free of the damn demon. Maybe I won't hear him. You said he's good."

"The thief is very good." She examined the check and placed it under the drawer in her cash register. "Now to the matter of the bait."

"Bait?"

"The *cuota*, so to speak. You will have to put something valuable inside your Goodwill case," she said. "Lure the thief just as you were lured with that promise of a corporate secret."

16

"I've been doing that, filling it thick and trying to get a mugger to—"

"Your efforts all failed, obviously. You've not been targeting the right thief. Nor have you been using the right bait."

"What will I need? Money? How much money? And how will you—"

"Nothing mundane, but something valuable. One hundred minimum, I would recommend."

Elijah knew the unspoken word was thousand. One hundred thousand dollars.

"Two hundred. Three hundred if you can afford it. Truly, *much* more to be safe. Something very, very old and worth a great deal. The thief I will send your way likes very old things, antiquities. Things that are singular, one of a kind. It should be ancient."

"An antique."

She laughed. "*Ancient*, I say. Babylonian, Assyrian."

"Babylonian?"

"Egyptian, Persian, Osirian, even Mayan or Aztec or from an Ugir tribe ... that is if you really want to be rid of your demon. Ancient, I said."

"A relic. You're talking about a relic. Museum pieces."

"To be certain the thief takes your bait."

"A relic would be costly. Sotheby's," Elijah said more to himself. "Something from Sotheby's maybe. Christie's—"

"Perhaps something instead from a place less reputable, something from one of the darker markets. Something more ... interesting."

Black market, he mouthed. "I have other sources. I can get something. Ancient, huh? I'll find something so old and so incredibly valuable this thief can't resist." *I don't care what it costs me. Anything! Everything! I'd give up everything!*

"Something that will fit in that briefcase."

"Of course. Something valuable. Who is this thief—"

"Not your concern."

Elijah stared at a spot next to him. Was the demon smiling? It was so very hard to read its expressions. "What's to keep him from just

17

taking the contents, leaving the damnable briefcase behind? What guarantee do I have that—"

"Elijah Stone, just as you took the Goodwill briefcase because you thought something important was inside, this thief will take your briefcase. Then it will be ... what is the expression? Yes, the demon will be the thief's cross to bear."

"I almost feel bad about this, giving the demon to someone else."

"Thieves, Elijah Stone, deserve damnation."

Elijah picked up the briefcase, the handle slippery in his sweaty palm. He noted that the demon squatted next to it, babbling and dripping.

"Buy something soon, yes. And something extra, something for me to use in the luring, a sweet treat to catch the mark's attention. I will need that, a seeding. Then call me to confirm that you have the necessary bait."

"I will buy something ... tomorrow, I hope," he replied. "Tomorrow somehow. Definitely." *Then soon this hellish ordeal will be over.* "Thank you, Adiella."

"My name, Elijah Stone, means ornament of the Lord."

He gave her a last look, all her jewelry and makeup and long, polished fingernails, flawless face with the creases gone from around her eyes. Maybe her name wasn't so inappropriate after all.

Out on the street, he heard a police siren, this one muted by the canyon of buildings.

3

Try it," Bridget said. "I had this meal prepared special."

Otter cut off a small piece and held it close to his eyes. "What is it?"

"Salmon and goat cheese crostini."

Otter wrinkled his nose. "Mom, fifteen, not fifty. I thought we were going out for pizza with Lacy."

Bridget raised an eyebrow.

"My girlfriend, Mom. Lacy."

"I thought her name was Samantha."

"So last year."

"Pizza. We could do that anytime." But Bridget knew that wasn't exactly true. The past two years the visits hadn't held to the schedule —high school field trips and sporting events, supposed cold and flu bugs, and her ex- having other plans. Bridget was lucky if she got to see Otter every other month. She hadn't fought for more time, like perhaps she should have. In fact, she hadn't fought for any time.

"The salmon was shipped from Alaska, caught on the Deshka River," Bridget said. "Delicate, tender flesh, I wanted to—"

"Impress me? Mom, this is what *you* like. This is an old fart's meal. Old fart's music, too. Don't you have any indie rock?"

A cello piece played in the background.

"Old." The word hit Bridget like brick. "I'm thirty-three, Otter." And she knew she could easily pass for ten years younger. Bridget kept in excellent shape. Not a single gray hair had dared to intrude in her curly red mane. "Thirty-three is not even close to approaching old."

Otter shrugged and took a tentative bite of fish and swallowed it. Then he took another. "All right. It's not horrible. Pretty good, actually."

Bridget grinned. Her ex-, when he didn't dine in his own restaurant, was all Hamburger Helper, canned green beans, and Hungry Man frozen meals. She wanted the boy to experience some-thing home cooked and yet refined on these few weekends together.

"I'm glad you like it, Otter. I—" She paused. Bridget always wondered what to talk about with her son: music, movies, thoughts on college and potential future careers ... all of them difficult subjects because she'd rarely paid attention to Otter's interests beyond swimming. Bridget knew she hadn't been the best mother even in the earliest years. Married too young. Pregnant too quick. She wasn't mother material, but she loved Otter and wanted him to think well of her.

"I was wondering about your swimming competitions. Do you have one coming up?" At least she knew her son was into that. The boy was named Otemar after his grandfather on his father's side. But because of the boy's proclivity to embrace anything to do with water, they'd hit upon Otter right away. Otter Madera was the name announced at the awards ceremonies and listed next to each swimming record broken at Léman Manhattan Prep. Though a sophomore, he was more than good enough to compete on the varsity team.

Otter talked for several minutes about an upcoming meet in New Jersey. "Lacy said she'd come," he finished. "Hey, do you think you might—"

"Because tonight's your birthday, I thought it would be acceptable for a little alcohol." Bridget rang a small bell to the side of her plate,

20

putting off the question of her attending the swim event. "Just don't tell your father."

Otter pushed aside the first course, having eaten more than half of it. He gave a smirk. "Fifteen, Mom. I've had alcohol plenty—"

Bridget didn't want the particulars and waved away the rest of Otter's words. She suspected the unfinished phrase was: *plenty of times.* She didn't want to know if her son frequently came by six packs of beer with a fake I.D. or if someone bought something harder for him. Neither did she want to lecture him about the ills of underage drinking, at least not tonight.

"So, by alcohol, you mean wine, right, Mom?" Otter looked from one glass to the next. There were three fluted ones in front of his setting, only one full, and that with Perrier water. "Wine. Probably dry as the Sahara and with a cork, no Mad Dog, no Riuniti on ice, no screw-cap strawberry zinfandel fruity stuff for—"

The chef saved Otter from more speculation. He brought out the second course. "Ceviche martini," he announced, looking straight at Bridget. "It is low calorie, one of my specialties. The acid in the lime juice pickles the shrimp to perfection."

Otter wrinkled his nose again. "A martini. Not the alcohol I was hoping for."

"Low calorie? Are you saying I'm fat, Dustin?" Bridget asked him.

"Not at all, *ma chère.* Far from it, in fact." Dustin winked at her. "I just want to make sure you don't get that way." He brushed Bridget's arm when he placed the martini in front of her, his fingers lingering against her wrist before returning to the kitchen.

Otter stared at his glass and selected a spoon out of order and played with the shrimp. "He's new, Dustin. Good looking. And young. Where did you find him?"

Dustin wasn't exactly "new," he'd been in Bridget's employ for about six months. But Otter hadn't been here before when the chef was around. "He's studying at the International Culinary Center—"

"Ah, a college student. He *is* young." Otter tried the shrimp and apparently found it palatable. He made short work of the martini.

"Dustin's not *that* young, Otter. He—"

21

"Are you sleeping with him?"

A piece of shrimp caught in Bridget's throat. "I—" She wanted to tell her son it was a rude question, and none of his business. "Sometimes."

"But not as often as you'd like, huh?" Otter stared at the kitchen door. "What's next?"

Dustin came back, presenting a Caesar salad. "Simple," he said. "But it is elegant and good for you." He cracked pepper over the top and disappeared again.

"He smells good," Otter admitted. "I'd guess he's closer to my age than yours. Dad would go for him."

Again Bridget wanted to say "it's none of your business," but she worked on the salad. Music continued softly—Mstislav Rostro-povich playing Bach's *Cello-Suiten*. It was the second suite, considered *Sorrow and Intensity*, a direct contrast to the first because of its pace and minor key. It was Bridget's favorite, musically vulnerable and sincere. She wished her son could appreciate the cellist's capacity to evoke the perfect sadness of the composition, but she knew Otter wasn't truly paying attention to it. "He's twenty-two, Otter." *If you're that damn curious*, she thought. *Eleven years younger than me. But you can do the math yourself.*

Otter nodded, and then said softly: "About the same age as one of Dad's last flings."

Dustin brought out the fourth course.

"Coffee and spice-rubbed lamb," he told Otter, as he arranged the dish. "I prepared it with pinot noir. The side is garlic mashed potatoes."

"Lamb," Otter said dully. "And the good china no less. Happy birthday to me." He ran his thumb around the edge of the plate; it was bone white trimmed with platinum. Then he traced the pattern in the Irish linen tablecloth. "Happy birthday, happy birthday—"

"Otter, I—"

"Sorry, Mom. I appreciate this, I really do. I just wanted you to meet Lacy, that's all." He cut into the lamb and started chewing. "Wow. This is really good. I—"

All hell broke loose.

The dining room window shattered, showering the table with glass. Three masked men in dark clothes somersaulted in, the one in the lead drawing a gun.

"No one move!" the gunman barked. "Hands up. Push back from the table."

Dustin screamed and dropped the cheese tray meant to be the fifth course. He swayed and fainted in a heap.

"Mom?" Otter glanced between Bridget and the men, her hands were up just like the gunman had ordered.

"No one needs to get hurt," Bridget said. She edged back from the table, her napkin falling to the floor. "What do you want?"

"Everything of value," the gunman said, clearly the leader of the trio. "Let's start with the cash and jewelry on you. If you're quick and cooperative, you live."

4

They were uncommon burglars. Bridget's formal dining room was on the third floor of her five-story brownstone, and so they had scaled the wall or jumped across from a neighboring building, either proposition requiring some athletic skill. Despite building codes, there was no external fire escape for them to climb; Bridget had that removed when she bought the place.

"If you don't cooperate," the tallest said. "Well—" He let the sentence hang.

Bridget realized their dark clothes had let them blend with the shadows, escaping notice by the block's elderly lookiloos who were usually perched by their windows and who would have called the police. The clothes were tight, at the same time not restricting their movements and revealing them to be muscular. What little skin that showed had been blackened.

Professionals.

"Money and jewelry first," the lead repeated, waggling the Glock for effect. He was the shortest of the three. "Be quick about it, eh? Then we'll get to the good stuff you have stashed. The stuff too good to keep in your shop. We're in a hurry. Places to go and all of that, you know. Chop. Chop."

He had a gentle southern accent; Bridget placed him from Georgia. The other two clearly looked to him for direction. He stayed to the right of the window, out of sight to anyone who might chance to look in, and gestured with his head to the others. They split up, the one in gray going to Bridget, the tallest to Otter. Each produced a black bag and opened it.

"Shit," Otter said, as he took off his watch. "Shit. Shit. Shit. Lacy gave me this." The tall thief took it, held it up, and promptly tossed it on the floor and stomped on it.

"Timex," the thief said. "Not interested. How about the ring?"

"Shit," Otter repeated. "I *just* got this." He worked the bulky class ring off and dropped it in the bag.

"Wallet," the tall thief said. "And that earring, too."

Otter wore a one and a half-carat diamond stud in his right ear; he grudgingly took it out and passed it over.

Bridget hadn't surrendered anything yet. "Leave the boy alone." She looked around the gray-garbed thief and got the attention of the leader. "The boy's just visiting. Understand?" She carefully removed her watch, a stainless steel *Cartier Pasha* she'd paid three thousand for but was worth double that. "The boy is just—"

The lead thief brought the gun up and around and aimed it at Bridget's face. "Shut up, you damn Mick. And where's the safe? A woman like you ... a place like this ... there's a safe. We want the good stuff."

Otter said glumly: "If only we'd gone out for pizza—"

The tall one in front of the boy cuffed him. "Close your mouth."

"Ow!" Otter hollered. "That hurt you son of—" Another cuff, this one harder.

"I said close it!"

The other thieves turned to look at the boy, and Bridget took advantage of the distraction. She brought her leg up in a roundhouse kick that caught the gray-garbed man in the hip. He was solidly built and Bridget only managed to unbalance him, but it was enough. While the man tried to recover, Bridget followed through with a lightning-fast uppercut that connected and sent a busted front tooth flying.

The man grabbed his jaw and doubled over, moaning.

"Marsh! You all right?" This came from the leader. "Marsh? Marsh!"

Marsh wasn't all right. Bridget struck him again with the heel of her hand and stunned him. One more blow and he crumpled in a heap.

"That's it! You move again and I *will* shoot. Ain't nobody gonna hear a gun go off, all their windows closed this winter." Once more the gun was pointed squarely at Bridget.

"All right." Bridget held still, hands to her sides. "All right. Easy. Just don't hurt the boy, hear me?"

"Tell me where the safe is," he retorted. "Tell me now!"

Bridget indicated an oil landscape hanging above a mahogany server. "It's behind that."

"I don't think so," the leader said. "Rob, no more nice and friendly. Grab the boy—"

"No! I said leave the boy alone. Please. The safe is in my office," Bridget said. "The safe with the 'good stuff' you're looking for."

"And where would that be? Your office?" This came from the tall man still menacing Otter. He had worked the boy around to the other side of the room, a good dozen feet away from Bridget. "Where is this office?"

"Upstairs and—"

"Don't tell them, Mom!" Otter moved. He barreled into the tall thief, sending him into the dining table and bending him backward over it.

"That's it!" the leader shouted. "You're both dead. You're both—"

Bridget crouched and sprang at the leader, fists forward and catching him in the stomach. The air "whooshed" out as he fell back with considerable force, upsetting a low table that was against the wall. The silver tea service on it went dancing across the hardwood floor and sugar cubes spun in all directions.

Another punch from Bridget and the gun flew out of the thief's hand and landed in a corner. A quick kick followed, and the man fell on his knees hard. Bridget swung again, but the thief dropped and rolled, then jumped to his feet. He whirled when Bridget came at him once more, bringing up his heel to deliver a solid blow.

It was Bridget's turn to fall back.

"Nobody had to get hurt," the leader hissed. "Not you, not the boy. Now you're—"

Bridget rushed at him, shoulder forward and driving into the thief's chest. Behind them, she heard Otter kicking the tall one.

"You're the ones in danger," Bridget said. She flailed to the right, fingers closing on the back of a chair. She brought it around and struck the thief with it.

"You think?" the leader retorted. He was panting, and he wiped at a line of blood on his mouth. When Bridget raised the chair again, the thief caught it with both hands and wrenched it away, slamming it against the wall. Then he flew at Bridget, ramming her back into the dining table, tipping glasses and toppling a crystal handle holder. The flames played against the linen tablecloth as Bridget got to her feet, winded.

At the same time Otter pressed his own attack, trying to draw the tall thief near the window. Otter was a head shorter than his opponent, but anger clearly fueled him. He grabbed a chair and pressed the legs at the thief.

"Don't call me 'boy,' you son of a bitch!" Otter managed to drive two of the legs into the man's stomach, forcing him against the wall. Their feet crunched over spilled sugar cubes and something crystal that had shattered. The thief's heel caught against the silver teapot and set him off-balance. Otter jabbed him again, but the thief was strong and knocked the chair aside and stayed upright.

"I'll call you whatever the hell I please, *boy*," the tall thief shot back. "I'll call you fancy boy. Pitiful little fancy dancy boy."

Otter dropped the chair and came at him, fists pumping. He swept his leg out and around, turning and smacking the tall man's kneecap.

"Fancy boy, huh?" Otter kicked at him again in the same spot, clamping his hands together to form one fist and swinging hard at the man's chest. "Fancy boy who took two years of taekwondo and six months of boxing."

The thief reeled from Otter's onslaught, but stayed on his feet and managed to dart deeper into the room, while narrowly avoiding Bridget, who was wrestling on the floor with the leader.

Grabbing the tablecloth, the tall thief yanked hard, sending plates and silverware clattering to the floor and keeping Otter at bay for a moment. The linen had caught fire, just enough smoke rising from it now to set off a ceiling sprinkler.

Water showered the combatants and made the floor slick.

"Fancy wet boy," the tall thief sneered. "Soon to be a dead one." He reached behind his back and pulled out a sap. "I'll beat you to death."

"And enjoy it." This came from the leader, who'd gotten the upper hand on Bridget. The thief had Bridget on her stomach and straddled her back. He pulled Bridget's head and shoulders up with a firm chin-lock. "I know I'm certainly going to enjoy finishing this Mick."

"No!" Otter shouted. He ignored his own opponent, whirled, and dove at the lead thief, landing a kick, but not one strong enough to dislodge the man. Otter came at him again, his heel catching the side of the man's face this time; blood sprayed in an arc. "Get off my Mom. Get—"

"That's enough!" This came from Dustin. "Stop it, all of you, before someone really gets hurt." The chef stood just beyond the doublewide doorway to the dining room, pistol in his hand, but pointed at the floor. There were three men with him, all in dark pants and sport coats, one wore a plaid vest. "Everyone up. Game over. I declare Bridget and Otter the clear winners."

The leader got off Bridget. "Hope I didn't hurt you too much, boss." He continued to wipe at the blood on his face. "Your kid's pretty tough, looks like. Gave Rob a run. Holds his own."

Boss? Otter mouthed. A pause. "Cool. Coolest birthday ever! This beats the hell out of my fourteenth." He beamed. "Thanks, Mom."

Bridget was slow to get up, nearly slipping in the water. She ground her teeth together; a couple of ribs were bruised or cracked. Straightening, she brushed at her blouse. Then she looked to the man in the vest. "See to having this cleaned up. And reset the sprinkler system." To the thieves and Otter: "We will convene downstairs in the study after I change." She grinned as she walked past her son and gave him a pat on the back. "Happy Birthday, Otter."

Dustin and the three men backed up to let Bridget through the doorway.

"Dessert for Otter and I," she told Dustin. "That cake you made. But none for our friends here. They won't be staying long."

5

B ridget stood in the shower, relishing the feel of the hot water pounding her back. Steam rose; she should have turned on the fan. It fogged the glass door, and she traced patterns on it, first a crooked smiley face, then a symbol for the Westies, an Irish street gang she belonged to during her teen years. Small then, truly insignificant in numbers now, the Westies had been her family, and she knew that the man who headed it had been a better parent to her than she was to Otter. Maybe not in the guiding hand sense to show her right from wrong, but in all the other ways that really mattered ... being around, being interested and supportive. She'd embraced the Irish-Brooklyn culture, held to some of the slang, and thought of Westies often. She brushed away the symbols and watched the glass fog over again.

At least she had provided Otter with a memorable birthday dinner, and she'd take the boy with her tonight as a treat. *Dear God, don't let the kid talk about any of this with Tavio,* she thought. Her ex- was so Catholic-straight-and-narrow-minded he'd never let her see Otter again. Or was that what she wanted, to completely sever her parental responsibility? That would make Tavio happy.

She was surprised the marriage had lasted as long as it had; her marrying so young and on an impulse, getting pregnant within the first couple of months. The sex had been frequent and good; and he'd bought her enough pretty things to keep her close for nearly ten years. But Bridget's business had lured her away an increasing number of hours—more than Tavio was willing to put up with and for dealings he grew less and less tolerant of. She feared on more than one occasion he'd call the police about her doings. Though Tavio was no angel, he told her she was a bad role model for their son. The divorce was finalized three years ago.

She turned off the water and drew the last traces of steam deep into her lungs, then stepped out and toweled herself carefully—the wrestling match with the thieves had resulted in painfully sore ribs. Already a bruise the size of a dinner plate was showing. She padded to her closet, which had once been a small bedroom, and selected an olive pair of skinny jeans and a black turtleneck. She dressed by the window, looking across at the nearby brownstones of Fort Greene.

It was a Brooklyn neighborhood on the edge of being upscale and trendy. Years past the area had been primarily black, and crime rates were high; now it was truly an ethnic melting pot of upper middle-class, touted by local politicians as being safe enough to walk your dog at three a.m. The sheen of Fort Greene, from Atlantic to Nassau, Flushing to Flatbush, had relaxed some of the residents, lulling them into a sense of security. An area with million-dollar condos? Bridget thought that kind of sparkle attracted criminals.

Rapes, robberies, and felony assaults were up a little, and there were reports of stolen cars every few months. A doughy woman directly across the street had flowers and a bicycle stolen yesterday. Realtors tried hard to downplay all of that.

None of those things worried at her, as she had state-of-the-art security ... though that would have to be analyzed as tonight's thieves had managed to find their way through it. Too, she was part of the criminal element that had crept in.

She loved this brownstone, remodeled and decorated to suit her perfectly, roughly twelve thousand square feet of space. Other buildings in the historic block were apartments and high-end condos that had shot up property values; Bridget's place had a dozen units in it when she'd purchased it four years ago and sent all the tenants elsewhere. She didn't like to share her quarters. She'd paid a little more than eight million for it, but it was easily worth double that now with all the improvements she'd made, including the outer facelift and the addition of a small elevator.

The nearby Pratt Institute gave Fort Greene a reputation of an artistic and cultural center, though the neighborhood's public school rankings were below average. There was a thriving business district a few blocks over—her shop was located smack in the middle of it.

"They're all waiting for you, *mon amour*." Dustin had entered so silently she started. He had changed into Dockers khaki and a bulky sweater that hid his muscles. His shoulder-length hair was pulled back so tight his face appeared sharp, all angles and edges. Handsome? Bridget thought beautiful was a better word.

"Lost in thought," she told him, turning.

Dustin rubbed against her, angling his chin down so he could stare into her face. "Penny for those thoughts, Brie dear. But I would give you a dollar."

She kissed him. He must have showered; he smelled of musk. The kiss was long, and he was the one to finally break it off.

"Otter did not know about you and me, did he?" Dustin thrust out his bottom lip in an adorable pout. "You keep things from him."

"He thinks you're too young for me."

He laughed softly. "He's probably right."

"I'm thirty-three. *Only thirty-three.* He called me old."

"I like older women, Brie. And I like your son. But he is so different than you, *mon amour*."

Bridget raised an eyebrow.

"Your skin." He touched her chin with an index finger. "So pale, you are. Like cream. And he is—"

It was Bridget's turn to laugh. "Otter enjoyed three weeks in Miami with Tavio for his Christmas break. I doubt he spent one minute more than necessary indoors."

"And his hair is like ink and short like a cap. Yours is red like fire."

A frown spread. "Otter has my ex-husband's looks," she sadly admitted. "I see Tavio so clearly in his face."

"But he has your eyes." Dustin kissed her again and tugged her toward the bed. "Let us take our dessert now, eh? I will make you forget all about your ex-husband Tavio."

She almost gave in, as she could never get enough of Dustin. It wasn't close to love, but she recognized that she held certain affections for him—and definitely a physical attraction. Bridget wasn't looking for anything beyond that.

"I will make you forget again and again." His teeth clicked lightly against hers.

Bridget normally had the stamina to keep up with Dustin in bed ... though after her struggle with the thieves, she knew she wouldn't last long tonight.

"Business, remember?" Bridget said reluctantly. "I've an appointment near the docks. I can't miss this one."

"I remember." Dustin sucked on her lower lip and shared her breath. "Business and then pleasure, my Brie." He backed away and went into the closet, returning with a pair of calf-high leather boots. Kneeling in front of her, he helped her put them on. "Then after this business, the pleasure will be mine."

Bridget felt a warmth creep up to her face.

"Your son, he is coming with us to the warehouse?"

Bridget nodded and took a last look out the window. "For his birthday."

"Sweet, odd name, Otter." Dustin paused. "I really do like him."

Bridget smiled. "I'm sure he likes you, too."

He shrugged. "He likes my cooking. I will take that as a good start."

Dustin served the cake on "Happy Birthday" paper plates. It was not lost on Bridget that Otter's piece was twice as big as her own.

"Incredible." Otter made short work of it and asked for seconds. "What is it?"

Dustin smiled. "White chocolate mousse with raspberry sauce, iced with vanilla whipped cream. I just learned it in my dessert class."

"I'm taking the leftovers with me when I go home tomorrow night."

Home. Bridget winced. She had no right to think that Otter would consider this place home, especially as infrequent as the visits had been. She just wished the boy was more delicate with his choice of words.

"If you keep eating like this there will be no leftovers." Dustin waited a moment. "Would you like a third?"

Otter patted his stomach. "I'm good."

Bridget only nibbled at hers. It was, indeed, delicious. But she'd eaten too well at dinner, and her thoughts of the three thieves on the leather couch a dozen feet away upset her stomach. Rob, Marsh, and Lou, the leader. She sat the plate on the coffee table and eased out of the chair, her ribs protesting.

"You're feckin' fools," she said, walking toward them. All three had removed their masks. Marsh, the one Bridget had cold-cocked, was still woozy, staring forward with a vacant expression.

Rob sat in the middle. Though he nodded in agreement, he looked puzzled. "So, how'd we screw up?"

"We didn't." Lou was wedged against the arm of the couch. He glared at Bridget. "We didn't screw up. We did just what the boss wanted. I don't see how that makes us fools. Boss, Rob didn't even complain when your kid beat the shit out of him. I'd say we passed your test with flying colors."

"Did what I wanted?" Bridget's face reddened with ire. "You were supposed to find a way in—"

"Which we did," Rob offered. "I got through your system. I'm first-rate. It didn't take a whole lot of—"

"—not let the neighbors spot you."

"Did that, too," Rob said. He straightened a little, and Bridget glared at the show of bravado.

34

"And you were supposed to rob me."

"You stopped us there," Rob admitted. "But, really, we didn't want to rough you up too—"

"Feckin' fools," Bridget shot back. "Test? You didn't come close to passing the test. You ignored Dustin. You thought he fainted, and so you concentrated on me and my son. You didn't see him crawl out of the room and summon help. He was effectively invisible to you. And so he was your downfall."

"Epic fail," Otter announced.

Rob shrank a little. "Yeah, well, there was that. Didn't consider him a threat, boss. A man in some cook's apron, in that outfit, he—"

"Everyone's a threat."

The lead thief spoke again. "Next time we'll—"

"I don't know if there will be a next time, Lou." Bridget continued the rant. Her words were fast, spittle shooting from her mouth as she stepped closer. "Worse, you brought a gun. Pissmires and spiders, you brought a gun. I told you no guns. No guns ever."

"It wasn't loaded, boss," Lou said. "Just used it as a prop, you know, a threat."

Bridget dropped her voice to a whisper. "Never bring a gun. It escalates everything. And if you get caught ... and with the skills you exhibited at dinner you will get caught ... the court will tack on years and years and years. A gun escalates everything."

"Sorry, boss," Rob offered. "We just thought—"

"No you didn't. You didn't think." Bridget's voice hissed like steam escaping from a kettle left too long on the stove. "You didn't think. And you lacked style. You lacked common sense, and you insulted my son."

"Oh, the Timex," Rob said. "Yeah, I should've just taken it. Bad form, huh, to tell someone they're wearing crap. Shouldn't have stepped on it, even if it was a piece of sh—"

"Hey!" Otter stood up from his chair.

Bridget waved him back down. "You treat your marks with a modicum of respect, understand? And don't underestimate them. The people we target, the places ... they have security as good as mine.

35

Maybe better. In some cases definitely better. If you can't defeat me, you can't rob them. Do you want to get caught? Spend your life in prison?"

Rob shook his head. Marsh was glassy-eyed, fading out again.

"Get him to the emergency room," Bridget directed. "Say he got in a bar fight."

Rob made a move to rise, but Bridget wasn't quite done. "Boss, I—"

"I thought you were better than this, especially you, Lou. I trained you better than this. Sloppy, cocksure, holding back for fear of hurting me. Scuttering gobshites. I see the excuses flitting behind your eyes. I should drop the lot of you, worthless as thieves!" She might not have been so furious if Otter was not here. She realized the boy's presence was coloring things; she wanted to look more dangerous and commanding in her son's eyes, to paint herself an authority figure that her underlings feared. *Let the boy think I am terrible and important.* And yet, she thought she should share some of the blame for the thieves' failure. She'd trained them ... perhaps just not well enough.

"I probably gave Marsh a concussion," she said, lowering her voice. "But all three of you deserved a crack in the head." She would apologize later to Marsh and pay his dental bill. She stood silent a moment. She heard a vacuum cleaner running upstairs.

"Maybe you knocked some sense into Marsh," Otter suggested.

The vacuum shut off, and furniture was pushed across the floor overhead.

"I thought you were among my best students." Bridget made a *tsk*ing sound. "What was *I* thinking?"

"Boss, we'll do better." Rob stood, hands in front of him in a pleading gesture. "Don't drop us. Honest, we'll—"

"You *will* do better," Bridget said. "Now get out of here. Get Marsh to North Central. The doctors in the ER there aren't too nosey. They're too busy to be nosey. Take him out the back."

Bridget waited until they'd left, then she finished her piece of cake, the sugar softening her temper. "We'd better be on our way," she told Otter. "Your birthday present is in a warehouse down by the docks."

6

They left the F train at York Street, where an aging saxophone busker leaned against a lamppost playing *All Bird's Children*. Bridget dropped a twenty into his open case; the bill stood out amid the collection of coins. They were halfway down the block when he started another Woods' piece: *My Man Benny*. The persistent honking of a taxi stuck behind a delivery truck ruined the intricate jazz melody. The drivers of both vehicles started cursing at each other in different languages.

"Maybe we should've taken a cab." Otter set his step in time with the blat of the horn.

"Cabs smell like Pine-Sol."

"Yeah, well, Mom, that subway smelled worse."

"And every other cabbie is a psycho." Bridget mentally corrected herself; things had gotten better, now it was every third cabbie.

Bridget did not travel by taxi, and did not own a car or possess a driver's license. She secretly loved traveling on the subway. None of her dealings in the city took her far from a subway stop. "We only have to walk two blocks."

"I couldn't tell you the last time I visited Dumbo, Mom. Nostalgic, huh? I think I was ten and on a field trip for some art exhibit. It was warmer then. Never been here at night."

"There are some amazing places to eat in this neighborhood," Dustin said. "Grimaldi's has coal-fired pizza."

"I like pizza," Otter said.

"The Brooklyn Ice Cream Factory," Dustin continued. "No preservatives, no eggs, freshly-made hot fudge. The River Café, a little pricy, but I think well worth it. Your mother and I ate there a few days ago. The Wagyu Steak tartare was an exceptional appetizer with its Cognac gelée, and the Mediterranean sea bass with chorizo sausage and shrimp stuffing was superb. I would like to try their roasted Amish chicken. The prosciutto served with it is said to—"

"I like pizza," Otter repeated. "Though the swim coach says we should all watch our carbs. Kinda blew that on your garlic mashed potatoes and the birthday cake, huh? But maybe I'll take Lacy to this Grimaldi's, if you think it's hot. She'd get a kick out of a date in Dumbo."

Dumbo referred to Down Under the Manhattan Brooklyn Overpass, a Brooklyn neighborhood that stretched to Manhattan across the East River. More than one hundred years ago it was called Fulton Landing because of the ferry stop that operated before the Brooklyn Bridge opened. In those early years it was filled with warehouses and factories. Through the decades that changed to primarily residential blocks with coveted loft apartments, art galleries, non-profit centers, and trendy restaurants.

Now a historic district, Bridget's destination was one of the oldest buildings that still actually functioned as a warehouse. The taxi had stopped honking, the delivery truck finally moving on. A siren cut in, and the flashing blue light of an unmarked police sedan bounced off the windows of parked cars. Bridget stood still until the sedan passed.

A boat out on the river sounded a long, low note. Another car started honking, and Bridget pointed at a dirt-brown building. "This is it."

"Doesn't look like anyone's here," Otter said.

"This time of night, that's the way it's supposed to look." Bridget led them through an alley too narrow to drive a car down and to a thick, steel side door. There was an electric key pad, and Bridget punched in a lengthy string of numbers, tugged the door open, and gestured Dustin and Otter inside.

It was well-lit, a fact hid to the outside world because of blackened windows. Big crates formed walls branching away from the center like the spokes on a wheel. The cavernous building smelled of old stone and dust.

"Do you own all this?" Otter craned his neck this way and that.

"Bought it two years go. Just the building," Bridget said. "The crates belong to some of the shops down here—we rent storage space to them. There's a loading platform in the back."

"Makes the place seem legit, huh?" Otter gave his mother a knowing nod. "Makes you the respectable businesswoman."

"And it brings in a respectable income." Bridget took the closest passage, then turned and directed them to the back.

A half-dozen folding tables that stretched end to end were covered with an assortment of objects, some of which glittered under the fluorescent lights.

Otter rushed forward. "Wow." He stopped just short of barreling into a table and stuck his hands in his pockets and whistled.

Four men came out of the shadows, and Bridget indicated that the boy and Dustin were her guests.

"Double wow," Otter said. "This shit looks old."

Bridget took in the display. "This is it?" She didn't hide her disappointment. "I expected more from this shipment. Last month I was told—"

"Boss, the mate said not everything got loaded. Said Spanish and Italian cops were crawling through Genoa looking for cocaine smugglers. Captain didn't want to get caught in the net by accident, so he left before the big pieces came on. Said that stuff is probably long gone. But he said this was the best of the lot anyway. Looks like this is worth a crapload."

"Triple wow." Otter seemed oblivious to the conversation and tentatively reached forward, stirring some old coins in a box.

"Hey—" one of the men warned.

"Some cool stuff, boss, don't you think? Said come late spring he'd make another run for you. And we got the ship coming in from England in a week with some paintings, and then the one from France after that. So, do you want—" Bridget waved him off, and the man stepped back.

"No, not bad then, considering," Bridget decided. "Definitely not bad." She'd been shorted before because of problems in port; smuggling was often a crapshoot. At first glance she estimated that these goods could bring in four to five million, with thirty three percent going back to the captain, who had some expenses on his end, and another fifteen percent divided among Bridget's crew. Bridget had other costs to take out of it too, but in the end she was certain to pocket at least a million for herself.

Bridget went to the first table, Dustin close enough behind her she could smell the scent of his soap. She cleared her mind and let the heavy silence of the warehouse close in. Bridget had spared no expense in having the building soundproofed so the city noise did not slip inside; nor did sounds from within travel out. The resulting quiet was eerie and thick, and helped Bridget focus and call up her talent.

A quartz bottle stopper capped with an oval cut sapphire caught her eye. She held her palm above it. Then lower, lower, until her skin touched the crystal.

She let the magic take over.

"Show me," she whispered.

An image formed behind her eyes, of an artisan chipping away at the sapphire, polishing it, then another man setting the finished gem into the housing of the stopper. The image shifted and a manic, yet regal-looking man came to the fore. Bridget absorbed the face and dipped deeper.

"Rurik," she said. The stopper had been crafted for Rurik in ... she strained to get the information ... 872. He was a Varangian chieftain who gained power over Lagoda ten years prior and went on to found the Rurik Dynasty, which ruled Russia until the seventeenth century. The history of the piece rushed at her now. The stopper was presented as a birthday gift along with a case containing three bottles of plum wine from the vineyards of a monastery. Rurik, a pagan, had served the "Christian brew" to his servants because he feared one of the monks had poisoned it. There was no sheet detailing any this information, but Bridget had "read" it clearly nonetheless because of her arcane sight.

With a little more effort Bridget saw Rurik's age-spotted hand touching the bottle stopper, holding it up to admire the facets caught in the sunlight spilling through the window of the chieftain's sitting room. There was pleasure in the man's wild eyes; he seemed to delight in shiny things. Today, Bridget placed the stopper's value at $11,700. Her gift of psychometry let her see—in her mind's eye—not only the person who had owned a thing or touched it or crafted it, but the actual worth of it. And she always translated that worth into today's American coinage. It wasn't automatic or unconscious—she couldn't simply touch a thing and discover its past. She had to center herself and concentrate before her mind could pull in the details.

Near the stopper was a heavy silver comb dotted with tiny pearls. Her palm hovered above it. Ufanda, Rurik's wife, used this, inherited it from her mother Umila. Bridget felt the beautiful Ufanda dragging it through her thick hair as she hummed a dissonant melody. Value in today's market, more because of its pure silver content rather than historical merit: $700.

Another elaborate comb, made of ivory and with a tine missing, could bring $400 from a collector if Bridget could prove the provenance of the tsar's family. Other trinkets from the same lot, a bulky cameo on a silver chain: $2,800; a battered brass chalice festooned with mismatched pieces of topaz once belonging to Rurik's grandfather Gostomysl: $2,100; a bronze cup set with a single large canary diamond also once held by Gostomysl: $38,500 for the stone alone; two balsa-rimmed mirrors inlaid with gold and ivory: $1,700 for the pair. Bridget saw Vadim, Rurik's cousin, stealing the mirrors from the bedchamber of a young woman who had refused his drunken advances.

There wasn't a single document to explain the age or significance of any piece. Bridget's gift precluded a need for such and let her differentiate originals from clever copies. She'd come into her "sight" when she was a little younger than Otter, but it took her a few years to fully develop it and understand that there was real magic in the world.

She had briefly considered taking on a legitimate job because of her amazing talent—museum curator, archaeologist, historian. There was so much trafficking in stolen and forged artifacts that her gift to determine genuine from fake would have been put to a good use.

But all of those occupations required an advanced college degree to back her up, and Bridget had never finished high school. By the time a friend suggested she could pay to have forged whatever diploma she needed, Bridget had decided that smuggling and brokering for the Westies was more interesting.... and allowed her to keep the choicest pieces.

There were more belongings of the Russian family: a chalice, two swords, a bejeweled glove with the leather rotted, a mug with crudely cut emerald inlays, a gold anklet that once belonging to Rurik's raven-haired mistress, a wood horse the size of a pumpkin; Bridget felt the hands of Rurik's young son carving it.

All interesting and all able to be sold above and below the counter in her Fort Greene antiques shop, but nothing truly outstanding. Perhaps the goods on one of the other tables could yield more.

"See anything here you'd like for your birthday, Otter?"

"Anything? I can have anything?"

"Of course." Bridget hoped the boy would not realize the value of some of the oldest pieces and would make a selection based solely on appearance. Still, tonight she was prepared to give away whatever caught her son's fancy.

"What about this?" Otter was several feet away, looking at a table filled with ornamental swords and daggers. Bridget sensed that they had once belonged to French nobles. She would have to get closer to pinpoint which weapon had been carried by which man. The boy held up a thin-bladed sword with rubies and citrines set into the hilt. "This is awesome."

Bridget joined him and concentrated on the piece. "Curious." The fingers of her left hand grazed the hilt and for an instant the air smelled of an overly sweet perfume. This was the one piece in the collection not owned by a French nobleman.

"This was actually a woman's, Otter." After a moment's focus she gained a name. "Diane de Poitiers, mistress to King Henri II." Bridget placed its value, for its history and gems, at $89,800. She hoped her son would select something else, as she knew a sword collector in Manhattan who would buy it.

"A woman's sword, huh?" Otter laid it down, apparently no longer interested. "Hey, look at this over here! This is kinda cool." He hefted a silver chalice. A mix of dark and faint blue stones were set in a fleur-de-lis pattern. "French, I take it. King Henri's? Or one of his mistresses?"

"Eventually Henri's." Bridget concentrated and sorted through the images that came at her. "Henri's grandfather owned that first, then his brother, then eventually Henri."

"I could set this on my desk at home. Too pretty to drink out of. But I could put pens and pencils in it."

Bridget smiled. The faint colored stones were blue-white diamonds, their size and clarity making the piece exceptional. It was, perhaps, the single most valuable piece on this table, perhaps of everything in the warehouse: $151,000 would have been her asking price. Maybe Otter had inherited some of Bridget's skills after all.

"I like it, Mom. I'll take this cup-thing," Otter said, the grin wide on his face. "Okay? Of course I know not to show it to anyone, 'cept Dad. I won't even show it to Lacy. None of this stuff ... well ... someone's probably looking for it, right?"

The majority of the items on the tables were stolen from the basements of museums and collections from estates, certainly none gained through any proper channels, else they would not be here, Bridget knew.

"Someone could be looking, yes," Bridget agreed. "But they'll forget about it after a while." *If they even remembered owning the pieces in the first place.* She knew that some of those estates and museums had so much inventory, they might never notice what was missing.

"Years," Otter supplied. "A lot of years, I'd bet, they'd be looking. Well, they won't think to look in Dad's condo. Thanks for the cup, Mom."

Bridget walked to the next table. She absorbed the history of the collection, discarding various images and locking on the visage of a fat, elderly man who seemed important and who had owned all of this lot. Bridget saw expressions flit across the heavily-lined face: anger, pleasure, sadness, confusion was the most prominent.

"A troubled man," Bridget decided. The ill-tempered portly fellow had a thin beard and moustache and fancied wearing elaborate collars that hid his thick neck. As Bridget's fingers brushed first a cloak clasp in the shape of a wolf's head, next a carving kinfe and fork, then a pipe bowl, and finally a ring, a name came to her: Albrecht Friedrich, a Prussian duke in the 1500s who had seven children. Bridget sensed that Eleanor was the duke's favorite, fifth-born and always in his thoughts, dying at age twenty-three while she gave birth to what would have been her first child. Bridget took on the duke's grief, then cast it aside, felt the man's smooth fingers wrap around the handle of the carving knife. Then she reached deeper and felt the duke's hunger and anticipation of a holiday meal. More, and she absorbed a disturbing twinge of ... what? ... Bridget directed all her attention to the collection, shutting out the pleasant scent of Dustin's soap and the sound of her son's continued oohing and ahing. What?

Odd, scattered, chaotic thoughts bordering on the edge of madness. Albrecht had been a conflicted man. The longer Bridget focused on the items, the more she absorbed, and the more her own thoughts became muddled. She picked through the disorder. Albrecht was named Duke of Prussia by the king of Poland, to whom he paid feudal homage. Fluent in Polish, he had tried—and failed—to gain acceptance to the Polish senate. A protestant, he enjoyed the backing of some influential Polish Lutherans, and so believed he could ascend to the Polish throne. But that did not happen. In 1572, four years into his reign as duke, his thoughts became even more ambivalent, and those around him questioned his sanity. Albrecht died more than forty years later, crying out the name of his lost daughter.

"Eleanor." A tear slid down Bridget's cheek. She shook off the connection and went to the last table, a mix of more Russian and Prussian antiquities ranging in value from several hundred dollars each to several thousand, and ...

A sudden sensation of giddiness threatened to drop her when her mind touched something valuable and out of place with the rest of the assortment. It was something very, very old.

7

Bridget fought off the lightheadedness and inched toward the very old thing, something carved from wood and sitting in the shadow cast by a black box inlaid with bronze. She pulled in a breath, feeling her lungs grow warm and her face absorb the heat that once beat down upon the carving.

"Wonderful," she breathed.

It was a wooden shabti statuette, roughly seven inches tall, and Bridget was careful not to actually touch it with her bare hands. She didn't want the oil from her skin to cause any damage, nor did she want to be overwhelmed by the images such intimate contact with something so old could give. That contact would wait for later, back in her brownstone, when she could savor it in privacy. She'd absorb just a smidgen of it now, a junkie taking a hit to tide her over until she could administer a proper fix. She moved her fingers to within an inch of it.

Talk to me, Bridget thought. *Where did you come from?*

She picked through a rush of images. This shabti had been placed in the tomb of Yuya, father of Tiye, who wed Neb-Maat-Re Amenhotep III.

A little more.

46

Centuries raced through her thoughts at a dizzying pace and she tried to grab the most important elements without being deluged. Buried in the Valley of the Kings, Yuya's single-chambered tomb was found in 1905 and dated to the Eighteenth Dynasty. Yuya and his wife held political influence during Amenhotep III's reign, and before that in the reign of Tuthmosis IV.

Titles tumbled from Bridget's mouth: "Lord of Akhmim, Priest of Min, Master of the Horse, His Majesty's Lieutenant Commander of Chariotry." All those things Yuya had been called. The tomb, like so many others, had been plundered. But not everything had been taken. Shabtis, including this one, carved statuettes that were meant to animate in the afterlife as servants, had been left behind to be discovered by archaeologists and placed in museums.

This piece had been in a museum.

Bridget gulped in the dusty air of the warehouse and the pleasant scent of Dustin. His hands were on her shoulders, steadying her. Dustin was talking to her, but she paid no attention, she was lost in the images emanating from the shabti. Drunk on it, she couldn't release the connection. Couldn't? Wouldn't. Didn't want to. Wanted to take the precious shabti back to her brownstone and shut everything and everyone else out and delve deeper into ancient Egypt.

"Bridget!" Dustin raised his voice and broke through. "Are you all right?"

"Mom?"

Bridget tried to wave them off, but her arms felt like lead. So old, this magnificent piece, so filled with history and memory and pictures.

Bridget pressed for more. This shabti, made of cedar, had changed ownership several times, ending up at the Malawi National Museum in Minya, Egypt, and put on exhibit. She saw it in a display case, as clear as if she'd been in the museum.

"A little more," she whispered, curious how it ended up in her warehouse in New York City. She heard chaos in her probing, a crowd, shouts, sirens, and whistles. It was August of 2013, and a riot was in progress outside the Minya museum. She watched armed thieves scurry in, break the case and steal the shabti, along with many other items. A jumble of news bits hit her like pellets from a scatter-gun. Looters had ravaged ancient sites and museums in that turbulent summer that year, stealing what they could carry away while demonstrators set fire to things all in a clash between Egyptian security forces and the supporters of the ousted president Mohamed Morsi. Bridget remembered the reports; hundreds died and thousands were injured.

In the bloody conflagration, this ancient piece within her grasp had gone missing. Bridget clearly saw the face of the men who had taken it—and the museum's other treasures—registered their names and tried to remember every detail about them, every scar and feature, heard the protestors in the background, felt the calloused and careless hands of the thieves on the wood, then felt it pass from one hand to the next to the next until it rested in one darkness followed by another and another.

The hold of the ship that brought it here? Yes, but more.

Its recent black surroundings did not have the feel of a ship.

The blat of a horn flittered at the edge of her thoughts. A ship's horn. Then a different sound, persistent. Honking. A jarring sensation. Foreign cursing.

The lurching of a damnable New York City taxi!

The darkness that had most recently cocooned this shabti had been the trunk of a cab.

"Mom?"

Bridget's throat had gone desert dry. She swallowed and worked up some saliva and broke the connection with the shabti. She was slammed by the sensation of awakening from a three-day bender. "This piece, this little statue ... it came with the shipment from Genoa today?"

"No, boss. Not that piece. One of Marsh's buddies lifted it from some rich dude's apartment on Eighty-Fifth. Marsh told him maybe you'd want that little statue for your antique shop, told him you like the old stuff. Ugly as hell, ain't it? Marsh was supposed to be here tonight, but I heard he had to go to the hospital and—"

"Marsh isn't feeling well," Bridget said, making a mental note to call and check on him later, pay the hospital bill and hope the concussion wasn't serious. "Marsh's friend. The one who brought this. What is his name?"

"Harold. No, Harry. That's it, Harry." He scratched his head. "Didn't get a last name for certain, though I remember it was a color. Black, brown, gray. Should've paid more attention. Sorry. He was a scruffy fellow. Dropped it off an hour ago. I gave him two hundred for it. I wasn't going to give him that much, but he kept dickering. Just an ugly piece of wood, but he wouldn't take less. Said there was more Egyptian—"

"Find this Harry Black, Brown, or Gray for me. Now. I want the address of the apartment."

Perhaps some of the other items stolen from the museum in Minya were also in the Eighty-Fifth apartment that Harry had plundered. Perhaps there were more ancient treasures to be had.

She loved very old things.

8

Bridget selected the darkest spot in the alley and scaled the wall. She used titanium hand claws, similar to Shiobi Spikes or what lumberjacks favored, but sharp enough to bite into the mortar between the bricks and give her purchase. The building was one of several prewar apartment complexes in the area. Its front had been given a serious and elegant facelift. The side in this alley had been left to deteriorate.

She knew other ways into this building, but tonight she craved the physical activity and the heady danger of the climb. Her skin itched with the anticipation of what she might find—another shabti, a piece of jewelry, a bowl, or maybe a death mask ... anything that might have been taken from the Malawi National Museum or Yuya's tomb, something valuable because of its age and significance, but more because of the images she would read from it.

Dear God, let it be another shabti. Let Egypt's misfortune from all those riots be my gain.

Bridget's target was on the tenth. There were only two apartments to a floor, and Bridget knew she had the correct side. The Internet was a marvelous thing, and a quick search on it had yielded various blueprints, notes about security, floor plans, a listing of tenants, and even pictures of the views from many of the windows. The Internet had also provided a little bit about the apartment occupant: Elijah Stone, forty-six, independent investment consultant. Born in Connecticut, Stone previously worked as a stock broker, operations manager for a NYC securities firm, and served as public relations director for a Manhattan medical device research corporation.

The sounds of the city came muted to her as she climbed, deadened by the cocoon of stone and the hour. Always there was traffic, but not a lot on the street at the moment. From her perch she spotted a *New York Times* van pass by, followed by a Greyhound bus. The scent of the belched exhaust was cut here, and the air did not smell too tainted. She breathed deep.

Scaling ten floors was not a terribly daunting task; even with her bruised ribs she could do this in her sleep. Bridget kept herself in shape by an unorthodox exercise routine that included regular hikes to the eighty-sixth floor observation deck of the Empire State Building. She even competed in the annual Run-Up, and held back just enough so she wasn't one of the fastest times; she didn't want her picture in the paper. One thousand five hundred and seventy-six steps, the lower third taken two at a time. Occasionally she would also jog up to the observation deck on the one hundred and second floor at the very top, but that stairwell wasn't always open, and she wasn't about to pick the lock in such a public place for the two hundred and eighty-four additional steps.

Ten floors by scaling the wall tonight? It was not so onerous, and yet it held a shade of risk to keep it interesting.

Her muscles bunched as she pulled herself up. She used her arms, letting her legs hang free. Bridget relished the burn she started to feel. She seldom burglarized apartments anymore; she'd done that often enough in her youth. Now, more the businesswoman, she made arrangements for illicit shipments and orchestrated elaborate heists wherein she rarely got her fingers dirty. But she retreated to her old ways every once in a while, like now, when the promise of something special was too irresistible to leave to one of her men.

A little more than a year ago she'd been lured into an apartment at

51

740 Park Avenue when she'd heard one of the tenants had purchased an intact Babylonian vase, a serious prize that was now in a place of honor in her study. The city's wealthiest lived at 740—once the Vanderbilts, Chryslers, Rockefellers, and now the people of new money: Schwarzman, Wang, Perelman, Koch, and Bronfman. This building on Eighty-Fifth wasn't in 740's class, and did not have as elaborate security, but it was out of the reach of the average New Yorker nonetheless. Apartments here started at $12,000 a month. The man she was going to rob had some money.

The burn in her biceps increased as she passed the fourth floor and headed toward the fifth. The ache in her side intensified. She'd glanced at her plate-sized bruise before heading out. It was a mix of purple and yellow, a sidewalk chalk painting that had been caught in the rain. Dustin had tried to get her to see the doctor, but she'd been injured worse before.

Past the sixth and toward the seventh.

Bridget had waited until Tavio came to pick up Otter before coming here. Tavio'd been handsomely dressed and smelling of too-sweet cologne, not a hair out of place, and offering a quick comment about rushing over after an "engaging dinner date." It was a jab, a "see what you're missing" poke meant to fester. He always came well groomed to pick up their son. It used to hurt and leave Bridget in a sullen funk for a few hours. But she'd gotten past it some time ago. Tavio probably knew his appearance and gentle digs didn't get to her anymore, but continued them anyway out of habit or lingering spite. Tonight, Dustin had answered the door and snaked his arms around Bridget's waist.

Bridget noted that Tavio's eyes flickered with a hint of indignation aimed at the young man. It hadn't helped that Otter had volunteered what a wonderful cook Dustin was and announced he was bringing home leftovers of the "best-ever birthday cake on the planet."

Bridget had waited another two hours, losing herself in Dustin's considerable charms, then left him to sleep, dressed in charcoal clothes, and took the subway.

Now to the eighth floor.

The climb tugged at her sore muscles, the burn spreading around her back and into her arms and becoming uncomfortable. Bridget continued to let her arms do all of the work, pausing when she heard a horn honking down on the street and making sure no one was coming into this alley. Sound carried even this high up in the gap between buildings, and she didn't want to be caught doing her Spiderman impersonation.

At the ninth floor she felt snowflakes dust her face.

One more, she told herself. One more floor.

One floor later, she pulled herself up on a three-inch-wide concrete ledge and to a narrow window that she knew from the Internet floor plans opened above the kitchen sink. Rich, paranoid New Yorkers often had alarms on their balcony doors, but practically no one this high up rigged their windows.

Bridget discovered that Elijah Stone, the lone tenant of this apartment, was no exception. The window she chose was safe, not even locked.

It was dark inside. At 1 a.m. on a Monday morning, Bridget had not expected the occupant to be awake. A quick and quiet search revealed a man sleeping alone in a king-sized bed, conveniently wearing a full-face CPAP mask. The sound reminded her of Darth Vader or a white noise machine, a constant airy whoosh. As the man exhaled, the volume rose slightly and made a harsher hiss. Middle-aged, a little heavy, hair thinning; Bridget thought the man looked sad and worn.

The apartment smelled of vanilla and apples and was large. Bridget knew from the floor plan it was two thousand square feet. Three bedrooms, three fireplaces, everything done in light, creamy colors that shouted money and refinement and seemed not to be the residence of someone who spent a lot of time here. There was no clutter, the knickknacks relatively few and tastefully arranged. Everything modern, she realized; nothing at first glance appearing obviously old —very old—like the shabti Marsh's friend had picked up here. But then no doubt such a treasure would be hidden.

She tugged off her gloves and moved silently throughout the

rooms, kept her breathing shallow and stretching out her fingers, brushing them against cabinet drawers and closet doors, searching for a hint of something ancient. A large silver candlestick on the dining table called up the image of a young woman on her wedding day when Virginia was a colony. If she could not find a true treasure in this apartment, she would take the candlestick for her trouble—the silver alone put its value at $1,700.

All the while she listened to the CPAP, setting its dull and routine rhythm to memory. If Elijah Stone roused, Bridget would know it because the sound of the machine would change, and she would dive for the window. Other sounds whispered in, just a hint of traffic and wind teasing the panes, someone moving around in the apartment upstairs.

There were only a half-dozen books on a narrow floor to ceiling bookshelf in the office, most of the shelves empty or holding odds and ends: a souvenir shot glass of Niagara Falls; a bikini-clad woman with long blond hair and big turquoise eyes smiling out of a silver picture frame; two shiny black coffee cups with the Café Grumpy logo, a commemorative Lucite block with a ghostly image of the Twin Towers etched on it; and another picture frame with a middle-aged man in a business suit—Elijah Stone—standing next to an elderly woman in black slacks and a sequin-dusted red sweater, a Christmas tree in the background. Nothing of value or particular interest. She turned, and then spun back.

The thickest book on the shelf managed to catch her attention. She touched the spine: printed a little more than a century ago, it was volume two of a Masonic history set. A very old man with slicked-back white hair flitted in Bridget's mind, likely the previous owner. The book was the most interesting thing she'd encountered so far, but not especially valuable, and not worth her time right now as it would no doubt sit in her shop too long to bother with.

There was a single shelf, decorative and attached to the wall over a widescreen television. Two items on it: a blown-glass paperweight with a purple blossom in the center and a baseball. The latter brought the scent of popcorn and dirt when Bridget touched the plastic sphere that held it and probed. The visage of a smooth faced black man came to the front. Bridget saw this very ball coming hard at the man. A crack and the ball sailed across an outfield carpeted with summer-parched grass. The man was fast, wheeling around the bases as the ball was snared and hurled back. "Safe!" Bridget heard an umpire shout. "Twelve seconds that took!" someone on the bench called. "Inside the park home-run for Papa!" a woman in the stands hollered. The umpire handed the man—James Bell was the batter's name—this ball. Years melted and the man, old now and sitting in a dingy apartment in St. Louis—the famous arch was visible through the window behind him—signed the ball and mailed it to a fan. "Cool Papa Bell," the signature read. He'd been a legend in the Negro leagues, Bridget registered. The ball wasn't the relic she'd been searching for, but a treasure nonetheless. Bridget put the ball in her pocket and moved on. She could sell it for nine hundred in her shop when she was finished enjoying all of its summertime memories.

A glance at her watch. She'd been prowling for nearly fifteen minutes. Too much time. She looked to the kitchen window and saw the snow coming down a little harder. The ledge would be slippery. Time to go.

One more pass, she decided. One more. If Marsh's friend had gotten a shabti here, there had to be something else, right? Something Harry Black or Brown or Gray had missed. She returned to the bedroom, fingers twitching in time with the CPAP. First to the closet, then to the bureau, the nightstand, and then the bed; all of it one more time. One more. Bridget froze. The bed.

Beneath the bed.

She crouched and reached under it, the fringe on the comforter tickling the back of her hand. She had the sensation of being watched, yet a glance confirmed the man was still sleeping. Next, she had the more welcome sensation of desert heat and a dry wind. The shabti hadn't been the only thing from Egypt in this apartment. Indeed, Marsh's friend Harry had missed something.

She stretched farther, careful not to move the comforter, holding her breath and stealing herself for ... there! A dizzying rush suffused

55

her, images of dark-skinned men with shaved heads and wearing symbols of Ra and Horus. Her fingers closed on the handle of a satchel, and she fought against the ancient glimpses that shot behind her eyes. Bridget forced the pictures down, and slid the case—a battered, oversized briefcase—out from under the bed.

It was heavy, promising something very interesting inside.

The leather looked old and carried the pong of dead fish, but Bridget didn't care about the smell. What an amazing thing it must hold! A treasure from the time of the pharaohs. She wanted to delve deeper, to look inside this very instant and run her hands over whatever it was, get high on the history of the object and trace its passage through the centuries. She stopped herself from reaching for the clasp.

Time for the discovery later, she thought, back at her brownstone. If she lost herself to the history here, she could well get caught.

The CPAP machine continued its sonorous accompaniment.

Bridget left the room, then the apartment, strapping the heavy briefcase to her back and climbing down the wall into the darkest part of the alley. The snow was coming harder still, mixed with ice pellets, so cold it was like shards of glass striking her face. She squinted through it as she hurried to the nearby subway stop at Eighty-Sixth and Broadway.

"Wait," she told herself as she settled onto a cold plastic seat. "Wait. Wait. Wait."

Bridget would force herself to not open the briefcase until safely back at her brownstone in Fort Greene. Then she would see what slice of the past she'd managed to lift from the tenth floor of the building at Eighty-Fifth and West End.

9

Locking herself in her study, Bridget sat cross-legged on a large golden-beige rug—an over-dyed Turkish oushak woven in 1910. She valued it at only $6,990 because one end of it was faded and frayed. Sometimes she meditated on it, palms against the nap and using her psychometry to draw out images of the long-fingered women who had deftly fashioned the flower and vine patterns and who she imagined to be her friends. Watching them weave soothed her, and the climate during the time the rug was woven was lovely and so far removed from New York City's winter. This morning, however, she kept the weavers away and fixed her gaze on the smelly briefcase.

She concentrated.

Oddly, she could not date the satchel; conflicting pictures danced behind her eyes. Likely a patchwork of hides—parts of previous garments and purses recycled and dyed to the same dull-brown shade, a myriad of faces from previous owners. Running her fingers over the leather, she felt it rough in some places, smooth in others, thicker along one side. Why a moneyed man like Elijah Stone in the Eighty-Fifth apartment would own it was a puzzle. Perhaps a hand-me-down from a relative kept only for sentiment's sake. Or maybe it was a convenient pick-up from a resale shop in which to hide something of great value. She saw flashes of Elijah, the man's manicured hands holding the case, but she was not interested in him at this moment, just in the treasure inside.

Who would think to look for a relic inside this piece of junk? A common thief would not have looked, and Bridget had only been drawn to it because her senses honed in on something *very* old. She would throw the briefcase away in tomorrow's trash. But at the moment, the briefcase was a box of Cracker Jacks, and she was going to find the prize inside.

The clasp was curious, tarnished silver with bronze inlay. Looking from one angle like a twisted face, from another like a gang symbol. She dismissed it; the clasp and the briefcase were not important—only the contents mattered. She unhooked it, opening the case and not yet letting herself look inside.

Savor this. Go slow.

She closed her eyes, fingers hovering above the opening, trying to block out the smell of dead fish which she attributed to the leather rotting and which had somehow gotten stronger. Her mind bore in.

Just a taste at first. Tease me.

Again she felt the heat of the desert. Bridget welcomed it; the imagined warmth helped to shake off the cold that had seeped into her bones from the climb up the apartment building wall. She had never physically been to Egypt, but her mental forays there because of her psychometry felt as real as if she'd stood on the sand long centuries ago. She owned several objects that had been culled from the Valley of the Kings, each precious because of the images stored, none obtained through legal channels. Each had given her many hours of pleasure as she absorbed the rare histories. It was like experiencing multiple and significant lives, a child's game of "let's pretend" become reality.

What are you, very old treasure? What? What?

Stone. She could tell that much, that the object inside was carved stone. The briefcase had certainly felt heavy strapped to her back, hinting at something substantial.

From which dynasty?

She couldn't tell that, despite her initial probing, and so she finally reached in, hands grasping and pulling out a limestone statue about thirteen inches tall. It was thick and had filled the entire briefcase. She automatically registered a value: one-point-two million, though to her such a treasure was without price.

How had Elijah Stone come to own such an interesting, valuable thing? And why hide it in a hideous briefcase rather than set it out to be admired? To own a thing and not be able to look upon it was foolish. In the same instant she asked the question, she answered it. The statue, like the shabti, had been stolen from the Egyptian Museum; her quick reading of it revealed that. Of course its new owner would hide it, at least until it could be displayed somewhere without fear of being recognized as an important antiquity. Or perhaps Elijah Stone was a smuggler or trafficker in goods like Bridget and had intended to resell it. One-point-two million would be a key haul for just one piece.

"It doesn't matter how you came to be in that apartment," Bridget said aloud. At least it did not matter at this moment. The important thing was that she held this wonderful, ancient relic. This piece of the past belonged to her now. Later, much later, she might check into this Elijah Stone. The man's source for very old things might need to become Bridget's source.

So beautiful in its simplicity, this statue.

She placed it reverently between herself and the briefcase. It was a rendering of a man in a wrap-around skirt in marvelous museum-quality condition. The man was seated in a high-backed chair that could have represented a throne. His garment was short. In the Middle and New Kingdoms men wore longer skirts or pleated ones, so this piece dated to the Old Kingdom, she was certain. About twenty-four hundred BC, Bridget placed it, probably the beginning of the Fifth Dynasty. She would narrow it down to the precise year it was carved much later. The statue was made to show elaborate jewelry and a headpiece, marking the figure as wealthy.

Who posed for this treasure? She pressed.

59

She drew out an image of a stately man, sun-bronzed and reasonably handsome and sitting regally still for the carver. Bridget felt the carver's hands run over the stone before making the first chisel cuts. It felt like a lover's caress.

"Kanefer," Bridget pronounced as she looked outward from the chunk of limestone. She nearly succumbed as a weakness washed through her; psychometry magic often exacted a physical price. She trembled like she was about to suffer a seizure, her teeth grinding together as she fought for breath. The sensation of the intimate contact with something centuries upon centuries old was amazing, and Bridget drank it all in, steadying herself and taking in more and more until she nearly lost consciousness.

The subject—Kanefer—had eyes as black as pitch, unblinking and looking like marbles set on a face that seemed too small for the tall, broad-shouldered body. Yet it was a striking face. The forehead was high and sloped, the head shaven, the chin and cheekbones sharp. His jewelry was considerable—a mix of gold and lapis lazuli that further indicated his wealth. Bridget let her senses spiral ever outward from the limestone, taking in the room in which the carver and Kanefer sat, seeing beyond it and espying impressive stone buildings—an intact Egypt before Roman armies, passing centuries, and vandals had broken down the structures.

Who? Bridget repeated. *Who were you, Kanefer?* Bridget previously owned nothing that had belonged to a man named Kanefer, and she would not lower herself to search a history book for information. She considered such books and Internet sites only scattered speculations; as far as she was concerned her psychometry gift was the only reliable way to learn about the past.

Who? Talk to me. Give up your secrets.

Days passed in the blink of Bridget's eyes. She gathered more memories from the stone, not wanting everything right away, and yet not wanting to shut out any details. She would return to this piece again and again, finding something new with each exploration. Now she would glean just enough to satisfy her addiction and yet leave her hungry for more.

She touched her forehead to the stone and pictured her mind flowing wholly into it to intensify the connection. Then Bridget felt herself rising as if someone had lifted her. She looked out through the statue's chiseled eyes and saw Kanefer holding up the finished art to admire. Stretching behind the man in the distance Bridget glimpsed the Nile Delta. Farmers carried wheat and flax that she knew would be woven into linen fabrics, perhaps into clothes that Kanefer would wear.

This indeed was the dynastic period of the great pharaohs, and by the structures around Kanefer and the dress of the men and women who worked nearby, Bridget placed it after the unification of Upper and Lower Egypt. She watched two men nod to Kanefer and speak in low tones. Historians had deciphered hieroglyphs, but they'd had no clue to the spoken language of the ancient Egyptians. Bridget heard the language clearly while connected so closely to the statue, and through her mental magic and nearness to the long-dead Egyptian, she understood everything as if she was a native speaker.

The men in attendance called Kanefer high priest and spoke to him in measured, respectful words, referring to him as "vizier" and "beautiful soul."

"He who called the world into being blesses us this morning, Kanefer," one said.

"The dreamer of creation brings the promise of rain for my field," said the other.

Bridget gripped the statue painfully tight. Of course! Kanefer was a high priest of Ptah, who the ancient Egyptians called the creator god. She opened her mind wider still and the lineage came at her in a rush. Kanefer was more than a priest, he was also a prince of Egypt, son of Sneferu, brother of Nefermaat I, married to a Hathor priestess and through that union was the father of Prince Kanefer II, Prince Kawab, and Princess Meresankh.

"Eldest son of the king," she heard someone in the background whisper of Kanefer as if it was a title. If this man was the firstborn, Bridget would not determine that now. Perhaps that would be revealed in a future visit. But she suspected Kanefer was merely the oldest living son at the time the statue was carved; she heard Kanefer mention to the carver about his brothers Nefermaat and Rahotep being buried recently at the royal necropolis of Meidum. So not an only son.

Greatest of Seers and Overseer of the Troops, Kanefer had been called.

Despite her intention to only give herself a taste of this time period, Bridget continued to direct all of her being in an effort to delve deeper and deeper.

Talk to me, high priest, she practically begged. "Talk to me like I am standing next to you."

Dear God, this Kanefer had been important. Images tumbled at Bridget far too quickly to be properly absorbed. She saw pieces, like highlights in an old newsreel fast-forwarding, this man leading a force and gaining control over the lands of the Sinai.

Bridget's chest grew tight and a part of her demanded she break the connection before she loose herself. But the greater part demanded that she continue the discovery. Sweat drenched her, both from the sensation of the desert heat and from the effort she expelled. She gasped for air and grasped the statue to her chest like a child would hug a beloved doll.

The images continued until the sand and the dark-colored men, all of the sounds and the desert breeze overwhelmed her and she collapsed from exhaustion.

She awoke sometime later, soaked, the statue next to her, the briefcase just beyond it. The air smelled putrid, of things washed up and rotting in the summer sun on the bank of the East River. The stench was so strong, and Bridget so spent after her delving, that she retched on the over-dyed Turkish oushak until her stomach was empty and she was weaker still. After several moments she pushed herself to her knees and froze.

Sitting next to the briefcase was a repulsive-looking creature that fixed its misshapen eyes on her.

The thing was size of a pit bull, but looked vaguely reptilian, squatty like a bullfrog with its long hind legs tucked to its side. Its hide was a mottled green-brown that bubbled and oozed, but was smooth and mustard yellow across its protruding stomach. Goo ran in thin rivulets down its skin and disappeared before hitting the rug.

The creature was clearly the source of the horrific odor.

Bridget was afraid to move. She was a dozen feet away from the intercom on the wall and the telephone on the desk. She didn't have a cell phone on her, nothing at hand she could use to call for one of her attendants or Dustin—not that they could do anything about this beast. For once in her life she wished she carried a gun. She could spring for the door, but she was woozy and ruled out that option. And so she didn't budge, waiting to see what the monster was going to do.

She knew that's what it was: a monster, not some figment of her imagination brought on by fatigue. There were such things in this world as true beasts, though she had never actually seen one, had only half-glimpsed their malformed shadowy images when she'd been mentally connected to ancient things of dubious origin or had ventured too deep beneath New York City. Where had this monster come from? And why? What did it want? Her life?

It had four eyes—one set perched directly atop the other. As Bridget stared, she saw a fifth eye open above them in the center of its forehead. The eyes shifted color and size, making her dizzy, and she dropped her gaze to the thing's mouth. The lips were bulbous, again conjuring up the image of a bullfrog, and when it yawned, Bridget saw a double row of fine, pointed teeth set against a black cave-like interior. It belched, the noxious cloud adding to the already overpowering stench, and then a long, thick tongue lolled out and swiped at a rivulet of goo running down its face.

The creature had no discernible nose or ears. It had a prehensile tail with a ridge of spiky hair on it. The tail flicked back and forth, and its front legs—Bridget noted they ended in twisted claws—bunched as if it was going to pounce.

No, not a monster, Bridget corrected herself. Calling that thing a monster would be too kind and understated.

10

You can't see it?" Bridget pointed at the beast sitting next to the open briefcase.

"That little statue? Of course I see it, sweet Brie. Egyptian? It looks old. And valuable. It should be in one of your display cases, the large one with the beveled glass, not on the floor." Dustin paused. "Is that what you slipped out to get last night? Is that what was so very important?"

"The statue? Yes." Bridget ran her fingers through her hair, curls still damp from sweating. She was shaking. "But do you see the ... thing? Next to the statue. Do you see *it*?" *How could the man not see it?*

Dustin thrust his hands into the pockets of his bathrobe and yawned. "I see the statue and an ugly old satchel. And I see that you puked on the rug and have made no attempt to clean it up. Is there something else?" He wriggled his nose. "And I smell something a little stinky. You maybe, or—"

"A little? A *little stinky*?" Bridget would have retched again over the foul stench of the creature, but her stomach had nothing left to give up. She stared at the monster, not meeting its disconcerting, fluctuating eyes. The rivulets of goo that trickled down its mottled hide pulsed like veins and looked purple-black in the morning light that

64

spilled in through the half-shuttered blinds. It belched and babbled a string of sounds she suspected was language, nothing she could understand. "Seriously, you can't see it, the ... monster?"

"Monster? No. There is no monster. Are you ill?"

She pointed vehemently at it. All the while the creature continued to babble. Dustin stepped closer and set the back of his hand to her forehead. The worry was evident in his eyes.

"You are clammy. Sick. So pale! I told you to call the doctor. You should not have gone out so late. Bridget, you ... oh, what is the damn word I need ... imagine. No, hallucinate. You hallucinate. Monsters! So sick."

"I'm not sick. And it's not 'monsters,' there's just one of the feckers. I just—"

"Drugs then. Did you—"

"I don't take drugs. I ... never ... take ... drugs." Bridget had experimented in her young years, pot a handful of times, cocaine only once, poppers at a dance club—twice with poppers, but she didn't like the effects. She rarely drank, as she didn't want anything to dull her special senses. Wine at dinner with Dustin, she did that sometimes, but not often. "And I'm not hallucinating," she said so softly she doubted Dustin could hear. Louder: "Call Michael, will you?"

He stuck out his lower lip and reached for the intercom. "I cook for you, Bridget O'Shea, and I share your bed a few nights a week. But I am not your servant." Nevertheless, he called for Michael. "I should, instead, call for the doctor. You have some nasty flu, or maybe something worse." He shuddered. "God, I hope I do not catch it. I have a sous-vide study session this afternoon—low temperature cooking."

Moments later, a stiff-backed man in a vest appeared.

"Michael, do you see it?" Bridget asked.

"The briefcase?" Michael glanced at it, and then gave Bridget an up and down before he noticed the vomit on the Turkish rug. "Yes, I see the briefcase," he said. "Would you like me to throw it out ma'am? Clean that up?"

"Yes." Bridget slapped her hand against her leg. "Of course, that's it!" If she'd been more alert, she would have realized it. The monster was attached to the briefcase, released when she opened it and took out the statue of Kanefer. It was like popping open a bottle and finding a genie inside. Elijah Stone must have had some sort of summoning ward on the briefcase to protect the million-dollar relic. Opening the case summoned the monster. Bridget had not looked for such a ward, thinking that Stone was just a normal man; only a small percentage of the populace was gifted with any sort of magic, or had any access to buying wards and the like. If she had opened the case in that apartment, the beast would have come out right there and then and woken Stone, and Bridget would have been caught and staring at serious prison time.

It was fortunate she had simply stolen the entire case and opened it here, Stone none the wiser. The monster was a temporary inconvenience.

"Yes, of course," Bridget said, relaxing. "Throw it out." Getting rid of the briefcase would get rid of the monster that had been warded to it. The creature was not connected to the statue; she would have learned that with her psychometry, and so it was linked only to the damn ugly briefcase. It did not appear to be vicious. It had not attacked her when she removed the statue—an alarm, nothing more, and a hideous and smelly one to say the least. A creature meant only to frighten and hold the thief in place until Stone could summon the police. "Yes, definitely. Throw the damn old briefcase out. Throw it out right away." Odd that Michael and Dustin couldn't see the monster, she thought. But perhaps only the ones designated by the ward were so unlucky—the thief and Stone; magic could be that quirky and specific.

"And that little statue, ma'am? What shall I do with it?"

"Leave that, Michael. I'll take care of it. Just—" The monster belched again, a visible gray-green cloud of noxiousness wafting from its maw. Bridget did not hold her breath in time and inhaled the biting, sulfurous reek. She felt the room spin and her knees gave out.

She was in bed, bathed, covered with a wool blanket, and had an IV needle sticking in her arm. Dustin and Michael stood behind Bridget's doctor, a fiftyish man who had retired from his practice a handful of years ago and made more money with his "house calls" to a group of select patients, Bridget on rare occasions among them.

"Fluids," the doctor told her, seeing Bridget staring at the drip. "And potassium before that. You were seriously dehydrated." He drew his thin lips into a line and shook his head in obvious disapproval. "And suffering from exhaustion. Bruised ribs." He paused and added a finger wag for emphasis. "I don't want to know how you came to be in such shape, Miss O'Shea, that's none of my business. But I'd advise you against future similar behavior. You're not a teenager."

Bridget caught Dustin hiding a smile at that comment. Dustin was dressed smartly in a sweater vest over a maroon shirt and dark gray slacks. She remembered him saying he had a cooking class to attend.

"Though you are—overall—usually in remarkable physical shape, you need to know your limits." The doctor's expression softened. "Seriously, Bridget, you had us worried for awhile. I wanted to put you in the hospital."

Bridget opened her mouth to offer a retort—several churned through her head, but changed her mind. "Thank you for coming over."

"Coming twice. The first to set you up this morning and make sure we didn't need an ambulance. This just to give you one more bag of fluids. You were in far worse shape then, I could've sworn you had a few broken ribs. Now, it looks only bruised. You're healing remarkably well. Still, take it easy."

"Thank you for checking on me," Bridget said.

"Twice." The doctor shrugged. "I was on my way to a late dinner anyway, Bati. Craving something Moroccan, you know. So not out of the way, actually." He patted his stomach and watched the last of the fluid clear the line, and then disconnected it. "But I'll dine easier knowing you're on the mend. I'll leave my bill with Michael."

Dinner? Bridget looked to the window. It was dark outside, motes of light from windows in the adjacent building glimmering. She'd been out for hours. Dustin wasn't going to attend his cooking course today, he'd already been there.

"Twice," Bridget said. "So you really have been here twice?"

"You'll see it in my bill. Now, if you don't mind, I don't want my companion to think I've abandoned her."

Bridget waited until Michael walked the doctor out, then pushed back the covers and swung her legs over the side of the bed and sat straight. She wondered who'd undressed her. Michael? Dustin, probably. She gripped the edge of the mattress, fighting off the dizziness that came from moving too quickly. Her stomach twisted and grumbled in hunger, obviously loud enough for Dustin to hear.

"Soup, I think," he said. "Nothing too heavy." He turned to leave.

"Thank you," Bridget said. She looked to her closet. She had a pair of sweatpants that would suffice and slippers; her toes were cold.

The briefcase she'd told Michael to throw out was sitting just inside her closet, the creature next to it, oozing rivulets of puss into a new pair of Jimmy Choo's.

"Dammit!"

Dustin stopped in his tracks and spun, giving her a puzzled, angry look. "What? You don't need more than soup and—"

"The old briefcase. I told Michael to throw it out."

"He did. This morning in the Dumpster. If you've changed your mind, it's far too late. The trucks came, and it's in some landfill now. That little stone statue is in the main display case. Quite nice, that statue. I believe it is very valuable." He dismissively waved his fingers. "About twenty minutes to heat it up, my soup. I'll leave it on the dining table. I'm going back to my apartment."

"Yeah. Tomorrow."

Dustin did that, retreat to his efficiency at least Monday through Wednesday, sometimes Thursday, and Bridget knew to give him space. She wondered if he saw other women then. She'd never asked.

"When you come down to get your soup, I suggest wearing a little something." Then he was gone and Bridget stared out the window, the lights of the building across the street looking like Chinese lanterns painted against black velvet.

The creature belched another noxious cloud, but Bridget held her breath this time.

"Pissmires and spiders." She stepped around the monster and avoided looking into its multiple eyes. Bridget grabbed the handle of the case, picked it up, and padded toward the window. With her free hand she opened the pane. The wintry air hit her, raising goosebumps. Then she leaned out and sucked in a deep breath of the frigid night. One more lungful and she held it, set the briefcase on the ledge and gave it a push. It thunked against the sidewalk five floors below.

"That ought to take care of you," she said to the monster. "Somebody'll grab it."

The creature had vanished, and Bridget smugly dressed in her comfortable sweatpants, Nicks T-shirt, and slippers, belted a robe loosely around her, and headed to the dining room.

The briefcase was next to the dining table, the monster a few feet away, bubbling and drooling, babbling, and fixing the thief with its disconcerting and very disturbing gaze.

11

By midnight Tuesday, Bridget concluded she could not rid herself of the briefcase through normal means.

She'd shoved it in a furnace.

Laid it on a subway track.

Tossed it into the river.

Gave it to Goodwill.

Left it in an alley.

Tucked it under a pew at St. Augustine's Church.

Mailed it to a residential address in India she randomly picked off the Internet.

Returned it to the apartment she'd stolen it from—no sign of Elijah Stone; in fact it looked like the man had gone on a trip; there was a telltale gap in his clothes closet and only a few pairs of underwear in a drawer.

Dropped it into the sewer.

Left it in the coat closet at Assumption Roman Catholic Church.

Paid a bicycle courier to whisk it away.

And "forgot" it under the table at Frank's Cocktail Lounge, where entirely out of character she drank four Jägerbombs in an effort to wash away the fetid-smelling monster while giving in to a bout of oblivion.

The briefcase returned every single time, unmarred, the creature appearing with it, and looking—if possible—surlier with each of Bridget's failed attempts. It would be comical, Bridget thought, where the monster not so repulsive and her predicament not so hopeless.

It's babbling was certainly language, some of it sounding vaguely familiar, but nothing Bridget could decipher. And though it had not harmed her, she suspected it capable of such. The thing flexed its claws and dug them into the plush carpet of her bedroom, arched its squatty back and narrowed all five of its eyes while it continued to ooze.

"I get that you're trying to communicate, you gobshite of a beast." Bridget had placed the briefcase by an open window in her bedroom. The winter wind that whistled in was uncomfortably cold, but the fresh air cut the absolute stench of the creature just enough so Bridget could keep her dinner and the alcohol down. She sat on the edge of the bed, as far from the satchel and creature as possible, her head pounding with the prelude to a hangover. "I can't feckin' understand you. I don't want to understand you. I just want you gone."

She'd elected not to share her dilemma with her staff or thieving underlings ... since it was obvious they couldn't see the beast anyway. She didn't want them to know she'd been cursed, and by her own doing when she stole the ugly briefcase. Such an admonition would be a sign of weakness.

But Bridget knew people who might help. She looked at the clock on the nightstand. However, those people would not be amenable to a visit at this hour—and they were not people she wanted to risk upsetting.

Finally, she tried to "read" the briefcase using her psychometry skill. Once again, contact with the odd leather yielded nothing useful, just a stream of faces she assumed were previous owners, all of them looking like shards of a broken mirror spinning and rearranging themselves in her mind as in a child's kaleidoscope. Elijah Stone's face came to the fore, expression desperate and hateful; Bridget could pick up nothing else about the man.

She was tired, but not yet to the edge of utter exhaustion, and she knew that's what it would take for sleep. Bridget thumbed the intercom to see if someone in her staff was still awake or could be easily woken.

B ridget stooped in the dusty attic. The light from nearby buildings faintly crept in through a dirty window and touched an assortment of boxes and oil cloth-wrapped bundles that were tied with string. The creature sat in the darkest corner, shining eyes and perpetual stench letting Bridget know just where it was. She couldn't tell if the briefcase was there for all the shadows. The thing continued babbling, louder than before, sounding angry.

"Volume isn't helping," Bridget said. In fact, the nonsensical racket was giving her an even worse headache. She peered out the window and waited, minutes later hearing measured footsteps across the beams behind her. She knew her companion could not hear the creature, nor would he be able to see it—Bridget was the only one so blessed.

"Sheesh, boss, something's a little stinky up here."

Her companion could, however, at least to some degree smell it.

"Ready Jimmy?" Bridget heard the young man yawn. She'd wakened him, wanting a sparring partner, desperate to be so fatigued she could chase away the last of the alcohol-buzz and sleep. Obviously Jimmy, who'd been living in a bedroom in the basement for the past year and a half, had known better than to take a pass on the opportunity.

"I guess, boss." Jimmy Hill was closing in on nineteen and done with the equivalent of high school, finally managing to gain his GED right before Christmas. That had been one of the conditions placed on Jimmy's employment, room, and board—an attempt to earn that treasured certificate. Another was indulging Bridget when she wanted company exercising.

"Let's be about it then." Bridget unlatched the window and swung it open, looking up to the sky that was gray from the city lights. She wore black leggings that she'd purchased through a mail order ballet supply store; many of her underlings, including Jimmy, bought similar garb. The leggings were not restrictive and were perfect for these activities. Over this she wore a loose sweatshirt the color of cold ashes. Jimmy was similarly dressed, but his sweatshirt was black with white block lettering that read: LMFAO. Pulled down over his ears he wore a dark green stocking cap with a Jets logo.

Bridget stepped through the window, seeming to float in front of it before she moved to the right and vanished.

"Coming, Jimmy?"

"I guess, boss."

One foot below the window was an impossibly narrow ledge slick with a layer of frost. Five stories below that was the thin alley that ran between Bridget's building and the next brownstone. Bridget climbed up the brickwork and listened to hear that Jimmy was following, but taking a little easier route, using the drainpipe.

"So, boss, what are we doing?" Jimmy pulled himself up over the edge and gingerly stepped out onto the roof. He shivered. "We got a problem with the chimney? I hope."

Bridget's roof was not flat, it had a peak, and that was one of the reasons why she'd chosen this building. "I'm getting some exercise, and you're getting a lesson."

Jimmy tried to stifle a yawn. "A lesson in what? It's really cold up here. I get that you want to tussle. But up here? It's friggin' freezing. What's that old saying, boss, about a witch's tit in January? It's colder than that up here."

Bridget usually sparred with Jimmy and some of the others in a well-padded room in the basement. But it was late enough, half past midnight, so few—if any—in the neighborhood would see them up here.

"Balance." Bridget reached behind her and unsheathed two shinai, lengths of bamboo with sword grips. She tossed one to Jimmy, who caught it, but nearly lost his footing.

Bridget glided across the roof, making navigating the pitch look as easy as strolling down a city street. She didn't look down, holding the shinai in her right hand and keeping her left arm out for stability. Jimmy tried to copy her, climbing slowly until both reached the top. Jimmy straddled the peak and crouched to meet Bridget's attack.

"I dunno if this is such a good idea, boss. It's pretty slippery." Jimmy looked nervously to his right and left. "And I heard you weren't feeling too well, that yesterday you—"

"Balance," Bridget repeated. The air was the sweetest that she had smelled since acquiring the briefcase. There was no sign of the wretched beast. Perhaps it feared heights or the slick slope of the roof. For the briefest of moments Bridget considered relocating her bed to this roof; but she couldn't live up here. Something else would have to be done to rid herself of the creature.

"Balance?" Jimmy asked. "I dunno boss, I—"

Bridget rushed him and the bamboo sticks met. Jimmy's stick was knocked aside and he almost lost his grip on it. His left leg stiffened to take the impact, but his foot shot out and he hit the slate with a spine-jarring thud.

Bridget remained impassive, extended her hand to help Jimmy up. Jimmy took it, pulled hard, and then jabbed his mentor in the ribs.

The air whooshed out of Bridget's lungs, as the youth nailed her hard in the ribs. They weren't even a little tender, and there'd been no sign of the bruises from only hours before. She'd healed amazingly fast. But he caught her off balance when he thwacked her again. For a heartbeat her head swam and she swayed, slipping, trying to catch herself and failing. Her breath came hard and fast in her throat and she slid down the roof stomach first, hands in front, scrabbling. Her shinai clattered into the gutter. The slate glossy with frost, Bridget couldn't find a purchase and wondered if she'd survive the impact with the alley.

Jimmy grabbed Bridget's ankle, stopping a slide that would have sent her off the roof. "Sorry, boss. I didn't mean to—"

Bridget righted herself and regained her balance. She laughed. "No, no. You did good, Jimmy. That was unexpected. You did good."

Jimmy looked nervous.

"Good job, really."

Jimmy appeared to relax, but only slightly. "We done, boss? Can we go back inside? You know, witch's tit and all that. Brrrr."

"Not yet." Bridget managed to climb back up to the peak, straddling it and walking to the chimney. She leaned against it and looked out over the city. In the distance, she saw barges on the river, wisps of smoke coming from buildings everywhere, adding to the grayness of the sky. She saw delivery trucks on a street to the north, their lights glowing warm yellow. She heard Jimmy climb up behind her. Still, there was no sign of the monster. She thought that just under the scent of smoke and grime she could smell the river.

Without warning, Bridget spun and leaped, twisting in midair and landing lower on the roof. "Jump," she told Jimmy. "Just make sure you land on your feet."

"Oh, crap. Really?" Clearly hesitant, the young man crouched and sprang, not making it half the distance Bridget had but staying upright nonetheless. "Wow." Jimmy paused. "Double wow. I am getting better, huh boss? Maybe I can go out with Marsh and Rob and them next time."

Bridget didn't answer, not one to hand out too many compliments. Jimmy had the body of a thief, compact, hard, lean, and he always appeared eager to learn. Bridget thought the young man would do well and advance in her illicit organization. She wanted Jimmy to take a few college business courses come the fall semester so he could understand bookkeeping, a pertinent component to the smuggling trade.

Leg muscles bunching, Bridget lunged at Jimmy, swinging with her fist. Jimmy staggered back, avoiding the blow, then turned and whacked Bridget with the bamboo, again hitting her with a considerable amount of force.

75

Bridget could swear she saw stars behind her eyes, but she didn't stop. She pushed off and leaped for the eaves, as close to the edge of the roof as she dared. Jimmy followed, and Bridget's hand reached, grabbing the young man's arm, lifting, and spinning him out over the side of the building, holding him suspended.

"Holy Christ!" Jimmy's shinai fell in the alley and he reached up with his free hand, finding Bridget's arm and holding on. "Shit and two is four, boss!"

"And four is eight," Bridget returned.

"You ain't paying me enough for this!"

"You're fine, Jimmy." Bridget dragged the young man up to the roof, where they boxed for a few minutes.

Spent, they sat side-by-side at the very peak, watching delivery trucks motor down side streets and spotting the flashing lights of an ambulance speeding through intersections before being swallowed in the silhouettes of taller buildings.

"I'm filthy," Jimmy said, looking down at his sweatshirt. "I'm bleeding. And I'm cold."

When a church bell bonged "one," Bridget stood and inched her way to the drain pipe. She shimmied down and crept along the ledge until she came to the open attic window. Jimmy was several feet behind her. She stepped inside and took a deep breath.

The stench was gone.

She looked into the darkest corner and didn't see the beast's eyes.

Bridget's heart raced with the possibility she'd somehow shaken the monster. Maybe the ward had a duration. Maybe the magic was used up and the beast had vanished back to wherever it had been summoned from.

"We done, boss?"

"Yes, Jimmy. You can go back to bed."

"After a hot bath, boss."

Bridget didn't see the creature in her bedroom either, and there was no sign of the briefcase. Indeed, the ward had a time limit. She poked her head out the window and looked down; the case wasn't on the sidewalk, hadn't fallen. Maybe Michael had managed to toss it out.

Maybe, but something didn't sit right.

Bridget stripped and eased herself into bed and was tired enough that she fell instantly asleep.

12

Bridget woke to an unrelenting tapping on her bedroom door. A glance at the clock: 2 p.m.; she'd slept for nearly a dozen hours. Stiff, but feeling considerably stronger, her bruised side only a minor annoyance, she sat up and swung her legs over the side of the mattress.

"Miss O'Shea?" More tapping.

"Give me a minute, Michael."

No doubt there was something Bridget needed to attend to; otherwise Michael would have let her sleep even longer. Bridget stretched and gagged. The stench and the monster were back. The creature and the briefcase sat side-by-side under the closed window ... the creature must have shut the pane, Bridget thought. She'd remembered leaving it cracked open when she returned after the sparring match on the roof.

It fixed its five eyes on her and started babbling.

Bridget recalled alternately dreaming that she'd finally ditched the beast or that the past two days had been nothing but a nightmare. But she could still faintly taste the alcohol she'd foolishly downed last night.

More tapping.

"Yes, Michael." Bridget raised her voice. "I said give me a minute!"

"It's rather urgent. There are policemen downstairs."

Bridget's mouth went desert dry, and the monster babbled louder. She needed a shower, but wouldn't take the time now. She dressed quickly, in casual, friendly attire—beige corduroy slacks and a slate blue sweater, thick socks and comfortable tennis shoes. She ran her fingers through her hair and tied it back, splashed some *L'Eau d'Issey* on her neck to cover the scent of her dried sweat, and came back to face the creature.

"Shut the feck up. Hear me?" Bridget kept her voice low, not wanting Michael to hear. "I can't understand you. And I don't give a damn what you're trying to say." She spun on her heels and went to the door. "And I am going to get rid of you today, you gobshite." Bridget counted to ten, forced herself to breathe evenly. She actually worried more about the police than the monster, which appeared to be only a smelly, vexing aggravation, like a wart that wouldn't dissolve. Bridget was meticulously careful with her smuggling operation, as one misstep would land her in prison forever—she'd done that many illegal things. She cracked the door.

Michael's face gave her no clue as to how bad the situation was.

"How many?"

"Just two." Michael paused. "Two policemen ... and your son, Otter."

Dear God, Bridget thought. Her son had shown the bejeweled cup to her ex-, Tavio, and in one of his fiery moods he'd decided to act on it, to turn her in. But Bridget could get around that one piece; having an antique shop, she could claim she'd bought the cup from someone who came in off the street, and she had no idea just how valuable or old it was. It could get ugly and uncomfortable, but the trail would end there and the cup would be eventually returned to whatever museum it had come from. Or maybe Otter had done something horrible. No, they would be at Tavio's condo if that was the case. Tavio didn't work during the day.

The police were in the entry room at the foot of the stairs, shoulder-to-shoulder with their hats in their hands, jackets unzipped. Otter leaned against the opposite wall, coat still fastened and scarf wrapped around his neck. His school backpack was on the floor near him.

"Dad's dead," Otter said as Bridget came down the stairs.

Bridget felt the color drain from her face and her knees threatened to give out. That wasn't possible. Tavio ... there was a mistake.

"Dead," Otter repeated.

"What happened?" Bridget went to Otter's side; hand on his arm, a dozen questions flashing through her mind and waging war with disbelief. She'd seen Tavio Sunday night; he hadn't looked ill. He was reasonably young—mid-fifties, roughly two decades older than her. "What happened? Was there an accident?"

Otter shook his head. "No. I don't know. He's dead. Dead. Dead. Dead. Someone killed him and—"

"Killed?"

"Your son's a minor," one of the policemen interrupted. Bridget didn't know which had spoken; her full attention was still on Otter. "Miss O'Shea, in school records you're listed as—"

"Yes, I'm his mother."

"The last names—"

"I took my name back after the divorce. My maiden name." Bridget swallowed hard. "What happened? With Tavio. Tell me."

Otter's shoulders shook. "Somebody got into the condo, Mom. Last night, this morning, I don't know. I was getting ready for school this morning and Dad hadn't come out of his bedroom. I thought maybe he had company, you know. He had company late sometimes. So I didn't want to disturb him ... them. I caught the bus. Then the cops pulled me out of world history and brought me here."

For several minutes Otter continued to sob and Bridget didn't move. The police were respectful, not intruding or interrupting.

"They said he was dead, in bed." Otter pushed Bridget away, wiped at his face with his scarf. "I should've checked on him this morning. Before I caught the bus, I should've checked. Maybe I could've—"

"—done nothing to prevent it," the same officer cut in. "Listen, Otemar, Miss O'Shea, we should—"

"I don't want to stay here, Mom." Otter said. "I want to go home, to the condo. I'm perfectly able to take care of myself at home. I want to go home."

"Fifteen, not fifty," Bridget said so softly she doubted the boy could hear.

Bridget finally regarded the policemen. They were both in their late twenties and rail thin, one with dark hair and the swarthy complexion of an Italian. That badge read: Bernardini. The other was Irish judging by the badge: McGinty. It was the Irish cop who'd been doing the talking, a sergeant by the insignia.

"How did it happen?" Bridget addressed the sergeant.

"Miss O'Shea, we're not really at liberty to discuss the case yet. Detectives are at the scene."

"He was murdered," Otter said. "They told me someone killed him. They wouldn't tell me more than that." He paused. "I want to go home, Mom. I can take care of myself."

"Miss O'Shea, we'd like to ask you a few questions about your ex-husband." This from the Irish policeman. "Is there someone here Otemar can stay with while—"

"Of course." Bridget gestured to Michael, who'd been keeping a courteous distance. "Michael, have Jimmy refresh Otter's room. I'll be going with—"

"I should call my grandmother," Otter said. "She needs to know."

Michael stepped forward. "In a little while, Otter. We'll call her together. Why don't you come into the kitchen with me until some things are sorted out?"

Otter looked to Bridget.

"It's okay. I won't be gone long," she told her son. "And I'll get us some answers. I promise."

Michael held out a heavy coat and Bridget took it and closed her eyes. The damnable beast was at the bottom of the staircase, babbling and oozing and adding to a headache that had suddenly sprang up behind her eyes. She prayed that the monster would stay behind, though she knew that wouldn't be happening.

It found a way to fit into the back seat of the police cruiser, babbling and oozing puss the entire ride to the 7th Precinct, the ugly briefcase on the floorboard, though Bridget had not placed it there.

13

The 7th was one of the smallest of the city's precincts, serving the lower eastside of Manhattan. Bridget felt queasy, more from being inside the old building on Pitt Street and surrounded by police officers than from having the babbling monster trail her. It was clear that no one saw the beast, but some smelled it, Bernardini making cracks to McGinty about needing to buy some Bean-O.

The precinct covered less than three-quarters of a square mile, with a big transient population, and a thriving business district on Orchard Street. Nearly half the permanent population was foreign-born, and a mix of races made up the clerical staff that moved between the desks in the precinct house.

Bridget was familiar with this area of Manhattan. She knew the blocks by heart around the subway stations on Essex Street at East Broadway and Delaney. But this building? She'd passed it often enough, never bothering to really look at it. Avoided it, actually. Rather squat and ugly, it needed some attention inside and out that the city coffers weren't likely going to allow.

They escorted her upstairs to the detective squad and put her in a room with a dingy olive green tile floor that smelled of ammonia-based cleansers. Elbows on a table under which the creature squatted and babbled, waiting for a detective to come interview her, Bridget figured she was the suspect. The ex- was always the suspect, right? F. Lee Bailey had written a book with something like that as the title. It had been in Tavio's collection of mystery and true crime books. CSI, Hawaii Five-0, Castle ... the ex- was always the suspect.

A few minutes into the questions, however, Bridget realized that wasn't the case with Tavio's murder.

It was two detectives, one Latino, one white, builds and ages like the pair of special agents in the Men in Black series. Though they'd introduced themselves, Bridget was so preoccupied she didn't catch their names. They just wanted to know Tavio's habits, and they didn't want to press Otter about it just yet, the boy being so upset. They'd get to that, though, they assured her. A detective would come to Bridget's brownstone tonight or tomorrow morning to talk to the boy.

"Look, I'm not sure this is any of your business, though I suppose it doesn't matter now. My ex- sees people from time to time ... men, women, even when we were married. Not that I knew about it at first," Bridget told them. *I was feckin' oblivious for a few years.* "Tavio didn't like being alone, and he didn't have much of a preference from what I could tell, race, sex, age ... though he liked young ones better. I don't have any names. I don't keep track. I don't want to know who—. I *didn't* want to know who—. Lately I'd see Tavio ... *saw him* ... only when he'd come to pick up Otter late Sunday nights. Sometimes he'd drop Otter off, but my son usually comes on his own. Tavio and me ... we'd really drifted apart since the divorce." *Had drifted apart,* she added to herself, *well before the marriage was over;* started drifting when she realized Tavio slept around—had probably always slept around on her. But she hadn't always been there to give him an excuse not to. It hadn't all been his fault. She hoped the detectives didn't press her on the marriage; she didn't want to talk about it.

The detectives gave Bridget nothing in return, no cause of Tavio's death, no hint of suspects, nothing other than that the body was with the Medical Examiner and they would prefer Bridget rather than Otter make the identification, though even that wasn't necessary.

They knew Tavio Madera was the victim; they had dental records. And it felt, to Bridget, like they were holding something back.

"In fact," said McGinty as he escorted Bridget away from the detectives and outside the building, "I'd take a pass on identifying your ex-husband. Trust me on this."

McGinty and Bernardini took her to Tavio's condo so she could gather clothes for Otter. There were two marked police cars out front and two unmarked sedans. A half block down the street a WNYW Fox News van was parked, so there must have been something interesting enough on a scanner to bring reporters here. A simple murder? There were enough of those in the city that they all didn't warrant a news van; sometimes they only got a few lines of type in the *Times*. But Tavio had been a restaurant owner, a bit of a socialite. There was no sign of any other media, so maybe the other stations had more interesting things to cover.

The WNYW reporters were in the lobby, getting "no comments" from a plainclothesman. Bridget's escorts rushed her into the elevator. She shivered, disdaining the close contact with police. When the doors opened on Tavio's floor, an officer holding a clipboard signed McGinty in. Bridget noticed the form detailed quite a few comings and goings.

It was a two-bedroom condo that took up an entire floor—the eleventh—of the twelve-story building. Tavio had purchased the condo right after the divorce—they'd sold their shared loft—and he grumbled that he couldn't get the one in this building that had direct access to the roof deck. Still, it was spacious, loft-style that he loved, and had been artfully and expensively decorated by a five-star interior designer that Tavio'd had a fling with. Bridget had been inside the place only once before.

"The ground rules are that you stay with us," McGinty said. He handed Bridget a pair of white, overlarge booties to slip over her shoes. "You're limited to only your son's bedroom and the big hall closet. We saw it has some empty suitcases in it you can use."

On first glance everything looked perfect to Bridget, like a center spread in one of the magazines Tavio was fond of. *Elle Décor* and

85

Veranda were fanned out on a coffee table next to stacks of *GQ and The Brooklynite*. There was a large arrangement of fresh-cut flowers in a vase, but Bridget couldn't smell them over the odor of the beast that trailed her.

"How ... who found him?" Bridget hadn't thought to ask that earlier. She knew it hadn't been Otter. In the ride to the condo she'd a chance to mentally berate herself. From the moment the police appeared at her brownstone she'd thought only of herself ... getting caught because of the cup she'd given Otter, and then worried she'd be a suspect in Tavio's death. She'd not really thought about Tavio. She'd truly loved him once—to an extent still had, and the sense of loss was only now seeping in. Bridget had been seventeen when they'd met, a random encounter at the restaurant he owned and that she and other Westies favored when they were looking for Italian fare. She married him when she turned eighteen, had Otter not quite a year later, probably should have waited on both counts. She'd been too young for the responsibility of a family. Tavio was two decades older, but so goddamn handsome the years hadn't mattered at the time. On their first wedding anniversary, Tavio purchased the antique shop for her. She'd been a frequent customer of the place, and he thought owning it would give her a legitimate hobby. Tavio knew she'd been involved with various illegal activities with the Westies, and while he knew she liked antiquities, he was unaware of her "gift" and her mental delving into the past; Bridget felt a need to keep a few secrets.

Tavio was what ... fifty-three, fifty-four? Hadn't he just had a birthday the fourteenth or fifteenth of December? Bridget'd always had trouble remembering the exact day. The fourteenth.

"He was fifty-four," Bridget said. "Only fifty-four." She raised her voice, thinking the police hadn't heard her the first time she'd asked: "Who found him?"

"Housekeeper." This from Bernardini. "She found your ex-husband. She called 9-1-1."

An evidence technician noticed Bridget and shut the double doors to Tavio's bedroom. Bridget had caught only a glimpse, bed covers on the floor, though that might have been of the police's doing. She'd noticed blood spattered on the white carpet, thought she'd seen some on the wall. If she was really all that curious she could come back here late tonight when no one was around and delve the bed. She knew the security in this building was good—had checked it out for Otter's sake, but it wasn't *that* good that she couldn't get past it. Maybe she could even use her psychometry on something in the bedroom not so bloody and repulsive to discover the murderer—though she would never tell the police about her arcane ability.

"Only the boy's room and the hall closet," McGinty repeated.

"I get it." Bridget retrieved two large suitcases and filled them with Otter's clothes, a hanging bag for the lone suit and two sports coats. She took a duffle out of Otter's closet and stuffed it with odds and ends—books that the boy might need for school, a couple of science fiction paperbacks, and the gem-encrusted cup that had been filled with pens and pencils and that the police didn't need to take a close look at. Maybe they had taken a look but hadn't realized what it was. Or maybe Otter's dog-eared copy of Michael Moorcock's *Tales From the End of Time* propped against it had hidden enough details.

Bridget smiled. She'd figured Otter for a Kindle or Nook or something, not real pages. Ah, there was an iPad. She took that, too, and the boy's laptop, which managed to fit in the duffle, leaving the bulky laser printer. She searched around for other things, finding a small framed picture of a dark-haired girl in a red sundress. She added that. Maybe it was the girlfriend Lacy; Otter had wanted Bridget to meet her. There were no posters on the wall, but there was a large framed print of the 1976 Montreal Olympics by LeRoy Neiman, numbered and signed, and an eight-by-ten photo on the bureau of Tavio and Otter after a swim meet. The photo had to be recent; it looked like it was taken outside the high school, the leaves on the overhanging trees orange and yellow. Otter was holding a trophy. There were a dozen trophies and plaques on a shelf above the desk. Bridget stared at them.

There wasn't a single picture of Bridget with Otter, though she knew a professional one had been taken of the three of them more than a few years ago. And other than the silver cup, there'd been nothing readily apparent in the room to tie the boy to Bridget.

"Your son is an accomplished athlete, looks like," McGinty said. Bridget had forgotten the police sergeant had been standing in the doorway.

"And I've been a shitbird mother. There was a reason I'd never argued for custody." Bridget selected two of the smaller trophies, wrapped them in T-shirts, and added them to the duffle, along with three ties. Otter would need the suit and a tie for Tavio's funeral. The demon squatted on the bed next to the suitcases. It uttered a string of something that niggled at Bridget's brain, and then belched sulfur. Bridget looked away. "But I guess that's going to have to change, the shitbird mother part."

"School records said you shared custody," McGinty said.

"Yeah. Sort of," Bridget said. "Otter's a good kid. He didn't deserve losing his father. Tavio was a good father." Softer: "And Otter deserves a far better mother than me."

"We'll find who did it."

Bridget didn't think McGinty's words had any real conviction. She might, indeed, have to secretly lend her talents to help.

"I can come back and get the rest later, right? Bring a packing crate or two. It doesn't look like there's all that much. Fifteen. How much stuff can a fifteen-year-old have?" Bridget pointed to a flat screen television that hung on the wall opposite the bed, then to the Neiman print. "I can come back, right?"

"Later, sure. When we're done."

"And when might that be?"

McGinty shrugged and looked over his shoulder. "Shoes. You're forgetting to take some shoes."

Bridget grabbed a smaller duffle at the bottom of Otter's closet, from the chlorine scent it had probably been used for swim gear. Underneath it were half a dozen *Playboys*. She fit four pairs of shoes in the bag and tossed it on the bed, trying to hit the foul creature, but it had sidled up to the pillows. Bridget gave another look around the room, surprised to spy a gray plastic model of the *Millennium Falcon* poised on a high shelf. She and Otter had put that together when the boy was six, and she'd never gotten around to helping him paint it.

"When are you going to tell me something about Tavio's death? Am I going to have to hear it on the news?" Bridget kept her eyes on the model, debating whether she should take it. She could use her psychometry to relive the experience with a six-year-old Otter; everything had been good then. She hadn't yet realized Tavio was running around on her. "Can't you tell me something? Anything?"

There were a few boxes on shelves in the closet, and she wondered if she should look through them. But the police would let her in later. She could sort through the rest of the things then, see what Otter wanted to take out of the other rooms. She'd let Tavio's mother deal with the rest. There were a couple of empty rooms in the brownstone to put the stuff in.

McGinty hadn't answered.

"Look, it was alright for detectives at the station to ask me plenty of questions. I cooperated. And I'm tired of not getting any answers to my own. Help me out here. Give me something. Tavio and I aren't ... weren't ... hadn't been close for a long time. But I certainly didn't hate him. I want to know something. Give me something."

McGinty let out a whistling breath. "Look, Miss O'Shea, I'm not the case detective. I'm not the primary or—"

"Something."

"Your ex-husband was killed late last night or early this morning. It was bloody, ritualistic maybe, and I don't really know much more than that myself. There was no sign of a break-in, so he probably let the guy—or gal—in. Like your son said, a guest, company. The case detectives think it must have been quick, the killing part, or your son would have heard something. And be very thankful he didn't hear anything, Miss O'Shea. Be thankful you still have your son."

Be thankful Otter hadn't heard Tavio scream, Bridget thought.

"So it was it quick? Did Tavio feel—"

"I don't know."

"You have a suspect."

"Miss O'Shea—"

Bridget fixed the Irish cop with a hard stare.

"We have ... and we haven't ... a suspect, Miss O'Shea. We don't

89

know who killed your ex-husband, but it's similar to some other murders in the city and—. We don't need a panic. There's a pattern, they all might be related. I'm leaving it at that. Maybe the investigative leads will release more later and—"

All? They all might be related. "A pattern? A serial killer? Tavio was murdered by—"

"I'm shutting up about it now, Miss O'Shea. Let's get you back home," McGinty said. "I'll help with the bags."

The monster didn't babble on the ride back to the brownstone. Again Bridget thought how much like a grotesque bullfrog the thing looked. The muscles in its mottled green-brown legs quivered as ooze continued to pump in rivulets down its sides and protruding stomach, disappearing before reaching the vinyl of the car's upholstery.

Bridget's gut clenched when the thing belched sulfur. It felt like canned heat had settled in her chest. She barely registered the colors of the city that bled by the window, and the pounding in her head drowned out the sounds of traffic and the crackle of the police radio.

It had started to snow by the time they eased up to the brownstone. Otter's face was pressed to the glass of a second-story window. The boy pulled back from the pane when Bridget got out of the car.

14

Bridget tried to leave the ugly briefcase in the backseat of the police sedan, and waved goodbye to McGinty as the car pulled away from the curb. But the briefcase appeared among Otter's suitcases and duffels on the front stoop when she opened the door and called for Michael.

"I swore I'd gotten rid of that thing," Michael said, looking at the case.

"I'm rather attached to it," Bridget replied as she set it inside and started carrying in Otter's things.

"Otter is in his room, Miss O'Shea. Jimmy is up there keeping him company, looking after him. Your son is taking this very hard. I've called your physician. He's going to prescribe something to help Otter rest and—"

"Did you call Tavio's mother?"

Michael shook his head. "I told Otter we should wait, see what you found out from the police and call her then. No use having to talk to the damned old woman twice."

"Don't call her. I'll go over and tell her in person."

Michael looked surprised. "That would be nice, Miss O'Shea, but—"

A wail came from upstairs and was followed instantly by pounding feet—Jimmy's.

Jimmy appeared at the top of the stairs and motioned wildly. "Boss, turn on the television. FOX. It's about your ex-" Then he was gone, assumedly back to Otter's room, and Michael rushed into the sitting room.

Bridget followed Michael, who had just clicked on the widescreen that hung above the fireplace. A few minutes after four, this was the early newscast's lead story. Bridget had missed the first of it, but there was Tavio's handsome face taking up half the screen, a black-and-white image from a newspaper society article.

"Single, affluent people in the New York City area are being targeted by a serial killer who extracts their hearts. Fifty-four-year-old Tavio Vāduva-Madera, the latest victim, was found dead by his housekeeper earlier today. Police initially refused to comment on the case, however a source in the coroner's office confirmed that Madera was brutally killed when his chest was ripped open and his heart cut out. No sign of the heart or—"

Bridget sprinted from the room and up the stairs, nearly tripping on the carpet runner at the top and racing down the hall and into Otter's room. The boy stood transfixed in front of a small television on the stand, Jimmy behind him.

"—a spokesman for the FBI admits authorities are looking for a serial killer, who profilers put between the age of thirty and fifty and who somehow charms single women and men into letting him into their homes. Madera is the second victim in New York City to fall prey to the killer this month. Three women were similarly killed in other states, going back to December, 2013; five in all solidly attributed to one slayer. But that might only be the tip of this bloody iceberg. And the FBI hints that the deaths could escalate."

Tavio's face disappeared to be replaced by four headshots which filled the screen then shrunk to take up half of it, allowing the anchor to be seen. The room spun and Bridget sagged onto the edge of the bed. Two of the women niggled at her memory. One was sixtyish with an ash colored bob; the other was young, with long blond hair and turquoise eyes.

Dear God. Her fingers gripped the coverlet. Those two women had stared out at her from picture frames in Elijah Stone's apartment.

"New York City Police were trying to keep the nature of this latest murder under wraps," the anchor continued, "in an effort not to panic the public. But FOX's investigative team has uncovered enough to report on this grisly situation."

Otter was crying, his shoulders shaking. He gulped in air and Bridget stared helplessly, the weight of the revelation anchoring her. Jimmy put a hand on Otter's shoulder.

"Jaylee Carter, twenty-nine, a freelance travel writer,—" The blond woman with the turquoise eyes from Stone's apartment was highlighted. "—was killed January second in her Brooklyn apartment. We reported on the case, but had not yet made the connection to serial slayings. The next image highlighted was the silver-haired woman from Stone's apartment. "Martha Stone, sixty-nine, of Freehold, New Jersey, was killed earlier, December eleventh." The reporter droned on about the additional two victims; both from a tiny resort town in Delaware, one slain in September, the other this past Christmas Eve.

"In all five cases, the hearts were not found at the scenes, and there is evidence the killer chewed on at least two of the women. FBI Spokesman Jane Tanis, admitted to our FOX team that the killings could stretch back to 2007 to include ritualistic murders still unsolved in Florida, Texas, California, and Washington state with enough factors in common to now raise suspicion they were committed by the same man. If that proves true, up to thirteen women, three men, and one boy ultimately may be traced to the serial killer, Tanis said."

The image shifted again, showing the reporter that Bridget had seen in the lobby of Tavio's condo, except the setting was outside the 7th Precinct. "Fox reporter Mark Ablee is live with Lieutenant Harold Grossman," the anchor announced.

Grossman's voice was measured, and he read from a card in his hands. "We discourage people in the New York area from inviting men they do not know into their homes. Further, if traveling alone,

93

keep to well-lit, populated streets. People who have been approached by strangers are asked to report any suspicious behavior to police. If anyone has helpful information, contact our taskforce hotline."

"We will have more on this breaking story at six and ten," the anchor concluded.

The scene shifted to a factory fire in the Bronx.

Otter's voice was a whisper. "Why didn't I check on him? Dad might still be—"

Bridget numbly left the room. She should comfort her son, but how? There weren't any words, and all the swirling notions centered selfishly.

How much was her life going to change because she now had a full-time son?

How could she hope to cope with Otter's grief, which must be a hundred-fold what she was experiencing?

Should she contact a psychiatrist for the boy?

Find an expensive boarding school to get him out of the way? Maybe put him in some military prep school that would keep him so busy he couldn't think about his father.

If Bridget kept him here, would she be forced to adjust her smuggling operations? Would she pull Otter into her dealings, welcome him into the "family business," or could she manage to keep the boy out of it? She paused at the staircase and stared down at the collection of suitcases and duffels.

And how the hell could she be so selfish to dwell on just how all of this could affect her? She should think about Otter instead.

"Pissmires and spiders." Bridget took a few steps down, intending to retrieve Otter's things and take them to the boy's room. Then she changed her mind. Michael could deal with it. She returned to the landing and instead took the staircase up. She needed a hot shower followed by a blessedly long subway ride with the ugly briefcase.

The monster was waiting for her in the bedroom, perched by the closet, the case next to it. The creature babbled again and oozed something even more foul-smelling than before.

"I get rid of you today," she told the beast. "In just a little while, in fact. I'm done with you stinking up my life and oozing into my expensive shoes."

The thing cocked its bulbous head, and the expression on its wide, warty face turned Bridget's spine to an icicle. It raised a front leg; the image of a dog attempting to "shake hands" came to mind. The misshapen claws, up to what would be the wrist-joint, were crusted with dried blood.

Elijah Stone had been connected to two of the dead women … and this beast and the briefcase.

Bridget had been connected to Tavio … and now the monster and the briefcase.

The beast belched a sulfurous cloud and Bridget grabbed the bureau when the nausea hit.

She was staring at Tavio's murderer.

The monstrous "serial killer" regarded her coolly and put down its leg. But it continued to babble shrilly.

15

Normally the subway relaxed Bridget. The train was her cocoon, comforting as a womb. Usually she could relegate the blathering of all the other riders to the background, the contemporary clamor spewing from radios, and let the sound of the car itself settle in, the squeaks and clacks and everything else a beat she imagined setting her heart in time to.

Clatter-clack-shuck-shuck-shuck-riders' conversations—and then the horn would come, and a bell sounding from somewhere far off. Clatter-clack-shuck-shushhhhh.

The rhythm of the ride was often good for getting rid of headaches and drowning worries. Her feet firmly against the floor, every vibration pulsed up through her soles. Today the vibrations seemed jarring.

Some of the riders in her car were texting; two looked at watches and tapped their feet as if that might provide the impetus to make the train go faster so they wouldn't be late to wherever they were going; a couple bobbed their heads to tunes playing on their iPods. There was a lanky man with a radio around his neck that was so large and heavy-looking she imagined it was curving his spine. The gaunt woman across from him nervously twitched as if she were either claustrophobic or an addict coming down from a high.

During some rides Bridget could see an entire slice of New York City's makeup inside a single subway car—all ages, races, rich, poor, religions—nuns fiddling with their rosary beads, Moonies selling jewelry, Muslims saying "There is no god but Allah," and the atheists arguing that there is no god.

Some of the riders were tense today, a few obviously sad, a couple clearly joyful. There were beggars, a local politician, and a rail-thin beauty with a perfect face who was likely headed to somewhere in the fashion district. Many of the people closest to Bridget chattered seemingly without coming up for air, the noise mixing with the screeching, clicking, shushing sounds the train made, the horn punctuating everything.

Clatter-clack-shuck-shuck-shuck-riders' conversations—and then the horn would come once more, and a bell sounding from somewhere far off. Clatter-clack-shuck-shushhhhh.

Bridget usually loved all of it, often arriving at a platform plenty early before her connection just to hear the train coming, the noise echoing off the walls of the tunnel and sounding like ghosts calling to each other. Then the crescendo of sound as one approached, the wind it created as it passed, the cacophony a symphonic tone poem she was comfortable with. Predictable clamor.

Clatter-clack-clack-shuck-shuck-schuck-conversation-shuck-schuck-conversation-a bell clanging-shuck-shuck-shuck-the demon babbling.

Today, Bridget didn't love the symphony of the subway. Today, all the noises were magnified and making her head pound so hard she wondered if her skull might crack like an eggshell. The warring colognes of the riders mixed with the stench of the monster, and all of it settling on her tongue like wet cement.

The demon babbled louder still, perhaps thinking she couldn't hear it.

The monster had splayed itself on the seat across from her ... and bubbled and oozed and appeared to hungrily eye a teen in an ankle-length wool coat. The beastly thing sickened her. Stomach roiling and breathing shallowly, she worried that she might pass out.

It had most certainly killed her ex-husband, and who-knew-how-many people before that. And she had to get rid of it before it killed someone else connected to her ... Otter, Dustin, Michael. Apparently no one but herself could see the damned thing. As jaded as New Yorkers were, they would have given the creature a wide berth if they knew it was among them. Or the brave among them would be taking pictures of it with their cell phones.

It prattled nonsensically, loud enough to be heard above the clattering and chattering.

"Shut the flying feck up!" Bridget gripped the sides of her head and leaned forward, chin between her knees. She tried to focus only on the subway car, her cocoon, which at the moment was miserably failing as a sanctuary.

Concentrate on the subway, she told herself. *Think about the subway, not the demon.*

There wasn't a mile of the New York City subway system that she hadn't traveled, and only needed to consult maps and schedules when they shut down certain routes for renovations. In Manhattan: Greenwich Village, Chelsea, Chinatown, downtown. In Queens: Sunnyside, Astoria, Long Island City, she could connect to all of them. The stops and lines were engraved in her memory, the sounds of the tunnels in the various sections a familiar favorite play list. To most of the eight million daily riders Bridget suspected the trains sounded pretty much the same, nearly entirely incomprehensible, the racket carried through distorted speakers. But when she listened closely, like she did to cherished classical music, the trains had different voices along the various routes, throatier, more powerful when it traveled from Hoyt to Lafayette to Franklin and Rockaway. Softer and almost lyrical from Steinway to Elmhurst to Woodhaven.

She couldn't hone in on the voice of this train today. Too much noise. And the demon. Her head throbbed.

Concentrate on the subway.

The line from Bergen to Grand Army Plaza keened mournfully most times. The one she took in Fort Greene, from the stop on Fulton and up to Court House Square, where she'd change lines, usually had the richest tones. From there, moments ago, she changed trains and took the line that trundled up Fifty-Ninth, Sixty-Eighth, up to One Hundred and Sixteenth, before turning and cutting toward Hunts Point.

"Dear God, make it all shut up." Bridget got off at the Elder Avenue stop and walked for a few blocks, hoping the cold wind would chase away the stench of the creature and being sorely disap-pointed on that account. At least the noise was more manageable.

Bridget sat the briefcase on the sidewalk outside her destination and looked up at the weathered sign hanging slightly askew above the door: DON'T JUDGE A BOOK.

She'd showered and managed to get here while the witch was still open. If Adiella Vāduva-Madera had heard about her son's death the place would have been closed up tight. But Bridget suspected the old woman did not own a television and only occasionally read the *New York Times*. News, unless it involved this rundown and crime-riddled street, was sluggish to reach her. The police at the station had asked Bridget about "next of kin" to notify regarding Tavio's death. She'd replied just Otter, plus some distant relatives in Mexico and Romania that she didn't have addresses for. She'd never known Tavio's father, who'd died twenty-five years ago. Adiella Vāduva-Madera? Bridget wished she had never met her.

The witch lived off the so-called grid and likely would not come up on any record search involving Tavio, who was an only child as far as Bridget knew. The witch didn't have an address, other than this shop. Tavio once told her that his mother lived in various "arcane pits" she'd established in and under the city. The bookstore looked like a pit, Bridget decided.

For the entirety of Bridget's time with Tavio, Adiella hadn't approved of the marriage. The witch hadn't bothered to show up to the fairy tale wedding Tavio orchestrated aboard a dinner cruise yacht. Adiella had made it clear she didn't consider it a real union, since the ceremony wasn't performed by a Catholic priest in a

99

Catholic church; they'd had the yacht captain officiate. Too, Adiella detested Bridget's association with the Westies and the smuggling business, regularly bringing up that she was a runaway without a proper family. Bridget simply was not good enough, a scamp and a thief not worthy of Tavio's affections. Bridget recalled how Adiella took every opportunity to announce her displeasure, calling the "Irish guttersnipe" a soiled piece of fluff that Tavio should have steered clear of—too young, uneducated trash.

Otter had been Adiella's weakness. Bridget's pregnancy had been difficult, labor arduous; she almost died and the doctor strongly advised her against ever becoming pregnant again. Adiella had attended the birth of what might therefore be her only grandchild and had put in appearances thereafter at Christmas to give the boy books. Adiella got together with Tavio and Otter on the side—lunches at Tavio's restaurant or other fine restaurants he wanted to sample, rare weekend trips where no doubt the witch's acid tongue rode Bridget into the ground.

Nearly 5:30. There didn't look to be any customers, so Bridget entered, briefcase in hand, reeking monster following her like a dutiful shepherd dog.

Adiella was behind the counter at the very back, reading a book. She looked up at Bridget, seeing through the shadows cast by the tall shelves and raising her lip. "What do *you* want?"

Bridget didn't answer. She slowly walked toward the witch, floorboards softly groaning, stepped up to the counter, and sat the briefcase down. She didn't want to deliver this news and was having second thoughts about not mentioning Adiella to the police. One of the officers could have come by and told her about Tavio's murder. But there was the matter of the briefcase, and so she needed to ask Adiella's help.

Adiella's eyes narrowed and fixed on Bridget's, drifted to the briefcase and widened like a pug dog's. In the span of a few heartbeats the witch's demeanor changed, the defiance Bridget was used to seeing vanishing, something else creeping in. Did Adiella already know about Tavio?

No, the witch wouldn't be sitting here if she knew.

"Your son is dead," Bridget said. No preamble, no easing into it. She'd intended to remain hardhearted, but the witch withering before her eyes softened her.

Adiella had looked like a young woman when Bridget first entered, skin smooth and flawless, hair tucked up neatly in a bright red scarf that matched her tailored jacket. She always dressed well and decorated herself with pieces of designer jewelry—big hoop earrings and necklaces with large, colorful beads. Bridget likened Adiella to a strutting peacock.

Small, not even five feet, she appeared to shrivel further. "Dead? My Tavio?" She wailed long and high-pitched like a banshee. Shelves tottered, and Bridget felt the floor vibrate beneath her feet. The keening was painful, and Bridget slammed her teeth together.

Wrinkles danced across the backs of Adiella's tiny hands and appeared at the edges of her instantly-rheumy eyes. Tears ran like rain down her cheeks. Her shoulders rounded and she stooped, gripping the counter to keep from slipping off her stool. The wailing stopped after a time and she appeared to fight for breath.

Bridget believed the witch was well more than a hundred years old and used spells to appear youthful. Maybe two hundred. Maybe three. Maybe she was immortal. But Adiella's concentration on her appearance had been sapped with this horrid news, and so the decades flooded her features.

Bridget wasted no time giving her the details, including the part about Tavio's heart having been ripped out. There was no kindness in her delivery, and yet she had to stop herself from reaching out a hand and touching Adiella.

It took several long minutes for Adiella to compose herself. Bridget saw the witch's lip quiver and fingers tremble; that coupled with her elderly appearance was a serious display of grief she'd not known the woman capable of. After Bridget finished her report, neither said anything for a while. A siren intruded on the silence, then a second, police cars a street over. A faint whistling crept into the shop, the winter wind picking up outside and finding its way in through cracks in the building. A door slammed and there were footsteps overhead, one of the apartment tenants come home from work.

"Do you think my Tavio suffered?"

"Most certainly. How could he not?" Then Bridget told her about the monster responsible, describing the beast in detail and pointing to briefcase. "I've acquired a monster. And it's what—"

"No monster was responsible. You are responsible," Adiella hissed. Her eyes practically glowed and she pointed a finger at Bridget. "Your monster. Your fault."

"So you can say that, say that it's my fault that Tavio is dead. I won't argue that point, and I can't get that point out of my head. Tavio indeed would be alive and well if I hadn't stolen this devilish briefcase."

"I will kill you!"

"Which probably won't save your grandson."

Adiella's eyes grew wide.

"There's a beast so clearly attached to it, this briefcase, and now attached to me. And the feckin' beast killed Tavio. If I die, what's to stop the beast from attaching itself to Otter? It's a damnable, heinous curse I've picked up, one I can't get rid of on my own. What's to stop the curse from passing to my son? Believe me ... I have exhausted all normal avenues to get rid of it. I know others who might help: Nuri Lakshmi, Beran, Goater in the Bronx."

"Lady Lakshmi is—"

"Not as powerful as you. None of them are as powerful as you."

"But she does not hate you, Lakshmi." A pause. "Beran, Goater of the August Moon, they do not hate you. I have *always* hated you."

"For whatever reason, yeah, I've never been in your favor."

"Because you are a pariah." She spit the last word out. "Let the thief no longer steal, but rather let her labor, doing honest work with her own hands, so that she may have something to share with anyone in need. Let—"

"Fine, I'm a pariah. No need to quote Ephesians. But right now, I'm the only thing standing between the monster and Otter. And I might not be enough."

"If Otter is harmed—"

"Listen to me, Adiella, this beast kills people close to the one who has the briefcase. It killed Tavio because he was close to me ... or at least the beast thought Tavio was close. The police are looking for a man, a serial killer. They think a serial killer got Tavio, and others before him. But I know better. It was this ... this ... thing that killed him." Bridget exhaled and unbuttoned her coat, easing out of it and letting it fall to the floor. It was warm inside the shop; she remembered that Adiella liked the heat. "I stole the briefcase from a man on Eighty-Fifth, and found out today the beast had killed that man's mother and at least one young woman he knew. It killed Tavio. No question about that. It kills and kills and kills."

Bridget had always been uncomfortable in Adiella's presence, but this was unbearable. The witch didn't blink, her eyes bored in, and Bridget felt her skin itch under the stare. Perhaps the witch was giving her some horrid rotting disease. "I didn't want the briefcase, Adiella, just what was inside it. But there was some powerful warding spell on the briefcase ... something vile and strong, and when I opened the briefcase I must have released the ward. Like I said, most definitely a curse is involved."

"Thou shalt not steal," Adiella said. "Treasures gained by wickedness do not profit, but righteousness delivers from death."

Whatever verse and chapter she quoted this time was a mystery to Bridget. "Adiella, I may well deserve this beast that's affixed itself to me—"

"Lay not up for yourselves treasures upon earth, where moth and rust doth corrupt, and where thieves break through and steal. But lay up for yourselves treasures in heaven, where neither moth nor rust doth corrupt, and where thieves do not break through nor steal."

"—but Otter doesn't deserve it."

Adiella growled. "You deserve it. You, Bridget O'Shea are a waste of human flesh."

"The beast kills people close to the one who has the briefcase," Bridget repeated. "Tavio's gone, that leaves Otter. You're the most powerful witch in the city, Adiella. Don't break the curse for me, break it for Otter."

Her expression softened. "This beast, Bridget—"

Bridget had to lean close to hear the witch. Adiella's voice had dropped to a mere suggestion.

"It's right here. The beast ... monster is too polite a word, I think. The beast is in your shop," Bridget said. "It is watching us. It's sitting right there." She gestured to her right, toward the base of a shelf stuffed with paperback romances. "It's ugly as hell, evil, and—as much as I truly hate to say it—I need your help."

"This beast ... it is a demon," Adiella pronounced, her voice a shade louder.

"Christ!" Bridget closed her eyes and sucked in a deep breath, the air in the shop filled with Adiella's perfume, the fusty odor of old books, and of the creature ... the *demon*. "Without casting a single spell, you know what it is? Can you see it? It's a feckin' demon?" Adiella indeed might be powerful enough to see the monstrosity. "Pissmires. I didn't think anyone but me could see it."

The witch shook her head, hoop earrings jingling. "See it? No. But I can sense it, Bridget O'Shea. I can sense that it is a dominant demon that has attached itself to your soul. Old, defiant, powerful. It wants something."

"No shit. I know it wants something. Blood ... hearts. Tavio's heart, life, women and men before that. A boy, too. The FBI thinks their so-called serial killer got a boy some years ago. It ripped the heart out of a boy. So Otter's probably next on its menu. The ... *demon* ... has been around this country a while, passing from hand to hand to hand and leaving a trail of bodies. I could probably find a way to have the damn briefcase stolen from me. That's how I got the curse, Adiella, I stole it. I took on the curse that was probably eating away at a fellow named Elijah Stone."

"Elijah Stone?"

"Yes, that is the man I stole the case from. And he's up and left the city. No wonder, huh? Probably vacationing in some tropics, demon free. God, but I was set up. Had to be. Stone needed the briefcase stolen and somehow I fell into his plan. A friend of Marsh ... hell, you don't know Marsh. And Marsh said he didn't know Harry Black or Brown or Gray. It was all a damnable setup."

"I see. Greed brought this upon you, and so greed is the trigger to the curse. Ever the greedy bitch, Bridget O'Shea. 'I was enraged by her sinful greed; I punished her, and hid my face in anger, yet she kept on in her willful ways.'"

"I don't need the Bible lesson, Adiella."

"Your greed—"

"I suppose in turn I could find another greedy bitch. I could certainly find a way to have it stolen from me. There are plenty of greedy bitches out there I could lure." Bridget took in another deep breath and nearly retched from the swirl of odors. The beast belched a sulfurous cloud. "But I don't want to go that route. I want to find a way to send this foul thing back to whatever hell it came from, no more killing people by ripping out their hearts." She paused and studied the witch. "I don't want to pass along the curse. I want to end the curse." Adiella had regained a measure of her composure, the wrinkles around her eyes and on the backs of her hands gone. "I don't want to take the chance that even if I do manage to get rid of the briefcase, to have it pinched by another thief, the thing won't go after Otter anyway." Otter was Adiella's weak spot, and Bridget needed to play on that. "I've not been a good mother, Adiella, I'll give you that. But I love my son, and I'm going to do what I must to keep him safe."

Adiella chanted as she pulled several books out from beneath her counter, not bothering to close her shop or flick off the fluorescent lights to create a magical mood. Bridget could tell she was panicked at the thought of Otter dying like Tavio. Then Bridget couldn't hear, the witch's lips working, but no sound coming out, her fingers trembling in her worry and grief and anger. Bridget couldn't hear the witch thump the books on the counter or turn the pages, and could no longer hear any of the traffic or sirens out on the street. She stepped closer, out of the bubble-like barrier Adiella had created to keep anyone upstairs or outside from hearing the magic.

Bridget didn't know what language Adiella spoke. Maybe Romanian, it had a Slavic feel. Her last name was a meld of Slavic and Spanish. She'd only once asked Adiella about her ancestry, and the glare she got in response kept her from asking again. The witch's fingers fluttered as she continued, like she was knitting something invisible. There was a pattern to the movements. One book, two, three. Adiella had seven on the counter now and it had grown dark outside, the streetlights coming on.

She went through the books again, and Bridget had to step back, her legs cramping. Bridget leaned against a bookshelf, out of the "bubble," hearing nothing again and not minding. She couldn't even hear the demon, which she was certain continued to babble. It always babbled. Only in her sleep had she escaped the hellish chatter. She realized when it had killed Tavio. It was when she went up on the roof to spar with Jimmy. The creature hadn't followed her ... because it went to visit Tavio. That it knew about Tavio had been disturbing. It had to have searched her mind.

And so it knew about Otter.

Dustin.

Michael.

And now Adiella.

Bridget choked back a laugh. If the beast ripped Adiella's heart out, she wouldn't overmuch mourn the witch. But she doubted the demon would find Adiella a choice target. The creature would select something with more meaning.

Otter.

Adiella's voice rose and then she collapsed. The sounds of the city came in through the cracks, the wind and traffic, music from across the street, a television program from an apartment overhead. Bridget didn't budge; she waited.

The witch dragged herself to her feet, spider web white hair poking out from under the red scarf that had slipped. Her chest heaved and she gripped the counter. For a moment, Bridget feared the witch was having a seizure.

"It defies me," Adiella gasped, regaining control and again chasing the wrinkles from her diminutive frame. "So very powerful."

"Try again." Bridget said. "Let's go to where your magic is stronger. Take me to one of your secret pits that Tavio told me about. Then try again and again and again."

"You will need your coat," Adiella said, her expression flat. "Though I doubt it will be enough to keep you warm."

16

Adiella bundled herself like an Arctic explorer, complete with knee-high boots trimmed in what looked to be real fur. She led Bridget to the nearest subway stop and waited for the train to arrive, load, and depart. When it was just the two of them on the platform—plus a homeless man sleeping against the wall, she climbed over the edge and down onto the track bed, having no difficulty despite her years and voluminous layers of clothing. Bridget followed, surprised at the witch's speed.

"The video feed?" Bridget asked, gesturing back toward the platform. "Won't someone have—"

"I did not allow it to record us."

Bridget carried the briefcase, though she briefly considered tossing it on the third rail to see what would happen. Before, she'd only let a train simply run over the damned thing, she'd not thought to try to electrocute the beast.

She decided against the notion, thinking that electrocution might only make the demon more pissed off and cause it to immediately go after Otter. The beast accompanied the case, and so if Bridget held onto its handle, she figured she was keeping her son safe—at least for the moment.

They'd traveled less than a block when she felt the ground tremble, another train coming. Adiella stepped onto a ledge and disappeared into a niche Bridget hadn't noticed. It took her a few moments to figure out where the witch had gone. There were service lights the length of the subway tunnel proper, but nothing in this narrow corridor. Black as pitch, she shuffled forward, holding a hand out to the wall and feeling her way. Somehow Adiella could see in this absolute black.

Bridget sorted through the sounds: the clatter of a train arriving behind her, the hiss of steam from somewhere overhead, the chitter of what she guessed were well more than a few rats, finding the slap-slap-slap of Adiella's footsteps, and judging that the witch was less than a dozen yards ahead. She focused on the slap-slap-slap and plowed blindly forward.

This place was ... *awful* ... no better word for it, she decided. In addition to the stench from the demon, Bridget smelled foul odors that were likely a mix of sewage and dead things. She'd wished she'd brought some peppermints, something to cut the horrid taste that had nested in her mouth, and a cell phone for a sense of security, though it was probably impossible to get a signal down here. She'd left the phone behind at her brownstone, not wanting to be disturbed. Plus, it was bone-cold here, evil-cold; she wore no gloves and her jacket wasn't sufficient. Adiella had been right that she wouldn't be warm enough, but she wouldn't let the witch know just how terribly cold she was. Bridget felt frost forming at the corners of her mouth and figured frostbite wouldn't be far behind. This place was wholly, thoroughly dreadful, one step removed from hell. And yet she'd suggested the witch go to one of her pits. Wonderful.

Sometimes Bridget's business dealings took her into closed subway tunnels to meet with brokers and smugglers. But that was usually under Manhattan, where the air was better, the nooks and crannies were cleaner, and where she was smart enough not to venture during the depths of winter. In her various explorations following Jimmy one day, she'd discovered people living in the city's hidden infrastructure—moles, they'd been dubbed in news reports.

Because of Jimmy, Bridget had connections to one mole community that numbered about a hundred and fifty and had an ersatz mayor. But, again, that was under Manhattan. Whatever moles might live down here … Bridget thought they might not be the human kind.

The tunnel sloped down, the air growing colder still, and several steps later Bridget felt frigid water—or something mostly liquid—swirling around her ankles. Awful? No, this was an appalling, horrifying hell-hole the witch was leading her through. And if she died here, no one would ever find her body. Suddenly the sound of Adiella's footfalls stopped and Bridget froze. The beast at her side started jabbering louder.

"Shut up!" Bridget spat. "Just—"

"Come along," Adiella shouted. "It's not much farther."

"Pissmires and spiders." Her teeth chattered as she sloshed forward, feeling the biting liquid swirl higher. Her toes had gone numb and her fingers ached. Would Adiella shed her of the curse and the demon and leave her in this dark labyrinth to die … justice for Tavio? A way to get Otter? For an instant Bridget considered retreating, but the demon belched a sulfurous cloud that spurred her on. The texture of the wall changed, her fingers now grazing bricks that were covered in frost and icicles in one spot, dry in another and dotted with the husks of insects that crumbled as she touched them. She sent her senses into the stone, thinking psychometry might provide a clue where they were going. Bridget focused, still walking forward but slow and cautious, finding a picture forming in the back of her mind and pausing to take it in.

Construction workers laid the bricks. The tunnel was well-lit way back then, but by lanterns. William Adams was the name of the man who'd put in place the very brick Bridget now pressed her palm against. William had just turned thirty-one on the day that Bridget observed him, born in 1860, which meant this double-barreled sewer tunnel was built in 1891. William was talking to his fellows, but Bridget couldn't hear for the loudening prattle of the demon. She gave up and discarded the image and slogged forward, hoping she wouldn't step in some depression that would drop her all the way into this icy muck.

Where the hell had Adiella gone?

As if in answer, Bridget saw a pale glow ahead. She quickened her pace, crouched, and slipped through a gap only as wide as a coffin and that might have served for sewer or rainwater runoff more than a century ago. The glow brightened and Bridget emerged into a chamber the size of her walk-in closet, the earth-and-brick walls covered with faded graffiti: "DiViDeD WE fall" in rose, blue, and white, the Statue of Liberty with a sword in her hand and a snarl on her face, "goofus '58," symbols that might represent various gangs—nothing Bridget recognized, caricatures of singers including Bob Marley, John Lennon, Captain and Tennille, and Jim Croce, hinting the place had been tagged in the early to mid-1970s. A generator sat in one corner, its purr powering a bank of overhead fluorescent lights and a state-of-the-art space heater. She spotted the outline of a larger doorway that was boarded over. The witch had no doubt brought the generator and furniture in through there, though clearly not by herself. There was a narrow bed piled high with comforters, a large crucifix hanging above it, a wide wooden rocking chair, a miniature refrigerator like you'd find in a dorm, with a single-burner hotplate sitting atop it, and a pristine wardrobe trunk that Bridget didn't need to touch to recognize its value: vintage Louis Vuitton circa 1920, an easy ten grand. She wondered if Adiella had purchased the trunk the year it was manufactured. Braided rugs were scattered on the floor. The place smelled of old stone and incense. The general stench of the tunnel had not encroached.

The demon?

It hadn't yet entered the chamber, was squatting in the opening, sniffing, all of its eyes rotating. If Bridget could ascribe an emotion to it, she'd call it nervous. After a moment, it edged closer, but only a few inches, looking angry and wary, and staying out of the chamber.

Adiella moved the rocking chair so it sat halfway between the space heater and the antique trunk. She opened the trunk and rummaged around inside. Bridget kept her attention on the demon. It

111

crept farther forward, but did not pass beyond an arc-like symbol chiseled in the floor and filled in with a silvery metal. The demon snarled at the line, then looked around like it was studying the graffiti.

"The demon doesn't like this place," Bridget said.

"It is consecrated in an old, old way. It should not be able to come inside. No demon should be able, no matter how powerful. Perhaps not even the devil itself."

"Well, that gobshite of a beast hasn't stepped past your line in the sand. So I suppose you're right. But I don't think it's happy."

"And well it shouldn't be. This 'pit' as you call it is sanctified and warded. I have the bone shards of three saints here." Adiella made the sign of the cross. "That it came as far as the doorway is another testament to its power. Still, it cannot pass my 'line in the sand.' It can look all it wants, but it can't touch. As I said, I doubt the devil itself could step beyond my ward."

Bridget wondered how many "pits" Adiella had in the city. And were they all sanctified and warded with saint bones? Tavio had talked of them, places in the earth where his mother had found a natural, arcane pulse that augmented her magic. Clearly the witch could live here if she had to, with the heater and the bed and the generator that probably bled electricity from a city power line. Maybe this is where she lived when she wasn't in her rundown bookstore.

Bridget noticed that Adiella was sweating and squinting at notes she'd pulled from the trunk and spread on the floor next to the chair. She'd brought out candles, too, thick misshapen things that she lit with a snap of her fingers and held to her nose, inhaling the smoke. She placed the candles in a semicircle. The marks on the wall—that Bridget had at first thought unfamiliar gang symbols—glowed. They were sigils the witch had put up, maybe protecting this pit, maybe boosting her spells.

Bridget's legs cramped, and still she couldn't feel her toes. She wanted to sit, even on the brick floor, but she resisted and continued to alternately watch Adiella and the demon, which had turned its warty, puss-oozing back to her.

There were odd symbols on Adiella's pages, some of which she traced with a gloved finger, some of which vaguely matched some on the walls. With the other hand, she drew invisible diagrams in the air above the largest candle, the smoke from the taper holding her designs for a moment, then curling toward the fluorescent lights. She spoke in a monotone, singsong voice that Bridget figured was a spell and that went on for many long minutes.

"The demon—"

"Is still here," Bridget said. "It reached a claw out, but it looked like something stopped it."

"Sanctified, I said. Protected. It cannot come in here." Adiella resumed chanting, padding again to her trunk and sorting through things Bridget couldn't see. She retrieved several stoppered vials, sat on the floor cross-legged in front of the pages, and arranged the vials in some sort of order. The chanting reminded Bridget of a CD she'd recently purchased, featuring Benedictine monks; there were no instruments involved, and yet the monks' chanting tones suggested such. Bridget flexed her fingers and shifted her weight from foot to foot, still having no feeling in them.

Adiella uncorked the first vial and gently spilled the powdered silver from it in a pattern. The next vial contained brass shavings, the final three appeared to be filled with red, green, and blue glitter that one could purchase in a craft store. She clapped her hands and a wind arose, swirling around her pit and whipping the various shavings and powders into a miniature twister that joined the tendrils of smoke rising from the candles.

Bridget blinked, grit spitting at her eyes.

The wind was gone as quick as it had come, and what spread across much of the floor were intricate lines of the powders and shavings. Glitter covered Adiella's brow except for where she'd rubbed at her hairline. Bridget stared: the lines intersected with some of the symbols and diagrams on the pages, and at sharp junctures blobs of wax from the candles hardened. Wisps of acrid smoke spiraled up from the blackened wicks. Adiella adjusted her scarf, tucked in a few errant white hairs, and chanted once more. Her age had come back upon her, wrinkles everywhere and her back rounded like a turtle shell. Her shoulders shook, and Bridget believed it was from grief. She'd not given the witch any proper amount of time to deal with the loss of her son. In truth, Bridget hadn't taken time to properly mourn either. Tavio had been her world many years ago, and no matter that the marriage had unraveled, that he'd repeatedly cheated on her, he hadn't deserved to die like that. There'd been good times, she'd been happy with him when the marriage was new. There was Otter.

Adiella had been right. Tavio's death was Bridget's fault. Had she not been tempted to pick up the ugly briefcase in Elijah Stone's place, Tavio would still be breathing. Otter would not be in danger.

And Bridget would not be freezing in this hellish pit.

All of this was her fault.

The numbness from Bridget's feet had spread up to her thighs. She considered stepping in front of the space heater, but stopped when Adiella let out a hissing breath and looked up.

"The demon—"

"Try again," Bridget remonstrated. "It's still here."

"The satchel. Set it in front of me."

Bridget edged forward, pausing and looking at the arcane mess on the floor.

"Anywhere here. Just set it down."

Bridget did, turning it so the buckle faced the witch. "That buckle, I was wondering—"

"Hush. Stand back, over by that crack." She gestured with her chin and Bridget took it to mean the coffin-thick crevasse they'd come through to get here. "Stand in front of that."

She complied, her legs feeling heavy and stiff like steel girders. From here Bridget could see everything in the room, and—if it was possible—it felt even colder in this spot. Maybe Adiella wanted her to block a draft or put her at the edge of pneumonia. Maybe if Adiella severed the demon she'd kill Bridget for good measure. Bridget doubted she'd stand much of a chance against the angered witch. Then Adiella would have Otter.

The demon looked over what passed for a shoulder and set all five of its eyes on Bridget. Then it snapped its attention to Adiella, who was chanting and fluttering her fingers, calling up another wind that sent the powders and shavings swirling around the ugly briefcase.

If only Bridget hadn't taken the damn satchel from Stone's apartment! Bridget wondered how she'd been set up, the tip about the ancient treasure not coming from one of her men, but a "friend" of one of them. A fellow named Harry Black or Brown or Gray. Somehow Elijah Stone had gotten the word out about some great treasure, and eventually that word had reached Bridget, who was quick to go after it. She could never have enough wealth or enough relics, the more ancient the better. Never satisfied, she'd brought this all on herself.

If only another thief in the city had cobbled onto the lure first.

Tavio would still be alive.

Otter would be at Tavio's condo.

Bridget wouldn't be shivering somewhere under the Bronx.

Dustin? Certainly he was in danger too. And Michael.

Her fault, but that blame was something she needed to discard. She couldn't undo what she'd done, and regrets couldn't bring Tavio to life or put everything back in its proper, comfortable order.

Bridget realized how quiet it had become. There was the faintest vibration, a subway train trundling on some track, and Adiella's monotone voice. But the beast was not prattling. It had quieted the moment the witch started on her serious magic. It was shaking.

"The demon—"

"Is still here," Bridget said. "But you have its full attention. I think maybe it's actually worried."

This time Adiella's words were faster and spirited, her hand gestures exaggerated and wild. Her scarf fell back and Bridget saw that the witch had a polished bald section on the top of her head, the white hair framing it, a tonsure like a friar's. There was some-thing like a tattoo on the bald space, but Bridget wasn't close enough to make it out; she guessed it was another arcane sigil.

Adiella's voice rose and the demon howled, a mournful baying that reverberated off the bricks and jarred Bridget to her bones. Bridget threw her hands over his ears, finding that the noise lanced its way in nevertheless.

As Adiella sprang to her feet the briefcase burst into flames, and the stench that billowed away brought Bridget to her knees. A wind came again, violent, mean, and wicked, disregarding Bridget's coat and shoes and settling a cold so deep inside her she feared it would be her death. The wind went on for minutes, the demon's scream accompanying its keening. When it finally subsided, Bridget raised her head to see Adiella slumped unconscious in front of the space heater, wrinkles thicker than she'd ever seen them, like old tree bark.

The briefcase, powders, shavings, candles were gone too ... not a trace of them even against the walls. But the demon was still there, in the entranceway, and it had started to chatter again. Its demeanor had changed for the worse, and the drool that spilled from its lips was acidic, striking the floor and sizzling.

Was she free? Had Adiella freed Bridget of the demon? She stepped into the crevasse, the demon edging toward her, stretching out a claw. Maybe Adiella had broken the curse, but had not chased away the creature.

"Christ on a tricycle," Bridget muttered. She looked between the beast and Adiella; the witch had started to stir.

Adiella struggled to her hands and knees, picked up something on the rug in front of her and tossed it to Bridget. She reflexively reached out and caught it. The buckle from the briefcase was searing cold like dry ice and she dropped it. But the freezing metal had done its damage. Leaving behind an image of the buckle's symbol scarred into the palm of Bridget's hand as surely as if she'd been branded.

"That clasp," Adiella said, as she levered herself up using the trunk. She righted herself and adjusted the scarf. Her breathing slowed and the wrinkles melted. "That sigil, clasp if you will, is what binds the foul soul beast to this world and to you. I can't destroy it. I can't get rid of the beast. That piece of metal, it is an anchor, ancient and powerful, and beyond my ability to affect. And unless you can get some unwitting fool to steal it from—"

"I said I won't do that. I won't let that thing pass to someone else, the slaughtering continue. It stops here somehow, and—"

"How the sigil came to be on that briefcase case is a mystery perhaps unsolvable, especially since the case is no more. That I was able to destroy that part of it, however, was some minor victory. But that odd clasp ... it was fashioned by a witch far more powerful than I, long long dead and from far away, certainly filled with a hatred or purpose stronger than even mine. The witch involved in the making of that metal, I get the sense that she hated something beyond demons, perhaps ironically championing them ... or at least the demon that crawls in your shadow. I get that sense from the magic."

"How can you tell—"

The witch waved away Bridget's question. "I used my strongest magic and could only best the skin of the briefcase." Her eyes tore into Bridget. "That creature—" she pointed a finger, guessing correctly at its position.

"—is still here," Bridget said. "Try again."

"I know it's still here." The witch cackled, the sound adding to Bridget's shivers.

"Then try—"

"There is no 'again' for me. I told you it defies my magic."

"But Otter—"

"Otter is the only family I have left ... you've seen to that, Irish bitch. And you'll keep him safe, no matter what you have to do to ensure that. On your very life—"

"The demon—"

"That demon is bound to you, Bridget O'Shea, and to a cause. Settle up with the demon. Maybe it wants something ... find a way to provide it." Adiella eased herself into the rocking chair and thrust her hands in her pockets. "Satisfy the soul beast, meet whatever condition it demands, and pray that it will be mollified and simply go away. The magic involved in its binding is complex, but I believe that somehow that is the crux of it ... satisfying either the demon or the condition of its binding. Now leave me to grieve for my dear Tavio. Leave me to grieve and find your way home."

"Adiella, I don't know what it wants. And I can't possibly figure that out. I just can't—"

"Can't?"

"It babbles. Not words. Not anything I can understand."

"Find a way to talk to it, Bridget. Find a way. You're a resourceful skel. Elijah Stone couldn't talk to it, so it killed the women in his life. The demon's attendants before Stone apparently couldn't communicate either ... hence the string of dead bodies you mentioned. Threats, those corpses were; threats to force the attendant to do its bidding, most likely. But you're inventive, creative, or so my dear Tavio believed." She puffed herself up, eyes red-rimmed. "If Tavio had never met you'd he'd be alive today. A curse to him you were, Bridget O'Shea. A poison pill he swallowed. So you find a way to communicate with that demon. Because if that demon kills my grandson, you Irish *târfă*, I will do far worse than kill you. Find a way to talk to it and give it what it wants, or you will discover that your personal demon is just the beginning of your troubles and pain. I'll find a way to bring all of hell's minions after your soul. Now get out of my pit."

1 7

Find out what the demon wants, she said. Satisfy it. The witch makes it sound so feckin' easy." Bridget stood in front of the gas-burning fireplace in her study, absorbing the heat; finally sensation returned to her feet. She thought about a hot shower, as she'd picked up some funk from the underground and wanted to steam the stink away, but that could wait, as she had no company that would be offended. Everyone else in the house slept. When she finally stopped shivering, she laid her coat across a chair and settled onto the over-dyed Turkish oushak rug.

The buckle—it wasn't really a buckle, but that word came to mind —was in front of her, faintly glowing in the light that stretched from the fire. Bridget was exhausted, having arrived back at her brown-stone slightly before three a.m. Adiella's magic had taken many hours, and now it was time to try her own.

Without realizing it, her fingers lingered on the rug fibers, and in the back of her mind she saw the image of one of the women who'd woven the oushak a little more than a hundred years ago. The weaver had a long face and kind eyes, and Bridget sometimes found a little peace just by watching this particular woman. She had a family, as Bridget had noticed a wedding ring on her very first foray into the rug and had spotted a young boy interrupt the weaver's work a few times, and calling out *"babaanne,"* which she'd learned was Turkish for grandmother. And once she'd seen an aging man shuffle by, kiss the top of the weaver's head, and move on. Perhaps a husband. Bridget had only briefly known what it was like to be part of a blood-family. Her father had brought them to New York when Bridget was eleven. He immediately joined the Westies, rose in their ranks, and was killed by police the day after Bridget's thirteenth birthday. He'd drawn a gun on a couple of patrol officers. Perhaps that was the reason Bridget refused to own any firearms.

Bridget's mother had never approved of the Westies and their illegal doings, and after her husband's death had tried to make an honest living working part-time in a department store and doing bookkeeping at night. She was so absorbed with work that it was easy for Bridget to sneak out. Their savings dwindled as the cost of rent rose. Bridget's mother decided the city was too expensive. And she feared Bridget would follow her father's dark path—disco-vering that the girl indeed ran with Westies boys despite her pleas not to. So she made plans to return to Ireland for a better life and to take Bridget with her.

Bridget, fifteen by this time, impetuous and bullheaded, ran away before she could be plucked from her beloved city. The Westies hid her and took her in, and that became her family, and in the gang's ranks she found purpose and clarity. If her mother had searched for her, she'd been unaware. But she had learned that her mother had eventually returned to Galway. Bridget sometimes wondered if she'd made a mistake, if she should have gone with her mother. Or at the very least, if she should have kept in touch.

She envied the little Turkish boy who again appeared in the back of her mind, hugged the rug weaver, and said: *"Seni seviyorum babaanne."*

"Seni seviyorum," the weaver returned.

Bridget couldn't remember if her own mother had ever said she'd loved her. Probably; mothers did that, didn't they? But her mother had worked so many hours that she'd spent little time with Bridget.

Bridget's grandparents? They'd been pictures only, faces of people from Kilkenny. Probably dead, maybe her mother was dead too. In the past eighteen years, Bridget had made no attempt to contact her mother.

She should have. One more regret to heap onto her soul.

One more.

Bridget had gotten her magical talent from somewhere in her roots—mother, father, or more likely grandparents or farther back, often talents skipped generations. Her parents had never displayed any arcane gifts. She knew that Tavio had inherited nothing arcane from Adiella, and for that, both she and Tavio had been thankful. Otter? Would some gift pass to him?

And could Bridget somehow satisfy the demon so Otter would be safe? How could she learn what it wanted?

The demon perched on a bench across the room, slimy face pressed to the window, the image calling up a dog looking out on the world. It babbled, but not loudly, the sound more of a susurrus that blended with the crackling from the fireplace.

"What do you want? So what the bloody blue hell do you want?"

It looked over its warty shoulder, four eyes locked onto her, fifth eye closed with its lid twitching. There was a definite pattern to its prattle, and it repeated something over and over.

Bridget dropped her connection with the rug and placed her hand against the buckle. The disturbing design of it had been frost-branded into her skin and looked shiny, like that part of her palm was wet. It didn't hurt. In fact, when Bridget pressed on the scar, she didn't feel anything.

She rubbed her thumbs against the metal like the thing was a worry stone, centered herself, and then concentrated. Sometimes the psychometry came easy. Dipping into the memories of the Turkish rug, for example, had become welcome and effortless, like looking upon the faces of old friends. The brick beneath the subway had not been difficult either; the brick had been thick with memories, the dipping almost effortless. Cool Papa Bell's baseball had been a simple read, too, even through its plastic case. But the buckle was taking serious work. To connect with the buckle was like jogging to the top of the Empire State Building ... with weights strapped to her ankles.

To communicate with the demon, she would first need to discover someone who spoke its language, and despite the difficulty to connect with the buckle, whoever fashioned this piece was Bridget's best bet to act as a translator.

"C'mon. C'mon." There was a barrier, something arcane. Serious magic had been involved in the piece's crafting, and it was acting like a ward, keeping Bridget's senses out. "C'mon!"

She could only use psychometry on inanimate objects, and so she needed someone from the buckle's past to mirror the language of the demon. Touching the demon would yield up nothing other than disgust. She couldn't talk to it that way.

"Give me your secrets," she urged the odd metal. "Stop fighting me."

The demon babbled in the background and returned to staring out the window.

After several minutes of effort, Bridget gained an image of a forge and a cloaked figure that was crushing and grinding ore on a stone table. Breaking through and gaining a memory from this piece had a price, it felt like Bridget's chest was being squeezed by a vice, her breath came in shallow gasps. She forced the connection stronger, and was handed a pounding headache for her success. The cloaked figure was a woman, she guessed, by the delicate thinness of the fingers. Old, judging by the wrinkles and age spots on the back of her hands. The figure, stooped and with rounded shoulders, painstakingly separated valuable bits of metal from the waste. She collected silver, copper, and gold particles as Bridget watched, then brought in lead and shiny grit, melting it all together to form an alloy that she poured into a mold to produce the buckle. Bridget had connected with the base elements of the buckle and was watching the piece being made.

There was someone in the background, but Bridget couldn't quite make out the figure—tall and with an odd silhouette, maybe just the play of shadows.

All the while the stranger worked, she spoke in a monotonous, flat tone that Bridget could not decipher. But it was tinny, an old woman's voice. Always Bridget somehow automatically translated words heard during a delving, turning it all into English in her mind. But this confounded her, what the woman was saying. And so she assumed it was a spell the metallurgist wove, the words having the same sense as Adiella's mumblings, and therefore her mind not able to comprehend. The ache in Bridget's chest and head intensified, but she didn't release the image. Instead, she searched for more and accepted the resulting pain.

Bridget didn't see her toady demon in the vision, though she'd expected it. The metallurgist must have called and bound the beast to the buckle somehow. So where was the demon? Not yet present at this stage in the buckle's existence and so not yet bound? Would the metallurgist summon it? Would someone else do that for her?

Bridget fought to stay linked with the buckle and continued to send her senses outward from the now-cooling metal, seeing the cave-like alchemist shop with primitive furnishings, and getting no better look at the cloaked figure, the hood keeping the face in shadows. The place smelled of charred wood, smoke, and stale sweat. There were tall shelves covered with broken clay bowls, narrow shelves arrayed with pouches and folded animal skins, more skins on the floor and hanging across the shop's door and window, a plate of dates on a low table. Bridget could not tell what time of day the buckle was being made, the fire from the forge the only light. Never could she see what was beyond the "line of sight" of the object she probed, and so she had no clue to the country or the year in which the alchemist worked. But she could hear beyond the object. Through a dark doorway voices crept into the workroom. Two voices, men; and they spoke a language that tickled her memories. Bridget had not heard this exact dialect before, though she had heard something *like* it. If circumstances were different, she would take time to delight in this new discovery. Again, there was that shadowy tall image at the edge of the image, and when it turned sideways, it looked to be wearing a bird's mask. Odd.

The headache worsened and her nose started to bleed.

Bridget understood the other speakers clearly—the men beyond the doorway, but she couldn't put a name to the tongue. The words had a similar quality to the demon's rants, but nothing precisely matched. And with no match, she could not understand the demon. She felt herself drifting off and deliberately bit her tongue, the jolt helping to keep her alert.

"She will bind," one voice said. "Others can catch. She can bind."

"This you promise?"

"This I pray. She can make a slave of evil that will in time conquer. That will allow us victory. A slave that she can bind like a mother unto a child. A free and powerful life for us."

Slave—that word matched with the demon's chatter.

Free.

Life—that matched too. Bridget had three words in the ancient tongue, and she stashed them in her memory. Slave. Life. Free.

The conversation went on, but turning to markets and the rivers, harvesting a crop called gongai, but Bridget found that uninteresting. She struggled to return her focus to the alchemist when one of the unseen speakers provided another clue. He ascribed a name to a river, and that translated into English as "Euphrates." One word was repeated three times: "enlil," and her mind provided no translation. The demon had uttered that—"enlil." Since in Bridget's vision the word did not have an English translation, it was therefore meaning-less. Unless it was name, maybe a person's name, Bridget guessed.

Bridget's nose gushed blood.

"Enlil." She tried it out, tasting blood on her tongue.

Bridget listened in for a while longer, and then the voices stopped. The alchemist destroyed the mold, curled on a rug on the floor and slept. The forge fire died, plunging the room into darkness. She considered pushing the image forward in time, but she was already spent. She could scarcely breathe. The connection broke, despite her attempts to hang onto it. She would delve again into it later when she was fully rested. Bridget couldn't remember a piece so difficult and exhausting to "read." And never had some-thing exacted so much physical pain.

"Euphrates." Bridget leaned back and tipped her head up, fighting the dizziness from exerting so much to get that brief glimpse. She wiped the blood off her face with a sleeve. A stream had dripped onto her shirt. She pressed her nostrils together and her voice came nasally. "Euphrates. Enlil. What else? Slave, life, and free." She worked a kink out of her neck and slowly got to her feet, feeling stiff and thinking another exercise session might help to reinvigorate her—that or sleep. Either way replenish her energy so she could send her pounding head into the defiant buckle again. But the demon might not follow her up to the roof or down into the basement for an exercise session. It might disappear and kill someone—Otter, Dustin, Adiella. Again she thought about her exercise session on the roof with Jimmy ... that was when the beast had killed Tavio.

She hated the witch who had been her mother-in-law—if only because Adiella had always tried to drive a wedge between her and Tavio. But Bridget actually might need the old woman now. Adiella had managed to destroy the damnable briefcase; maybe she could still prove necessary. And the demon had certainly looked nervous in the pit in the subway tunnels.

"I'm stumped," Bridget told the demon. She tugged her shirt up, found a clean spot, and wiped more blood off her face. At least it was easy to breathe again, but her temples still throbbed. "I can't try again, not for a little while, not with the buckle." She couldn't stay connected to any one object indefinitely; her gift didn't work that way. Psychometry taxed her, save for with her beloved oushak, and there was too little inner energy left at the moment to have another round with the buckle. "I should get some sleep." She knew she desperately needed it, but more than that she needed to keep her eyes on the demon. "Christ on a tricycle. What the hell am I going to do?"

It looked away from the window; still its fifth eye was closed. The thing hissed and a thick line of acidic drool spilled over its lower lip and extended to the floor, sizzling and smoking when it hit the hardwood.

"That's endearing," Bridget said.

Its four open eyes narrowed and it raised its incomprehensible voice.

125

"Slave. Life. Euphrates. Euphrates." Bridget wiped the sweat off her forehead. "Euphrates."

The demon cocked its head and parroted the last word. Bridget clearly understood: "Euphrates," though even in that one word, a guttural-sounding accent was evident.

"Euphrates." Bridget's heart sped. "Tigris," she tried.

Recognition danced on the demon's hideous face.

"Babylonian," Bridget pronounced. "I think you're speaking Babylonian. Dear God you *are* old. And now I have your language. Babylonian. How much deader of a language could you have spoken? Ugh. And how the hell could a demon from Babylonian times end up in present-day New York? Have you been on a murdering spree for centuries?"

A little more than a year ago Bridget had ventured to an apartment at 740 Park Avenue. Through a trusted contact she'd heard one of the tenants had purchased an intact Babylonian vase from an auction house. The vase was now in a place of honor in Bridget's study, and she carefully removed it now and brought it to the rug.

"Fuck the Euphrates." Bridget had delved into this vase several times before, and so was familiar with it. She might find just enough inner spark for it, and reading the vase couldn't possibly make her headache any worse. "What do you want?" she asked the demon again. "What the bloody blue hell do you want?"

The vase was glazed, hardened clay, and that it was intact made it exceedingly valuable. On one of her forays into it she'd looked outward from the piece, seeing a lithe girl carrying it across a stretch of plain. Pushing her senses, she'd learned that the girl walked across the fertile alluvial ground between the Tigris and Euphrates Rivers, the heartland of Mât Akkadî, the Babylonian Empire. The vase had been fashioned eight hundred years before Christ, and the girl was carrying it to collect silt from a certain spot along the bank that her mother favored as fertilizer for a trough herb garden.

Bridget's other mental journeys with this vase had taken her through a considerable patch of barley, chickpea, and sesame. And one foray placed the vase in a marketplace, when the girl had become an old woman and had traded it for a sack of dates and fresh fruit. Bridget searched for that particular memory from the vase now, as in the marketplace there were many people chattering, and she could "browse" the various stalls until she could find words to match the demon's. It would be a far simpler delve than the buckle.

Bridget sensed that she hovered on the edge of collapse, but her fingernails dug into her palm, the competing pain helping her focus.

"Give me just a little," she begged the vase. "A hint to mollify the beast." She needed something to start a conversation with the demon, something that she could use to guarantee Otter's safety. Something more than the name of a damnable river. Her mind settled comfortably into the glazed clay, her senses spiraled out, and she took in the chatter of passersby in the marketplace. Again there were similarities to the words, but not a direct match. Bridget tried out one word after the next, repeating aloud what the Babylonian shoppers said and looking up to see if the demon recognized something.

"Euphrates," it said. "Tigris. Life. Slaves."

"Enlil." Bridget heard that one word again, though she couldn't see who spoke it, a shopper behind someone else; a disembodied voice. "Enlil," Bridget repeated. Then louder: "Enlil." None of the other words matched anything the demon had uttered. Nothing else!

"Enlil," the demon returned, hawking out a gob of acidic spittle, like the word was a piece of rancid meat.

She browsed the marketplace for several minutes until she felt too lightheaded and the connection with the vase broke. Bridget knew she was too physically and emotionally exhausted to stay linked. "So maybe not Babylonian after all."

"Euphrates."

"Not exactly Babylonian. But something close. Something that has to be close to Babylonian, or that at least shares a few of its words. So what language, then? And you know 'Enlil.'" Maybe that was name of the woman who'd forged the buckle. "But if you don't speak Babylonian, then what the hell language is it? What? What could—"

Something *earlier* maybe?

127

What might be earlier *and* include references to the Euphrates and Tigris?

This time it was a struggle getting up off the oushak, the muscles in her legs feeble as wet noodles. Bridget stumbled to her desk and leaned on it for support, reached in the top drawer, and pulled out an iPad.

E-U-P-H-R-A-T-E-S.

The first thing to come up was the Wikipedia entry.

Tigris & Euphrates, a board game.

"No. Try something else."

E-N-I-L, she typed into the search bar. She tapped "enter" and watched the various headers scroll on the small screen.

Enil: an entertainment company based in India.

Enil: an American corporation focused on student reading assessment and teaching.

Enil: European Network Information Literacy

Enil: Dr. Enil Jimenez Blish, a California optometrist.

"Shit." Bridget typed again. "Missed a letter."

E-N-L-I-L.

This time something entirely different came up.

Enlil: Solar Wind MHD model of the heliosphere.

Enlil: Enlil-bāni, tenth king of the First Dynasty of Isin who reigned twenty-four years, known for the apocryphal manner of his ascendancy to the throne, 1798–1775 BC. Interesting, but probably not it.

Enlil: Sumerian god. More interesting.

"Sumerian."

Bridget selected the Wikipedia entry for the Sumerian god and sagged into the desk chair. She never relied on the research of others, but this Internet search was worth a try. Could the demon and the buckle stretch back that far? To Sumerian times? It was the right region of the world.

She scanned the document. Enlil was called the Lord of the Storm and primary deity in the Sumerian pantheon. The name was found in later writings, too: Hittite, Canaanite, Akkadian, and other

Mesopotamian cultures. Ellil, a variation. The god of wind, birthed in the exhaled breath of An and Ki—gods of the heavens and earth—after they'd coupled. When Enlil was young, he was banished from the gods' home for raping the deity called Ninlil. Apparently licentious, Enlil was said to have fathered at least four children in the underworld and was eventually allowed to return to the gods' home. Later, Enlil schooled his god-offspring in how to capture and slay demons.

Demons.

"Interesting," Bridget said. "Demon-slaying. So I expect Enlil is a dirty word to you, eh, demon?"

"Enlil," The demon growled. "Sumer."

"Great. So if I've guessed right and you're Sumerian, now I have to find something Sumerian so we can share more than a handful of words. Something easier than that damn buckle."

"Sumer," the demon pronounced louder. Its fifth eye opened and gleamed malevolently, the multiple eyes adding to Bridget's dizziness. "Sumer."

Shivers shot through Bridget's spent frame.

"Feckin' Sumerian it is," she said.

1 8

Bridget tossed her shirt away, and changed into a clean sweater, padding through the brownstone quiet like a cat.

She checked just to be certain, but she had nothing Sumerian in her display cases. All the while the creature followed, chattering, drooling, and belching clouds of noxiousness. Bridget feared she would drop from fatigue and the stench, and though it might do her some good to actually give in and sleep for a few hours, she worried what the demon would do during that time. The buckle had found its way into her pocket; she'd not put it there. At least it was easier to deal with than the damnable briefcase.

She glanced at her watch: 4:11 a.m.

She listened, no one was moving around yet. Michael got up early, but not quite this early. Otter should sleep as long as he could; sleep would keep the grief at bay. Jimmy? She could call Jimmy, but to what purpose? She didn't have time for another sparring session.

Bridget left for her antique shop. She recalled having a couple of Sumerian pieces there, not on display, of course, waiting "under the counter" for the right buyer. It was just a matter of searching her inventory to find something and then sinking her mind inside a piece so she could finally communicate with the demon ... beyond the handful of words she already had. Bridget remembered delving into at least one of the pieces when she'd acquired them several months past, and not finding the memories entertaining enough for a return visit. But there had been a man talking, if her memory served. That wasn't much to go on, but it was something, an avenue to hopefully find more words in common. And trying to reconnect with that piece would not be as physically exerting as the buckle had proved.

A woman bundled in a faux-fur coat walked her dog, letting it piss on a lamppost and leave a steaming gift near a neighbor's stoop. She didn't pick it up, just kept going. The sheen of Fort Greene, Bridget mused, wasn't so terribly bright this morning. She'd walk to her shop; it wasn't far, and she didn't fear any criminal element that might be skulking about.

Yea, though I walk through the valley, I will fear no evil, she mused, *for I am the biggest, baddest bitch in the valley.* And an even worse son of a bitch trailed her, oozing rivulets of reeking goo.

Always there was noise in the city, but it was not as noticeable this time of day. A siren, muted, a car door slamming and an engine starting—a neighbor heading to work. Winter added to the quiet. A lot of people stayed inside when the temperature dropped. Bridget shivered, remembering just how very cold she'd gotten last night going to Adiella's pit. Now the chill—and the walk—were helping to rouse her. There was a small coffee shop a few doors down from her antique store. It would be open, and she fancied an extra-large drip-grind; today she'd get the dark-roasted blend that was overly strong and with enough caffeine in it to startle an elephant. Maybe she'd order two to be safe.

Bridget thrust her hands in her pockets. This time she'd stuck a cell phone in one. Michael would be up in an hour or so, and Bridget would call to have him check on Otter and fix the boy whatever he'd like for breakfast. Jimmy could keep Otter enter-tained for a while; no need for school today. And then when Bridget got back she and Otter would face the unfortunate tasks of planning Tavio's funeral and picking a time when Adiella could visit her grandson.

Crap. And they'd have to deal with Tavio's estate, too. Michael had

131

left her a note that an attorney had called. Apparently Tavio had left almost everything, including the restaurant, to Otter. Adiella figured into some of it, Bridget suspected, or maybe some charity her ex- had favored. The attorney could be put off for a while. Nothing for Bridget in the will, but then she didn't need any of Tavio's wealth; she had more than enough of her own.

Bridget turned down a side street. The snow from yesterday had been pushed against a curb, heavy enough that the wind hadn't taken it away. It spilled over the sidewalk in places, and she walked around it and stepped over the cracks in the concrete … something she'd done ever since childhood, the poem about her mother's back playing in her head. A thought struck her as she reached the next intersection. She whirled, looking at the snow. In the faint glow from the street-lights that were still on she saw prints in a low drift, webbed misshapen tracks. The demon left tracks … at least that Bridget could see. Could others see them?

Three more blocks to go. She stepped into the intersection. Paying no attention to the traffic lights and distracted by the notion of the demon leaving a visible trail, Bridget didn't see the bakery delivery van bearing down on her. The van had been going a little too fast, and it struck Bridget dead-center. The impact sent her up and over the hood, against the windshield and breaking it, then across the driver's side and into the center lane of the street.

Bridget's head hit the pavement hard.

Everything was a blur. The van screamed to a halt, the driver pried himself out from behind an airbag and ran to Bridget, thumbing an earpiece phone and shouting at the 9-1-1 operator. A car had been coming from the other lane, and it stopped, too, a man in a long, wool overcoat getting out and waving a cell phone, taking pictures with it, and then also calling 9-1-1.

"Oh God, Oh God, Oh God." This from the van driver. He circled Bridget and flapped his arms against his sides like he was an overly plump bird trying unsuccessfully to take flight. "Oh Dear Mary Mother of God." The man interrupted his flapping long enough to cross himself and bend over Bridget. To the man in the wool overcoat, he shouted: "It wasn't my fault. She stepped right in front of me. Oh Sweet Jesus."

Bridget blinked and things came better into focus. The van driver had a face the shape of a jug, with a three-day growth of beard and a plaid coat that didn't meet in the middle.

The frazzled man touched his ear. "That's right, operator. I'm at the corner of—"

"No. I'm fine." Bridget pushed herself off the pavement and shook her head She untangled her curls with her fingers. The cell phone in her pocket starting buzzing, but she ignored it.

Bridget wished she would have worn gloves, her fingers were cold. She was a little dizzy, but that was clearing up too. And she ached from where she'd impacted with the van, but all things consi-dered, the pain was bearable. Nothing broken. "I'm fine, really. Nothing's broken."

That revelation hit Bridget like the so-called ton of bricks. She *really* was fine for the most part. Not a busted rib or tooth, though she felt tender places. She could have been killed, at the very least seri-ously injured. Her face was cut from where it had met the van's wind-shield, but not as badly as it should have been. So she was damaged ... but only a little.

Otter's birthday dinner fight had caused her more pain.

"I don't want an ambulance." Bridget brushed at her slacks, and then straightened her coat. She shook the disbelieving van driver's hand, and jogged away, around the man still taking pictures with his cell phone. She took the very next side street, a little detour, to avoid an ambulance or a police car that might respond to the 9-1-1s. Bridget didn't want any paramedic trying to check her out and delaying her from reaching the antique store. And she'd had enough of police for a while.

She was fine.

Sore, but she could live with it.

Bridget swallowed hard. She was fine like the briefcase had been fine when she tried to burn it in a furnace.

Laid it on a subway track and watched a train trundle over it.

Tossed it into the river and saw it sink.

Dropped it into a sewer and let it float away in the muck.

"Christ on a tricycle." The revelation hit: the buckle protected what it was "affixed" to, apparently, and so now that it was "affixed" to her, Bridget had walked away relatively unscathed. A blessing in that respect, she thought. But it was a blessing she'd rather do without if it meant losing the demon.

The demon followed her around the corner and into the coffee shop, babbling and oozing and malevolently eying the woman behind the counter who took Bridget's double extra-large coffee order. It followed Bridget back out and to O'Shea's Antiques & Appraisals. Bridget held the two big coffees against her chest with her left arm and with the right hand started keying in the security code for the front door. The cell phone in her pocket buzzed again.

"Hey lady, bet you've got a lot of money in a shop like that," came a voice from behind her.

The sheen of Fort Greene, Bridget mused once more. "The day keeps getting better."

She spun, intending to get a look at the robber before deciding how to deal with him. But the man was quick and had been making a move, thrusting forward with a knife, the blade slicing right through Bridget's coat and into her stomach. The man was Bridget's height, thicker, younger, with long sideburns and a New York Yankees stocking cap. She immediately registered that he fit the description of the man who'd four times held up people outside the Capital One Bank on Fulton earlier this month. In those cases he'd only brandished a knife. In this case he'd used it.

Bridget dropped the coffees, the hot liquid splashing up from the sidewalk on her legs. "Son of a bitch!" Bridget shouted. "This, I don't need." The knife still in her, and causing a considerable amount of pain, she jerked a knee up, catching the robber in the groin. As the surprised man doubled forward, Bridget brought both hands in to chop at his exposed neck, the most vulnerable part given that he was otherwise thoroughly bundled up for the weather.

The breath whooshed out of him and Bridget pressed the attack with an uppercut to the jaw. The man took it, and he raised his hands to ward off Bridget's next blow, stepping back to get away, catching his foot on a raised piece of sidewalk and teetering off balance. Bridget kicked him again, this time landing a solid blow to the man's thigh. A second whip-kick and he fell back, half on the sidewalk, halfway into the street, lying at an ugly angle over the curb. Bridget kicked him one more time for good measure.

"Get the hell out of—" That would be the easiest route, let the guy go. Bridget pulled the knife out of her gut, seeing blood on it. She'd felt it go in her … it had hurt like the devil, *still hurt*. The knife, the van … they'd hurt, but not been as bad as she'd expected. Well, honestly, she'd expected to be dead. Already, the pain from the blade was dropping to a dull, persistent ache. She knew the wound was starting to heal.

"Pissmires and spiders." She *should* let the guy go. That would be the easiest course. Then there'd be no dealing with police, no report to fill out, and above all of that no questions. All she wanted to do was swallow a couple of aspirins, find the Sumerian pieces inside her shop, and somehow manage a way to talk to the demon.

Her free hand found the cell phone in her pocket and she punched in 9-1-1. Fortunately the phone still worked, despite everything she'd been through. She brought it up to her face. "The Fulton Street Yankee fan—" That's what the local *NY Times* blog had labeled him. "I've caught the scuttering asshole. Can you send someone to pick him up? And make it quick."

Bridget waited, sitting on the curb next to the woozy robber; hand pressed to her stomach where the knife had went in. Glaring, she ignored the passing cars that slowed out of curiosity, and all the while getting angrier for "doing the right thing." If the thug hadn't been pestering people on Fulton, she would have let him go. But Bridget actually liked some of her neighbors, and she didn't want any more criminal element creeping into Fort Greene, especially if Otter was going to be living here too. And she certainly didn't want anyone else in the neighborhood getting stabbed by the damn thug. She'd cleaned off the knife on a napkin from the coffee shop and when the first officer approached, she passed it to him.

"My jacket saved me," she lied to the four officers who showed up. "Knife got caught in it, stopped it. Then ... I dunno ... I was having a bad day. I just lit into him, beat the shit out of him. Went all-out Bernie Goetz I guess." At least the latter part was true. "You better not charge me for that. It was self-defense, really."

"We'll need you to come down to the precinct."

"Of course you will," Bridget said. She hoped the robber wouldn't find a way to sue her for the beating.

"It won't take long."

"Of course it won't." But this time Bridget knew it was the cops who lied.

There was just enough room in the backseat for Bridget and the demon, both of them reeking. The cops cracked the windows open and the winter whistled inside.

19

He went to school?" Bridget talked on her cell phone to Jimmy. "You and Michael let him go to school? You're thick, the both of you. Why did—"

"Said he had a history test, boss. Said he wanted to stay busy, not think about things. Said he had to get out and—"

"Put Michael on—"

"Michael went with him, boss. Thought he should see if there was any paperwork at the school to deal with, change of address and such, you know. They took a cab, not even an hour ago. Michael said he tried to call you. Said he—"

Bridget remembered her phone buzzing earlier; no doubt Michael had been calling. She thrummed her fingers against the detective's desk. The detective had stepped away to get them more of the precinct house's lousy coffee. Across the room, she saw Sergeant McGinty, who waved and headed over.

"Boss?"

"Yeah, Jimmy?" Bridget pressed the phone to her face and thought she ought to get one of those ear-bud things.

"It was a good idea, Otter going to school. He needs to be busy.

And he needs to stay with school. I should've kept with school, boss, and—"

"I know, Jimmy." Bridget hung up and forced a smile for McGinty. "What brings you back to the precinct, Miss O'Shea?"

An officer dropped Bridget back at her shop. Bridget had somehow managed to talk the police into leaving her name out of the arrest report the press would have access to—citing not wanting to deal with reporters and all the over-the-top coverage that Good Samaritans often had to endure. She looked at her watch: 8:05 a.m. She had fifty-five minutes before the shop opened for business, so a half hour before her manager and two employees would show up. Maybe she could find the Sumerian pieces on her own.

She had to key in the security code three times; she was that out of it, her fingers not cooperating with her brain. The demon patiently waited, then was the first to enter when the door opened.

It was a two-level shop, each floor a reasonably spacious twenty-two hundred square feet. The larger pieces were on the first floor, such as period furniture—currently including showpieces like a Spanish colonial bench, and two hundred-year-old Marquetry cylinder desk, Bregeres upholstered armchairs. In the aisle ahead of her sat a lavish 18th century Biblioteque marriage armoire and a fine Ottoman inlaid table with mixed woods and mother of pearl. To the left were shelves with porcelain, china, and silver. Paintings, including one "Old Master," hung on the walls. Smaller pieces, sports memorabilia, dolls, books, and all of Bridget's "under the counter" goods, changed hands on the second floor, which is where she headed after making sure the surveillance cameras still worked. The camera at the door had caught the footage of the New York Yankee fan knifing Bridget, and her subsequently wiping the blood off the blade. She erased the footage, not wanting evidence of her walking away basically unscathed from what could have been a fatal stabbing. She'd told the police her security camera hadn't been working.

Bridget's employees—members of her smuggling operation—kept the shop spotless, the furniture gleaming, silver polished, floor dusted, and cobwebs off the restored tin ceiling. She liked the way it looked and smelled ... though the scent was impossible to detect between her own sour pong and the assortment of stinks the demon produced.

Her store was a real asset to the area, customers a mix of upscale clients with lengthy "want lists," common folk, occasional tourists, and those who knew they could acquire special treasures. Her goods ranged from little odds and ends that could be had for about $40 to large pieces that would bring in thousands. She took the staircase, listening to the familiar creak of the steps and appreciating the slick feel of the mahogany banister against her fingers. There was an elevator, but sometimes it jammed, and it would be her luck for it to do so this morning—leaving her in close quarters with the demon until help came. She was surprised the cops hadn't made some crack about her foul odor, but maybe they figured she'd picked it up from her tussle on the filthy sidewalk with the Yankee's fan, not from her foray into the bowels of the city last night.

Bridget flicked on the lights upstairs, glanced at the shelves that spread away from the landing, and turned and went into her office that was between the elevator and the restroom. There were two more levels, both with lofty ceilings. The third floor was crammed with stuff that hadn't yet been cleaned and cataloged, and items that had been cataloged, but not put in the official books. The fourth was vacant, the floor dicey and likely to give way if a fat man walked across it. At one time it had featured one of those spring-floors for ballroom dancing, but the sections were rotting, and so she'd had it busted up and removed.

Bridget sat at her desk, pulled out a ledger from the hollow spot in the tub drawer, and started scanning the coded entries to find Sumerian pieces. Dear God, please let me have something from Sumer here, she thought, and not sold to some antiquities fancier.

The demon hopped around the room, appearing to take in the details, and for a change chattering in a thankfully low voice. Bridget

139

picked out the occasional word: Euphrates, Tigris, Enlil. Bridget. Life. Slaves.

"You're a broken record," she told it.

Rob arrived early. He still wore the bruises from Otter's birthday dinner, but it looked like he'd used some sort of pancake makeup to cover the worst of them. Still, some of the yellow-green showed through.

"Do we have anything Sumerian?"

"Sumerian? Geeze, that's really old. Ever see that movie, boss? Conan the Sumerian. Just kidding." Rob scratched a spot on the back of his hand. "I think so. I think we do. Hard to keep track of everything, but I think so." He brightened. "Yeah, we do, two pieces. Had three, but Alvin sold one last week to a history professor who said we were asking too much. Alvin's a helluva salesman, boss. He's do in, oh about twenty from now. I'll have him dig up the two we got left. Maybe we should set the pieces out somewhere, eh? One of the counters. They're pretty small, if I remember right. I'll have Alvin get them for you as soon as he comes in."

"Please."

It took Alvin, one of Bridget's oldest employees and an expert forger, only a handful of minutes to find the Sumerian pieces. Each was boxed and tied with a string, coded with tags. He left the boxes on Bridget's desk, wriggling his red-veined nose when he got too close to her.

"We do have a third piece, Miss O'Shea," Alvin said. "It's sold, though. A history professor paid a good deposit for us to hold it. He's coming by Tuesday to pick it up. It's a Sumerian astrology tablet, a rock about the size of a skull."

"These two should be good enough. Thanks, Alvin." Bridget thought Alvin and Rob might be due a little raise for putting up with her odd requests and behavior.

Alvin was pushing seventy, though he dressed like a teenager, jeans and rock band T-shirts—no matter how cold it was. His hair was long and silvery, pulled back with a suede cord. He had startling Paul

Newman blue eyes that twinkled, and that, coupled with his rich voice, was an asset in dealing with customers.

"These two small pieces, they're rather plain, Miss O'Shea," Alvin continued. "And despite being five thousand years old, are not especially valuable. We're getting four grand from the history professor for the tablet. But these little pieces ... he wasn't interested. Doubt you'll get more than six hundred or so. We have them overpriced. They came in on a shipment early last year, and I recall that you touched them and went all silent, said they were 'interesting but not outstanding.' We've been keeping them under the counter so to speak, but—"

"I do remember," she said.

According to the tags, she was only asking eight hundred for each, and realized they should go in a display case downstairs, as these were likely to never be noticed as ill-appropriated. Yeah, they could reduce them to six hundred, and take five if someone offered. The first was slightly more remarkable, a ram carving, weighing about two pounds, with curled horns and the body simple, front and back legs together, tail short, workmanship average for the time. The other was a round stone seal about three inches in diameter, rare because of its size; most seals were smaller. The stone was light with dark red bands shooting through it, alabaster with a smooth patina. It featured drill holes to illustrate a horse that would appear when pressed against wet clay. Bridget revised her estimate; she'd actually ask a grand for the seal ... when she was done with it, and take an offer of nine hundred. Simple, but rather pretty for something so very old.

"Will there be anything else, Miss O'Shea? There's a few Greek pieces I want to—"

"No. No. This is all. Good work on selling the tablet, Alvin." Always Alvin, never Al, she knew. Not even his brother, another of her questionable employees called him Al.

He left, and she heard the rattle-hum of the elevator. Alvin never took the stairs.

"So tired." She was talking to herself, but the demon cocked its head, listening. "I have never been this tired." Her watch read: 10:35.

141

Bridget's probing of the buckle had put the icing on her fatigue. She'd not used her psychometry on anything so heavily laced with magic before.

The Sumerian pieces *should* be easy reads, but in her exhausted state, that might not be the case. She held the alabaster seal against her palm, closed her eyes, and listened to the harsh breath of the demon and the creaking of the stairs. Rob was leading a customer up, their voices flowing under a gap in the closed door. They were talking about the sets of early Bowman baseball cards and a near-mint Mickey Mantle rookie. A woman was looking for a special gift for her baseball card-collecting husband.

The seal had come from Umma, an ancient city on a river in what was now Iraq. Bridget's arcane senses took in the image of a reed-thin man using the seal. She'd remembered seeing this image before, when she'd first acquired the seal many months ago. The man was a scholar, and there were baked clay tablets with writing on them around him. Sumerian written language predated Egyptian hieroglyphics, and Bridget knew that much of the early writing that had been discovered was not translatable. No one living knew what the language sounded like—except Bridget and the demon. The thin man with the seal addressed a boy, maybe his son. There was a similarity in tone to what Bridget had heard spoken by the Tamils in southern India. She listened closely, trying to find words that matched what the demon spewed.

From the previous foray into this piece, and into a handful of other Sumerian relics Bridget had through the years acquired and sold, she'd learned that Sumer was the name Babylonians had applied to the country. The earlier Sumerians had referred to it only as The Civilized Land, and they called themselves the Black Headed Ones. The few Sumerians Bridget had glimpsed in her visions before appeared fastidious and shaved their heads, probably to avoid lice. The land was fertile, agriculture and hunting fed a population that traveled by boat on the river and that had a bartering system of commerce. The land was wet, not like the desert that covered it today. The ancient people practiced irrigation, conducted complex business transactions, raised livestock, and their various dealings were recorded on clay tablets. There were slaves, and even they had limited rights. The man who'd once owned this alabaster seal had a slave—the boy, Bridget realized. Not a son, a slave, and the man ordered him to bring water and dates. The boy vanished, and the man stopped talking, his fingers moving over the clay tablets, reading to himself.

"Talk, damn you," Bridget said. She nudged the vision forward, and she sat uncomfortably in the chair in an attempt to keep from dozing. Some time passed before the boy came back, and then left again, with no more words exchanged. Forward again, and the man rose and slept on a pallet of woven reeds, woke, and resumed reading the tablets. This was why Bridget had not returned to the piece after she'd first acquired it. The man was boring, probably a hermit, and Bridget was ready to give up on the seal and try the ram. The man paced in the confines of his baked brick home, then strung the seal on a cord around his neck, exited, and strolled down a path between buildings.

"Finally." Bridget chewed on her lip and fought the urge to look at her watch; she didn't want to drop the connection to the piece. "Now you're being interesting. Now you're moving. Now all you've got to do is talk to someone. Talk to—"

There were people on the path, all clean with shaved heads, some toting bowls filled with fruit, a woman carrying a child. Everyone chattered, but it was a cloud of sound she didn't have time to pick through because the man with the seal picked up his pace. He went to a larger home, this one two levels high and also made of baked bricks. Two men came to the doorway and started a conversation with the seal bearer. Bridget directed all her concentration at it. Words started to match the demon's prattle. Her mind started to translate.

Liberate.

Unshackle.

Forever.

Clay.

Stone.

Enlil.

Bridget tried to memorize the words, repeating them softly in the ancient tongue while the men in her vision continued to talk. She discovered that the man with the seal was a priest, and the women in the home—distant relations of the king—sought the blessing of the gods. The priest was invited inside, all five people present chattering now and providing Bridget with information about the society's religion. It was at its heart nature worship, the wind, animals, water, all deified as humanlike entities. Enlil was at the top, and Bridget heard the priest assure the women that the wind would be kind this season and not uproot the recent planting; that Aldî-nîfaeti would be kept at bay, harnessed if possible and stopped from causing havoc.

Liberate.

Aldî-nîfaeti—demons.

Unshackle.

For an interminable time Bridget managed to stay connected to the seal, as the priest made his way through the city, boy-slave following and meeting every request. Bridget soaked in the words as she became soaked in sweat from expending so much mental energy. She set as much as she could to memory, but she feared it wouldn't be enough.

"You want freedom," Bridget said. The demon in her office desired to be liberated from Bridget and the buckle, to go home, to not be tied to anyone. "I get it. I want that for you. I want you the hell out of my life. But I don't know how to achieve that. I don't know how you were hooked to this buckle, how to undo it. And I don't know how in the hell you ended up in New York."

The demon babbled almost angrily.

Liberate, Bridget said in the ancient tongue. "So we're crystal clear on that part. Liberate."

The demon nodded and parroted the word in English, coming out *liburrrrate.*

Bridget concentrated on the vision and pushed the scene forward again. At the end of that long-ago day, the priest went into another home, this of an apparently wealthy family, said a prayer, and called for the blessings of Enlil, Enki, and Ninhursag, the latter considered the mother of the gods. The priest and his boy-slave watched as a woman festooned with gold and silver jewelry mumbled over four small alabaster bowls that had been etched with symbols Bridget couldn't get a good look at. She placed the bowls upside down, one in each corner of the home's lower level. They were similar to the clay bowls that had been in the forge room of the woman who had made the accursed buckle. But these were intact. The ones in the forge room were all broken. The intact bowls were similar to other pieces Bridget had seen elsewhere, in a museum perhaps, none had come through her shop.

"If Lord of Storm desires, Aldî-nîfaeti will be taken here tonight," the priest in the back of Bridget's mind said. "In this home and that of your brother. Taken forever, if Lord of Storm's blessings fall here, no longer will Aldî-nîfaeti ruin the crops and slay the livestock." The conversation continued.

Prison.

Forever.

People.

Know—understand.

Aldî-nîfaeti—demons.

Unshackle.

Freedom.

Freedom.

Freedom.

Bridget repeated all of these words. When she couldn't maintain the connection any longer, she slumped forward on the desk. When she woke, still slick with sweat, she looked at her watch: 12:41 p.m. Her stomach rumbled. The demon had wedged itself into a chair across from her, folds of pus-riddled fat hanging over the arms, and fetid goo running down the chair legs, disappearing before hitting the floor. Its tail twitched in time with the second hand ticking away on the wall clock.

Four of its eyes were closed, but the upper one—the fifth eye—was open wide and locked onto Bridget, holding her firmly in place. This time when the beast spoke, Bridget understood just enough.

"Bridget break prisons. Bridget unshackle Aldî-nîfaeti," it said.

"Bridget gain. Bridget break. Bridget unshackle. Bridget does not unshackle Aldî-nîfaeti ... people of Bridget unshackled from life. Unshackled Tavio."

Bridget's people—Otter, Dustin, Michael. Bridget dropped the seal and ram into a pocket, with them and the buckle it felt like she was carrying a three-hundred-pound weight.

"Unshackled Tavio from life." It had a smug look.

Bridget did not need the reminder that it had killed her ex-husband. She couldn't get that burning thought out of her head. Neither could she successfully tamp down the guilt she felt. If she hadn't taken that damnable briefcase out of Elijah Stone's place, Tavio would be alive.

"Unshackle Bridget people from life." Now it appeared to leer. "Unshackle all Bridget people."

As the demon had apparently unshackled the loved ones of the buckle's previous owners ... owners without the ability to understand the ancient Sumerian dialect, and thereby unable to know the demon had a task in mind for them.

"Bridget gain prisons. Bridget break prisons. Know?"

"Yes, I know. I understand. If I don't find the Sumerian demon bowls and break them, you will keep on killing. I'll get the prisons, all right?" She tried to convey that in the Sumerian words she'd memorized. "There can't be all that many intact demon bowls can there? "I'll break them. I'll break every damn one of them. I'll let demons loose in New York City." Whatever it took to keep Otter safe. "And I'll find a way to free you, too."

"Bridget gain prisons. Bridget break prisons." The Sumerian tongue was coming easier to understand.

The prisons—demon bowls. They were relics Bridget had indeed seen in museums, and one had almost changed hands in this shop a few years ago. But the seller approaching her had asked too much, and Bridget knew there was no profit in the transaction. Babylonian relics ... Sumerian relics. Pieces of etched pottery she'd thought products of primitive, superstitious societies that were valued by archaeologists and collectors because of their age. Like the alabaster bowls the woman in the vision had placed in the four corners of the Umma home. Like the bowls in the alchemist's cave-like room.

Apparently the bowls had really worked to capture demons and to keep the occupants of a home safe. And now the demon sitting in Bridget's office was demanding the release of its captured kin. Finally the beast had found an attendant who could communicate and who had the skills and shady connections to acquire the ancient pottery.

"Break prisons. Liburrrrrate. Unshackle Aldî-nîfaeti," the demon said. All of its eyes narrowed. "Else unshackle Otter from life."

"This day just keeps getting better and better and better," Bridget said.

20

D o an Internet search," Bridget told Rob. "Search on demon bowls, see what eBay has to offer. Get me a list of museums that display them. Sumerian, Babylonian. Sumerian preferably, but get both to be safe. We could've bought one a couple of years back, but the guy wanted too much."

"But you want them now?"

"Auction houses that have some coming up for bid, antique stores. And call the captain, the one that does the Italy run. See if he can give you some leads for any bowls that might be attainable in Europe. See if Alvin and his brother have any contacts to check."

"Okay. Then what?"

"The ones on eBay, at auction houses ... buy them ... however much it costs, I don't care. Buy them now. Any of them. No, all of them. The others, in museums, we'll make arrangements to get them somehow. As many as we can find, and as soon as we can get them. Christ, there can't be many of them intact, as old as they are. Thousands of years old. Maybe one dozen, two at the most."

"Sure, boss." Rob looked only mildly puzzled. He still wrinkled his nose in her smelly presence. "You starting a pottery collection? If it's bowls, we got some Depression-era—"

"Starting now. And Rob—"

"Yeah, boss?"

"Keep this as quiet as possible."

"Sure thing, boss. Hey, Alvin just sold that cylinder desk downstairs. The old goober's pretty good, eh?" He quirked the corner of us lip up in a weak smile. "You look down, boss. Thought the cylinder desk deal would help your mood."

"You finding those bowls ... that's the only thing that's going to help, Rob." Bridget took a different route back to the brown-stone, not wanting to revisit the intersection where she'd been briefly airborne because of the speeding van. She got home a little before 1, and she thought about stopping in the kitchen and throwing something together for lunch; her stomach continued to rumble. When had she eaten last? Instead, she opted for a shower first. She couldn't stand the smell of herself, and she could do nothing to appease the demon until Rob managed to find some bowls for her to smash into little pieces. She'd written down the best approximation of the pronunciation of the Sumerian words she'd learned, not wanting to forget them. She put the sheet under her cell phone on the bureau, placed the buckle next to it, stripped, and went into the shower.

She continued to let the words tumble through her mind as the hot water pounded away at her stench.

Prison.

Forever.

Clay.

Stone.

People.

Know.

Aldî-nîfaeti.

Unshackle.

Freedom.

Life.

Freedom.

Freedom.

Freedom.

"Freedom for Aldî-nîfaeti," Bridget said. "Unshackle the demons. I understand." Bridget prayed the demon understood that she was working on its demands. It sat just beyond the shower, waiting for her and looking utterly bored.

She turned up the pressure and the water came angry against the back of her neck, as hot as she could stand it, steam rising all around and fogging the glass. Her fingers fluttered to her stomach, finding no trace of the knife wound. Maybe there was a scar, though.

The door clicked opened, and Dustin reached a hand in to turn the knob so the water ran cooler.

"Mind if I join you?"

She hadn't expected him to visit today. "Dustin, I think—"

"Shush. Don't think."

But she couldn't stop thinking … about Otter, poor dead Tavio, and how was she going to find enough of the damnable ancient bowls to satisfy the demon. One dozen? Two?

"Don't think, Brie," Dustin said. "Not for a little while. Don't think. Just feel."

The water temperature apparently to his liking, Dustin slipped in behind her and ran his hands over Bridget's shoulders. He kneaded the muscles in her neck. "Tight, *mon amour*. So much on your mind, I know. I am sorry about Tavio. I heard it on the television. I called, and Jimmy said the police look for the man who did the terrible thing." He pressed himself against her. "Where is Otter?"

"School. He went to school."

Bridget let him turn her around.

"He will live here now?"

"I don't know. Yes. I just don't know. But at least for the time being. At least until … oh, hell, I don't know. Yes. I think yes. I hope yes. I think—"

"Brie, stop thinking." Dustin kissed her, light at first, then deeper. "I like him, Otter. And I like that he liked my cooking on his birthday." Dustin tipped Bridget's face up, the mascara and eyeliner running from her eyes in thin, black rivulets. "But I am sorry for him, too, *mon amour*. A boy should have his father also. A boy should have a mother and a father."

Bridget instantly recalled her own mother, all the hours she'd worked, too many for the two of them to be close. The memories were far away, and she'd done just fine without a mother. She'd done fine making a family in the Westies, then with Tavio, and now alone. Bridget was a rich, successful woman, and she really didn't need anyone. "Otter deserves better than me, Dustin."

"You are a good woman, Brie. A good provider."

"A good provider? Sure. But I'm not a good woman, Dustin. You know that. I'm—"

"A criminal?"

"Yes, and—"

"I know that. But not a common one."

"Well, no. But—"

Dustin cut off the rest of her words with another kiss, his hand on the back of her neck to pull her close, holding her tight. Dustin breathed into Bridget's mouth and with his free hand stretched for the soap. It was a French milled, organic bar—he'd given Bridget several. This one smelled of grapefruit, tangerine, and musk, and he leaned away slightly and brought it up to Bridget's nose.

"Your clothes outside on the floor," he said, "stink." He started lathering her. "You stink a little too. What did you get into?"

"Nothing good," she said, remembering Adiella's pit in the subway. "And nothing I can tell you about."

"You have too many secrets, Brie. But I'll let you keep them. I like you mysterious."

She'd intended the shower to be short, just enough to pound away her awful odor. Then she'd planned on a brief nap, setting an alarm so she'd be awake before Otter returned from school. And so she almost stopped Dustin, but his hands were at the same time insistent and relaxing, his lips too soft and traveling everywhere. Bridget couldn't get enough of him, soft skin, hard muscles, and gorgeous eyes.

She'd dally with him in the shower for just a little while—she'd allow herself that small pleasure. Bridget coaxed him to gently scrub her down to her toes. He lifted each foot in turn, cupped her heel and lathered her ankles. When he was finished, he stood and pressed the bar into her hands, turning his back to her.

"Your turn." His voice was husky, and his eyelashes looked long and thick because of the water, like an artist had used a charcoal pencil to gracefully apply them.

Neither said anything for several moments, the only sound that intruded was the spat-a-tat-tat of the water jetting against them.

"Dance with me," Dustin said when Bridget took a turn soaping him and sluicing off the scented foam. "Dance with me, Brie," he repeated louder.

Bridget raised an eyebrow.

"Dance with me, I say, Brie O'Shea. Dance with me before your son comes home from school and you have to talk with him about unfortunate things, a funeral for his father. Dance with me to music only we can hear."

She shook her head. "Not now, Dustin, I—" Bridget turned off the water and opened the shower door, stepped out and grabbed a towel. They shared it. She noticed the demon had squatted on her discarded clothes, probably fouling them. Bridget would toss them out in the morning. The demon belched; the cloud more visible than usual because of the damp air from the shower.

"Dance with me."

Dustin bent and hooked his arm under the back of Bridget's legs, picked her up and cradled her against his chest. She nested her face against his neck and nuzzled it, and let him carry her to the bed and slip her between the sheets. The demon followed and settled itself next to the nightstand, all eyes trained on the couple, no longer appearing bored.

"One dance," Bridget said, riding a wave of pleasure that followed where his fingers traveled across her bare skin.

"One long and wonderful dance," Dustin said.

She gave herself over to the rhythm and feel of him.

152

Bridget woke to a persistent tapping on her bedroom door. Dustin's arm was draped across her, pleasantly pinning her, his eyes hazy with sleep. She looked at the clock on the nightstand: 6:03 p.m. The "4" dropped down, then the "5." The demon's eyes were closed, and it appeared that it was oozing less than usual. Perhaps it slept sometimes, too.

The tapping continued. "Miss O'Shea?"

"Yes, Michael. I'll be out in a minute."

"Dinner, Miss O'Shea. In the formal dining room. Otter is used to eating early and so asked that it not be postponed any longer."

Bridget disentangled herself from the sheet, kissed Dustin's cheek, and hurried to the closet.

"We will dance again after dinner, eh?" Dustin laughed. "Dance and dance. I hope dinner is something tasty. I've worked up quite an appetite."

"I suspect we're having pizza. Otter said he likes pizza."

It was pizza, two large pies served on silver platters on the dining table. Thick, one was topped with broccoli, mushrooms, eggplant, and peppers, the other with sausage and pepperoni.

"From Vesuvio's," Michael said. "I warmed them in the oven, Miss O'Shea. They were getting a little cold."

Otter grabbed two slices of the meat pizza and gave Dustin a slight smile. "Glad you're here." He tucked the linen napkin into the collar of his shirt. "That veggie thing is all yours, Mom, since you seem to be counting calories."

"Otter, I am very sorry about your father—" Dustin began.

"I know," Otter said. "Thanks."

"After dinner," Bridget directed this to Otter, "you and I will—"

"Make arrangements for Dad? Already did that. I picked Carle-Rotzski's, they do cremation. Stopped there after school. I want Dad cremated. I know what happened to him. They were talking about it at school. All tore up by the serial killer. I don't want any closed casket thing. I want him cremated. I picked out the urn. It's better this way. Who goes to cemeteries really? I'll have the service catered by Dad's restaurant ... *my* restaurant ... it would be appropriate, don't you think. Mom, you'll have to sign papers or something, pay for it, the cremation. The funeral home said you'd have to sign. I've set it all up and e-mailed a notice to be printed in the *Times*. I had enough on my debit card for the newspaper announcement." He took a breath and kept going. "Cops aren't releasing his body for a few days anyway. I stopped there, too, at the precinct, but the cops aren't telling me anything. Nothing more than I heard at school. And they didn't ask me as many questions as I thought they would. It wasn't like the cop shows I've seen on TV." He took a bite of the pizza, and nodded his approval. "Grandma Adiella's going to help me go through some photos tomorrow ... for the service. You know, put them up on a couple of posters, Dad's life in review. Gotta have something like that for people to look at. I called her, Grandma Adiella, and I'm going to meet her at the condo, go through photo albums and see what pics he has ... had ... on his laptop. Download some on a flash drive so Carle-Rotzski's can display them on their big TV."

Fifteen, not fifty, Bridget thought. Otter had already planned Tavio's funeral. "Otter, I can help with all of that and—"

"Dad's attorney called an hour ago," Otter cut in. "Seems I'm the only beneficiary. I get everything, the condo ... which I've been thinking about. I'm going to sell it. I don't want to live there after Dad's ... you know. It would give me nightmares. You'll probably have to sign some of the paperwork, the attorney said, 'cause I'm a minor. I get the restaurant, too. Dad owned the building, apartments above it and everything. He owned half of some famous restaurant in Italy, too. Explains the vacations he'd take there. I didn't know that, about the Italian place, he probably hid that from you in the divorce. Anyway, he'd sold his Microsoft stock to buy into that restaurant. Besides that, he had a good amount—but nothing amazing—in an investment portfolio. Looks like I'll be set for life if I'm not extravagant. But it's all fixed so I can't withdraw anything or move the assets around until I turn nineteen."

"Otter, I—" Bridget was flabbergasted: not that Tavio owned part of a restaurant in Italy, but that Otter was going to be so well off that he wouldn't need her. And he'd likely leave her in the proverbial dust when he hit the magic age of nineteen. At best, she'd have four years with her son.

"I'm keeping the restaurant open here, I called Enrico earlier. Told him to keep everyone working, keep everyone paid, that someone'll go over the books with me next week. Figure maybe I'll use one of your accountants. Don't worry, Mom, everything'll get handled." Otter stuffed his face with pizza, and his next words came muffled. "I have an appointment with the attorney early next week to sort through things." He waved at Michael. "Get a plate and join us, Mike. This is a lot of pizza. And I'm not touching that one with the eggplant. Hey, I want to go to Italy when school breaks at Easter. I want to see the restaurant there that I own half of. I suppose you'll have to come with me."

Bridget reached into her slacks pocket, the buckle was there, though she'd thought she'd left it on the bureau—apparently it was indeed affixed to her just like it had been affixed to the briefcase. She felt rested enough, so she might venture into the buckle tonight to watch the ancient alchemist at work and try to get more information; that might keep her mind off her quickly-growing-up son. Her stomach rumbled loud enough for Dustin to hear, and he cut her a curious look. She grabbed one of the veggie slices. Certainly not something she would have ordered, though Dustin was refining her tastes and coaxed her to try new things. But she was hungry enough to eat just about anything. She held it to her nose—the sauce smelled good, and the cheese was considerable. So not completely healthy. She took a bite and found it actually quite good.

Bridget was debating whether to tell them she caught the New York Yankee's fan this morning when the dining room intercom buzzed and Michael got up to answer.

"Miss O'Shea," the voice on the other end said. "Is Miss O'Shea there?"

"Yes." Michael looked to Bridget. "But she's eating dinner with her son and—"

"Mike? That you?"

155

"Yes."

"You tell Miss O'Shea she's got to come see something downstairs. In the basement. Her dinner isn't going to be sitting too well afterward. You tell her she has to come right now."

Michael dropped his hand from the intercom. "Miss O'Shea—"

Bridget pushed back from the table so fast that she tipped the chair over. "Michael, don't let Otter out of your sight. Dustin, stay with them. Stay together. Understand? All of you stay together!"

She thought the demon had been sleeping by the nightstand in the bedroom. It had been making a noise that could have passed for snoring, all of its eyes closed. Though she had the buckle in her pocket, she realized the demon hadn't followed her down here to dinner.

Bridget had a very bad feeling that it hadn't been sleeping at all.

21

Jimmy was in the weight room and apparently had been doing bench presses. On his back, the bar of the two-hundred pound weight rested on his throat, his mouth open. That alone would have been enough to kill him, cutting off his oxygen; eyes bugged out like a something in a horror film, as though he'd fought for breath. But it was the gaping chest wound that had done it. Jimmy was ripped open down to his lifting belt, ribs broken and protruding at grotesque angles. Blood had spattered the wall behind the bench and had pooled on the floor. Blood continued to drip into a box of chalk, the powder Jimmy had used on his hands to help his grip. Shimmering bright red, Bridget couldn't shake her gaze away from the growing pool of blood.

"Bridget." Louder: "Bridget!"

Bridget looked away and into the face of the Aidan Murphy, her head domestic. Aidan was in his sixties, a Westie who had come to work full-time in the brownstone after it had been renovated, the only employee who never addressed Bridget as Miss O'Shea. It was Aidan who had summoned her.

"I was doing laundry, Bridget." The brownstone featured a state-of-the art laundry facility in the basement. "I heard Jimmy scream and came straightaway. I'd thought he'd hurt himself, not having a spotter. I saw the weight had dropped on his neck, and before I could get to him his chest exploded. His heart came right out and disappeared in front of my very eyes." Aidan reported this matter-of-factly, with little fluctuation in his low, thick brogue.

Aidan's visage, however, revealed his utter shock and disgust. Aidan was bone pale, and blue veins on his nose stood out starkly. Blood had spattered on his shirt and pants and the tops of his shoes.

Bridget again looked at the blood pool beneath Jimmy and saw that a line of it led away, ending at the demon, which squatted in the shadows between the scale and a rack of dumbbells. Of course, Aidan couldn't see the demon.

The demon opened its maw, so wide that Bridget saw Jimmy's heart inside. It deliberately chewed with its lips pulled back so Bridget could get the full effect of the atrocity.

Bridget tottered and felt the bite of pizza rising into her throat. She leaned back against the doorframe.

"I know you don't favor the police, Bridget," Aidan continued.

"We can't call them," Bridget croaked. She hadn't been a suspect in Tavio's death, but calling the police for this would bring down far more scrutiny than she could manage, and would put her under a spotlight that could jeopardize not only her freedom, but the people who worked in the brownstone and the antique shop. And then what would happen to Otter? He'd be shoved off on Adiella. Dear God, Bridget couldn't let that happen.

The police wouldn't believe an invisible demon was respon-sible. So very few people in the world knew there was magic. "No cops. No cops ever. The cops won't—"

"I understand." Aidan closed his eyes and crossed himself, lips working in a prayer.

The sound of a dryer tumbling a load of clothes and a washing machine draining seeped into the weight room.

"He was a good one, Jimmy." Aidan opened his eyes. "Wanted to please you, Bridget, and fit in." He gestured to a couple of college cata-logs next to a stack of folded towels and the boy's LMFAO sweatshirt.

The blood hadn't yet reached that side of the room. "Told me he was going to enroll in some business courses come the next semester, at your suggestion."

Tears slid down Bridget's face and her hands shook. "We can't call the police."

"I understand," he said again.

A four-bar chime sounded, signaling the washer had finished. The dryer continued to softly rumble.

"I have seen things in this city," Aidan's voice had grown quiet. "Things that defy explanation. Dark things, Bridget. Mouldy, desperate, diabolical things."

Another chime played, the dryer shutting off,

"There is something very dark in this house."

Bridget nodded.

"I will make the calls and have this taken care of, his room cleaned out. Jimmy had been so long out of any system that no one—save us—will notice he is gone."

"Thank you, Aidan."

"And then Bridget—"

"Yes?"

"Consider my resignation tendered. I will be gone before the morning." Aidan slipped toward the elevator, leaving Bridget alone with the carnage and the demon.

"Bridget break prisons. Liburrrrrate. Unshackle Aldî-nîfaeti," the demon said. Four of its eyes were closed, but the fifth widened and held Bridget in place. "Else unshackle Otter from life." It tongue lolled out and it wiped the blood off its lips. "Mmmm. Jimmy."

"You feckin' gollier! I'm working on freeing your damn demons!" Bridget raged at it, feeling her face turn instantly red and veins standing out in the sides of her neck. Her anger broke whatever hypnotic hold the beast had used with its fifth eye. "I'm gonna buy a gun. And I'm gonna blow your slimy brains out! You've ruined my life! Everything!"

"Unshackle Aldî-nîfaeti," the demon repeated coolly in its long-dead language, all eyes open now and looking unfixed, like they were trying to find a place to settle on its hideous face. The effect was dizzying. "Else unshackle Otter from life. Unshackle Otter. Mmmmm Jimmy."

"I'll damn well unshackle you!" Bridget rushed it, knowing with every step it was the wrong thing to do. Fueled by grief and fury she dropped her shoulder and barreled into the beast, feeling it give like a rubber ball, like the thing had no skeleton. "You can't hurt me, monster!" The buckle in her pocket made her indestructible, didn't it?

The warty skin of the demon felt like sandpaper, and the goo that ran in streams from boils that appeared and disappeared was thick and blistering hot. It seemed like Bridget had stepped into a fire. The demon could indeed hurt her. She dropped to her knees in front of it, ignoring the heat and driving her fists into it, treating it like a punching bag. Connecting with it produced the same sound as pounding a bag.

The demon laughed, the sound deafening and horrifying and reverberating off the walls of the weight room and growing impossibly louder. Bridget was certain the entire neighborhood could hear the hurricane of malevolent cackling.

Then the monster slammed its enormous mouth shut and reached a blood-soaked claw up, thrusting Bridget back. Acid bubbled from nostrils that flared wide below its eyes. Still Bridget wailed away, pummeling the creature's outstretched leg since she could no longer reach its body. It leaned forward, like a dog on all fours, twisted its head curiously, then swatted Bridget with its tail, the impact sending her halfway across the room and into the bench.

Bridget fell into the blood pool, and she slipped trying to stand.

The demon casually padded over and flattened Bridget, pinning her to the floor with a talon that felt like a sledgehammer had come down on her chest. It brought its head close to her face and opened its maw, belched up a cloud smelling of sulfur and death and of foul, foul things that there were no names for. Bridget felt her bowels release.

She'd known fear many times in her life, especially in the past few days since she'd acquired the buckle. But the fear that coursed through Bridget now was absolute, and she was certain the demon would kill her in a horrible, painful manner, rip out her heart, her soul relegated to some abyss. The things Bridget had done; there would be no eternal salvation.

Bridget had never begged for anything, but she tried to do that now, for her life and for Otter's. But her throat was desert dry and nothing would come out; her tongue felt swollen and unwieldy.

The demon laughed again—long and loud and terrifying—and it looked from Jimmy's body to Bridget. Then it spoke in its dead language, a string of words she couldn't understand. But it ended with: "Break prisons. Unshackle Aldî-nîfaeti. Liburrrrrate. Else unshackle Otter from life." It spat a gob of acid for emphasis and backed away to circle the weight bench. Making sure Bridget was watching, it stretched a claw up, broke off one of Jimmy's ribs, and proceeded to pick its teeth with it.

Bridget crawled toward the door, pulling herself up by grabbing on the bar of a treadmill. She sucked in air that was filled with the demon's stench.

"Break prisons. Unshackle Aldî-nîfaeti," Bridget said, her voice cracking from the effort. "Break prisons. Liberate all the feckin' Aldî-nîfaeti in the world." She reached into her pocket for her cell phone and pulled it out, nearly dropping it, hand so slick with Jimmy's blood. She thumbed it open and called up Rob's number.

"Hey boss."

"Anything?" Bridget's voice was hoarse. "On the demon bowls, Rob? Anything?"

"Oh, yeah boss. I spent all afternoon doing some research. An antique shop in Manhattan has two, both Sumerian. Go figure, eh? Some for sale right here in the city. I offered enough cash that the manager will deliver them here after he closes up. Want me to—"

"Bring them over as soon as you get them."

"Sure, boss. Another thing, the Metropolitan Art Museum has some in a near-east display, three of them, also Sumerian. I saw it all on the museum website, but you know they ain't gonna sell them, it being a museum and all. Got a bid on two on eBay—Babylonian for

161

those. Neither had that buy-it-now option. Four days to go on the one, five on the other. We'll win them."

"Thanks, Rob. Keep looking, okay? And bring those two as soon as they're delivered."

"Oh, I will, boss. As soon as I get them. But it's gonna take a while to nail all of these friggin' bowls down, you know."

"And any demon bowls that previously sold on eBay ... see who bought them. Get names, addresses, phone numbers. Buy them. Buy them all."

"Do my best, boss."

"Do better than that, Rob." Bridget breathed more evenly now, but each breath brought more of the noxious odor deep into her lungs. Her mouth was filled with an acrid taste that no amount of saliva she worked up could cut. "Work on it all night if you have to. Call Marsh and if he's feeling better, get him to help. And don't forget to call the captain."

"Boss, mind telling me what this is about?"

"No."

"Boss?"

"Yes, Rob?" Bridget noticed that the demon had returned to the spot between the rack of barbells and scale, looked to have comfortably settled itself, and was rotating its neck the way a man might work a kink out.

"Boss, I figured there wouldn't be all that many, demon bowls you know, seeing as how old these things are, and made of clay and all. But boss—"

"Yes?"

"A link off the museum page says there's about two thousand intact. If they're real expensive, it could wipe out all the ready accounts. I suppose we could steal some of them—"

"Two thousand," Bridget whispered.

"Break prisons. Unshackle Aldî-nîfaeti," the demon repeated. "Liburrrrrate."

Despite being a bloody, disheveled, mess, Bridget stopped in the dining room to make sure Otter, Dustin, and Michael were still there. She hadn't been physically hurt by her brawl with the demon, not a scratch, just the temporary sensations of heat and pain. Indestructible.

The trio gasped and stared opened-mouthed and kept her at arm's length.

"Mom?"

"What the hell happened to you?" Dustin said.

"You okay? Omigod, what happened? Mom? You're bleeding!"

"It's not my blood," she said.

"Mom?"

"Listen very carefully." Bridget had their complete attention. "The three of you need to stay together, understand? Just like I told you. Together. Nobody goes anywhere alone, not to the bathroom, not to bed, nowhere. Stay together like you're all joined at the hip. No matter what. There's—"

"I-I-I don't understand, Mom. Is someone in the house? Should we call the police? What—"

"No cops."

"Mom—"

"Otter, there's a demon in the city. In the house. A real demon. A feckin' ugly demon from some pit of hell. But it will be leaving with me shortly."

"A what?" The boy had a look of disbelief on his face and started to interject.

Bridget kept going. "I know. Demons don't exist, right? Wrong. It's a horrid gobshite of a beast, and it's hell-bent on killing people to get what it wants."

"Not possible," Michael said.

"Don't believe me. Hell, I know you don't believe me. I wouldn't believe me. You think I'm a real header, off my nut. It's okay if you don't believe me. But believe this—you three need to stay together. Michael, make some calls and get a few men over ... with guns if they

163

have them. It killed Jimmy. Get Rob, Marsh. Get Alvin and his brother Quin, too, the Halm brothers love guns."

Dustin's expression turned from worried to cold to shock. Bridget had told him how much she hated guns. "I won't be part of any madness," Dustin said. "Right now, I am going. I will not—"

"I can't keep you here, Dustin," Bridget shot back. "But there's safety in numbers. And I'd rather you not turn up like Tavio or Jimmy. 'Cause if you go off alone, that's a very good possibility." She shouldn't have said it that way, especially seeing Otter's face, but she couldn't take the words back. "You're safer together. You're just … safer."

She wheeled and stalked from the dining room.

"Where are you going?" Otter shouted.

"To the art museum," Bridget returned. After a shower—alone—to wash off Jimmy's blood and everything else. And after one more change of clothes, something nice and dark and nondescript. "To the museum so I can free some demons and save all of you. And damn myself to the deepest pit of hell."

22

Jimmy had been a random act of compassion on Bridget's part, proof that she wasn't quite as cold or badass as she tried to make people believe.

Bridget had spotted him roughly three years ago. He was with two other teens, panhandling on the platform—the same platform she'd stood on moments ago before transferring to the train taking her toward the museum.

She'd offered to buy the trio dinner at the sandwich shop that sat streetside above the platform—the popular 2nd Ave. Deli, which was oddly named because it was actually on 33rd Street. The other two beggars declined, picked up, and moved to another spot where they could mooch unbothered. But Jimmy had taken her up on the offer.

That's how Bridget knew that Jimmy was an "honest beggar," down enough on his luck to accept food, rather than money. Not a professional panhandler at any rate. The city had plenty of those, who treated begging as a full-time job and who raked in a good bit of unreported income and only sought monetary handouts. She'd read an article in the *Times* that said the average beggar on a NYC street made only $50 a day, but the really good ones made enough to buy a Mercedes and a nice house in the suburbs.

165

Jimmy had been overly skinny then, wrists and elbows protruding, all bones and hard angles, but he'd had the appetite of a linebacker. He wolfed down a big bowl of matzo ball soup, followed by two corned beef sandwiches, before coming up for air, saying "thanks, ma'am," and engaging her in conversation over a piece of cherry pie.

Could the demon tell she was thinking about Jimmy? Trying to recall the good times with the boy in an effort to blot out the image of him being gutted on the weight bench?

The demon sat one row in front of her, gaze apparently drifting from one passenger to the next. There were eleven other riders in this car, many of them chattering, the words indistinguishable white noise coupled with the rattle and hum of the train.

Four women were together, dressed smartly, reasonably light on the jewelry, heavy on the makeup, and in long winter coats, maybe headed to a play or some society function; they had that look. Two teenage boys were in matching jeans jackets, one wearing garish checkered pants, his long hair in a ponytail. The other had a spiky black mohawk and a plethora of earrings—four in his left ear, five in his right, one in his nose, a couple in his eyebrows, a small silver hoop in the center of his lower lip. Earring Boy held the hand of the youth with the ponytail and leaned into him. The other five passengers looked to be on their own. A businessman with a leather briefcase, maybe a lawyer; two middle-aged women, one with mismatched shoes, grocery bags nested in a wire pull-cart; a subway worker that by his weary face hinted he was heading home from a shift; and a homeless-looking soul hunched on a seat at the very back, shoulders so rounded and head so shadowed under a hood that Bridget couldn't determine an age or sex, could hardly tell the figure was breathing.

The demon seemed most interested in the teenage boys, who were talking close and conspiratorially. The one with all the earrings in particular had the demon's attention.

Jimmy had spilled his life story to Bridget over a second piece of pie. He'd told her he had just turned fifteen, had dropped out of school after junior high, was the youngest of five siblings, all scattered to the winds in foster homes.... he hadn't talked to any of them in a few years and suspected they were all probably old enough to be on their own now. He'd been shuffled from one foster home to the next since he was ... Bridget remembered that he scratched his chin before settling on "five." He couldn't recall why they'd been taken from their parents, though he knew the police had visited the apartment often before all the kids were finally plucked.

Jimmy said he didn't like any of his foster parents, though he admitted that none of them were "bad folks" and honestly had seemed to care. They made him go to school, follow rules, and those things had not appealed to him at the time. So he cut out after the third family he was stuck with and fell in with the city's homeless population, which eventually led him under Manhattan. Jimmy had been Bridget's introduction to the mole-world.

Bridget couldn't recall just what had possessed her to offer Jimmy a "job" of sorts with her crew. Maybe she felt sorry for him, or saw something of herself in him ... running away and joining a gang. He didn't accept her offer at first; it had taken two more lunches when she ran into him panhandling again. And after a year and a half of doing odd jobs for her, she invited him to live in the brownstone and become a full-time part of her smuggling operation. Maybe it was because of Otter she'd reached out.

She'd felt she had failed her own son, and believed it was far too late to rectify that with Otter ... though now fate had given her another chance with that. So maybe she'd reached out some sort of helping hand to Jimmy at the time in an effort to balance the karmic scales. If she'd left him alone three years past he might still be alive.

Bridget tried to picture Jimmy sparring with her on the roof, wolfing down corned beef sandwiches, poring over textbooks because she demanded he study, waving his GED certificate under her nose.

But she couldn't hold any of those memories for more than a heartbeat. In the end all she saw was his bloody, ripped up body on the weight bench and the demon munching on his heart.

"Jimmy. Mmmmm." The demon looked over its warty shoulder and licked its lips.

It had been reading her mind! In the instant she'd thought that,

Bridget discarded the notion—or rather, the essence of it. If the beast could read minds, it would have found a way to communicate with its previous attendants, or even with her. She wouldn't have had to go to such lengths to connect with a Sumerian artifact and cobble together a conversation through it. Perhaps the demon could capture images or a focus.... Jimmy for example, and before that Tavio. Bridget had been thinking of basically nothing but Jimmy since leaving the brownstone. Likely the demon had some empathic qualities, but couldn't make a solid mental connection. Tavio, the demon had plucked her ex-husband from her head and must have been able to hone in on him, find him, just like it had found the women important to Elijah Stone.

Images and connections, but apparently not complete or complex thoughts.

It was an important realization, and maybe something she could use to her advantage.

Bridget left at the 86th Street station, the demon following. It felt like the temperature had dropped a dozen degrees in the short time since she'd left home; a snowy-sleet mixture spit down. The sidewalk was slick and forced her to a slower pace than she would have liked. Her breath puffed away and she thrust her hands into her pockets, her fingers feeling cold despite the gloves, all of her cold and empty because of Jimmy. She briefly considered catching the westbound M86 bus that would drop her off right in front of the museum. Instead, she hoofed it the few blocks and jogged up the museum front steps, which had been thoroughly salted. The demon dogged her.

It was Friday, and the museum was still open. Fridays and Satur-days, and sometimes for special exhibits, the museum stayed open until 9 p.m.

"You'll have less than two hours," a woman at the big octagonal desk told her. "We start clearing the halls at 8:45 and—"

"I know. That's okay, I only want to catch the exhibit on the medieval treasures from Hildesheim." Bridget paid the $25 admission fee. She'd grabbed three ten dollar bills before she left, not wanting to have a wallet on her. The five remaining ought to get her a good-sized cup of coffee for the trip back. "I read about the exhibit in the *Times*."

"I suggest you hurry then," the woman said, supplying directions. "It's a large display, about fifty works. Gallery five-two-one. You'll find it one of the most complete and elaborate collections of church furnishings from Europe." She prattled on a little more, Bridget catching something about Bishop Bernward of Hildesheim, bronze doors, a baptismal font, and illuminated manuscripts. She left the desk and rounded a corner, following the directions on the map the woman had pointed to, then taking a turn and heading elsewhere.

Bridget had heard a news spot about the exhibit and really intended to see it, just not tonight. Bishop Bernward of Hildesheim was supposedly the greatest patron of the arts in the Middle Ages and was said to have commissioned numerous illuminated manuscripts. The Golden Madonna was advertised as part of the display. Oh, to delve into something he'd worked on; that would be a historical mind-trip she'd like to take.

She loved the museum and had been through its entire two million square feet many times—though she'd never been able to traipse through everything in one visit. Her first visit had been with her parents when they tried to teach her about the Old Masters. But she was too young to appreciate the works then, and so was bored stiff. The highlight had been visiting the museum's gift shop, where her father bought her a puzzle featuring a reproduction of Adolf Dehn's Spring in Central Park. They'd put it together on the kitchen table, and she still pictured it in her mind, a watercolor view south from Sheep Meadow toward midtown Manhattan.

Bridget came to appreciate the museum as a teenager, when she and some of her Westie pals would pickpocket the more affluent-looking tourists come to see whatever new exhibit was being promoted. She took time then to soak in the art and afterwards would spend her pilfered money on a dinner in an expensive restaurant. Restaurant? Her son had just inherited one; she'd try to talk him into selling it. Otter should go to college and pursue a solid career, maybe train for the Olympics swim team. Tavio had mentioned that once to her, that a swim coach said Otter should cast his eyes in that direction. A boy didn't need to worry about running a restaurant.

Keep focused, Bridget thought. Keep your mind on the museum. She believed she knew as much about this museum as any of its employees did.

The museum traced its roots to 1866 in Paris, where a committee of Americans traveled with the notion of observing French art galleries so they could establish something similar in New York City. Civic leaders, artists, collectors, businessmen, and philanthropists pooled their talents and money, and in 1870, the Metropolitan Museum of Art opened its doors. A decade later the museum moved here, to Fifth Avenue and 82nd Street. The building continued to expand, the various additions encasing the original structure.

To this day, the place was one of the world's greatest art centers.

She and Tavio had visited together a few times years ago. His favorite haunts had been the Florence and Herbert Irving Asian Wing, filled with calligraphy, sculptures, lacquers, and textiles, and the Arthur Ochs Sulzberger Gallery with rotating exhibits from the museum's arms and armor collection. They only took Otter once, when he was six or seven, the boy finding the place stuffy and boring. However, she knew Tavio had taken him rather recently. Again Bridget chastised herself. Tavio had shown the boy some culture, and she'd shown him the inside of a warehouse filled with ill-gotten treasures.

She took advantage of a clump of people gathered past the entrance to the Kingdom of Benin Gallery, part of the Arts of Africa, Oceania, and the Americas collection. Their numbers effectively cloaked her from the cameras, allowing her to slip around a corner and into a blind spot, the demon following her the entire way, babbling and oozing. She waited for another group of people to pass her position, and she melded in with them, going from blind spot to blind spot, losing herself amid tall men, until she eventually made her way to an employee area, which was thankfully unlocked, and folded herself into a large and mostly empty cabinet. Bridget fiddled with the catch on the inside so that if someone tried to open it they'd think it jammed or locked, but she doubted this late anyone would even come into the room. And if they did? Bridget was usually one to carefully plan, but tonight she was pretty much winging everything. Somehow the demon managed to squeeze inside the cabinet too, its stench overpowering. Her eyes watered and she breathed as shallowly as possible, checked the luminous dial of her watch, tugged off her gloves, unbuttoned her coat, and waited.

"We have to stay here," she told the demon, though she knew it couldn't wholly understand her. "Until well after this place closes."

The interior of the cabinet wasn't completely dark, a crack between the doors let in a little of the room's fluorescent light. Enough to see the shape of the creature and to tell that all five of its dizzying eyes were open and regarding her; they appeared to have a ghostly luminescence. She couldn't see the ooze that dribbled down its mottled hide, though she heard its soft trickle, and she heard it belch and smelled the resultant cloud of sulfuric gas, which was followed by what sounded like snoring. Bridget turned her face away and pressed it against a seam in the wood. The scent of varnish couldn't compete with the rankness of the demon's breath, but it helped.

She shut her eyes, tried to get the image of Jimmy's bloody corpse out of her mind, and prayed that the demon would stay in the cabinet with her and not lose patience and disappear to rip out someone else's heart.

23

ridget waited until nearly eleven. She was stiff from sitting in a cramped position, and she rubbed her thighs as she climbed out of the cabinet, the demon sluggishly following and growling. The employee room was dark, but enough light seeped in under the crack in the door that Bridget could orient herself.

She once again pictured the various halls of the museum, the route she'd taken to get to this room and where she needed to go to reach the bowls ... and in the end what might happen if she got caught, all things that had tumbled through her mind while she'd waited in the cabinet. There were motion sensors, video cameras, alarms, and security guards to contend with, and her heart seized at the notion of being discovered inside this place. She wasn't *this* kind of a thief, she told herself, at least not anymore. She didn't break into museums. She brokered and smuggled and dealt under the table. She used connections and courted the black market.

She didn't do ... *this*.

But she was doing *exactly this*.

Excuses tumbled through her head that she might use if confronted—she got lost, hadn't realized the museum closed ... somehow hadn't heard the repeated announcements, fell asleep in a lounge. She'd fallen down some stairway and hit her head, only now coming to. Hopefully, though, she wouldn't need an excuse—all of which would be lame anyway.

"Aldî-nîfaeti. Unshackle," the demon growled.

"Sure," Bridget said softly. "Unshackle Aldî-nîfaeti. Unshackle all the feckin' Aldî-nîfaeti in this museum … if there are any."

While she had no trouble accepting and reselling museum pieces—that someone else had stolen and brought her way—she had not personally taken a single object from a museum. Too risky maybe, or against some flimsy moral code that hovered in the back of her mind. But what was the difference between accepting stuff swiped from a museum's basement across the ocean and from taking something out of a display case in the Metropolitan Museum of Art? If there were lines to be crossed, today she'd cross them and pluck something right out of an exhibit—three somethings according to Rob … if all went well.

The demon continued to hiss and babble, most of the words in the long-dead Sumer tongue she couldn't fathom. A scattered few words she understood.

Prison.

Unshackle.

Jimmy. Mmmm.

Otter.

Aldî-nîfaeti.

Freedom.

Otter.

Freedom.

Aldî-nîfaeti.

Unshackle.

Michael.

Otter Otter Otter.

"Shut up you damnable gobshite and I'll unshackle the Aldî-nîfaeti. But if you don't shut up, maybe you'll have to find some other sorry fool to—" Bridget stepped to the door, held her breath, and pressed her ear to it. Silence. She stepped out into a dimly lit corridor and

173

started toward her target. The hallway smelled strongly of lemon floor polish and musty things.

The Metropolitan Museum of Art had serious safeguards, but Bridget figured that she was up on the technology. She worked her way through the halls, either tilting cameras or passing through blind spots, using a few of the large air vents to move from one area to the next, and making her way through stairwells used only by employees and security, pressing herself against walls the entire time. She saw and avoided half a dozen different security guards before reaching the wing where a sign read: ANCIENT NEAR-EASTERN ART. Rob had e-mailed her about where precisely the bowls were in this hall, according to the museum's interactive Internet site. He'd also noted in his message that there were two hundred and sixty-nine Sumerian pieces on display.

She stood where the shadows were thickest and took in the collection—cow and duck-shaped amulets, figurines, the feet from a broken statue, cuneiform tablets ... and the bowls, everything eerily illuminated by the after-hours lighting.

The demon hopped at her side, chattered louder, and gestured with a talon at the case that held the bowls.

"Unshackle Aldî-nîfaeti," the demon hissed. "Unshackle Aldî-nîfaeti. Unshackle Aldî-nîfaeti. Unshackle—"

"Yeah, that's why we're here, eh?" Bridget had managed to disconnect the video feed from the chamber, was pleased there were no motion sensors here—that she could find, and disabled the alarm on the case.

"Gotta work fast," she whispered. If someone was monitoring the various screens, they'd realize that the feed to this room was out and eventually would send someone to investigate. She just hoped that with so very many rooms in this place, it would take a while before anyone noticed the missing feed.

She pulled a small tool from her pocket and worried at the case's lock, swung the side panel open—some sort of heavy Plexiglas that looked clear as crystal, and reached inside, over an ox-like figurine and to the first bowl, small and shallow, like something a kid would eat cereal out of. She gingerly lifted it, brought it out, and noted that the demon had stopped moving. All five eyes were wide and fixed on the bowl, its mouth drawn tight. Bridget carefully sat the bowl on the floor and reached for the second, this one twice the size of the first and deeper; it felt like it weighed three to four pounds.

"One more," she whispered. "One more." This time she had to lean into the case, as the final bowl was well inside the cabinet, engraved cylinders on either side of it. Similar in size to the larger one she'd just brought out, this one looked thinner and quite fragile, and she held her breath when she cradled it with her gloved fingers, lifted it up and over the other objects in the case, and pulled it out. She sat this down, too, then reached back inside the case, removed the exhibit cards for the bowls and stuck them in a pocket, and then rearranged the other Sumerian pieces. With luck, the bowls' absence might not be noticed right away.

Squatting, she nested the bowls inside each other and gingerly picked them up, headed away from the case. She stopped when the demon rushed by her and raised its gaze to meet hers. "Unshackle Aldî-nîfaeti. Unshackle Aldî-nîfaeti."

"Not here," Bridget whispered. "I'm not going to break a piece of pottery in here." She wanted to get out of the museum as fast as possible and deal with the bowls outside, preferably a few blocks away, some nice dark alley. She wanted to delve into the pottery first with her psychometry, see exactly what was trapped inside.

Bridget wanted time to discover what—if anything—she'd be letting out. She started around the beast, but it moved and planted itself again, all eyes glaring defiantly.

"Unshackle Aldî-nîfaeti."

"Yeah, I get that. I'm going to do that." Still she kept her voice to a whisper. "Unshackle Aldî-nîfaeti, but outside. Eventually. Outside."

"Mmmmm Otter." The demon made a smacking sound.

"Pissmires and Spiders." Bridget sat the bowls at her feet and gestured. "All right. All damn right. Go ahead and bust them to pieces yourself. Free your damnable Aldî-nîfaeti buddies."

The demon skittered back, eyes on the nested bowls, acid bubbling

175

at its lips. If Bridget could ascribe an emotion to the beast, she'd say it was nervous.

"You don't want to touch the bowls, do you?" She nudged them closer with the tip of her shoe, and they rattled together, the edge of the lowest one flaking. "Maybe you're afraid one of them will suck you up inside it."

"Unshackle Aldî-nîfaeti," the demon snarled.

She nudged them closer still, all the while worrying that she'd been in the museum too long, that someone would notice the cut video feed to this room. "Maybe there's some über-powerful witchery scrawled in the clay, something that threatens you." A nudge even closer.

The beast slogged back, growling out a string of words she couldn't understand. Its dizzying eyes narrowed. "Unshackle Otter from life." It turned away. "Unshackle Otter. Mmmmmmmmmmm. Otter Otter Otter."

"Wait, I'll unshackle one of your buddies." She picked up the smallest bowl and brought it down hard against her knee. The impact sent an image into her head, of the woman who'd fashioned the bowl, who spoke in the demon's tongue, and whose face was deeply lined and hard-looking.

Bridget stared at the two pieces of the bowl, half-expecting to see some monstrosity filter out with the falling clay dust. But nothing happened. The demon fell silent and twisted its front claw against the floor, making a skritching sound. Acidic drool spilled out over its bottom lip and hissed against the polished marble. It shook its ugly head.

"Okay, so I did it wrong. Or it was empty, eh? So what am I supposed to do? You tell me what I'm supposed to do."

"Unshackle Aldî-nîfaeti."

"Yeah, yeah, yeah. I got that you feckin'—"

It made a gesture with its claws, and Bridget got the intent. She flipped one of the bowls over, so its rim was against the marble floor.

"Now what?"

The beast snarled and raised a claw, balled what amounted to its fist and drove it down, with the other claw it pointed to the over-turned bowl. "Unshackle Aldî-nîfaeti."

"So break it while the bowl's inverted." In one of her psycho-metry delving she'd spied a bowl turned upside down in the corner of a room. All right, but—" She picked up the mid-sized bowl, studying the markings inside it, not able to see it very well because of the faint after-hours lighting. But she managed to spot two figures etched in the clay, odd creatures she guessed represented demons, their hands tied. Words that resembled bird tracks circled out from the center of the bowl and wrapped around the etched demons. Cradling the bowl against her with one arm, she used her teeth to pull off a glove so she could directly touch the clay. "All right, I'll break the bowls, but I have to take a closer look first."

Bridget shut out the sound of her demon's harsh breathing, and spilled her senses into the ancient bowl. A woman appeared in the back of her mind—most of her face hidden by cowl, shadowed thin lips quivered as she muttered in the very old language. Bridget could clearly understand the woman; her psychometry allowed for that. The woman used a tool to etch words into wet clay—what was becoming the very bowl that had survived the centuries and was in Bridget's hand.

"Huseff, son of Nogress," the woman intoned. Her words had a flat sing-song feel, like a chant or maybe a spell or counter-spell. Bridget wondered if the woman was reciting what she was engraving into the clay or if the spoken and written words were completely different. "From Huseff's men-sons I heard the voice of the frail and of other men fighting and of angry weeping women. All are cursed and afflicted, pained by Yadun and Yaqrun and Azada. Yadun and Yaqrun and Azada, one will be taken with this bowl, seized by its scales and hair tufts upon their heads—"

"Unshackle Aldî-nîfaeti," Bridget's demon snarled. "Else Unshackle Otter. Mmmmm Otter. Unshackle—"

Bridget's mind bore in deeper and she continued to listen to the woman.

"—grab them by the tufts of hair about their heads, by their broken

177

horns. Sahtiel help in the binding. Grab them by their high broken horns and say 'remove the curses and the pain from the hearts of those you have raged against.' I adjure you in the name of Prael the great and Ruphael and Sahtiel. Bother no more Huseff and his men-sons. Descendants of Nogress must be teased no more, cursed no more, demon-vexed no more. I am the healer and the binder. I turn away fetidness and sickness. I protect the descendants of Nogress, the men-sons of Huseff. I bind. I bind in clay and words. I heal and annul. With these words I coax and catch I bind. Weapon of clay, mother wet-earth, in the names of angels Sariel and Barakiel—"

"Unshackle Aldî-nîfaeti," the demon spat. "Mmmm Otter."

"—free the hearts of Huseff and his men-sons from darkness. Ease the troubles of the descendants of Nogress. Protect this house from all vileness. Bind and seal and capture forevermore the Aldî-nîfaeti."

"Unshackle Aldî-nîfaeti," the demon growled, apparently oblivious to Bridget's delving into the pottery. "Unshackle."

Bridget's head pounded. Her connection with the clay bowl had gotten increasingly difficult and painful as the woman's chanting continued. And with that last sentence it felt as if an ice pick had been driven into her brain, so hurtful the link had become. It was all Bridget could do to stay on her feet and hold the bowl. Psychometry came almost effortless to her with some pieces, but apparently when an object had been witched, it was another matter entirely. She fought for breath and struggled to keep the image of the woman in the fore-front, watched from a distant place as the woman finished the engraving and ran a watery paint around inside the bowl so that the color collected where her tool had dug into the wet clay. Then she poured the remaining paint out onto the dirt floor.

Bridget's chest was tight and she felt feverish. The demon paced and hissed, mumbled "Unshackle Aldî-nîfaeti. Unshackle Aldî-nîfaeti" like it was the chorus of a catchy pop tune.

"I will," she told the demon. "Give me a moment more." She wanted to see what happened next, pushing the image forward, leaning against the display case for support and watching the woman bake this bowl and others she must have inscribed earlier, all sitting in a brick oven. The woman bent, grasped this bowl in crooked fingers, and shuffled outside into the night, to a home that Bridget knew must belong to Huseff, through a door opened by a tall man. Two boys stood behind him. Bridget kept all her attention on the woman and bowl, and for a moment it felt as if she was the bowl and could feel the woman's calloused sandpaper fingers against her skin and sense the arcane energy gathered anxiously in the clay.

"Unshackle Aldî-nîfaeti," the demon hissed. It nudged her leg, but Bridget managed to keep the connection with the clay.

The woman shuffled to a corner of the room, the floor of which was hard-packed earth. Ever-curious, Bridget wondered who Huseff was, and his sons ... were they important? Of any consequence to their community or to history? Had they done something to be vexed by demons? Her knees threatened to buckle and she felt lightheaded; she was breathing so shallowly now, and she saw flashes of light behind her eyes, the headache caused by this connection almost to the unbearable stage.

"A little more," Bridget whispered. "Please finish this."

"Unshackle Aldî-nîfaeti. Mmmm Otter. Unshackle Otter from life."

The woman turned the bowl over and placed it where the walls met at a forty-five degree angle, repeated the words Bridget had heard her intone when etching the bowl, finishing with: "Ease the troubles of the descendants of Nogress. Protect this house from all vileness. Bind and seal and capture forevermore the Aldî-nîfaeti."

There was a light behind the woman, a torch or lantern, something that made the shadows on the wall dance. At first Bridget thought the shadows were cast by Huseff and his sons, but as she focused, she saw they weren't at all human shaped. They were grotesque and alien looking. Two fled like leaves cast away by a strong wind, but the third writhed against the wall and shadow-claws stretched up as if trying to hold onto something.

"Yadun and Yaqrun and Azada, one will be taken with this bowl, seized by its scales and hair tufts upon its head," the woman chanted. "One will be grabbed by the tufts of hair and its broken horns. Sahtiel help in the binding. The others will flee this protected place, Huseff, fearful to return."

"Unshackle Aldî-nîfaeti," the demon snarled and nudged Bridget more firmly. A talon pierced her slacks and pricked the skin underneath.

Bridget ignored the beast and watched in her mind's eye as the remaining shadow-thing detached from the wall and took on fleshy form. It flailed with lobster-like claws, trying to gain a purchase, and it keened shrilly as it was sucked down and down, circling the over-turned clay bowl, then disappearing underneath it, like garbage disap-pearing down a drain, screaming and raging ... and then there was silence. For a moment Bridget thought she'd gone deaf. Then a soft sound intruded, the woman's feet scuffed across the dirt floor and she and picked up the bowl and cradled it to her. Again Bridget felt the calloused fingers against her skin and the arcane energy in the clay—she was that connected to the bowl. But she also felt an immense darkness that threatened to smother her, the snared demon inside the clay. And she wondered if her mind had been caught by the etchings just as the beast had.

Caught? Yes. She couldn't break the connection.

"Unshackle Aldî-nîfaeti," her demon growled.

"I can't," she tried to say. Bridget didn't think she'd actually managed the words, that she was only thinking them. "I can't." This time she managed to speak. "I can't. I'm caught like the damnable Aldî-nîfaeti." Caught with Yadun or Yaqrun or Azada—whichever one of the three shadows the woman had sucked down into the clay. Bridget realized it was not the same woman who had forged the buckle in her pocket. This woman had used clay, the other had used metal. Why? Was Bridget's demon different? Did it matter what mate-rial was used in the catching of demons? Or did each witch use what-ever material most appealed to her?

Bridget couldn't see the woman any longer, only the etched-words, black against the dusky-red clay cocoon that held her. She couldn't feel the woman's fingers, only an oppressive heat. The woman had "felt" powerful, almost a palpable aura that had surpassed what Bridget sensed in Adiella's company. Bridget could still hear, her beast grumbling over and over: "Unshackle Aldî-nîfaeti. Unshackle Otter. Mmmmm."

Bridget tried again to break the connection, picturing Otter. Get free for him, she thought. For Otter.

"Otter. Otter. Otter. Mmmmmm."

Get free.

Finally! Her senses were out, feeling like she was a child who'd just gotten off an especially long, dizzying tilt-a-whirl ride.

"Unshackle—"

"Fine." She flipped over both remaining bowls and placed them lip-down next to each other, stared at them. "Fine, you fecker."

Her demon mumbled and closed four of its eyes, the fifth locked onto the bowls. Though she couldn't pick out a single word from its ramblings, she found a pattern in them, like a song chorus. The demon's voice rose and its fifth eye widened so it appeared double-sized.

There was a warning in her head to get the hell out of the museum, not to do this. She ignored the warning, thinking of Otter. "Fine. Fine. Fine." She brought her leg up and angled her heel, drove it down over the bottom of the bowl she'd just delved. "Let's see what happens, eh, you scuttering gobshite. Let's see—"

The demon chanted louder still; Bridget had never heard it manage this volume before. Its fifth eye turned blackest black, as if it tried to draw in all the meager light in this room. She watched in horror as the broken pottery shards started to shift and skip against the floor. Her demon was playing a role in freeing the Aldî-nîfaeti.

"Holy crap," she said. "Something's really coming out of—"

"Hey! Don't move, you!" That was a new voice. Strong and gravelly. "Joe, this is Carl. I've got a thief in four-eight-one. Repeat, section four-eight-one. Call for a squad. Probably more of them around. Check the feeds." To Bridget again: "Don't move, you."

Bridget spun, intending to run from the room, back the way she'd come; couldn't allow herself to get caught. But she was suddenly struck by something. Jolting, jarring, painful. Two needle-tips in her

181

arm connected to electric cables. "Christ on a tricycle." She'd been tasered.

Bridget's legs gave out and she dropped to the hard marble floor, falling and striking the second bowl and shattering it as the electric current from the guard's weapon cavorted through her.

"Bridget unshackled Aldî-nîfaeti," the demon pronounced. "Aldî-nîfaeti liburrrrrated." It began its horridly loud, songlike chant again and the shards from the second bowl started to dance.

24

Bridget grabbed the thin cables and tugged the needle-tips out, fighting the effects of the electric jolt. She got to her feet just as the security guard dropped the taser, drew a Glock, and fired.

His target was what she had freed by smashing the bowl. At first it looked like oily smoke that rose in a thick, lazy spiral from the jittering potty shards, resembling one of the shadows she'd glimpsed on the ancient wall with her psychometry. She jumped back to buy herself some distance, watching as the form expanded quickly, and he fired again. The emerging creature lightened until it became the shade of early morning fog with solidifying tendrils that flowed away across the floor.

Bridget darted farther back and saw that the color of it changed once more, and with that the scent of the thing became pronounced, like something burnt and biting. Her own demon was still singing or chanting or evoking ... or whatever the hell it was doing. And the shards from the second bowl were becoming more agitated.

"Sweet Mary Mother of God!" the guard fired on the tentacle-beast and advanced, the bullets either missing and striking the display case or passing through the creature with no effect. At the same time, he talked into a microphone on his shoulder. "Joe, you're not going to believe this. Joe! Get everyone over here. Everyone, hear me! Section four-eight-one. It's a monster! A God's honest monster! Trigger the main alarm! Do it now! Now!"

The newly-formed creature looked nothing like her demon, which hovered at the edge of her vision, its song finally ended and all its eyes open.

It looked worse.

"Bridget unshackled Aldî-nîfaeti. Unshackled!"

The tentacle demon was easily the height of an NBA center. It had a dozen or more octopus-like appendages at its base that twitched against the marble floor, and a cylindrical body that rose in the middle of them, smooth and straight like a Roman column. It sprouted two mannish arms, furry and black and ending in snapping lobster-shaped claws, and a head that was simian and topped with broken horns. Everything but the arms was a mottled green-beige, patches on the tentacles scaly, and a few places on its head where tufts of dark green hair stood up at odd angles like stubborn crabgrass.

Bridget's stomach flip flopped and she grabbed the edge of a case to center herself.

What had she expected?

That nothing would happen? That in coming to the museum and breaking bowls no demon would pop out because it just didn't seem possible—despite the images from her delving?

Or had she thought that if something did come out, it would be a carbon-copy of the demon that dogged her? Certainly not something this massive and even more threatening.

And what *should* be happening now? The guard *should* be killing the thing, splattering its otherworldly guts all over the display case and sending its soul to hell.

Which, of course, wasn't happening.

The guard fired twice more, the bullets striking the beast squarely now, but doing nothing other than maybe pissing it off.

The column-creature opened its mouth and let out a sound like a thousand fingernails scratching across a blackboard. The guard shouted into his mic, but Bridget couldn't hear him over the demon.

Indecision held her. Flee, that would be the safest thing. Don't get caught, run back to the brownstone, and think. Think. Think. Think. The police would be coming soon, and more museum security was certainly on its way—though that might take a few minutes, the museum being so spread out. She couldn't get caught ... what would happen to Otter? Let all the security deal with the monster.

Flee, that would be the best course.

Flee.

Or do something rash and stupid like helping the security guard and risking her own capture.

The tentacle creature slid toward the guard, making a "slorping" sound against the marble and leaving a slimy trail. The pitch of its screeching changed and suddenly ceramic objects inside the Plexiglas display cases cracked, and some of the fluorescent tubes in the cases exploded. Bridget slammed her hands against her head and darted toward the security guard, skidding to put herself between him and the demon. She thought: invincible, right? If getting hit by a car and stabbed by a robber didn't kill her, this demon couldn't touch her, right? Her own demon wouldn't let it. If something happened to her, how would the rest of the damnable demons get released?

"Stay back!" she hollered at it. "Stay the hell away!"

A lobster-claw grabbed her wrist, picked her up and hurled her into a display case as if she was a near-weightless ragdoll.

Bridget watched the guard fire again and again until the Glock was empty and he dropped it. Then she saw a second patch of oily smoke rising. It had taken the other demon longer to escape its shattered prison.

"Noooooooooo!" Once more she darted toward the guard, who was screaming for help into his mic. She was intent again on interposing herself, but this time she was a heartbeat too late.

Flames flowed away from the demon's tentacles in a great "whoosh," reaching the guard and enveloping him.

"No!" Bridget wailed, stopping in mid-stride and leaping away,

185

narrowly avoiding the flames herself. The fire continued to wash over the floor and she sprang to grab the top of a display case, hanging there, listening to the flames crackle and the guard scream, faintly hearing the pounding of feet—more guards coming.

"God, no!" Bridget pulled herself up on top of the case and lay flat, aware she was triggering probably a dozen alarms. "Stay back!" She hollered to the approaching guards. "Stay out!"

The fire swirled across the marble, casting everything in a hellish orange glow and engulfing the four guards who charged into the room. The stench and heat were incredible, and at the edge of it she saw the second freed demon. It had finished forming, looking like a giant slab of Silly Putty, almost comical in its appearance. It rolled itself into the flames, and like a cocoon wrapped itself around the closest burning guard. Within heartbeats it moved onto the next guard and the next, the flames dying down and showing … nothing. The gray putty-demon had dissolved the bodies. It rolled itself toward the first charred victim and started devouring him, just as more security guards arrived and the tentacle demon sent a wave of fire crashing toward them.

Weren't there sprinklers? Shouldn't they be coming on and stopping the fire? She looked up and spotted a few strategically placed so they wouldn't damage the exhibits. The sprinklers had been melted.

Bridget could hardly breathe. What she'd witnessed … and what she held herself responsible for because she'd released the two monstrosities … kept her lungs captive. She turned her head so she wouldn't have to look, certain the putty-demon would dissolve the rest of the burning corpses. Bridget had thought her stomach empty, but she managed to retch something up. She peered over the edge of the display case and saw her personal demon; it was grasping one of the column-beast's tentacles. Faintly, she heard them talking in the long-dead tongue.

Her lungs felt seared, and she was unable to work up any saliva. She wanted to scream at the demons and to holler out a warning to more guards; she heard the slap of leather against the marble, and the shouts of men. But her tongue was sandpaper and she could muster no sound.

How many more were going to burn?

Get out of here, she thought. You can't help the guards, but maybe if you leave, the demons will follow. Save the guards by fleeing. She eased herself over the edge of the case and dropped to the floor, feeling the heat through the soles of her shoes.

Really, what had she thought would happen by releasing demons in the museum? That nothing bad would happen? That they would happily skitter away and start new lives in some dark alley, subsisting on rats and trash? She had to have known something horrid would result. Or maybe she'd thought that breaking the Sumerian bowls would release nothing at all. The first bowl had not spilled out a demon. What right-minded person would think that clay bowls could possibly contain ancient creatures of nightmare? She'd never doubted that such monstrosities could exist. Bridget had half-glimpsed enough things when Jimmy took her on a tour of the city's subterranean communities. But a part of her had truly doubted that they could be caught in a bowl ... and subsequently released...

... and then to embark on a fiery slaughter.

She rushed from the room, keeping her eyes down so she wouldn't have to see the demons or the guards who were burning; she heard the screams of the new batch of victims. Darting down a hallway and finally catching her breath, she still couldn't find her voice. What the hell had she been thinking?

She'd been thinking about Otter; that if she broke a few bowls maybe the demon that dogged her would leave her alone and go away. Otter would be safe.

Otter.

She had to get back to her brownstone. The screams and crackling flames receded as she hurried down a back staircase, climbed a display case to get to an air vent, and shimmied toward the back of the museum, all the while working to stay in the shadows and away from security cameras. Bridget pictured the various wings, turning here and there, popping out and taking another staircase, always mindful of the cameras, worrying that she might have been caught on a video feed somewhere.

She felt in her pockets—cell phone, lock picks, a shard from one of the pots she broke, cards from the three broken bowls ... along with the damnable buckle that bound her to the demon. Bridget wanted to make sure she'd not dropped anything that could be traced back to her.

As she neared the back of the building she heard sirens—several, muted, suggesting that the police or fire department were not directly behind the building. Bridget trembled all over, sweating; she'd never felt a fear so thick. Still clinging to the shadows, she held her breath and pushed open one of the back doors, triggering a shrill alarm that competed with the police sirens. The air was cold and warred with the heat that still held to her lungs. She nearly fell on a slick of ice as she ran from the building, watching the play of red, blue, and white emergency lights that bounced off the brickwork all around. It was all so loud ... the sirens, shouts, cars honking, her heart hammering ... and her demon jabbering. Suddenly it had appeared at her side, talking about God-knew-what, its words coming fast and with a brittle hardness to them.

She picked out "Otter."

It continued to say Otter every so often, mixed with words she couldn't understand. She would have to delve into the Sumerian seal back at the brownstone to gain more words. Bridget had to more effectively communicate with it, explain that she couldn't release more demons, couldn't be responsible for anyone else dying. She couldn't get the image out of her head, of the museum guards being incinerated and devoured.

"Otter," the demon said.

"You'll not hurt him," Bridget said, as she slipped into an alley and stopped to catch her breath. She'd finally worked up enough saliva to talk.

"Otter. Otter. Otter."

"You'll not feckin' touch him."

"Mmmmmmmmmm."

25

There were more police cars and fire trucks arriving, judging from the crescendoing sirens and the increasing light play against the buildings. And there were plenty of lookiloos drawn out onto the sidewalks despite the hour. Bridget cut through a throng of young people with drinks in hand who'd emerged from a dance club, their breath puffing away from their faces like they were all smoking invisible cigarettes, the sequined dresses of the women glittering under the streetlights.

She took the steps down into the subway two at a time, her demon following.

Lord knew where the other two demons were. She hoped they weren't still in the museum immolating police and firemen. She hadn't the ability to stop them. Could anyone? Call the National Guard or drop a tactical nuke on the Metropolitan Museum of Art; maybe that would do it.

"Are you okay?" A doughy-faced woman with an ankle-length winter coat gave Bridget an up and down as she claimed a spot on the platform. "Young lady, you should see a—"

"Doctor? I'm fine, thanks." Bridget brushed past her and stood farther away, rocking back and forth and still hearing the sirens. What

189

the hell had she done? Releasing demons? What she had to do, she told herself, to keep Otter safe.

There were only a dozen people on the platform, two of them pointed at her. All of them regarded her curiously. She knew her clothes were singed and she likely smelled like a charcoal briquette. The stench of the museum fire and the charred bodies had coated the inside of her mouth; it was all she could taste and smell.

A train rumbled into view and she hopped on as soon as the door slid open. It wasn't the one she needed to get back home, but it would take her to where she could make an easy connection, probably adding ten to fifteen minutes to the trip. She needed to get home, but she also needed to get away from the vicinity of the museum.

She shuffled to the far end of the car and sat; the plastic so cold she felt it through her pants. Rarely were the cars heated to a satisfactory level, but there were usually enough bodies to make up for that. Not at this hour, though. Bridget and her demon were the only riders in this car. The lighting, what there was of it with some of the lights out, flickered eerily. Still, there was enough to reflect her face in the window. There were soot smudges on her chin and forehead, and her once-long red hair was about a foot shorter on one side; it had caught fire and melted, her cheek and ear burned, making her look like a Goth freak. Bridget hadn't felt the flames that had done it, but then she was numb during much of what had happened minutes ago in the museum.

She gripped the bar in front of her, the metal chilling. "Damn." Bridget stared at her bare right hand. She remembered taking off one of her gloves in the museum to connect with a bowl. She must have dropped the glove. Probably wouldn't come back to bite her, though, it was no doubt ashes. Her demon settled across from her and closed its eyes, oddly—thankfully—quiet. She couldn't even smell its stench for the taste of the fire.

Three riders entered her car just before the door hissed closed. The train lurched forward. They were men.... boys, she mentally corrected, maybe Otter's age. Shouldn't be out so late. Should be home in bed, like Otter should be—though she was certain her son wasn't. Please let him be safe, she thought. Dear God, please let Otter be safe.

The tallest of the three swaggered toward her. He was dressed in jeans—pants, jacket over a hooded sweatshirt, tattoos of steer skulls on the backs of his hands. "Smells like a fire sale over here," he said. He gripped the pole for balance as the car wobbled, and flashed her a yellow-toothed smile. He made an exaggerated sniffing sound.

"I've got no money," she told him. "Well, five bucks. Here." She pulled the bill out of her pocket.

He shrugged and took a step closer, plucked the bill out of her fingers and made a show of tearing it in half, then quarters, the pieces fluttering to the dirty floor. Then he thrust his right hand in his pants pocket.

"You'll live longer if you leave me alone." Bridget noticed that her demon watched the boy and made a smacking sound with its bulbous lips. "Go away," she added. "And quickly."

He laughed. "Well, I ain't interested in money." He looked over his shoulder to the other two, who sniggered and elbowed each other. Bridget was certain they were no older than Otter. No business being out this late. They all had tats on their necks, but she couldn't see the designs clearly because their collars were turned up; meager protection against the winter cold. Probably gang members, and certainly up to no good. Definitely up to no good. All three reached to the backs of their jackets and pulled the sweatshirt hoods up over their heads.

"Seriously," she tried again. "This isn't going to end well for you. Back off." Crime had been going down, politicians and cops touting New York City as safer than Chicago, Detroit, and LA. But there were still too many assaults, including in the subways in the late, late hours to lone women on empty platforms or in uncrowded cars where not all the lights worked.

The closest youth drew a switchblade out, flicking it open. "Don't put up too much of a fight, fire sale, and you'll live through this. I promise."

"A little bit of a fight though," one of the others joined him. "It'll be more fun if she fights a bit."

191

"I dunno Joey," this came from the third youth, who'd not budged from the opposite end of the car. "This doesn't feel right. Why don't we—"

"Why don't we hurry up and do her, then," the tall one said. "Train's gonna make a stop real soon. If you ain't gonna participate Zin-Zin, stay at the door so no one gets on at the next stop."

"Or comes along from another car," Joey added, as he unbuckled his belt.

"Me first, Joey. You got to go first the last time." The tall youth lunged for her, leading with the knife, and trying to grab her arm with his free hand. Bridget jumped to her feet, and he took advantage of that, sweeping forward with a leg and catching her, setting her off balance.

She fell back, hitting the cold, hard floor of the subway car, and he was on top of her, blade pressed to her throat. He ground his pelvis against her.

"I'll be quick, Joey," he said. "Zin-Zin, watch how it's done."

Bridget got her hands against his shoulders and pushed up. She wasn't afraid of the knife; she'd been stabbed to no effect from the Yankees Fan early this morning. Her assailant didn't budge, and he pressed down harder.

The train stopped and the door hissed open. Bridget screamed to hopefully catch the attention of someone outside.

"Move along," she heard Zin-Zin say. "Move!"

She screamed again and the tall youth head-butted her. The door hissed closed and the train lurched on its way again. The demon rocked with the motion and continued to watch.

"Get off me, you fecker!"

"A fighter, eh? This'll be fun." Fast as lightning, he dropped the knife and grabbed both of her wrists and pinned her harder, brought his face close to hers and licked her cheek. "Gotta love a fire sale. Yum, you taste like burnt steak."

The demon hopped off its seat and loomed over them. Bridget had figured it would strike her assailant. Instead, it just continued to watch curiously and babble words she didn't understand.

"Get off me!" she hollered again, as she redoubled her efforts, twisting and trying to raise her legs to kick him, but found her ankles held by one of the other youths. Bridget was strong and should have bested both of them, but she was also spent from the museum outing and everything else that had transpired today, and they were young and angry. "Get off—"

The demon leaned in closer still, its ugly face brushing Bridget's forehead. It babbled something. She made out "Aldî-nîfaeti," as she pushed one more time and dislodged the tall youth and kicked hard enough to loosen the grip of the other; she was pretty sure she'd landed a heel to his face. A second kick and she was free. She scrambled out from underneath them.

"Hey!" The tall one was on his knees and made a grab for his knife. Bridget was fast and fuming and kicked it farther away and then drove the tip of her shoe into his neck. He made a gacking sound and crawled back a few feet.

She caught her breath while he picked himself up. The youth behind him, shorter and thicker, had a knife too.

"Get her," the shorter one said.

"We're comin' to another stop." This from Zin-Zin back by the door. "Maybe we ought to—"

"Kill her is what we ought to do," the tall one said. "Kill the bitch." He reached behind him, and his fellow passed him the other knife.

"Aldî-nîfaeti," the demon said, babbling a mix of other words and craning its stunted misshapen neck back and forth so it could see Bridget and her assailants.

"Pissmires," Bridget said. "Pay attention to Zin-Zin back there. Walk away while you gutter punks can still breathe."

The tall one rushed her again, ducking low to avoid her wild punch. Bridget hadn't been trying to actually hit him, just keep him back. Too many people had already died tonight ... all their blood on her hands. Bridget stepped back and adopted a boxer's stance; at that moment the train stopped again and she wasn't ready for it. Set off balance, he rushed her once more, grabbing at her clothes and pulling hard to knock her down. Her punch only grazed his shoulder. The demon hopped excitedly, apparently enjoying the action.

Undaunted, she brought her elbow down on the top of his head, but the blow didn't deck him. Undeterred, he pressed the attack, ripping her jacket and spilling out her cell phone, the damnable buckle, and the shard of pottery she'd intended to delve.

"That's it you feckin'—" Bridget tried to knee him in the groin, but missed the mark and only landed a strike against his thigh.

"Move along, people. This ain't the car you're looking for." This from Zin-Zin. "Move. Move. Move."

The tall youth growled and tugged harder on her jacket and pulled her to her knees. She punched him squarely in the face, breaking his nose. But he landed a punch too, against her jaw, momentarily stunning her.

The tall youth hit her again, and she sagged back, head hitting the floor of the car, legs bent at an awkward, uncomfortable angle. Her tongue lolled against the sharp edge of a broken tooth and tasted blood. She tried to get up, but her limbs had other plans, and she flopped like a wounded fish.

"Aldi-nîfaeti," the demon said. It had waddled over to her, ugly face looking down at hers. "Unshackle Aldi-nîfaeti. Otter. Mmmmm." Then the demon disappeared.

"Wonder if its gold?" The short thug picked up the buckle and held it high in the flickering light. "Joey, my man, look what fire sale had. Odd looking thing, huh? Bet it's worth something." He grabbed up the cell phone too, but left the pottery, which had broken into even smaller pieces.

Bridget could smell the redolent swirl of subway scents. She still tasted blood and the museum fire, but the stench of the demon was gone.

"Joey, if it's gold think we can swap it for that used Cobray at Broad Street? We need another nine."

A gun, Bridget realized. They were going to try to trade the buckle for a gun. But they couldn't trade it. The damn buckle would come back. Over and over and over.

Bridget spit out the broken tooth and shook her head—which did nothing to clear her senses. She rose up on her elbows and straightened her legs. The subway car shifted in her vision, and the young toughs blurred. "Dropsit," she said, hearing her words slur together like she was drunk. Probably concussed. "'S'buckle. Jus dropsit. Pleash."

On second thought, don't drop it, her hazy mind said. Take the thing and get off at the next stop. Leave me here or kill me … either way Otter should be safe now since you stole the damn demon. *Let the demon go after your loved ones. Let it wipe out your whole feckin' gang and do the city a favor.* She was certain her assailant had taken on the curse, just as she'd taken it on from Elijah Stone. He'd taken it and she could no longer see or smell or feel the presence of the demon.

She was free.

"Must be valuable," Joey said, looking around his companion. Joey's hood had fallen back and the gutter punks were coming better into focus, though her head hurt horribly. Bridget saw the tattoos on their necks. She stared and they came clearer, stylized initials—ICG— Insane Gangster Crips members. Joey leered at Bridget.

The car stopped and the doors hissed open.

Dear God, leave, Bridget willed them. *Get the hell away from me. Take the demon with you.*

The youth who'd stolen her buckle didn't see the demon yet … otherwise he'd be hollering or pointing or running from what was clearly a monster. But Bridget hadn't seen it at first either, not when she'd initially stolen the briefcase from Elijah Stone in his fine apartment, and not when she'd rode home with it on the subway. It wasn't until after she'd had it a few hours, when she was safe and sound and alone in her brownstone, studying the amazing Egyptian piece the briefcase held. Maybe it took time for the demon to transition from one owner to the next. Or maybe it liked to appear when its new owner was alone.

"Pissmires." Bridget grabbed onto a nearby seat and pulled herself up, just as the doors hissed closed and the train moved again. Didn't they have video surveillance on these trains? Didn't anyone know

195

she'd been assaulted by a trio of gutter punks? Older car, she realized. The MTA only installed the cameras on the newer ones where they wouldn't have to rewire everything.

"Not the 'droids you're looking for. Move along," Zin-Zin had told whoever had been going to board from another car. "Go somewhere else." A pause: "You, too, dick-wad. You don't want this ride neither."

"So fire sale, you told me you didn't have no money." This from the tall one. He looked from the buckle in his buddy's hand to her, and back to the buckle. "So that was a lie. Maybe you got more lies in your other pockets. Maybe you got more treasures."

Bridget turned her pockets inside out. The three exhibit cards she'd taken from the museum fluttered out.

"Joey, Bo," Zin-Zin slapped the side of the car to get their attention. "Next stop, I'm out of here. You should—"

"Get me a piece of the fire sale before I'm heading out," the tall one said, as he made a slashing gesture with the knife.

"Me too," the shorter one said. He slipped the buckle into his pocket. "I want to do her too. Just leave her breathin', Bo. I don't do dead ho bagels."

Like hell, Bridget thought. These junior Insane Crips weren't going to "do her" no matter what. Despite the lingering wooziness and the jackhammer of a headache, she lashed out. Grapping a seatback with both hands for support, she kicked as hard as she could, aiming for Bo's hand, but nailing his arm instead. It was good enough, the knife went flying and Bo was momentarily surprised. She followed through with a roundhouse kick, high above the seats and catching him in the chest. He fell back against the one named Joey.

"Don't let that scud bitch beat you up!" Joey pushed Bo toward Bridget and she kicked him again, aiming for his crotch and connecting solidly. He dropped with an "ooooooooooh!" She slid past him and was on Joey, pounding him like she was trying to tenderize a tough hunk of meat.

He fought back, but he was slow and lacked skill, and had he been even a little sharper Bridget would've been in trouble. She was pretty certain she'd broken a few of his ribs—the "invincible" part of the demon curse hadn't kicked in yet. She could still hurt him. He threw his hands up to defend himself and at the same time kicked at her; steel toe shoes from the feel of a blow landing against her calf. She heard the tall punk getting to his feet behind her, moaning and cursing softly. She jammed her elbow back, hitting him and keeping him off balance.

The train eased to a stop and the doors hissed open. Zin-Zin was good to his word and darted out. Joey looked over his shoulder and Bridget capitalized on that, delivering a solid punch to his chin, harder than she'd intended. His head snapped back and he dropped like a rock. She wheeled on Bo. He'd grabbed onto a pole, his dark eyes filled with hate and lip curled up.

"Filthy ho bagel," he spat. "You're gonna die, bitch. I'm gonna—"

As much as the confines of the car allowed, Bridget spun and kicked, her heel driving into his knee. She kicked again, and as he fell, she kept up the assault, fueled by ire. The doors slid closed and she grabbed a seatback to keep from joining the thugs on the filthy floor of the car as the train moved on.

"You feckin' fool!" She kicked him until he stopped moving. Then she leaned over him; he was still breathing. So was the other one. Good, she didn't need two more deaths on her head. She sat between the two, waiting to get off at the next stop ... wherever that was. For the first time in her life she had no idea where her subway ride was taking her.

"You sad, sad fool," she continued to rail. "Now whatever family you have, whatever friends ... they're all going to die because you can't speak Sumerian." She wiped at her nose, blood coming away on her fingers. "Shit." She pinched her nostrils and tipped her head back, seeing a poster advertising a high school production of The Odd Couple taped to the ceiling. "Their hearts'll be ripped out because you won't know what the demon wants." Good riddance to them, she thought. Fewer Insane Crips members in the city wouldn't be a bad thing.

Bridget felt the train slow and she stood, the quick movement setting the jackhammers off in her head again. She'd had nothing but

197

one headache after the next since stealing the briefcase from Elijah Stone. Well, thank God she was free of the curse. Thank God she'd gotten on this old subway car and that some clatty dirtballs decided to assault her.

The car stopped and the doors hissed open. She gave Joey one last kick, bent and reached into his front pocket and pulled out the buckle and palmed it.

"A stupid fecker, I am, stealing this again," Bridget said. She made it out and onto the platform just as the doors hissed closed behind her and the train continued on.

26

Two men were on the platform, bundled in parkas and carrying duffels, sailors she could tell from their pants and hats. They paid her little attention and she shuffled by them and to a restroom. Should've grabbed her cell phone back from the thug while she was at it, but she'd been in a rush. She could've called the brownstone, checked on Otter. Bet she couldn't find a payphone anywhere nearby, not that she had a single coin to put in it. Payphones were practically obsolete.

What the hell had she done ... taking back the buckle, and the demon? She'd been rid of the curse! That's what she'd wanted, to be rid of it! What the bloody blue hell had she been thinking?

She smelled the beast, and then heard it, saw that it had appeared at her side. "Bridget unshackle—"

"Shut up. Shut up. Shut up." She angled her head in the bowl of the sink and ran water on her face. She shivered, the water cold like ice, but she kept at it, scrubbing her cheeks and drinking and spitting until the taste of the fire was gone. Her mouth ached from where the thug had broken at least one of her teeth. She looked in the mirror. "A feckin' double bagger," she pronounced herself. Her jacket was torn, everything singed, her hair ... Dear God, her once-beautiful red hair.

One side was a riotous tangle crusted with blood and subway car crap, the other side practically non-existent, melted in the museum conflagration. It looked like she'd glued orange Brillo pads behind her left ear.

Bridget paced, her heels clicking against the hard floor, the demon watching her and growling that she needed to "unshackle Aldî-nifaeti."

"What in all the levels of hell was I thinking?" She was thinking that she wanted this nightmare to end—with her. That she didn't want the demon to keep passing from one thief to the next to the next, the string of corpses with their hearts ripped out stretching on indefinitely. Who else could communicate with the damn thing? Who else could divine pieces of its language?

Probably no one.

No one *living* in any event.

"Bloody hell." Bridget had put Otter and Michael and Dustin in jeopardy again—and to her their lives were worth more than the lives of whoever was related to the subway thugs. How bad would it have been for the demon to rip out the hearts of Insane Crips members?

She stormed out of the restroom and set her feet in time with the pounding in her head. She knew how to use the subways without money or tokens. Always there were places to get on and off. She took the next train and made two more switches before she emerged from the stairs two long blocks from her brownstone. It was snowing, a sleety mix that stung her face. Salt remained on the sidewalk from a previous application, but there was not enough of it, and so the pavement was slippery and she fell twice in her rush. By the second tumble she was so weary that she crawled to a streetpost and used it to pull herself up.

There wasn't another soul out on the street in her block, though a late-model Buick cruised by, slowing when it came even with her, and then moving on. She heard something going through garbage piled up in a narrow gap between condo buildings.

A glance at her watch under the streetlight. The crystal was cracked, but she could read that it was 1:45 a.m. Her adventures in the museum and the subway had swallowed more time than she'd realized.

"Bridget unshackle Aldî-nîfaeti. Bridget unshackle, else Otter unshackled from life."

"Shut up."

It kept blathering.

She found them on the fourth floor in the theater room—Otter, Dustin, Michael, Marsh, Rob, Alvin, and Quin. They'd been watching one of the Lethal Weapon movies, but she stopped it with a flick of a switch at the back of the room. She brought the lights up.

"Mom! What the hell happened to you?" Otter stood and spun, spilling a bowl of popcorn he'd been balancing on his lap.

Dustin vaulted over his seat back and was at her side in a heart-beat. Behind him, the others stood slack-jawed. "An ambulance—"

"I don't need a hospital. I'm not going to a hospital."

Dustin gingerly touched the side of her face where her hair had burned off. "What—"

"It's a long story, and not a good one. And we don't have time for it." Bridget looked around him. "Michael, Marsh, Alvin ... grab a couple of duffle bags, suitcases, whatever, and go to the kitchen. Fill them with food ... cans, bottles, boxes, soda—"

Michael straightened his collar. "See here, Miss O'Shea. It's two in the morning and you'll not order me—"

"—around like this?" Bridget bent and put her hands on her knees. Her sides ached, and she grabbed a deep breath. "Michael, I want you to live. I want all of you to live. Just ... oh, hell, just shut up and do it." A few more breaths and she straightened and talked fast. "Trust me. I'll make it up to you. Just trust me and live. Dustin, Otter, Quin, grab some coats, the heaviest in the closets, and flashlights. Stay together. Meet up in the kitchen. Quin, you've a gun, right? Meet up in the kitchen. We have to—"

Dustin put an arm around her shoulders. "I care for you, Brie, but not enough to put up with—"

"Pissmires! I'm trying to keep you alive. Keep all of you alive. And I don't have time to argue." She flailed an arm behind her. "You can't see it, but there's a demon behind me."

"You said that before, Mom, a demon, and—"

"—and it's still behind me. We don't have time to argue this, Otter."

"Okay." Otter nodded. "Okay. C'mon, Dustin, Alvin, let's—"

"No. Sorry, Brie." Dustin brushed his lips against her cheek, wriggling his nose at the scorched scent of her hair. He gently tipped her face up. "Call me when—if—you come to your senses."

Then he was gone.

"Mmmmmmmmmm," the demon said.

Bridget spun and put her face down to the beast. "Listen you feckin' monster. Leave him alone. You want your Aldi-nîfaeti unshackled?"

"Unshackle Aldi-nîfaeti," it said.

"Who's she talking to?" This came from Alvin.

"I assume a demon," Michael said. "An invisible one."

"Otter, Quin, coats. Spare blankets if you're fast. We're going camping." Bridget turned back and pointed to the exit. "Michael, Marsh—"

"Yes, Miss O'Shea," Michael said. "Duffels filled with food for your camping trip."

"*Our* camping trip. Rob, you and me will—"

"Boss ... what do you want me to do with this?" He held a package the size of a breadbox. It was wrapped in brown paper and tied with a string. The stamp on the side was smeared. "I think he ripped me off, but—"

"Bowls."

"Two, boss, I told you—"

"Move. Move. Move." Bridget waved at the others. "Coats, food. Move. Meet in the kitchen."

A moment later she and Rob were alone.

"The antique guy, boss. He brought over two bowls. Eleven hundred bucks. Bet he ripped us off." Sweat had beaded up on Rob's forehead. Bridget could tell he was nervous, probably the one person in the house who really believed they were in the midst of something very bad.

"Bring them with us. We've got to—"

"Hurry. Yeah, I get that." Rob headed toward the doorway. "Boss, you look like hell."

"Yeah," she agreed. "And hell is surely where I'm going." Then she raced to her bedroom and tugged off her singed clothes and boots, seeing that the sole of the right one was partially melted. She listened to the demon babble the entire time. She struggled into tight leggings, put loose sweatpants over them, and found her heaviest sweater and most comfortable shoes. Last, she grabbed her wallet and Swiss Army knife off her dresser and jammed them in a pocket; she'd not taken her wallet to the museum, not wanting any identification on her. She flipped up a false bottom in a drawer and pulled out a stack of hundreds that she wedged into another pocket—just in case she needed some ready cash. She filled a tote with items from the bathroom: a few bars of the milled soap Dustin had given her, a razor, bottle of shampoo, two hand towels, a package of unopened toothbrushes, all for the "camping trip." A glance in the mirror as she rushed from the room: Rob was right. She looked like hell, barely human.

They weren't waiting in the kitchen; they were sitting in the adjacent dining room, two stuffed backpacks, a bulging duffle bag, and the wrapped package from the antique store. Coats were draped on the backs of chairs, and all of them were red-faced from rushing.

Rob had been talking, something about the package with bowls in it, but he shut up when she hurried in.

Michael stood. "I have worked for you, Miss O'Shea, for—"

"Can it," Bridget was purposefully terse. "Oh, the hairy word! I said I'm trying to keep you alive. There's a feckin'—"

"Demon. Yes, Miss O'Shea. You already—"

In a fast, fluid movement that belied his age, Alvin rose from his seat, pulled a Walther from his pocket and fired two shots at something behind Bridget. In that same moment, Otter jumped up so fast he tipped his chair over.

"Mommmmm!" Otter hollered.

They could see her demon? Bridget whirled and jumped back so quick she ran into Marsh and knocked him down. She saw her demon, but she also saw something else—the tall, tentacled thing she'd released in the art museum.

Lava flowed from the demon's tentacles, spreading across the floor and scenting the air with something foul and acrid.

Bridget stared, incredulous. She hadn't thought the beast would come here. How could it know where she lived? "Christ on a tricycle! Run! Otter, run! Grab everything all of you and run!"

Otter acted first, snatching his coat and a backpack and dashing out of the dining room, knocking a serving tray over and sending china flying. The others shouted and grabbed for the bags and coats, save Alvin, who kept firing.

"Outside!" she shouted after them. "Rob, the package! I'll meet you on the sidewalk!" Marsh hesitated only a moment and she waved him away. "Look after Otter. Stay together! Alvin, get out of here. Bullets won't work."

Alvin turned and ran, replying, but she couldn't hear him. The lava had caught the drapes on fire and flames crackled and danced toward the ceiling. The sprinklers kicked on, but they weren't enough to put out the flames. The entire room was becoming engulfed, and she watched in horror as part of the floor gave way, taking chairs and the table with it.

Amid the flames, her personal demon squatted, regarding her with all five of its eyes. It was talking too, but she couldn't hear it over the fire.

Bridget felt her blood boiling. The lava reached the tips of her shoes, more of the floor fell away, and she jumped back just in time. The lava and flames had spread toward the hallway, leaving only one way out of the dining room now, and that was into the kitchen. She wheeled around and dashed through the doorway, past the stainless steel counter, and hit the intercom. Her tote bag fell from her shoulder. "Fire! Everyone out of the house now!" Bridget didn't think anyone else was inside, but she gave the warning nevertheless.

"Everyone out!" The sprinkler kicked on in the kitchen as she grabbed up the tote again. The marble floor was as slick as an icy sidewalk, and her feet shot out from under her and she went sliding. She crawled to the far door and grabbed onto the jamb and pulled herself up.

Another "whoosh!" and everything wood in the kitchen was blazing. She took the steps two at a time. She was going to lose the brownstone, all the treasures inside it. An image flashed into her mind as she raced down to the next floor and then the next. She saw a little Turkish boy hug the weaver of her prized oushak. "*Seni seviyorum babaanne.*"

"*Seni seviyorum,*" the weaver had returned.

It had been many years since Otter had told Bridget he loved her.

Out the back and slipping through the narrow alley to get to the street out front, the icy snow spat at her, providing a sharp contrast to the heat that blasted out in waves from the brownstone. The others were gathered in the middle of the street, their faces glowing orange in the light from the fire. Neighbors were up and out, too, coats thrown over pajamas, several of them on cell phones, a few taking pictures. Bridget heard sirens: someone had called the fire department. She knew the building couldn't be saved.

"Move!" she called to Otter, rushing toward him, falling on an icy patch and landing hard, tote bag flying lose. Rob was closest and picked her up, cradling the package with one arm. She grabbed it from him and nodded to her tote bag. He retrieved it and turned his attention to the fire. "Move," she said breathlessly. "We got to move!"

Through a high window she saw a column move amid the flames, the tentacle beast. Her own demon hadn't come out of the house; maybe it was reveling in the fire. Maybe it reminded the demon of hell and it was having a grand time.

"Move," she said again, no power in her voice. "This way. Move. Move. Move."

She ignored the neighbors, their voices swirling with the ashes and the snow.

"There's Bridget O'Shea. Get a look at her."

205

"Like a bomb went off there. I knew she and all those men were up to no good."

"Looks like she's hurt. Did someone call an ambulance?"

"Look at her hair!"

"Bridget! Bridget!" This from one of the neighbors she was friendly with. Bridget waved the woman away and shouldered through the growing crowd, keeping her head down.

"My condo! It better not get my condo!"

"Gotta be arson. Nothing goes up that quick otherwise."

"Hey, where's O'Shea going?"

"Mom, where *are* we going? With all this stuff? Shouldn't we wait for the fire trucks? The police?"

"No cops," Bridget said, steering her group toward a side street.

"The demon," Otter continued, walking backward in front of her. "That ... that ... octopus-monster. Won't the police—"

"I don't think the demon will let the cops—" living cops, Bridget mentally amended, "—see it. I don't think it likes witnesses."

"My stuff," Otter said, turning around and falling in step at her side. Behind them Marsh, Rob, Alvin, and Quin walked double-file. She noticed Michael was in the rear, reluctant, but keeping with them. "My stuff, mom. It's toast. My books, clothes, all of it. My school—"

"I'll buy you more stuff, Otter."

"Mom, my laptop and—"

"Please shut up." Bridget said, as she led them down three more side streets, picking a subway entrance that was far enough away that the sirens and the fire and the conversations of the lookiloos were deadened by the urban canyons. Sparse traffic shushed by, sluicing up the sleety snow mixture. The steps down were an icy mess, and Bridget took them slow; she didn't want to risk dropping the package, hoping it contained what Rob advertised: two demon bowls.

"Mom, where are we—"

"Going?"

"Yeah," Alvin said. "I'm old. Not used to this walking."

"Not used to seeing monsters, either," Quin said. Softer, but still

Bridget could hear him. "I'm quitting, Alvin. After this, I'm retired. To Florida, I'm going."

"Where we going?" This from Marsh. "Boss?"

"To a pit," Bridget said, stopping on the bottom step. "Three connections from here."

"A pit? Mom?"

"It's nowhere you're gonna like, Otter. But you'll be safe there. All of you will be safe." She squared her shoulders and headed toward the turnstiles. Good thing she'd grabbed money; she wouldn't be able to sneak them all through. "One of you brought a flashlight, I hope. Please tell me we have at least one flashlight."

27

Bridget glanced at her watch: 3:44. It looked black as night in this godforsaken neighborhood, the sky so overcast, most of the streetlights in this block broken, apartment windows dark, the sidewalk empty. As crowded as New York City was, she found it odd and disconcerting to be alone, save for the company of her babbling demon—which had rejoined her after she'd stuffed her entourage into Adiella's pit and made a stop in a subway bathroom to cut her hair, leaving about an inch all the way around and wondering if she should have just shaved it all off. Bridget had no clue where the other two beasts were, and didn't want to think about them right now. She knew the tentacled beast had visited her antique store; she'd stopped there to retrieve the other Sumerian piece, the astrology tablet the history professor was buying, thought she might delve into and gain more language and insight into ancient Sumer. But she discovered fire trucks on the scene, watering down what was left of her place. It would be a total loss, most of the treasures ashes or slagged. The astrology tablet? It was a rock and would survive; maybe she'd come back and sift through the rubble for it later.

It was snowing again, fat flakes that settled on top of the curb drifts and cut some of the sooty-cityness that made winter look dirty.

208

Bridget loved New York and normally couldn't envision living anywhere else. But a beach in the Caribbean wouldn't be so bad, would it? Blue sky and sunshine, sipping something sweet and intoxicating with a paper umbrella in it, not a demon in sight.

She couldn't stop the tears, and her shoulders shook as she walked. She'd been crying since the squatty demon rejoined her. It had blood on its claws and on its lower lip.

Bridget knew it had killed Dustin.

And it was her fault. She could have let the subway tough keep the buckle.

The last thing Dustin had said to her: "Call me when—if—you come to your senses."

"Mmmmmmmmmmm," the demon had said as Dustin left.

Bridget could have stopped him. She could have used Alvin's gun … and what? Threatened to shoot him if he didn't go with her little entourage down into Adiella's pit in the subway? She could have tied him up, carried him if necessary. She could have kept him alive. She should have. Her feckin' fault Dustin was dead. One more body because of her.

One more.

She'd *known* the demon would kill him, *known* it the moment she let Dustin walk out of her house.

Her fault. One more death on her fingers.

One more.

Empty. Bridget felt wholly empty. Had she loved Dustin? Maybe, or close to it. She loved the way he made her feel, loved the way his hands and lips traveled over her skin, loved the scent of him, loved the sex, his cooking, his smile, that he called her "my Brie" and *mon amour.* She hadn't let anyone else get so close to her, not since Tavio. Hadn't let anyone into her heart.

Now all she had left was Otter.

Her crew? She had them, some would remain loyal and with her while she rebuilt her smuggling operation. No doubt she'd have to start from scratch. If the lava demon had burned her brownstone and her antique store, it had certainly slagged her warehouse too.

Her crew was a family of a sort, but it wasn't the same ... it wasn't Tavio or Dustin. It wasn't like her "adopted" son Jimmy.

Why the hell hadn't she let the subway thug keep the damn buckle and the damn demon? Why did she have to grow a feckin' conscious and go all righteous about saving strangers? Dustin would still be alive. And maybe, just maybe, she wouldn't feel like worthless garbage.

Could she keep Otter safe? She couldn't make him spend the rest of his life in Adiella's pit.

A crumpled up fast food bag scudded past her in the wind, coming to rest against a snowdrift wrapped around the base of a street sign. A skinny mongrel poked its head out of an alley, regarded her with matted eyes and worked its nose.

"Nothing to feed you," she told it. "And you better disappear or my demon might eat you."

The dog made a snuffling sound, and then darted away.

Not a two-legged denizen to be seen. Within an hour or so that would change. The Mexican bakery a handful of doors down would open, renters would come out heading to work. Cars would chug by with more frequency on the street. The noise would ratchet up to its comfortable and cacophonic New York City level.

Where the hell was the witch?

Adiella had not appeared in the hole where Bridget had left Otter and the others. Granted, the witch had other pits in the city, probably all of them underground, and maybe Adiella was sound asleep in one of them right now. Or maybe she had an apartment somewhere in this very neighborhood. Bridget had figured some magical gewgaw or ward would have alerted Adiella that they'd trespassed last night in one of her holes, and that the witch would have arrived out of anger or curiosity.

Though Bridget hated the woman, she didn't know where else to turn right now. And since the witch hadn't showed down in the subway, and since Otter had fallen asleep, Bridget set out to find her. Was it possible the demon had slipped away sometime in the past few hours and killed Adiella like it had killed Tavio and Jimmy and no doubt Dustin? Yes, possible, Bridget had to admit, but she doubted it.

The demon only seemed interested in eating the hearts of people Bridget cared about.

It didn't look like Adiella was in the bookshop. The front window was softly lit, displaying an array of hardcovers and paperbacks, some new, some used. Bridget pressed her face to the glass and made out the shadow-images of shelves upon shelves farther back, but nothing else, nothing moving in any event. But the shop was deep, and she couldn't see all of it. "Pissmires. Where the hell are you?"

She reached into her back pocket for a small leather case. She selected a thin metal pick and started working on the lock, using her body as a shield to hide her hands. Bridget hadn't seen anyone on the street, but that didn't mean there weren't early-risers or all-nighters up in apartments overlooking this sidewalk. Let any lookiloos think she had a key and was supposed to be here.

It was an old brass lock and an almost-effortless pick. She twisted the knob and swallowed a scream as a burst of fiery pain hit her. Bridget was a statue. She couldn't move and the agony intensified, turning from fire to ice, then again a searing heat hit her that was even worse than the previous jolt.

The witch didn't need traditional security or burglar bars like the other establishments in the block. All Adiella required was her accursed bone-numbing magic. Bridget had expected some sort of arcane defense, but nothing this severe.

The alternating waves of extreme heat and cold chased each other through her body as she finally managed to inch forward. One step, two, pushing the door wider, and then feeling like her teeth had been replaced by constant lightning strikes. A third step and the pain wholly consumed her, all of it scalding now. Bridget fell into the shop and fought for air. Her pulse, the rush of blood pounding in her ears, was as loud as a crashing wave.

She didn't know how long she lay there before she could move again, though likely only moments, curling into a fetal position but able to crook her foot and give a kick that closed the door behind her. Faintly, she heard the latch catch, and in that moment the fiery pulses stopped and the crashing noise in her head died away. The pain lingered, though.

The demon had followed her into the bookstore, apparently unaffected by Adiella's magical ward. The light that spilled from the front display window made its warty hide faintly gleam. It scuttled close and sat in front of her face, babbling in its ancient tongue and Bridget of no mind to attempt to pick out familiar words. Rivulets of pussy goo continued to trickle down its hide, wider than before. Or maybe the rivulets hadn't changed at all and only her perspective had; she'd not been this close and eye-level with its repulsive skin for more than a few seconds before. One thing that certainly had changed was its odor. The demon still reeked, just as horribly, but there was a different component to the stench, a strong sulfuric acid odor that clung to the roof of her mouth.

"The feckin' witch," Bridget cursed through clenched teeth. "Where the hell is she?" She waited for her pain to lessen to a more manageable level, and then started to uncurl herself.

Was the ward meant to kill a burglar or just discourage one with a thousand volts of eldritch energy? Kill the sucker, she guessed. If Bridget hadn't been so blessed and cursed with the demon buckle— the thing she was certain had saved her when the Yankee Fan jammed a knife in her stomach—she would have died to Adiella's security measure, and maybe been incinerated in the process. The witch's magic probably would have wholly eliminated a normal burglar, not left a body behind that had to be explained or disposed of.

She got to her knees and grabbed a nearby shelf, using it to help pull herself up.

"Adiella?" Bridget called for the witch a few times. The only reply was the demon babbling. "Yeah, I heard you. Free the Aldi-nîfaeti. You're a broken record. Well, I did free two of them. You ought to count that as one in the plus column."

Bridget had no intention of freeing even one more demon. She had too much blood on her hands and wasn't going to add another drop to it. Again the image of the museum guards popped into her mind. There had to be a way to keep Otter safe ... other than him living in one of Adiella's holes for the rest of his life.

There had to be a way to get rid of the demon.

The demon snarled at her, acid goo spilling over its bulbous lip and hitting the floor, sizzling. It belched a cloud of something noxious that made her head spin.

"Free Aldî-nîfaeti," it said, adding a string of words she couldn't comprehend.

"Adiella!" Bridget walked to the back of the shop, the demon stopping under the poster of the dog with a Frisbee and seeming to study it. "Frisbeetarianism is the belief that when you die your soul goes up on the roof and gets stuck," she read. "My soul's not going up."

She paused a moment, listening. Then: "Adiella!"

Maybe the witch would show up here if Bridget kept hollering. Maybe her painfully triggering the ward at the shop door would alert Adiella, and the witch would arrive soon. Or maybe Bridget could find Adiella's other holes if she rummaged around here for clues: that was what she'd anticipated doing by coming here.

Bridget padded to the back counter, flipped the switch on a single fluorescent light that hung above it, and laid her hand flat against the side of the cash register. Maybe by using her psychometry to call up an image of the witch, Bridget could discover the woman's whereabouts.

Bridget's palm tingled and her mind pressed in. The cash register gave up its details: Model 356 Brass National Cash Register, manufactured in 1909, a crack in the marble plate below the keys, good working condition, not cleaned or restored, value $900 dollars. Looking out from the cash register she caught a glimpse of the witch's fingers, smooth in this image from yesterday, bedecked with baubles that might have been costume jewelry.

Bridget watched Adiella ring up a customer's purchases—a stack of more than a dozen paperback fantasy romance titles with scantily clad busty women and shirtless musclemen on the covers. The buyer was an elderly woman with wrinkles poorly masked by too much pancake makeup. The smile was nice, though, and her eyes looked engaging. She spoke Spanish.

"*Espero que la lectura de todos estos,*" the old woman said. Bridget understood every word: I look forward to reading all of these.

"*Podrá disfrutar de ellos,*" Adiella returned. "*Vuelva cuando se necesita más.*"

Yes, lots of romance books, Bridget noted from the sign above a wide set of shelves. Still looking out from the cash register, she saw Adiella close up the bookstore and leave.

Bridget removed her hand from the cash register, balled her fists and set them against her hips. What the hell had she really hoped to accomplish by coming here? Listening to an image of Adiella say where she was going, hopefully. Catching some comment about where the witch lived, where her holes were under the city. Bridget indeed might get one of those crucial tidbits of information, but it could take some time, delving deeper into the cash register or the counter or the stool worn smooth by the witch's posterior, flipping through days or perhaps months with her psychometry. Or simply waiting until the witch showed up to open the store.

The demon waddled toward her and reached out a claw, nudging her leg. "Unshackle Aldî-nîfaeti."

"Yeah. Yeah, I know, unshackle all the Aldî-nîfaeti feckers in New York." Good thing the beast couldn't wholly read her mind. It would know she'd never bust another Sumerian bowl again.

Bridget unbuttoned her coat and took it off, draping it over the counter. Adiella obviously craved the heat and didn't bother to turn down the thermostat even when she wasn't here.

She sat on the wooden stool and steadied her breathing, looking over the cash register to see the demon squatting in front of the counter, tracing a whorl in the wood floor with a talon. It still babbled, but softly, and nothing Bridget could understand other than "Aldî-nîfaeti" and "Dustin. Mmmmmmmm." She wished she would have brought some coffee ... or anything for that matter to drink. So thirsty. There was a small refrigerator under the counter, and Bridget cracked it open to see three bottles of Jarritos grapefruit soda, a package labeled chili-flavored salted plums, and a half-full jar of pinto bean dip. Maybe the witch had warded her larder, too; Bridget didn't want to be on the receiving end again of Adiella's magic. Besides, grapefruit soda didn't sound thirst quenching.

Just work, dammit, she told herself. *Get to work and delve into this and find Adiella.*

Bridget reached for the cash register again, and then stopped, noticing an open shoebox just under the counter, filled with scraps of paper and business cards. Perhaps there were bills in there. Even though Adiella lived off the grid, chances were she had to pay bills for the shop, and maybe some other address or a phone number was listed. It was worth a look.

The demon squatted in front of a sale rack and appeared to study the titles on the lowest shelf. It looked over its bumpy shoulder and regarded her. "Unshackle Aldî-nîfaeti. Else unshackle Otter." It paused. Streams of putrid goo ran out of sores on its sides, disappearing before they struck the floor. "Mmmmmmmm."

She did her best to ignore the demon, brought the box out and sat it next to the cash register, started rifling through it, her fingers stiffening when something caught her eye. An ivory business card that felt like it had a linen content, dark brown small caps printing: ELIJAH STONE. And beneath that: CONSULTANT. There were phone numbers and a FAX number.

215

28

W hy the hell would Adiella have Elijah Stone's business card?" Had the witch been researching the demon for Bridget? Trying to find out more about researching its previous owner? She turned the card over and spotted an ink scrawl on the back that matched the address where Bridget had stolen the cursed briefcase.

Researching the demon? Researching Stone? Bridget doubted it.

"Well, let's break the devil's dishes and take a closer look." Her heart felt like it was being squeezed, and a part of her said: put the card back, keep looking for Adiella, you don't want to delve into this. But Bridget didn't listen to that part. She closed her eyes and rubbed her thumb across ELIJAH STONE, felt the raised ink on the linen-stock business card, and let her senses dip inside, concentrating until she felt Stone's manicured fingers on the card. Easing outward just a smidgen, she noted the card—and his hand—were in his pocket; and that there about a dozen other cards there.

"More," she coaxed, centering herself and hooking the tips of her shoes behind a rung in the stool to give her more stability. "Follow the card."

"You have acquired a demon," Adiella pronounced.

Bridget nearly lost her perch, hearing the witch's voice. For an instant she thought Adiella had come into the shop, and then she realized the voice came from the image pulled from Elijah Stone and the card he held, from her exploring the memories of the paper. Adiella had appeared only inside her head.

Bridget closed her eyes to better concentrate. Her senses spiraled outward, seeing Elijah in the bookstore, feeling his fingers nervously play with the corner of the business card inside his pocket, pull the card out.

Then she saw Elijah push back from the counter. "A demon? You know for certain that's what it is? It's a demon? A *real* demon? Fire-and-brimstone from hell?"

"An old demon, a soul beast." Adiella shook her head. Bridget noted that the witch looked old in this image, cobweb strands of white hair protruding from a colorful scarf wrapped around her head.

"Can you see it? This demon?" Stone asked. Bridget got a good look at him. Middle-aged, librarian-complexion pale, slightly paunchy, good-looking face though, strong chin. Fancy shoes, an expensive overcoat that he'd unbuttoned.

The damnable briefcase at his feet.

Bridget felt her blood boil. The witch had known about the briefcase prior to Bridget stealing it. She continued to let the image play out. She'd known about the demon affixed to it.

"Did your ... spell ... whatever it was you did ... let you *really* see it? The demon?"

"See it? The beast is here? In my shop?" Adiella looked furious. "You brought a demon into my shop? You dare?"

"Of course it's in your shop." Bridget noted that Elijah was sweating, probably had been for some time. Nerves or the heat of Adiella's bookstore.

"You dare! You brought it with you? You dare!" Adiella made the sign of the cross.

"I can't help but bring it with me! It goes where I go. I could have explained that if you'd—"

Adiella interrupted him by mumbling. Bridget realized she was

217

casting some sort of spell. "I cannot see the demon, no, Elijah Stone. "Where is it?"

"Right next to me. *It's always right next to me.* It's staring at you."

"Ah, that is what I feel. I feel its eyes on me."

"So ... get rid of it! That's what I'm paying you three thousand an hour for, right? Get rid of it. That's what I came here for, what Lady Lakshmi sent me here for. Just get rid of the damn thing."

Bridget's heart hammered as the scene progressed. Her throat tightened as she realized how this was going to play out.

"Is it gone?" Adiella asked after a fashion.

"No. It's not gone. It's still watching you, and it's babbling in some language I can't understand. It's always babbling. It only shuts up when I'm sleeping."

"This demon, describe it to me, yes."

"It's fuckin' ugly."

"In detail, please."

Bridget ground her teeth together, and she felt the card twist between her fingers. Still, she held to the image. Elijah Stone had described it accurately enough, though he'd left out the part about the rivulets of goo that ran down the beast's hide.

"It is not a demon I am familiar with, Elijah Stone. And I have faced many demons. I have exhausted my magic in an effort to sever this particular beast from you. It should have worked. My magic is strong. It should have worked, but it is a dominant demon that has attached itself to your soul. As I said, old. Very, very old. It defies me. And that it can hide from my sight ... its power is great. You say it babbles?"

Yeah, constantly, Bridget thought. In fact, when she opened her eyes to check on the demon, she saw it, still chattering in the background about its fellow Aldî-nîfaeti. It had moved along to the "classics" shelf, its claw running across the bindings. She kept watching the image nested in the back of her mind.

"Powerful," Adiella pronounced.

"Powerful? Horrible is what it is. And it's caused me nothing but grief. It's ruined my life, ruined everything. It's killed. Because of that ... that ... *thing* I have no one left in my life. My girlfriend, gone. My mother, sister, a niece. It's never hurt me, just the women in my life I cared about. It's just me now and that ... that ... damnable demon."

Oh. Dear. God. Bridget worked not to fall off the stool. Adiella had been told the demon was murderous and that it killed women close to Elijah Stone. Had the witch thought that because women were the victims ... wait ... had she *wanted* Bridget to be one of the demon's victims? The witch hadn't deduced that it also killed men. Apparently only the holder of the buckle was safe.

"Lakshmi could do nothing, not exorcise it. And I cannot sever it—"

"So why the hell am I here? Why—"

"But unlike Lakshmi, I can save you, perhaps save your soul. I cannot sever it, but I can provide a remedy. And it is not such a difficult one, Elijah Stone."

"You can't get rid of it, but you know—"

"—someone who can."

"You came by this demon, Elijah Stone, by stealing it, yes?"

"Pissmires and spiders," Bridget cursed. "Yeah, I was set up." She had a little trouble believing it was her ex-mother-in-law.

"My magic told me that much, that greed is the trigger to the horrible curse. The covetous pockets of darkness in your soul stirred the demon and attached it to you. That man, the previous attendant, he lured you—perhaps not intending you specifically, but lured someone, you—to steal the demon. He must have divined the nature of his curse ... and the remedy. You solved his ugly problem by willingly ... eagerly, in fact ... taking it on yourself. It is how the curse and the beast pass from one to the next. Greed, desire, ambition, those pockets of darkness, all of those things wrapped in the trigger."

"Curse. I am cursed. I stole the briefcase," he admitted.

"Thou shalt not steal," Adiella whispered. The words were as loud as thunder in Bridget's mind.

The witch had never approved of her, of the thieving, smuggling, was openly happy when she and Tavio announced their divorce. And

219

here Elijah Stone had walked into the bookshop and presented Adiella with an opportunity to curse Bridget. Adiella's hands would be relatively clean.

"I know someone who will steal it from you, Elijah Stone. I know an individual who will unwittingly take your soul beast and your curse and thereby save you."

"You do? How? When?"

"Your address," she said. "I will need that."

He smoothed out a crinkle in his business card, turned it over and scrawled an address. "That's where I live."

"Eighty-Fifth and West End. Expensive." She took the card and placed it in the little box where Bridget had found it.

"How much will all of this—"

"You owe me twenty-seven thousand, five hundred—"

So Adiella made a good chunk of change *and* managed to get Bridget cursed in one of those proverbial fell swoops.

"And this thief—"

"Is very good."

Good? One of the best, Bridget thought.

"The thief is very good." Adiella put his check under the drawer in her cash register. "Now to the matter of the bait."

I took that bait, Bridget fumed.

"The *cuota,* so to speak. You will have to put something valuable inside your Goodwill case. Lure the thief just as you were lured with that promise of a corporate secret."

My greed, Bridget thought, caused this. My greed, Adiella's hatred. She missed some of what was said in the image.

Adiella was talking again. "Nothing mundane, but something valuable. One hundred minimum, I would recommend. Two hundred. Three hundred if you can afford it. Truly, *much* more to be safe. Something very, very old and worth a great deal. The thief I will send your way likes very old things, antiquities. Things that are singular, one of a kind. It should be ancient."

"An antique."

Adiella cackled. "*Ancient,* I say. Babylonian, Assyrian."

"Babylonian?"

"Egyptian, Persian, Osirian, even Mayan or Aztec or from an Ugir tribe ... that is if you really want to be rid of your demon. Ancient, I said."

"A relic. You're talking about a relic. Museum pieces."

"To be certain the thief takes your bait."

Adiella knew Bridget's weaknesses. What was the saying by Gauguin? Concentrate your strengths against your competitor's relative weaknesses. Adiella had done that.

"Something that will fit in that briefcase."

"Of course. Something valuable. Who is this thief—"

"Not your concern. I will tease the thief, Elijah Stone, to take the bait that you dangle."

"What's to keep him from just taking the contents, leaving the damnable briefcase behind? What guarantee do I have that—"

"Elijah Stone, just as you took the Goodwill briefcase because you thought something important was inside, this thief will take your briefcase. Then it will be ... what is the expression? Yes, the demon will be the thief's cross to bear."

"I almost feel bad about this, giving the demon to someone else."

"Thieves, Elijah Stone, deserve damnation. Buy something soon, yes. And something extra, something for me to use in the luring, a sweet treat to catch the mark's attention. I will need that, a seeding. Then call me to confirm that you have the necessary bait."

The seed had been the shabti at the warehouse, the lure that led Bridget to Stone's apartment and to the damnable case under his damnable bed and had started this damnable mess.

Set up by Adiella, who clearly had no idea it would turn out like this.

Adiella's only son slain by the demon.

Her grandson in jeopardy.

What Adiella had wanted was for Bridget to suffer.

At least the witch had gotten her wish on that count.

Bridget crumpled the card and squeezed it so tight her fingers ached. She kept the scene playing in her head, watching Adiella smile and stretch like a cat, hearing the witch softly hum. The witch practically floated toward a shelf labeled "Occult and Supernatural," depressed a whorl in the wood, and the case slowly swung out. A second set of shelves was behind it, loaded with shoe boxes and file folders and mason jars filled with things Bridget didn't want to get a closer look at. Adiella reached for a box at the bottom, opened it and rifled through some index cards, tugging one out and returning to the counter, still humming.

The witch picked up the phone. It was an old rotary model, and Bridget watched her perfectly manicured index finger spin the numbers. Someone must have picked up immediately.

"Harry," Adiella said. "I have an assignment for you. This will settle your debt with me. I'll need you to take something to a warehouse in Fulton Landing, DUMBO, yes, that's the area. She rattled off the precise number and street, provided a description of Bridget's warehouse, and told him that he'd need to contact the men on the loading dock.

"No, I don't know what this 'something' will be. I don't have it yet. I'm certain I'll have it tomorrow though. My client is desperate and wants to act quickly. So come to the bookstore tomorrow before closing. The package? It's for Bridget O'Shea." A pause. "Who is she? No one who matters and not your concern." A longer pause. "Yes, Harry. This settles our account."

Adiella kissed the card and returned it to the box, closed the secret panel and smiled even broader. Bridget had never seen the witch so happy.

"Glorious day," Adiella said as she made the sign of the cross and whirled giddily like a child. "Praise God for the glorious day."

Bridget felt sick and dropped the connection. "Glorious day," she parroted. Instantly she thought of Tavio and Jimmy and again of Dustin. "A feckin' glorious day." Bridget closed her eyes and leaned on the counter, fought with the image of her demon feasting on Jimmy's heart. It had killed those close to her as a threat … free its fellow demons or it would keep on killing. But what would happen when it killed them all? Bridget didn't have that many people who meant

222

something to her. Kill everyone in her smuggling operation? Kill whatever Westies members still remained? Her contacts overseas? Could it travel that far from her? Would it continue to pull person after person from her mind until she did as it bid or until she got someone else to take on her curse?

Why the hell hadn't she let the thug in the subway keep the damn buckle?

When Bridget opened her eyes again, the witch was standing across the counter from her.

29

What the hell are you doing in my shop?" Adiella glared daggers.

Bridget wondered how the witch got in. She hadn't heard the door open, or the floor creak. Was Adiella so powerful that she could appear out of thin air?

"Irish guttersnipe!" Adiella continued. "You've no right to trespass. I will—"

Bridget dropped the crumpled business card on the counter, smoothed it out, and pushed it toward Adiella. Though with all the creases and in the poor light it couldn't be properly read, apparently Adiella recognized it. She folded her arms in front of her chest and put on an imperious look. The witch might indeed have appeared out of nowhere. She wasn't wearing a winter coat, just a thick cable knit blue sweater that looked expensive. Her customary overly large jewelry—a brass and wood bead necklace with a stylized sun fob, earrings that dangled to her shoulders, and bangle bracelets, were probably made to her unfashionable specifications. Her long nails—Bridget likened them to claws—were painted a shimmery gray and tipped with black lines. Odd to be dressed to the nines so early, she thought. Or maybe it was late; maybe Adiella had been at some coven gathering.

"You will help me," Bridget said, tapping the card.

"You want to know why I did it?" Adiella glanced at the card. "Why I seized upon the opportunity?"

So the witch was actually admitting it. Bridget hadn't expected that.

"No. I honestly don't care why you did it."

"You're a thief, Bridget O'Shea. You stole my son and his affections, kept him from finding a good woman. Kept him from giving me more grandsons. You steal the air from the righteous that walk the streets in this city, defiling it with your presence. You steal. 'If a thief be found breaking up, and be smitten that she die, there shall no blood be shed for her. If the sun be risen upon her, there shall be no bloodshed for her, she should make full restitution—"

"I can quote scripture, too," Bridget cut in. "Once upon a time I was a 'good Catholic girl.' Suffer not a witch to live—"

"You can't even get that right," Adiella spat. "Exodus: Thou shalt not suffer a sorceress to live. And I am no sorceress."

The demon trundled closer, looking between Bridget and Adiella, its fifth eye closed tightly, but the other four open and glimmering with obvious curiosity. It belched, the noxiousness wafting up and smelling like a carton of rotten eggs.

Bridget came around the counter and watched as the witch's expression withered. Fear? Did Adiella fear Bridget? "Well, you damn well better hope you can cast spells like a sorceress, 'cause you're going to help me."

The witch backed up, giving herself more space; the demon watched only Adiella now. "I told you I cannot dispel the demon. I didn't lie to you. It is an old one, a powerful one, more powerful than anything I've encountered before. It can hide from my vision. Satisfy it, you Irish *târfă*. Find out what it wants, I told you. Do whatever—"

"Oh, I damn well know what it wants, Adiella. I managed to share a handful of words with the beast. It wants me to free all the demons in the city. I already let two loose."

"Then just keep—"

"Letting demons run amok? Hell no. I'm done trying to satisfy this warty gobshite. Now I'm going to send it back to whatever layer of hell it came from. And you're going to help me. Send it back and catch the ones I turned loose."

Adiella opened her mouth, but Bridget didn't give her a chance to protest.

"You're going to help me, or I'll suffer a witch not to live ... just for spite. Your blood on my hands? That's nothing next to what I caused last night. And you set it all in motion by saddling me with a feckin' demon." Bridget took a breath.

"Unshackle Aldî-nîfaeti," the demon said. It was staring at Bridget now.

"You didn't have to steal the briefcase from Elijah Stone. I didn't *make* you steal the demon, Bridget O'Shea. I didn't *force* you to do anything. I might have presented you with the opportunity to steal it, but you didn't have to do it. Your decision. Your action. It's all on *your* head. Tavio's death. It's on you. Thou shalt not steal. Thou shalt not ever steal!"

Bridget grabbed Adiella by the arm and tugged her toward the front door. "Too bad you didn't wear a coat. You're going to be awfully cold until we reach your pit."

"How dare you, Bridget O'Shea. Trespass in my—"

"Yeah, well, Otter's trespassing there too." And Michael, Marsh, Rob, Alvin, and Quin. The witch was just going to love having Bridget and her entourage gathered in her bones-of-saints sanctified hidey hole.

They made one stop, at a rundown twenty-four hour corner bodega above the subway entrance. It sold questionable looking fruit, as well as cigarettes, snacks, and soda. Bridget found energy drinks at the bottom of a cooler and bought all of them: four cans of Red Bull, two Monster, three Rockstar, and a one Full Throttle. The clerk claimed not to have change for the hundred she slapped on the counter, so she added a half dozen packs of Twinkies, a stack of Hershey bars, a *New York Times* and a *Daily News*, and a cheap-looking keychain flashlight. The clerk double bagged it all in plastic sacks that appeared to have been used several times before.

"Do you have any notebooks? Notepads? Anything to write on?" Bridget craned her neck this way and that in the cramped, dirty confines of the convenience store. She saw a large cockroach meander slowly across a shelf. The place was probably infested with them. Adiella stood just inside the entrance, making sure she didn't touch anything, shivering, and glaring at Bridget the entire time. "Anything?"

The clerk shrugged. "Postcards. I have postcards."

"Great." Bridget grabbed the entire stack and pocketed a pen that was on the counter. "Keep the change." Then she ushered Adiella outside and down the stairs, waited for the train to pass, and disregarded a pair of beggars who tried to stop them from climbing down near the tracks. She turned on the tiny flashlight, and prodded the witch toward her pit.

The demon seethed. It squatted in the crevice at the entrance to Adiella's pit, acid drool dripping from its lower lip and hissing against the floor. It had tried to enter the chamber several times, and tried once again now as Bridget watched. It closed its four main eyes and opened the fifth, made a scritch-scritching against the stone with a talon and then tentatively raised that talon and prodded forward. Rebuffed again, it appeared to doze.

"It's there," Bridget told the witch, pointing. She talked softly. "My demon. It's angry."

"I can feel that. It is palpable," Adiella said. She also kept her voice to a conspiratorial whisper. "You have trapped us here, Irish *târfă*. If one of us dares to leave, that thing will—"

"—rip out your heart. That's what it does. And eat it." Bridget sat cross-legged in a corner, under the spray-painted caricature face of Bob Marley. The pit smelled fusty and damp, but the air was ten times better than usual because the reeking demon could not get close to her.

"Jimmy's heart," Michael said without turning around. His back was to Bridget. "It ate Jimmy's heart."

"Then by my hairy word we had better be successful, eh, Adiella? Or these men will either die of old age here or die to the beast you've saddled me with."

Thou shalt not steal, Adiella mouthed.

Otter still slept, thank God, on the bed against the opposite wall. Alvin and Quin sat side by side, coats pulled tight, guns on their laps, watching her and the witch, but with eyes that could hardly stay open. Their heads bobbed; they'd be sleeping soon. Rob and Marsh were on either side of the vintage Louis Vuitton wardrobe trunk, using it as a table and playing cards, both feasting on the Twinkies she'd bought. But both men were clearly more interested in what Bridget was doing than in their game. Michael sat in front of the space heater, deliberately not looking at her, running his thumb around a can of one of the energy drinks.

Bridget knew Michael would be leaving her employ if she managed to find a way free of the demon mess. He'd seen Jimmy's body, and so the threat of that happening to him was holding him in place at the moment. Alvin and Quin, she knew they'd be done, too. Despite them witnessing the tentacle beast turn her brownstone into so much kindling, she'd had to practically physically force them through the abandoned tunnel and into this graffiti-coated den. "We're too old for this shit," they repeatedly told her.

Rob and Marsh? The latter would probably be on his way; she'd beat him up pretty bad at Otter's birthday dinner, had never treated him with much respect ... one more regret to add to the ton she'd already logged.

One more.

Rob would stay, to the death of him. He'd grown up in the Westies with her, and she knew he'd always harbored a crush ... and also always known nothing would ever come of it. Rob was more of a brother than a love interest. With the exception of Tavio, she hadn't allowed herself to get so close to another. Dustin? Had she loved him? she wondered again. Maybe. But not with the intensity she'd once felt for Otter's father. She'd never allow herself that intensity again. She started to cry and brushed away the tears.

"Got something in your eye, boss?" Rob asked.

"Just memories," Bridget answered.

"What is it you want me to do?" Adiella was in the rocking chair, stack of postcards in her lap, pen ready. "What am I supposed to write?"

Bridget carefully unwrapped the package Rob had brought. She noticed the demon had its eyes opened again, thin slits that added to its evil-looking countenance. Again it tried to breach the entrance, and again it couldn't come an inch closer. She moved aside the shredded packing material and brought out a small bowl. The lighting in the pit was just enough so she could make out the details. It was etched, like the ones had been that she'd broken in the museum, and there were little stick figures ... people maybe, or demons.

"What am I supposed to write?" Adiella persisted, raising her voice enough so that Otter stirred. The boy rolled over and continued sleeping.

"Whatever I say." Bridget could tell that the other bowl was a little larger. The packer had nested them together. She didn't have a lot of room to work, so many people in this chamber made it rather cramped.

The demon saw the bowl and became more animated. "Unshackle," it said. "Bridget unshackle."

"I want to find the spell written on this bowl, Adiella. I want to somehow be able to repeat it and for you to record it. Then I want you to use it against my ... companion ... over there." Bridget didn't know if it would work, but the demon hadn't wanted to be too close to the bowls when they were in the museum. She'd thought the beast nervous then. Now, it was clearly furious, and yet also seemed excited at the prospect that she might release another of its fellows. It pantomimed flipping the bowl over, just like it had in the museum.

Adiella was right, Bridget thought; the beast would no doubt slay whoever left this room.

She popped the top on a can of Monster and started slugging it down. The taste was strong and sugary, like liquid carbonated bubble gum. She nearly spit it out. Bridget had never tried an energy drink before; it had better work to keep her awake. She managed to chug the rest of it.

"I have to pee," Rob announced. He stood and brushed his hands against his pants and took a step toward the crevice. "Is it all right if I—"

"No!" Adiella and Bridget shouted practically in unison.

Otter woke and sat, the bed creaking. "What's ... mom? Grandma Adiella? Mom! What happened to you?"

Bridget pulled up the hood of her coat to cover her nearly-bald head.

"Really, I have to pee," Rob said. He shifted his weight from one foot to the next. "It's gonna be running down my leg if I don't—"

Adiella gave him a dirty look. "There's a pot, under the bed. Use it."

"In front of God and—"

"—everybody," Bridget said. "If you want to keep breathing. Don't leave this hole. And Otter, I'm fine. Had a little hair trouble."

"No hair, no trouble," Marsh whispered.

"Christ." Rob looked under the bed and found a polished brass chamber pot. Marsh sniggered. "Laugh it up, buddy. Wait until you have to take a turn." He squeezed behind the witch, apparently thinking her and the rocker afforded some measure of privacy. "What the hell? Where did my—"

"You think I would have my warren fouled with the smell of waste?" Adiella said.

"It disappeared," Rob said. "My piss. It just..." He shrugged and zipped up, replaced the chamber pot and reached out to tousle Otter's head.

The boy pulled back. "No-no. I know where that hand's been."

Rob returned to the card game. And he and Marsh passed cards back and forth while keeping an eye on Bridget and Adiella.

"This might take awhile," Bridget told the witch. "Just listen, and when I repeat something that sounds like a spell—"

"I know, write it down," Adiella said. "Whatever it takes to keep Otter safe." She smiled sweetly at the boy. Bridget thought the expression did not suit the witch.

Bridget gently rested her fingers on the edge of the bowl and dipped her senses into the clay. She hadn't read the ingredients on the side of the Monster drink, but whatever was in it had given her a burst of energy. The delving came easy.

Maybe too easy.

30

Bridget was enveloped, the sensation bringing to her mind the image of being wrapped tightly in blankets. There was no warmth or comfort, just an oppressive sense of binding. It was as if she'd gone blind, but instead of a sheet of solid blackness, it was red-brown.

Clay.

She was seeing the clay of the bowl, effectively inside it and trying her damndest to look out, mind all jittery from the energy drink, heart racing. Fighting down a sense of panic, she explored further, her senses circling and finding the wall of red-brown interrupted by slashes—the characters that had been carved into the bowl's interior. The symbols were artful and precise, laid into the clay with an expert hand. Her mind continued to circle the bowl, around and around like a merry-go-round, traveling up and down and all the while around, finding the stick figures that either represented men or demons.

Bridget felt water sloshing against her as she dipped her mind farther back into the bowl's history. The clay she was inside came from a riverbank, dug by hand—the fingers of the digger thrusting into the ground and pulling her up, casting aside stones and the bones of fish. Her clay self was plopped into a wooden bucket and carried somewhere, the distance traveled not seeming far, listening to the measured footfalls of whoever toted her. Birds cried, and children laughed nearby. A man shouted. The strains of a wind instrument briefly played. She nudged time forward and felt herself lifted from the bucket, plopped on a hard, flat surface, fashioned by strong but elegant female hands, turned on a wheel. The spinning sensation relaxed Bridget, like hands working her muscles at a favorite massage parlor. Around and around like a merry-go-round. The sound of the wheel, and of the potter softly singing, was restorative.

Like Dustin's feathery touch on her bare skin.

Around and around, hands sluicing up water to make the bowl she was becoming uniform and perfect, clay pulled off to make the bowl small. The song mesmerizing.

Around and around and around. She should be dizzy, a child trapped on a carnival ride, but it was so very calming. For the first time since she'd acquired the buckle, she felt true peace. Bridget knew she should be seeking a way to trap a demon, just as whoever had made this bowl intended it as a trap. Fast-forward, she told herself. There was Otter to consider.

And Michael, Rob, Marsh, Alvin, and Quin to protect.

She should be using her psychometry to pursue the information she craved. But she'd suffered so much, physically and emotionally these past few days. Tavio's brutal death, Jimmy's heart ripped out, Dustin most assuredly slaughtered by her demon, Otter in her less-than-stellar mother care, the beloved brownstone in ruins, her antique store and its precious and priceless treasures slagged, on and on and on and on.

Around and around.

The wordless song of the potter continued, like it was a spell cast on her.

The hands working the clay-that-she'd-become felt like a lover's caress, sluicing away at the horrid memories of the past few days and making her memories of Dustin clearer.

Around and around.

Enjoy this for just a little while.

233

The woman's hands on the clay-that-she'd-become were restful and addicting and at the moment oh so necessary to ease her tortured, splintering soul.

Around and around.

Enjoy this for just a little while longer.

The potter's sweet song became her breath.

Around.

There was Otter to consider.

Was it that she wouldn't pull herself from this relaxing sensation ... or *couldn't*? Would this be the closest thing to heaven Bridget would ever experience? She'd damned herself, with her thieving, but more by releasing the demons in the museum. Ashes to ashes, the guards' bodies. Their deaths on her. Her soul destined for the bottom of hell.

Around and around. Make the memories go away.

Around.

For just a little while.

One more turn.

One.

More.

Wait. What was that? A different impression. Suddenly a cold and prickly wave rushed through her, no longer the welcome massaging pulse. But whatever uncomfortable numbness it had caused, it was fleeting, and so Bridget again concentrated on the strong, elegant fingers, the water sluicing up, and the rhythm of the wheel. The beautiful song.

Around and around.

Seeing the red-brown of the clay she'd become, cut here and there by the stylized characters, vaguely wondering what they meant, and then—

—being assailed by the cold and prickly touch again.

Bridget was jarred as if she'd just slugged down another of the syrupy sweet Monster drinks. She tried to press her mind outward, to get beyond the present memory of the clay and away from the prickly sensation, like forcing the fast-forward of a CD. This time the painful chill did not pass. It persisted. Think about Otter! Get free!

But something prevented that and held her fast. She felt a coil loop around her and tighten. The rhythmic sound of the wheel and the potter's song that had been worked into the fabric of the pot vanished to be replaced by a sibilant string of words. Foreign and exotic-sounding, it was as if a sultry Etta James was speaking ancient Sumerian. And because she was part of the bowl, her gift mentally translated each word.

"Morsel you are, come to share my prison." The coil rose higher, circling all of her essence; she felt like she couldn't breathe. "Morsel feels sweet."

I'm not a morsel! Bridget raged. *I am a visitor, passing through the clay.*

"Not I think," the voice continued, deepening to a baritone. "Not passing through. Staying in my prison, sharing my prison. Wonderful company for eternity. Companion until the end of everything."

Bridget felt the chill increase, like she was stuck in a forming ice cube.

"The end of time."

No! I am passing through.

"Caught as Ku-Ninsunu is caught."

Is that your name, demon? Ku-Ninsunu?

"Aldî-nîfaeti."

Is that your name, Aldî-nîfaeti?

"Ku Ninsunu is my beautiful name. My beautiful self. She who was spawned by the river, it means, though no river was involved. Caught as Ku-Ninsunu are you—"

Bridget.

"Bridget is caught with Ku-Ninsunu forever."

The demon was female? Did her own demon have a sex? Male? Female?

"Ku-Ninsunu and Bridget caught until the end of time. Caught by Hilimaz, Ku-Ninsunu and Bridget. Together forever. I will eat you slowly. Nibble by nibble so you last a very long time."

No!

"Else unshackle Ku-Ninsunu. Together unless Bridget unshackles Ku-Ninsunu. Eat you ever-so-slowly, piece by piece, unless Bridget unshackles Ku-Ninsunu."

Hell no!

She was indeed trapped ... with a demon named Ku-Ninsunu inside the bowl she'd dipped her mind into. Trapped as tightly as if she'd been placed in manacles, sucked in like the demon had been pulled inside however many centuries past. What would happen to Otter now? Had she done this to herself? In allowing herself a few moments of pleasure feeling the potter work? Had Bridget doomed herself to an endless mind-locked existence with a piece of ancient pottery?

"Forever with Ku-Ninsunu. Eat you piece by piece."

By all that's holy!

"No, Bridget. Nothing holy is here."

Just passing through.

"Pass back, Bridget, and unshackle Ku-Ninsunu. Pass back. I will not let you go farther. Only despair is here. Captured until the end of time. Free Ku-Ninsunu, or Ku-Ninsunu will not free you."

No. I am passing through!

"Pass back and unshackle Ku-Ninsunu." The voice was louder and hurtfully angry now.

No! No and no!

The red-brown clay cut through with the characters became a wall of black, changing again to swirling shades of grass and ocean. The colors shifted and settled and sharpened to form the blue-green scales of the coil that had wrapped around her.

Ku-Ninsunu. She was seeing the demon.

"Yes, Ku-Ninsunu. I am the vexer of farmers, wilter of crops." The demon was a long snake, its hues transitioning in brightness until they glowed electric. As it coiled more of itself around Bridget's delving presence, the colors ran like a sidewalk chalk painting caught in the rain, the edges coming in and out of focus. The scales seemed to grow and shrink in size, but she realized that was just the beast breathing. It relaxed its grip and the coils dropped farther down so that its head lowered even with her eyesight.

As beautiful as the shades of its scales were, the head that crowned the body was in even measure hideous. Looking like a plague-pocked mandrill, the face was twice the size of a human's. Its lips were covered with thumbtack like spikes, and the tongue that darted out over them was bloated and black and dotted with open sores. The beast's eyes were round, the irises a dark purple, and the pupils shiny red like drops of fresh blood. When it turned, she saw that instead of ears it had nickel-sized holes from which ooze trickled, reminding Bridget of her own demon and its never-ending rivulets of goo. It had a second set of eyes, one above each ear, both with hot red pinpricks in their centers. It was not bald, but neither did it have hair, rather a gray-green mass of short wriggling worms, each with tiny bright eyes that flared like matches being struck.

The Aldî-nîfaeti stank of myriad spoiled things, reminding her of the garbage-choked alleys she'd chased the Westies boys through twenty years ago. Two decades, that was but a heartbeat compared to the eternity she was facing inside this prison with this hell-born monstrosity.

"Unshackle Ku-Ninsunu. Free the wilter of crops."

Seriously? Instead Bridget decided she had better free herself.

If the beast could hold her inside the clay, her mental presence might also have some sort of a physical quality. She envisioned herself moving her legs, meeting resistance against the Aldî-nîfaeti's coils. Working harder, imagining that she was pumping her legs in a run up the Empire State Building's stairs, she made a little progress. Eighty-six floors, she'd managed the run several times. One thousand five hundred and seventy-six steps, the lower third taken two at a time.

The muscles in her legs strained.

The coils seemed to loosen.

Faster, the steps two at a time, she imagined that her arms were swinging at her side, that she was working to keep her feet free of the other runners, her breath puffing and her lungs filling with the demon's stink.

Faster! Bridget pushed out with her imagined arms against the thickest coil that pressed against her chest. The scales were smooth and cold and felt oddly good against her palms, one big muscle that she fought against to get her more breathing room. She fancied that she was lifting weights, which she often did to keep her mind off her business worries. But when that connotation came to mind she saw Jimmy laid out on the weight bench, ribs broken and a gaping hole where his heart had been.

"Unshackle Ku-Ninsunu."

Like bloody blue blazes I will, you Aldî-nîfaeti fecker! Bridget's simmering hate fueled her, and she pressed harder still, the snake-demon a three-hundred pound weight she was hell bent on lifting. In her mind's eye she saw her knees raising and lowering like pistons.

One thousand five hundred and seventy-six steps.

"Caught forever," the demon purred. "Unshackle Ku-Ninsunu."

You sons of a bitches don't have much of a vocabulary. Unshackle Ku-Ninsunu. Unshackle Aldî-nîfaeti. Bridget strained that she imagined the veins in the sides of her neck were going to pop.

"Morsel for Ku-Ninsunu."

One more step!

One more!

Sol's Gym had been an old clothing factory on Fourth Avenue in Brooklyn. It was near a stretch of row houses and rundown ware-houses, and it had recently been converted into a boxing gymnasium. Bridget and some of the Westies boys went there after the place closed for the night and they were certain the infrequent cleaning crew was long gone. They'd sneak in through a side window over an alley. It never latched properly, and they would have to climb on a Dumpster to reach it. They'd shimmy in and turn on only a few lights, none in the front of the building where someone passing by might see. Though who would have called the cops? It wasn't a good neighbor-hood, and it wasn't a store someone would break into to steal from. Looking back, Bridget realized they were needlessly worried of discovery.

Bridget and her friends were thieves, but they never stole from the gym, they only used the equipment for a few hours, taking turns holding the punching bag, and then setting up matches in the ring. They didn't let Bridget spar the first several months of their forays. They said it wasn't that she couldn't fight; they well knew she was strong and quick. They said that they didn't want to fight her, didn't want to risk marring her pretty face.

So while they boxed she hit the weight equipment, her presses in time with their swings and grunts. Sol had posted signs on the ceiling for the boxers to read while they bench pressed. DIG DEEP, was the largest. WANT IT MORE THAN ANYTHING. AMBITION IS THE ROAD TO SUCCESS AND PERSISTENCE IS THE VEHICLE YOU DRIVE. WHAT ARE YOU WAITING FOR? NEVER GIVE UP. GREAT EFFORT SPRINGS FROM GREAT ATTITUDE. ONE MORE.

That last slogan had become Bridget's catch phrase for all her teen years.

One More.

One more push up, sit up, bench press. One more set at the punching bag.

One more match with her Westies friends who had finally relented and fought with her.

And lost to her.

Not one of them had bested her, though she wondered now if they'd pulled their punches to "not mar her pretty face." And one night she'd clobbered Seamus Doyle so hard he hit the mat like a dropped sack of potatoes. They had to carry him out, and it hadn't been easy sliding him through that alley window. He didn't come to until they were halfway down the street and in the shadows the row houses cast in the streetlights.

One More.

The memory of that one sign on the ceiling became thicker in her mind than the coil that tried to tighten its grip.

One more, you Aldi-nifaeti fecker! One more push, one more kick. One more run up the thousand five hundred and seventy-six steps, the lower third taken two at a time.

One more!

Free!

The binding she'd felt was gone, and there was a sensation of air moving around her. The scales were gone and Bridget thought she was peering through a dense fog. But after what seemed like several minutes, things cleared. The bowl she was delving and that she now looked out through sat high on a rough wooden shelf in what appeared to be a potter's shop. Bright light streamed in through a doorway, letting her see every bit of the one-room building. The walls were wattle and daub, the roof tightly packed reeds. There was a fire-place filled with logs, but no ashes and no odors to indicate it had been used in a while.

The image was so intense that Bridget could feel the breeze playing across her. She spiraled out from the bowl, seeing pottery everywhere ... on shelves, a table, large pieces on the floor against the hearth and set against the walls, on the windowsills. Jars with matching lids that might be intended for honey or butter, narrow ones for oil and wine. Pitchers, vases. The vases were extraordinary; some had pointed feet made to resemble animal claws, some were on stands or set on rectangular wood frames, a few were flat-bottomed. A couple of the containers were sealed with clay, and there were dishes of all sizes.

A pottery wheel sat under the largest window, a tall woman worked diligently at it, her hands so smooth Bridget guessed her to be a mere teenager. She hummed a haunting tune, perhaps the one Bridget had heard while she wrestled with the demon. Clay tools were arrayed on a bench next to the potter, including a variety of wedge-shaped reeds, some with dried clay on their tips. Bridget realized those were what the potter used to engrave words and pictures into the bowls.

Bridget hadn't known the art of making pottery on a wheel stretched back so many centuries; primitive man wasn't so primitive, after all.

"Join me," the potter said. "There is no one else here, no one else to see you." She continued to work the clay.

The potter's eyes were closed, but she turned her face toward the shelf Bridget's delved bowl sat on. One side of her face looked young and smooth, but the other was a mass of ugly scars that made the skin look wet, and on that side, no hair grew.

"Come join me," she repeated. "You are not Aldi-nîfaeti, and I have no fear of ghosts. There is no need for you to hide on my shelf. There is no need for you to fear me."

31

She can see me? Not possible.

Bridget's gift of psychometry was a one-way street. She could look into the past through an object she held and concentrated on, but *just* look and listen and mentally translate the language of the speakers. The object, the bowl in this case, was a window that she could see and hear through. She wasn't truly there.

Right this very moment Bridget was in Adiella's pit off the winter-cold subway tunnel, her back against a graffiti-covered wall, and the ancient bowl nesting in her hands. She was looking into that bowl's past, to a land that was now called Iraq or Iran; geography and politics were not precise in her mind.

A one-way window.

It was not possible for anyone on the other side of time to look back at her. Such a person was millennia dead, and the place ... Sumer ... no longer existed. The building, the potter, dust, memories of the earth tramped on by soldiers and buried by centuries.

"Of course I can see you," the potter continued, her eyes were closed. She turned her head back to the bowl she was shaping. "And I welcome you to my shop. Come visit with me." She reached an arm to her side and indicated the bench next to her. There was an empty space amid the clay tools. "Come. Come, little ghost."

Not possible.

Or was it? Bridget was more than six thousand miles away and more than six millennia disconnected from ancient Sumer.

"Come sit with Hilimaz."

Hilimaz … that was the name the demon in the bowl mentioned.

"I'll not entreat you again, little ghost. Come sit with me or be on your way."

Bridget nudged her senses toward the bench and imagined herself sitting on the rough wood.

"Ah, that is better. Who are you, little ghost?" The potter put the finishing touches on her bowl, fashioning a lip around it, and sluicing water up to make it smooth.

"Bridget." Bridget had thought the word, but it came out as clearly as if she'd spoken it. "My name is Bridget O'Shea."

"Pretty. Does Bridget mean anything?" The potter understood her, so the translation apparently went both ways.

"Mean? I don't—"

"Your name, little ghost. Does it have a significance?" The potter removed her foot from the pedal and the wheel slowed and then stopped. She appeared to scrutinize the bowl, and then turned to face the bench. Her eyes were still closed. "Your name, does it mean anything? Mine, Hilimaz, means beauty, though I am not. I was, though, years ago, and always in my mother's eyes I was lovely." She stood and walked to a nearby barrel, dipped her hands in and sloshed them around. She wiped her hands on a rough-spun cloth, hung up her apron, and returned to her stool. "But my mother died before she saw me like this. So always in her view I am beautiful. Your name, little ghost?"

"Bridget is Irish, inspired by St. Brigid of Kildare. She was a nun, and she founded the Convent Cill-Dara, the Church of the Oak it came to be called. She also founded an art school, and the students were proficient in metalwork and illumination. My mother taught me all of that when I was very small. The name Bridget means strong-willed and virtuous. I am the former, but certainly not the latter. And I am nothing like the nun I was named for." A pause: "How is it that you can—"

"See you?" Hilimaz smiled. Half of her teeth—those on the side of her scars—were broken. She opened her eyes; they were milky white. She was totally blind. "I see with my mind, Bridget the strong-willed. And I listen with my heart."

Hilimaz smoothed at her robe and closed her eyes again. It seemed to Bridget like she was waiting. A silence eased around them. It was almost unnerving. Bridget expected to hear sounds beyond the potter's shop—people moving in the community that certainly must stretch beyond the doorway. Or the people in Adiella's pit talking or slapping down playing cards, the distant rumble of a subway train. But there was nothing, not even trees rustling in the breeze that continued to wash into the shop. Not even Otter's voice.

"I'm from very far away," Bridget said. "A land you wouldn't know of. I came here—I came here—"

"—because you need Hilimaz's help." The potter's smile turned sad. "So an Aldî-nîfaeti troubles you."

"How did you know—"

"—people come to me to rid their homes of Aldî-nîfaeti. And to sometimes trade for my wares. But Bridget the strong-willed ghost would not need my pottery, and so you need my help with a demon. But tell me, how can a demon vex a ghost?"

"I'm not a ghost. Not exactly." Bridget regaled the blind potter with a tale of New York City, her psychometry ability, the ancient pot she delved to get here. She finished with her tale of the buckle and her personal demon, as well as explaining about letting the pair of demons loose in the museum.

"A curious thing you are, little ghost. I think I like you, but I do not think I would like your New York City."

"It is rather noisy," Bridget said. "Hilimaz, I know you can catch them, the demons. The pot I delved. It has a demon in it."

"That pot? That one contains Ku-Ninsunu."

244

"Yeah, that's the fecker's name. I had a hell of a time getting past her and—"

"—into my shop."

"Yes."

"And so you have come to Hilimaz to learn how to catch the Aldî-nîfaeti that you released in New York City."

"Yes," Bridget said. "Essentially yes." To learn a spell that she could get Adiella to cast into a bowl. So she could catch the demons she let loose and maybe save some small part of her soul. And hopefully find a way to be free of her own demon.

"Tonight I go to the place of Enmebaragisi, little ghost. He and his wife have been troubled by a persistent Aldî-nîfaeti. I will catch the creature and add it to those on my shelf."

"Catch it in a bowl like you snared Ku-Ninsunu?"

The potter nodded. "You may come with me and watch. I am very good at capturing the Aldî-nîfaeti. I will teach you, Bridget the strong-willed. Then you will be very good at capturing the Aldî-nîfaeti too." The potter rose and reached her hands toward the bench and selected a reed tool, flicking the dried clay away from the end, and then turning back to her wet bowl. "Watch me now, little ghost, this is part of the learning."

"You are engraving a spell."

Another nod. "Each spell is different and yet the same. You must have the name of the Aldî-nîfaeti, and that must be woven into the words. Names are power. In all ages names have been powerful. Saying the name calls it to the bowl. The Aldî-nîfaeti cannot resist. I say it now as I write it, and I will repeat it at the place of Enmebaragisi. You must invoke names of gods, too, as that righteous touch makes the clay stronger. Now watch and listen."

Though the potter was blind, her marks were precise and even. She started at the center of the bowl, where she drew a stick figure, then etched characters in a spiral away from it. "I Hilimaz call Pua-tuma-sin, Aldî-nîfaeti of the house of Enmebaragisi. I take her by the scruff of her twin necks and her many horns. I poke out her dark and evil eyes that she may no longer look upon the family of Enmebaragisi. Sahtiel help me in this catching. Aid me that I might grab Pua-tuma-sin by her thick necks and her many horns and say 'remove the curses and the pain from the hearts of those you have raged against.'"

Bridget remembered that particular sentence from delving the bowl at the museum: "Remove the curses and pain from the hearts of those you have raged against." There were other similarities to the spells, but that part was word-for-word. Distracted, she'd missed some of what the potter had said.

"—I adjure you in the name of Ruphael and Sathietl and in the name of Prael the great. Bother no more Enmebaragisi and his wife Shag-ana. Descendants of Ekur must be teased no longer, teased nevermore, cursed no more, Aldî-nîfaeti-vexed no more. I am Hilimaz the binder and the cleanser. I turn away all things fetid and foul. I protect Enmebaragisi, descendant of Ekur, and I protect the wife of Enmebaragisi, Shag-ana and her coming child. I bind. I bind in clay and powerful words. I heal and annul. With these words I catch I bind. Weapon of clay, mother wet-earth, in the names of angels Sariel and Barakiel—"

Ruphael, Sathietl, and Prael, they'd been mentioned in her previous delving. Ruphael, Sathietl, Prael the great, and she thought Barakiel, too. Bridget committed all those to memory.

"—I, Hilimaz, shackle the Aldî-nîfaeti named Pua-tuma-sin. In so doing I free the hearts of Enmebarasis and Shag-ana and her coming child. I ease the troubles of the descendants of Ekur. I, Hilimaz, protect this house from all vileness. Bind and seal and capture forevermore the Aldî-nîfaeti named Pua-tuma-sin." The potter rubbed the wet clay off her engraving tool.

"You said you were going to catch this demon tonight. But the bowl won't be dry by then."

"Dry enough," Hilimaz tutted. "Wet or dry, if I handle it with care it will work well. I do not want Shag-ana and Enmebaragisi to endure their Aldî-nîfaeti even one more day. Shag-ana is big with child, and I fear Pua-tuma-sin waits for its birth. Aldî-nîfaeti are known for eating the young."

"And killing in general," Bridget muttered.

"Come, little ghost, I will show my city."

Bridget thought of Otter sleeping and wanting to return to him. All she needed was the spell. "But I haven't time for this. I want to watch you catch the demon. That's very important. I need to listen to the spell again. But that's all I have time for." And repeat it to Adiella so she can write it all down. "I want to watch the spell work, and then I need to be on my way. I have demons to catch in my city."

"You will see my city first. It is not yet time to go to the home of Shag-ana and Enmebaragisi." The potter poked out her bottom lip and shook her head. "Bridget the strong-willed, it will take more than one catching for you to understand and learn. You will see my city and learn my spells, and that will require time."

"I don't have time," Bridget argued. She thought about Otter stretched out on the cot in the witch's pit. She had to be over and done with this and to find a way to keep him safe. "I need to catch two demons and banish one back to the hell it came from."

The potter rose and stepped to the doorway. "You will see my city first, on this I insist."

Bridget felt compelled to follow, like she was a fish tugged on a line.

"You have no choice in the matter, Bridget the strong-willed. You gave me your name, and so I have power over you. I will make you my apprentice, for there are not enough witches in this world who can capture demons. And you are no competition to me here."

"I'm not a witch—"

"Yes you are."

No! Bridget railed against that notion. "I am a psychometrist."

"I do not understand that word—"

"Psychometry, object reading," Bridget explained. "It is a form of ESP … extra-sensory perception … that allows me to learn the history of an object I hold. The object, your bowl in this case, has an energy, and that energy transfers and translates its past and experiences."

"So it is you who does not understand. That is being a witch," the potter continued. "You will make an apt student." She reached to the back of her robe and tugged a hood up and over her head. Only her

247

chin showed. "Come, little ghost." She stepped through the doorway and beckoned with her hand.

Bridget followed, but she wasn't sure it was of her own volition.

"I will teach you my craft and then you can catch your own Aldínífaeti," Hilimaz said. "As for banishing? I cannot do that. I catch them only."

"But I need—"

"You need to learn. You gave me your name, and so you will be mine for a time. Until I judge that you are ready."

"I have your name, too," Bridget said.

"Ah, but Bridget, ghosts have no power over me, even the strong-willed witches among them."

32

It must have been early spring, Bridget guessed, from the looks of all the flower buds sprouting outside Hilimaz's pottery shop. Sounds assailed her the moment she passed through the doorway: the happy cries of children were the loudest, a dozen played in an open field. Like Adiella, Hilimaz must have been able to keep out sound on a whim, letting her craft pottery in her shop undisturbed.

The area was green as far as she could see—grass, fields being readied, the air mildly warm and thoroughly pleasant. The scents were rich. Bread was baking somewhere, everything so very far removed from the desert-like conditions of the country in Bridget's day. The dampness in the air hinted a body of water was nearby.

Men and women wore simple robes, some with beautiful feathered headdresses and gold armbands, a few were heavily perfumed. As she followed the potter, Bridget looked through open doorways of homes, one side of the road wattle and daub construction, the other side larger buildings made of clay bricks. It was as if she was looking from a middle- to upper-class neighborhood in New York. She noted beds, stools, and chairs, some carved with legs that resembled those of oxen. Fireplaces, small fire altars, some appearing recently used. Tools were laid out in many of the homes, knives, wedges, something that looked

249

like a saw, drills. There were weapons on a few of the people passing by. She noted that only one woman had nodded to acknowledge Hilimaz, the others all looked away from her.

At the far edge of her vision, a woman worked at writing on a large clay tablet with a metal engraving tool. Closer, inside a building that was a rather large smith's, she saw three men hammering copper, silver, and gold into plates and jewelry.

A few nodded to Hilimaz, only one spoke. He addressed her as Ruabi-ruve. Later, Bridget heard others whisper and point, again calling the old potter Ruabi-ruve.

"It is the name I go by here, Ruabi," Hilimaz said, apparently aware of Bridget's curiosity.

"Because names are power," Bridget mused. "And you do not want the people to have power over you. But me ... it's all right that I know your name because a ghost can't have power over you."

"Clever student."

"But in the pottery. You use Hilimaz there."

"Because names are power. The people I help with my spell and bowls, they never notice. They never hear me use my real name in the spell."

"Because they don't pay close enough attention to what you're doing."

Hilimaz nodded. "Their fear and worry keeps them from being clever, little ghost."

"There is our leader." Hilimaz nodded to a man standing in a doorway. He had a shaved head and carried a feather headdress loosely in front of him. "He is largely responsible for invoking the laws that prevent women from taking more than one husband. To be caught now doing so is to risk stoning."

Bridget shuddered. She'd delved into pieces before that revealed cultures' barbaric practices, and she would never be able to accept violence against women.

"I will not take another husband," Hilimaz said. "Mine died many years ago to an Aldi-nîfaeti, the first we tried to capture together. My husband and I were just learning the necessary spells and how to shape the bowls. Taught by his mother, we were. Always women are the more powerful witches. My husband, he died horribly, and I was forever scarred by Yaqrun, a most formidable Aldî-nîfaeti, and one I much later caught. I am lu, a free person now."

Yaqrun. That name! Bridget had heard it. Where? Yaqrun, it niggled at her brain.

"The demon, the Aldî-nîfaeti that killed your husband and scarred you. Its name was Yaqrun."

The blind potter growled. "A foul, foul Aldî-nîfaeti, that one. My husband and I ... we took it on too early in our training. And we paid the price. Would that I had died instead of him. Pursuing Yaqrun was my idea."

Yaqrun. The museum! When she'd delved one of the bowls in the museum. Bridget remembered that delving. "Huseff, son of Nogress," the potter had intoned, the words sing-song and flat. "From Huseff's men-sons I heard the voice of the frail and of other men fighting and of angry weeping women. All are cursed and afflicted, pained by Yadun and Yaqrun and Azada. Yadun and Yaqrun and Azada, one will be taken with this bowl, seized by its scales and hair tufts upon their heads—"

"Hilimaz, does this demon, Yaqrun, spew lava? Does it have tentacles for feet? A head like an ape? Is it tall?"

"Arms like snakes?" Hilimaz stopped and cocked her head. "Little ghost, how would you know this demon?"

Bridget told her. "I need to recapture it. I need—"

Hilimaz's sightless eyes narrowed and her face drew forward until it looked painfully pinched. She made a hissing sound and Bridget saw the potter's hands clench. "—to most certainly imprison her again. She is most foul, one of the worst. She was too strong for my first attempt, I told you. Yet I later caught her, on the anniversary of my husband's death, when she kept the company of Yadun and Azada. You had best be a most apt student, Bridget the strongwilled. That Aldî-nîfaeti is a difficult one. To set such a beast loose—"

"I don't know the name of the other one I freed."

Hilimaz made a scratchy *tsk-tsk*ing sound. "Names are power. Without the name, the Aldî-nîfaeti you loosed remains free."

"So how do I learn the other name?"

Hilimaz didn't answer; she turned and resumed her walk. Her hands did not relax.

There were sheep, goats, pigs, and cattle, all tended by young men, and all clearly domesticated. In a field past a row of small homes, Bridget saw oxen pulling plows to work what appeared to be a hard, stubborn field.

By the side of a larger home was an enclosed garden with ornamental trees. Other homes had plants growing in pots and vases, perhaps herbs. There seemed to be at least one date tree outside each residence. Ancient Sumer was much more civilized than Bridget expected. She tried to take it all in as the potter walked down a main road and then turned down a path between long buildings. In the distance she saw irrigation ditches.

"Here we honor our gods, Bridget the strong-willed. Do you still recognize them? Enlil, god of wind—"

Bridget remembered her demon spitting that word out like a hunk of something spoiled. "Yeah, I've heard of Enlil."

"He is one of our most powerful gods, controlling the fertility of the soil and the destructive nature of storms. It is good to fear and respect Enlil." She gestured to a three-walled building, the front of which was opened. Frescoes covered the walls, and there were impressive sculptures of bears and bulls. "Enki, god of the earth, also directs our rivers and wells and is responsible for crafts."

"How do I learn the names of the Aldî-nîfaeti, Hilimaz? I need to catch what I let loose. And I've another demon, one that seems to be attached to me. A horrid gobshite of a demon that is a murderer. I need to find its name. And I need to get rid of—"

Hilimaz raised a hand to cut her off. "All demons are murderers. You are the student, little ghost. I will teach you everything you will need to recapture Yaqrun, slayer of my husband."

"How long—"

"It will take as long as it takes, little ghost. I will not let you leave until you are ready."

"I have a son." Bridget tried to pull her senses back into the bowl, not caring if she had to battle the Aldî-nîfaeti-snake-thing again. She thought of Otter and the pit in the subway. But she couldn't budge from Hilimaz's side. "I need to be with my son."

"Then you had better learn quickly, little ghost." Hilimaz pointed to another fresco. "You will learn about our gods and our way of life, for the Aldî-nîfaeti are a part of that."

"Go on then," Bridget said, intending to hurry the teacher along. "Tell me more."

"Ninhursaga is the goddess of mountains and vegetation. I believe she is the mother of all of us. Utu is the god of the sun, Nannar of the moon, and Inanna of the morning and evening, war and rain. Divine and immortal, yet we can influence them and learn their will."

"Enlil," Bridget said. "Tell me more about Enlil. I remember reading that Enlil was banished from the gods' home for raping Ninlil."

"When he was young and lacked wisdom," Hilimaz returned. "When he thought passion was love."

"That Enlil eventually was forgiven, right, that he had several children—"

"Godlings."

Interesting term, Bridget thought. "And that he taught the godlings how to slay demons."

She nodded. "Yes, when he was banished to the underworld, he studied Aldî-nîfaeti and learned how to defeat them and control them. The godlings passed onto a few mortals the tricks of the spells and clay."

"You're one of those mortals—"

"No. My husband's mother was. Enlil's eldest godling taught her directly. Then, she taught me. And I will teach you. Women have the true power, I believe. Men can try. But a woman's mind can better handle these things."

253

"Quickly," Bridget added. "I am in a hurry. Teach me quickly, Hilimaz. My son—"

"Again I say that it will take as long as it takes, and you will not leave before I have given you the skills, Bridget the strong-willed. You will stay by my side, I say again, until you are able to deal with Yaqrun. And as for the other demons, taking them is your concern. Yaqrun, with all my soul I despise that one. You will stay with me until I am certain you can catch Yaqrun."

"You don't understand."

"I understand with all clarity, little ghost. You will have the tools to recapture Yaqrun, slayer of my husband and tormentor of my soul. Few in this world have gifts such as you and I, and those gifts must be enriched and practiced. You should not concern yourself with time. To a ghost, time means nothing. Be pleased that I am willing to teach you. Be very pleased that I demand that you learn."

"As long as it takes," Bridget mused. "And how long do you think that will be?"

"If you work hard, my student, I believe you will be ready in three or four years."

"Three or four—I don't have—"

Hilimaz gestured to an open doorway. "Now, we will pray to Enlil to bless our efforts this coming night."

"I'm Catholic," Bridget thought, but her words were vocalized. "And it can't take three or four years."

"Catholic? Maybe Enlil knows your god, Cathol. And maybe your Cathol will not mind you praying to Enlil." The potter motioned and Bridget felt herself tugged through the doorway. "Maybe they are related, our gods. Or maybe Enlil fathered some of Cathol's children. Maybe Enlil fathered Cathol."

33

The home they went to that night was opulent. It sprawled at the end of a street, rising two stories with a flat roof rimmed by plants that draped over the sides and in some places veiled windows like curtains. Lights glowed from only one side of the home, but the stars were so bright in the cloudless sky that the ornate details of the place showed clearly.

Bridget had never seen so many stars.

"Enmebaragisi is a prominent merchant," Hilimaz explained. "The wealthiest of men from a line of wealthy men. Yet all his gold did not keep the Aldî-nîfaeti Pua-tuma-sin at bay."

Enmebaragisi greeted the old potter, bowing deeply and gesturing her inside. Bridget guessed him to be in his sixties, his dark face deeply lined like a crumpled paper sack, and his hands were wrinkled, his hair sparse white wisps that hung down to his shoulders. The wife, Shag-ana, could have passed for a teenager, and her belly was so swollen it looked like she was going to give birth any moment. There were two others in the main room, both young men that appeared roughly the same age as Shag-ana; maybe the man had been married before and they were sons. Bridget forced down her curiosity and thought of Otter.

Hilimaz paced the room, the damp bowl cradled in her hands. She didn't bump into the people or the furniture, but she shuffled slowly and hummed softly, the same tune Bridget had heard when she'd first spied the potter during her delving.

Hilimaz was clearly intent on whatever she was doing, and Bridget turned her thoughts to Otter. She thought about Adiella's pit in the subway, and for an instant heard a voice with a distinctively Brooklyn accent. The Brooklyn accent became clearer: "Marsh, you suck at cards, you know." Faintly she felt a vibration beneath her, the rumble of a subway train.

Bridget pried her mind away from Adiella's pit and focused on Hilimaz. Oil lamps hung from the ceiling and set the shadows of the room's inhabitants against the walls. Hilimaz' shadow traveled, as did another, they looked to be dancing. Bridget stared at the twin shapes, one no doubt the Aldî-nîfaeti Pua-tuma-sin that the potter had come to catch. Why didn't the demon flee the house? Why risk getting snared?

Interspersed with Hilimaz's dissonant notes was "Pua-tuma-sin." Perhaps the demon couldn't flee because Hilimaz had its name, that being the hook that had caught the fish. Over and over and over she'd told Bridget names were power. Yaqrun—that was the name of the lava-spewing tentacled beast Bridget had released in the museum and that subsequently had burned down her brownstone. What the hell was the name of the other one? And, more, what was the name of the Aldî-nîfaeti that dogged her and had slain people she'd cared about? The warty, puss-oozing son-of-a-bitch that had gnawed on Jimmy's heart right in front of her?

Bridget sensed the air growing hot and dry and saw the disparate-aged couple and the teenage boys huddle together. They all breathed shallowly, and it looked like Shag-ana was in distress. She clung to her husband with one hand, and the other on her belly visibly quivered.

The tempo of Hilimaz' tune increased when the potter reached a sharp corner and turned the bowl upside down. Bridget felt as if the air had been sucked from her lungs, the sensation so intense and hurtful, like she was physically present in Enmebaragisi's house. Her senses spun and she felt herself circling downward. Just how deep was her mind in ancient Sumer?

The demon's shadow looked like shiny black paint running toward the corner where Hilimaz placed the upended bowl. The creature took on dimension as it fought to stay free, half extricating itself from the wall. It was a hideous thing, man-shaped but with elbows and knees grotesquely oversized and covered with spikes. It had no flesh on its legs and arms, just blackened bones, and it had no feet. Its torso was covered with flesh, or rather a writhing mass of insect-things that expanded and contracted as the Aldî-nîfaeti breathed. The monstrosity clawed at the air with its seven-fingered scabrous hands, and it opened its maw and keened. The head of it was vaguely simian, like Yaqrun's, and its tongue was a serpent that unfurled and snapped at Hilimaz, striking her again and again.

The potter had been speaking, but Bridget had been so caught up in the demon's manifestation that she'd not caught most of it.

"—I heal and annul. With these words I catch I bind. Weapon of clay, mother wet-earth, in the names of angels Sariel and Barakiel. I, Hilimaz, shackle the Aldî-nîfaeti named Pua-tuma-sin. In so doing I free the hearts of Enmebarasis and Shag-ana and her coming child. I ease the troubles of the descendants of Ekur. I, Hilimaz, protect this house from all vileness. Bind and seal and capture forevermore the Aldî-nîfaeti named Pua-tuma-sin."

The demon's keening became a knife, so sharp and painful. Had Bridget been able to physically react, she would have held her hands to her ears and slammed her eyes shut. But her senses locked in place, she was forced to watch and listen as Pua-tuma-sin's serpent tongue continued to lash out at the potter and its scream became so high-pitched it dropped Enmebarasis and the others to their knees.

Then in a heartbeat the noise was gone, and the demon with it. Bridget glimpsed its scabrous claws dig at the earthen floor as it was pulled under the bowl. Hilimaz bent, turned the bowl upright, shuddered, and collapsed. Bridget feared the old potter was dead, but after a moment she saw the woman's chest slowly rise and resume a normal rhythm. The family recovered and hovered around Hilimaz.

257

Bridget heard them all clearly, though they spoke the long-dead Sumer tongue.

"Praise be to Enlil and Utu and Nannar," one of the teenage boys said.

"The gods are good," Shaga-ana said. Both hands were pressed to her belly, and her feet were apart as if she had trouble balancing. Sweat was thick on her forehead. "The gods keep my baby safe by freeing this home of the ruinous Aldî-nîfaeti."

Enmebaragisi gingerly touched his young wife's chin and tipped her face up to his. "Our child will not be eaten, beloved. Enlil and Utu, Nannar, and Prael blessed us."

"It was her," the other teenage boy said, pointing to Hilimaz's prone form. "Not the gods, father, it was the witch who saved us. She—"

"It was the gods," Enmebaragisi countered. "They worked through the blind woman, she is their focus in this city, their vessel. She is nothing more."

The young woman pulled away from the group and went to a chair, eased herself onto it, still holding her belly. "We must pay her, husband. We agreed—"

"Of course." He waved a hand and the boys retreated to a room out of Bridget's sight. She kept her gaze on Hilimaz, worried that the potter had been gravely injured. It was selfish, Bridget was concerned about herself and Otter, needing the old woman to be all right so she could continue the lesson.

The two boys returned with a small chest. Enmebaragisi opened it. Inside were jewels and pieces of gold. He selected a thin gold bracelet and what looked like an uncut sapphire. He closed the lid and gestured again, and the boys took it away.

"That is not enough, husband," Shaga-ana said. "Not for ridding our home of the Aldî-nîfaeti."

The merchant laughed. "She is an old, blind woman, my heart. What does an old, blind woman need with wealth? This will buy her food and tools for her clay. She does not need more." He handed the pieces to his wife. "I have business to attend, my heart. When Ruabi-ruve awakens, pay the witch and send her on her way."

Bridget smoldered. The merchant didn't act grateful, pleased, yes, but he hadn't even displayed the courtesy of helping Hilimaz off the floor. The two boys did that, but after Enmebaragisi left and the young woman asked them to. They settled the potter in a chair, and when she came to, they gave her something that smelled like strong coffee.

"Thank you, Ruabi-ruve," the young woman said. "You have made my home safe, and my child-to-come will live without fear." She tentatively stretched a hand forward, took Hilimaz's free hand and placed it on her swollen stomach. "If this is a girl, I will name her for you."

Hilimaz left several minutes later, the gem and bracelet in her pocket, the damp bowl held carefully against her.

"That man is rich." Bridget still fumed.

"Certainly," Hilimaz replied. "But I am an old, blind woman, and what do I need beyond food?"

Even unconscious, Hilimaz must have heard the merchant. Bridget studied the potter's face, looking for some trace of ire at the sleight the merchant had committed. The old woman's expression was serene, though Bridget noticed a horrid mark on the scarred side of her face, where the demon's snake-tongue had bit her.

"Still," Bridget persisted. "He should have paid much more for what you did."

"Bridget the-strong-willed, do you not believe he will make atonement for his rudeness in the world after this? Do you not believe there are repercussions for unfortunate behavior?"

She did believe it, and worried that her own soul was bound for some very dark place. "He has so much wealth. I saw gold and gems and—"

"And in your Catholic world so far removed in time and distance from this place, little ghost, what has wealth gotten you? Has it made you at ease? Joyful? What has it provided for your soul?"

259

34

Yaqrun."

"Yes, Bridget the-strong-willed, that is the name of the demon you released, and the one you must recapture. Say the name again and again so you will never forget it. Say it each hour of each day until you are ready to catch the beast. And if you do not say it often enough, I will say it for you."

Bridget worried that months had passed in the blink of an ephemeral eye, based on the crops growing and being harvested—chickpeas, lentils, onions, lettuce, leeks. Barley and wheat were growing tall. She and Hilimaz traveled near the river, where homes were made of tightly woven reeds, and watched fishermen bring in their catch, from across the fields, hunters toted gazelle they'd speared. She worried that Otter and the others had left the pit, perhaps had been slain. She couldn't pull her mind back to look in on them, Hilimaz held the leash too tight.

"I need the name of the other one, Hilimaz. The other one I released." Again Bridget described the massive slab of Silly Putty that she'd watched devour the flaming museum guard. "More than that, I need the name of my demon, the toad-thing that shadows me. You promised to help on those counts. And I need to know if my son—"

260

"I promised to teach you. I've done that. Provide names?" Hilimaz shook her head, as she had the many other times Bridget had asked. "I never promised that. Enlil has not provided the names, little ghost, not today and not on the other days. Perhaps there are Aldî-nîfaeti Enlil does not know, and so you may never know their names and never have power over them, never be able to summon them into a piece of pottery. But you know the name Yaqrun."

If Bridget had kept a piece of that broken pot she could have delved it and discovered the name of the Silly Putty beast through the memory of the person who'd trapped it. But she'd lost that shard on the subway.

"Maybe we should try to find the other witches who trap demons."

"And how many times have you suggested that?"

"I have lost count."

"And how many times have I said that is a foolish thought?" Hilimaz laughed. "What makes you think, little ghost, that because I catch Aldî-nîfaeti, I know others who catch them also? I do not. The mother of my long-dead husband, she caught Aldî-nîfaeti, and she taught me. And now I teach you. Before many more years pass I must find another one in this city to teach, pass the craft on." She stared out across the river as if she was actually seeing something. "You may teach whoever you please when we are done."

"I know only a couple of witches in New York. Lady Lakshmi, Goater, Beran, Adiella." She said the last name like it was profanity. "There is not one of them that I would—"

Hilimaz made a huffing sound like sand blown across dry ground. "I say you are a witch, and that makes the learning easier for you. But one does not need to be a witch to catch the Aldî-nîfaeti. You need the name and the words, you need clay and the words. A strong heart helps. Anyone can say the words, Bridget the-strong-willed. Anyone who can learn the words and can stand up to fear."

"Then ... then ... why aren't there lots of people in this city who can catch the feckin' Aldî-nîfaeti?"

Hilimaz laughed, long and musical. "I am old and ugly and blind, little ghost. If others knew how to snare the Aldî-nîfaeti in this village,

261

the people would have no use for me at all. Better that I am needed and whispered about and feared and revered, that I am the only demon-catcher here. Better that they think I am important and mystical. So I will not teach my craft to anyone else here until my days grow even shorter. These people who I have helped ... if they paid attention to my words, they could learn the snaring, too. But these people do not notice my words, the catching spell, they notice only the Aldî-nîfaeti that vexes them, and they are too afraid to notice anything else." She paused. "You, I teach you because you are not really here. You are not a rival for my attention. You, I teach because you are a mystery and because I have your name and some power over you. You, I teach because it gives me something interesting to do. And above all things, you I teach because Yaqrun is in your very far away time and place city. I hate Yaqrun more than I love life, and you will catch that Aldî-nîfaeti."

"My son—"

"Do not worry about your son, little ghost. The time you spend here is nothing."

Bridget thought often about Otter and prayed that Hilimaz was correct, that he'd be there in Adiella's pit when she returned.

"Now, we will recite this new spell again and again."

Time shifted as Bridget committed more spells to memory and watched as the old potter engraved bowls, certain now that she could duplicate the characters. Each spell was a little different, various gods' names invoked, but all had a central theme.

"Yaqrun," Bridget said again one morning. It was fall, the crops were being harvested and the air, though still pleasant, had the faintest chill to it. "I am ready, Hilimaz."

"So you believe, little ghost. But what of the other that you released? And what of this toad-thing you tell me follows you? Are you ready for them?"

"I have no names for them. And each damnable day I spend here you tell me you have no way to gain their names."

"Sad little ghost." Hilimaz's expression was forlorn. "And that your toad-thing is bound to metal?" She made a tsk-tsking sound. "Metal cannot capture the Aldî-nîfaeti, or truly imprison it. Only clay. I have told you this in all the days you have spent here. I have told you this again and again, and yet you do not hear. That toad-thing is not a prisoner. It is something else. When will you listen?"

Bridget did nothing to hide her ire. "And I have told you in all the days that the feckin' Aldî-nîfaeti who dogs me is caught, bound...." She stopped herself. "Bound." It wasn't caught, not *inside* something, like the other Aldî-nîfaeti had been snared in the clay. Her demon had a presence and waddled around New York City at her heels. It had killed Tavio and Jimmy and certainly Dustin. It had killed women Elijah Stone knew and how many others through how many other years. It was a feckin' serial killer. "It isn't caught," she said. "It's attached, but not caught."

"Finally. So long it took you to say those words, little ghost." Hilimaz's expression turned smug. "This Aldî-nîfaeti you speak of is bound, yes, but not imprisoned."

"My curse."

"Maybe," she stroked at her chin. "Maybe it is not a curse. Who would bind an Aldî-nîfaeti? And why?" Bridget noticed the old potter had dry clay on her hands. Hilimaz had been missing things lately, the clay on herself, bumping into her bench and stumbling. The vagaries of age were catching up.

Just how long had Bridget been inside the bowl?

"Four years," Hilimaz said. "You have been here four years, little ghost. And yes, you are ready for Yaqrun. But the others ... with no names ... you will have no power over them. Neither your god Cathol, nor Enlil, has given the names to you. Maybe you will never gain those names and those beasts will be forever free. A demon lives forever, you know. But you are ready for Yaqrun, and that is my only concern. Come visit me again, little ghost, and once more give me something interesting to do."

263

"Mom? Mom!"

Bridget opened her eyes. Otter was on his knees in front of her.

"Mom!"

She opened her mouth to say something, but her tongue was like sandpaper and her throat was dry.

"Mom!"

Marsh shouted too, and Rob, Quin. She felt the rumble of a subway trundling along, and heard her demon babbling ... and through the racket, she understood every single word the beast spewed. She'd learned Sumerian in her time with the old potter.

"Mom!" Otter shook her shoulders.

"M'okay," she managed. Bridget realized the bowl wasn't in her hands, it lay next to her like it had fallen out of her lap.

Rob thrust one of the awful energy drinks at her and she took it. The too-sweet syrupy drink felt amazing going across her tongue and down her throat.

"Mom! What happened? Are you okay?" Otter jostled her shoulders again.

She nodded and drank more of the Monster.

"You've been out of it for a while, boss." This from Rob, who hovered. "Like two days. We've been stuck down here the whole fucking time."

Two days? Bridget had hoped she'd pull her senses back to the present shortly after delving the bowl, Hilimaz had suggested that would be the case, and that no "time was nothing." But two days was better than four years—which the old potter had claimed she'd spent in ancient Sumer. It could not have been that long, could it?

She groaned and stretched, realizing nature and taken its course and her bladder and bowls had emptied while she'd been linked to the past. Her legs and arms and neck were stiff like she'd been turned to concrete.

Rob and Otter continued to chatter, her demon babbled too: "Bridget must unshackle all of the trapped Aldî-nîfaeti. Bridget must leave this cave under the world and unshackle us all, else I will unmercifully rip the heart out of Otter, unshackling him from life. Bridget unshackle Aldî-nîfaeti and release me. Please, Bridget."

Every word. The demon spoke Sumerian, and Bridget under-stood every syllable.

"Two days nearly," Marsh said. "We're like mostly out of food 'cept for one can of Pringles and half a jar of pickles. We didn't know what the hell to do. Couldn't snap you out of it. And we tried just about everything until—"

"—until I told them to leave you alone." Adiella was in her rocker, hands folded in her lap, postcards spread on the floor nearby, nothing written on them. "I told them you would snap out of it ... eventually."

"But Alvin didn't want to wait, Mom. He ... he went out there." Otter gestured behind him, to the crevice that led from the tunnel to Adiella's pit. Bridget's demon squatted there, four eyes opened and looking from one person to the next, fifth eye so tightly closed that it appeared to be a wrinkle on its warty forehead.

"We didn't see what got him, boss," Rob said. "Had to be that demon, the one that set your house on fire."

"We heard my brother scream." Quin was sitting on the cot, elbows on his knees and head hung low. "Heard him die."

"I kept him from going after Alvin." Rob again, pointing to Quin.

"*You* kept him? It took all of us," Marsh said.

They continued to chatter, one question after the next as she sat in her own waste and tried to gain some feeling back in her limbs. "Did you kill the old man who left this pit? Bridget asked her demon in the Sumer tongue.

"Mmmmmmmmmm," the demon replied. "Tasty, that old man."

"Where were you, Mom?" Otter's hands were still on her shoulders. "I mean, you were here, but you weren't. Adiella said you look through things, like the bowl you were holding. She says it's what you do, that you like very old things 'cause you can see their story. Is that where you were? It's what you were doing in the warehouse, too, wasn't it? Looking inside old things?"

"Yeah, Otter." Bridget flexed her fingers. "I was inside the bowl, my mind anyway." Feeling was coming back, along with the uncomfortable sensation of a thousand little bees stinging her. "I was delving the bowl. I call what I do delving."

"Delving. To figure out what to do about the demons, right? Somehow you were doing that?"

"Yeah, Otter. I got some of it figured out."

"Good, then we can get out of here, right?" Rob started pacing, a short course because he had little space in the crowded room. "We can—"

"Help me up." Otter tugged Bridget to her feet and she shifted her weight back and forth. "God, but I stink."

"Well, yeah, there is that," Otter said. "You sort of … sort of …."

"Yeah, I stink."

"So you can get us out of here now? I've missed school. I'll get in trouble for that. I'll need a written note. I've Dad's funeral. Geeze, Mom, that's tomorrow night. I'd set it up for tomorrow night. We gotta pay the place, and I'd set it up, put a notice in the paper, on-line, and for—"

"We'll take care of it, Otter."

"So you know what to do about the—"

"Demons? Give me a minute." Bridget took a good look around. Rob paced. Marsh leaned against a wall, hands in his pockets, scraggly growth of beard. Everyone looked tired, bags under their eyes, fatigue clear on their faces. Except Adiella; the witch looked like she could step behind the counter of her bookstore and open it for business. Adiella met Bridget's gaze, then looked toward the crevice.

Bridget approached her demon.

"Bridget is well. Good. Now Bridget must unshackle all of the trapped Aldî-nîfaeti. Bridget must release me, please. Together we will master the realm, crush the skulls of those who oppose us. Unshackle us all, Bridget, else I will unmercifully rip the heart out of Otter and eat it before your innocent eyes. Bridget unshackle Aldî-nîfaeti and—"

She crouched until she was eye-level with it, her still-stiff legs protesting. "You listen to me you gobshite." All the words except for the last were spoken in Sumerian. "You're not going to kill any more of my people. I'm through with your threats. Free you? Hell, I'd do it in a heartbeat if I knew how."

"Release me, Bridget. Release me and I vow not to eat the hearts of those you love."

"And how the hell do I manage that? Releasing you?"

"Say the words," the Aldî-nîfaeti said. "I will tell you the words to say and—"

Bridget bolted upright. "What did you say, demon?"

Behind her Otter and Rob talked softly.

"What's she saying?"

"Is that a language? Is she growling?"

"Do you think she's talking to a demon? An invisible one? Michael said there was an invisible one."

"Think there really is an invisible demon there?"

"Is that what got Alvin?" The last was whispered. "An invisible demon?"

"Bridget, I spoke that I will tell you the words you need to free me. I have no power with the words, but you do. And you must say them and—"

"So I can release you? Just like that? Just like the spell that caught your feckin' Aldî-nîfaeti fellows in the bowls?"

"Say the words. I will tell you—"

"What if I don't release you, eh? What if I keep you bound to me until my last breath?"

"Please, Bridget." The beast's voice had changed. It was softer, and its eyes were cast down. "Freedom, please. Else I will rip out Otter's heart and eat it before your innocent eyes. I will kill your son."

"No you won't. I forbid it." She felt the vibrations of another subway train and heard Otter and Rob talking. Quin mentioned something about his brother, and Michael grumbled and sat on the cot next to Quin. "You're bound to me. I didn't understand that before. And because you couldn't understand me ... because I couldn't communicate."

"Please, Bridget. I will eat Otter's hot beating heart unless you—"

Bridget slammed her fist against her hip. "Dear God." This she said in English. Instantly the pit behind her quieted. "Oh, dear God." She went back to the Sumer language. "You're bound to the buckle. You're bound to me."

"Bridget, please—"

"I'm right, aren't I? You're bound."

"Yes, Bridget."

"I can order you around. You have to do my bidding, not the other way around. It was never ever the other way around. I don't have to free the damn demons that were sucked up in old pieces of pottery. That's just what you *want* me to do."

"Yes, Bridget, I want my Aldî-nîfaeti brethren free."

She remembered what Hilimaz had told her only minutes ... years ... thousands of years ago: "Your toad-thing is bound to metal? Metal cannot capture the Aldî-nîfaeti. Only clay. I have told you this in all the days you have spent here."

She thought back to her delve of the buckle while she sat in her warm study on her oushak rug. A man's voice had said: "She can make a slave of evil that will in time conquer. That will allow us victory. A slave that she can bind like a mother unto a child." Bridget had heard then that her demon was an instrument; she just hadn't understood. She'd let it be the master.

"Unshackle Aldî-nîfaeti, Bridget. Free me. Together we can—"

Again she dropped to a crouch until her eyes were even with it. The stench from it overpowered her own stink and her eyes watered. "You're bound to me, demon, to this metal. She pulled the buckle out of her pocket and dangled it in front of him. She'd delve the buckle again later, when she was clean and rested, no matter the physical and mental cost. She'd delve it to be certain. But she played her hunch now.

"You're bound to this metal and so to me."

The demon regarded her icily.

"You're mine," she continued in the Sumer tongue. "Aren't you? It just took me some thousands of years to realize it. And if I'd been able to *really* talk to you from the very beginning all of this would have played out differently, wouldn't it? *You're bound to me.*" Her lip curled up in anger. "If I had figured it out, Tavio would still be alive."

"Mmmmmmm Tavio."

"What's she saying?" This from Otter, who must have recognized his father's name.

"Jimmy, he'd be alive." A pause. "Did you kill Dustin? Did you eat his heart?"

"Mmmmmm Dustin," it said.

"You fecker."

"Bridget unshackle all the—"

"What's your name, you damnable beast?"

"Ijul," it replied.

"Yaqrun," Bridget said.

"You unshackled the mighty Yaqrun," the demon said. "Slayer of farmers, burner of children, destroyer of—"

"Yeah, I freed him. Your name is Ijul."

"Ijul of the Seventh Waste, decimator of—"

"Let's just go with Ijul." She stood again, her legs cramping.

"Mom, what's—"

She waved Otter's question away with an impatient gesture.

"Close your eyes, Ijul."

The demon did.

"Turn around, Ijul."

The demon complied.

"Christ on a tricycle," Bridget said, those words in English. She felt a wave of weakness crash through her. If only she'd realized, she could have saved Tavio and Jimmy and Dustin, kept the museum guards alive. Hell, she wouldn't have released the Aldî-nîfaeti in the museum.

Sumerian again: "Turn around again and face me, Ijul."

The demon did.

"Twitch your tail, Ijul."

It did.

"You are bound to me." She continued to speak in Sumerian, so effortless a language now. "Ijul, you are not to eat another human

269

heart. Ever. You are not to harm my people. Do you understand? I command you."

"As you command, Bridget," Ijul said. "As you command, I obey."

"You are not to disappear on me, Ijul. You are not to leave my side."

"As you command, Bridget."

Son of a bitch! Bridget thought. If only she'd commanded it from the first, ordered it—in a language it could understand, used its name as that was power over it—she could have kept Tavio and Dustin and Jimmy alive. Otter would not be with her now; he would be in school, chatting with his girlfriend, talking about swim competitions. The museum ... it never would have happened. The buckle had never been meant as a curse, it was a means of control. The buckle was the leash that connected the dog to its owner. She'd just not known she could tug on that leash. Her demon, not commanded, had been free to roam on its own and slay who it desired. The dog analogy fit: a dog with no boundaries, no instruction, was free to wander and do what it will. She wouldn't free it—not yet—even though she wanted to be free of it. It would go bounding away to cause death and havoc. If she kept it, she could keep it in check.

"Yaqrun," Bridget repeated.

"Slayer of farmers, burner of children, destroyer—"

"Yeah, that son of a bitch. We're going to get Yaqrun, Ijul. You understand?"

"Please, Bridget. Please do not—"

"Please, Bridget your sorry ass. You're going to find Yaqrun for me. Can you do that, Ijul?"

"As you command, Bridget."

"Yeah, I command. We're going to deal with the slayer of museum guards and the burner of children." And then we're going after the other fecker, too.

"Mom?" Otter had crept up behind her. "Mom, what are you doing? Is there something there? Are you possessed? You're talking gibberish."

She stood and rubbed her thighs. "Is there any more of those nasty sweet drinks?"

Otter shook his head. "We're pretty much out of everything. Are we gonna—"

"Get out of here? Yeah, in a while. I need you ... all of you ... to stay here a little while longer. Can you do that? Just to be safe? I'll come back for you. Then we'll all go out to a fine dinner. You must be hungry." She looked around Otter. "Michael, Adiella, please keep everybody here." A pause. "Adiella, do you have a spare change of clothes in that trunk?"

"Please, Bridget," the demon said. "Do not do this. Together we can crush the skulls—"

Bridget grabbed the clothes Adiella reluctantly offered, stepped through the crevice and beckoned her personal Aldî-nîfaeti to follow.

"Yeah, well together we're going to deal with Yaqrun."

"The slayer of farmers," the demon said.

Bridget paused as she stepped over the heartless body of Alvin, crossed herself, and felt the vibrations of a subway train purr up through the souls of her boots.

35

Bridget borrowed a phone book at a corner convenience store and scanned the Yellow Pages. The clerk behind the counter gave her a serious up and down. She'd cleaned up in a restroom in the subway as much as possible, discarding her old clothes, save the coat, and changing into the outfit Adiella had provided. The witch was smaller than Bridget, and so the pants fit tight and were effectively capris. They were orange, the sweater—three-quarter length sleeves to her—was a thick cable knit mud brown, the colors looking more suited for fall and pumpkin harvesting than walking the New York City streets in the height of winter.

Bridget thought she still smelled funky, the sink and hand soap not enough. Maybe it was the demon's stench. She wrinkled her nose and traced her fingers down the entries. Outside, she heard horns blaring, sirens keening—though softly, indicating they were several blocks over. She'd emerged in the wee hours of the morning, and so the sidewalks had people, but not the rush of to-work or to-breakfast or heading-home. Music played, some Latin station with words she couldn't understand. Maybe that's why her finger gravitated toward a Latin-owned pottery shop. It had a small boxed add: Full Range of

272

Classes for Children and Adults, hand-thrown, and wheel. Eight-week sessions, low-cost materials fees. It was on West 26th, only a dozen blocks from here, between Sixth and Seventh Avenues.

She and Ijul would hoof it; the cold air would keep her alert.

"Thank you," she told the clerk, passing back the book and handing over a five for a steaming cup of coffee, which she finished it before the end of the first block.

Lord, but she loved this city.... the bigness of it, the brassiness, all of the clamor and the color, the people of all stripes, the trash and the glitter, and the buildings that stretched like long skinny fingers into the sky grasping for the clouds. Bridget loved the feel of it too, from the brush of women hurrying past her on the sidewalk to the swish of air caused by a passing subway car to the vibrations that pulsed up through her feet. Sending her mind back to Sumer had intensified her passion for New York. The land was so quiet, and though that ancient city was sizeable there'd been nothing tall, no steel fingers aimed skyward, and no rattle from cars. She smiled at the recollection of the goats and sheep, and their funny sounds; she'd enjoyed watching them, rather relaxing while Hilimaz pulled clay from the riverbank. But she hadn't been able to touch anything there. Odd that she could feel the breeze and smell the air that was so clean it barely carried a scent, and she could sense the warmth of the sun. But true tactile sensations had been denied to her.

Bridget stopped outside of the shop and placed her fingers against the building. It was red-brown brick, sooty from the city, cold to the touch and rough as her fingers rubbed against it. She concentrated on the feel of it as she caught her breath. Bridget had taken the dozen blocks at a fast clip. She hadn't realized she'd been delving, the brick's memory flooding at her as easily as the memories had come from her prized and lost Turkish oushak rug.

"Momma I don't want to wait here." In her mind's eye, Bridget saw a girl, about twelve, leaning against this wall, back of her head pressed against this brick. Judging by her clothes, it was the 1960s, and it was summer. The brick held other memories, but this one was the strongest. It flashed forward and Bridget saw the girl wait until dark, mother

273

never returning, but eventually a policeman came and tugged her away. Bridget shook off the memory and went to the front of the shop: ARCILLA MUNDO, the sign read. Smaller words under it were in English: CLAY WORLD.

She'd walked around the city long enough that hours had melted. It was a little past ten; Bridget saw a clock through the storefront window. They didn't open until eleven. She retreated to the corner and leaned against the building, letting her fingers play over the bricks and—with a little work this time—taking their memories. The conversations in her head helped deaden the chatter of the damnable demon. God, if only she'd known, if only she'd been able to truly communicate with it from the beginning. She pushed thoughts of Tavio, Dustin, and Jimmy from her head and listened to the bricks.

"Ijul," Bridget said an hour later when she heard a bell jingle and the shop door open. "Follow me."

"As you command, Bridget."

The shop was warm and the strong scent of clay reminded her of Hilimaz's pottery shop. Finished pieces were arranged on shelves. Some were beautiful with bright, glossy glazes, solids and patterns. Others looked crooked and primitive, and the signs underneath indicated the young age of the potters.

At the back of the shop was what Bridget was interested in.

"Can I help you?" The woman who walked up between the aisles of pottery was tall and stocky, gray-brown hair pulled back in a bun, and her face was dusted with only a smidgen of makeup. Bridget guessed her to be about sixty.

"I want to throw a couple of pots. I see you have a wheel."

"We have afternoon classes. Eight-week sessions—"

"—for three hundred dollars. I saw your ad in the Yellow Pages."

The woman smiled. "Beginners to advanced and—"

"I'm a little of both."

The demon started chattering at her side. "Rip out the heart of this woman, Bridget, I could. Smash the skulls of—"

"How about I pay you three hundred for a couple of hours?" Bridget still had a wad of cash from when she'd escaped from her brownstone. She peeled off three hundreds and pressed them into the woman's hand. "I only want to make two pieces and get them fired."

A few minutes later, Bridget was working the clay on the wheel, sluicing up the water like Hilimaz had done. At first her efforts resulted in something silly and crooked-looking, but she kept at it, the demon softly babbling the entire time about his Aldî-nîfaeti allies and what all of them could do to "take control of this land with Bridget leading the way." Though she'd not worked the clay in ancient Sumer, she'd watched Hilimaz each time she'd made a bowl, so closely it seemed like her own hands were doing the forming. Bridget recalled an old movie she'd watched many years ago: Patrick Swayze's *Ghost*. There'd been a sensuous scene where Demi Moore was working clay on a wheel, and Patrick Swayze was there with her. At the time she thought pottery might be a good activity. But the movie over, a young Bridget lost interest in that notion.

She actually liked the feel of the wet clay against her fingers, and she wished she'd brought Otter with her. It would have been a good idea to let him watch, hear the spell she would work into the clay. Hilimaz said anyone could catch a demon if they knew the words. And though Hilimaz also said that women were better suited to such work because of their clever minds, Bridget knew her son was very bright. She ought to teach him this one arcane thing; if demons indeed lived forever, who knew how many were wandering around in this present day? She had half-glimpsed odd and shiver-inducing things during some of her forays into the subway and particularly with Jimmy. Maybe there were demons down there.

The shop owner was fortunately busy with other customers when Bridget started engraving the spell. She kept her voice low, with a melodic sing-song lilt that she'd heard Hilimaz use.

Bridget started at the center of the bowl, where she drew a stick figure using the tip of a key she pulled off a ring. The key was useless; it had been to her beloved brownstone. The characters she etched spiraled away from figure. "I Bridget the strong-willed call Yaqrun, Aldî-nîfaeti, slayer of farmers, destroyer of children. I take her by the tentacles. I pierce her dark and evil eyes that she may no longer look upon the people of New York. Sahtiel help me in this catching. Aid me that I might grab Yaqrun by her many limbs and by her thick neck and say 'remove the curses and the pain from the hearts of those you have raged against.' I adjure you in the name of Ruphael and Sathietl and in the name of Prael the great and under the eyes of Inanna of the morning and evening. Bother no more the people of New York City. They must be teased no longer, teased nevermore, cursed no more, Aldî-nîfaeti-vexed no more. I am Bridget the strong-willed, the binder and the cleanser. I turn away all things fetid and foul. I protect the people of New York City. I bind. I bind in clay and powerful words. I heal and annul. With these words I catch I bind. Weapon of clay, mother wet-earth, in the names of angels Sariel and Barakiel and Prael the great. Under the gaze of Inanna of the morning and evening, I Bridget the strong-willed shackle the Aldî-nîfaeti named Yaqrun, slayer of farmers. In so doing I free the hearts of the people of New York City. I ease their troubles. I Bridget the strong-willed protect this city from all vileness. Bind and seal and capture forevermore the Aldî-nîfaeti named Yaqrun."

"Bridget, please do not do this thing," her demon practically whimpered.

She placed the finished bowl aside and reached for another clump of clay, starting the process over again. "Ijul, what is the name of the other Aldî-nîfaeti that I released with Yaqrun?"

"Bridget, please! Together we can attain greatness and rule this land, crush—"

"Give me the feckin' name of the putty-beast, Ijul. Now."

"Kaliv-re, Bridget."

She stopped herself from saying "Thank you." This bowl did not take as long, and she'd made both relatively small and thick. In her time with the old potter she'd learned that the size of the bowl didn't matter—so long as they were large enough to hold the words to the spell. Hilimaz had made them various sizes depending on her mood and how long she wanted to work at the wheel. Neither did any glaze or paint need to be poured across the characters for them to be more easily read; that was just for esthetics, to make her customers believe more work and magic had been incorporated.

"I need them fired," Bridget told the shopkeeper. Hilimaz hadn't always waited for her pots to dry before using them to catch Aldî-nîfaeti. But the ancient Sumer city was nothing like New York. There were so many people here in a hurry, jostling each other on the sidewalks and in the subways and on the busses. Bridget had never seen a soul bump into Hilimaz. "They're stronger fired."

"Definitely. I'll have a load ready to fire in three or four days."

Bridget peeled off another hundred. "I need them fired now."

"Well ... all right. Still, it takes time. I mean, I fire them now, you're not going to get them until—"

"How long?"

"If I fire them now, the kiln should be cool enough to open tomorrow. We open at eleven. So you could come back then."

Bridget pulled out the rest of her money, keeping a hundred and twenty back in case she needed something for bus or subway fare. "Open early. Really early." She waved the money at the woman, who screwed up her face in puzzlement.

"Eight," she said.

"Seven. And all of this ..." Bridget counted the money, reserving the hundred and twenty. "Three hundred and sixty-three dollars. I'll give it to you at seven tomorrow morning."

Bridget didn't stick around waiting for the potter to ask what the rush was for.

Ijul in tow, she stopped at a Chinese take-out place and spent the hundred dollar bill on an assortment of dishes and a two-liter bottle of Coke, then went back to Adiella's pit to tell Otter she hoped to have the demons caught in plenty of time for Tavio's funeral.

"I'm not ready to say it's safe out here yet. Give it a while longer."

"Dad's funeral tomorrow," Otter prompted.

"We'll make it in time."

She ordered Ijul to stay put in the crevasse, and to not touch a single human, even though he mentioned to her again just how delicious warm hearts tasted. Bridget briefly entertained the notion of

277

delving the buckle. Indeed, she intended to do that—get to the crux of the entire matter with Ijul, but not now. She worried that she might encounter another witch like Hilimaz who could hold her in the past; she didn't want any more days passing by down in the subway. She wanted Yaqrun and Kaliv-re securely ensconced in clay, Tavio laid to rest, and Otter and the others safe.

Then she'd peer into the buckle.

Bridget propped herself against a wall and closed her eyes, pretending to sleep. She didn't want to deal with all of their questions, especially with Quin asking if she'd seen his brother Alvin. She would tell Ijul to move the body before the night was up. Through the stone, she felt the faint and pleasant vibration of a subway train and inhaled the scents of Chinese cooking.

36

Bridget and Otter had to walk a few miles to the Red Hook Grain Terminal.

"I needed to get out," Otter said. "That cave, pit, hole, whatever you want to call it. Felt like a coffin."

She didn't say anything. Bridget had said plenty earlier, demanding he stay in Adiella's pit until this matter was resolved. He decided otherwise and promised to sneak out if she didn't take him along. So rather than risk that and risk him running afoul of something human or otherwise, she'd grudgingly agreed he could come with her ... after demanding that Ijul protect him.

"Three days down in there, Mom. Really, it felt like I was in a coffin, you know. I need a hot bath. I just feel so friggin' dirty. I'm going to All is Well when you're done doing whatever you're doing here." All is Well was a men's spa in the Flatiron District. Bridget knew Tavio used to go there and no doubt had introduced Otter to the place.

Otter had no trouble keeping up, despite the fast pace Bridget managed. One thousand five hundred and seventy-six steps, the lower third taken two at a time, in the Empire State Building run. Maybe next time she'd invite Otter to participate in the Run Up.

279

But "next time" was going to be a while off, she suspected. As much as she loved New York—and never in her adult life had been out of the city—she was starting to question staying here. Her brownstone gone, her antique store and the warehouse. She had plenty of investments so that she could rebuild. But should she?

Should she start over somewhere else?

"This is a creepy place we're going to." Otter pointed ahead. His breath was puffy against the frigid air, like he was smoking an invisible cigarette. Bridget thought his face appeared hard and had lost the boyish charm she'd noted only a handful of days ago during his birthday dinner. His eyes were marbles, the sparkle gone.

Fifteen, not fifty, she thought. Losing his father, seeing a demon burn down the brownstone. How much had all that aged him? Certainly there were things he'd never un-see and would disturb his dreams for all the decades of his life.

"Maybe we should've taken a cab.... provided a driver would've risked coming here. The place looks haunted."

Bridget had to admit that it did look eerie. And if it had been just her, she would've taken a cab from the last subway stop. But with Otter along the fare would have exceeded the twenty bucks she'd left herself. And the banks weren't open yet to replenish her funds.

"Looks like it would make a great set for some horror movie, Mom."

It is the set for horror, Bridget mused. The Red Hook Grain Terminal was where Ijul directed her. The demon said Yaqrun was living somewhere amid the concrete silos. Her demon could apparently sense where others of his kind were.

"Place hasn't been used for half a century." Bridget finally said something. A heavy layer of frost covered everything, but the black mold on the concrete was still visible beneath. "When the barge canal was dug, rerouting the Erie Canal, they built this place. The Red Hook waterfront used to be a busy place, Otter."

She'd first discovered the place in her youth in the company of the Westies boys she ran with. There were fifty-four silos, and once upon a time grain was mechanically hoisted into them from the bellies of ships that had pulled up. It was considered an engineering miracle in its day, but it had too-fast become obsolete as the grain trade in New York declined. It had become cheaper to unload grain in Philadelphia and Baltimore. So the jobs vanished, the docks decayed, and the area's residents took up living in "Red Hook Houses," ugly public housing projects. The place became thick with crack cocaine, and despite the gentrification in the area—all the specialty shops and wine bars that were moving in—drugs were still around.

Bridget hadn't been back since she explored the place with the Westies boys. Even they had been intimidated by the criminal element that clung to the abandoned terminal's fringes and they'd never ventured there after the sun went down. There were scattered news reports in the past few years that the owner of the industrial park was looking to build the property farther out into the bay by laying in a landfill made of sludge and concrete.

Cradling her box with the fired bowls nested inside, Bridget nudged Otter toward the closest silo. "See there?" She kept her voice down and nodded toward an ash-gray van. "Security." It must have pulled up recently, as there was no trace of frost or snow on it.

"Who'd want to protect this dump?" Otter worried his foot against a piece of cardboard frozen to the ground.

"They're probably not protecting this place so much as trying to prevent people from getting in and hurting themselves."

Otter chuckled, and then dropped his voice. "Oh, I get it. Urban explorers, huh? The urban explorers ought to go check out Grandma's little cave in—"

A piercing "ahhhhhhhooooooo" sliced through the air. Bridget thought it might have been a boat horn. But it came again and ended with the loud clanking of metal on metal, coming from a nearby silo.

"Yaqrun," Ijul said. "I told Bridget I smelled Yaqrun in this direction. Yaqrun cries a kill."

"Wonderful," Bridget said.

"What's wonderful? This place is—"

Bridget's scowl stopped Otter from saying anything else.

"Bridget, once more I ask you not to do this horrid thing. Do you not realize that with Yaqrun at our side, you and I can defeat an army? With the powerful Yaqrun, we can—"

She scowled at her demon too, but that did not shut it up. The thing continued to prattle on about conquering New York City and then the land and the sea beyond. The ooze that ran down its sides this morning was thin and sluggish, and frost covered its warty hide. She wondered if it felt cold or heat.

"I still think this isn't the best idea, Otter, you coming along." But she hadn't stopped him, and she hadn't given him the slip when she could have. She really was considering teaching him the art of demon-snaring. But she hadn't even practiced it yet herself, only lived it vividly by watching Hilimaz.

"Better idea than staying down in that hole with Michael and—"

"Then c'mon, and watch yourself. I'll be too busy to watch out after you." She cut a look to the demon.

"Protect Otter," it said.

Everything inside that wasn't concrete was rusted. Evidence of urban explorers was on the walls—spray painted initials, gang symbols, a caricature of a big-nosed woman who was perhaps a singer or other celebrity. A door had been painted turquoise; it looked recently done, with IOII stenciled in bright white on it. All the details were easy to see as light came in through broken windows. Not a pane of glass was intact. An attempt had been made to cover some of the windows; dingy plastic hung over a few in tatters, flapping like agitated ghosts. Through a gap in the plastic, Bridget saw part of a building a hundred feet away that had collapsed into the canal.

"So ... this demon you're hunting," Otter said. "It's in here?"

"Apparently," Bridget returned. "And they're actually called Aldî-nîfaeti. I think I'm going to teach you a little Sumerian when we've some quiet time. A pretty language; you'll probably catch on quick."

"Cimmerian?"

"Su-merian. Conan the Barbarian is not involved."

A rust-covered ladder with high steps led up. Her demon squatted at the base.

"Yaqrun is above," Ijul said.

"Yeah, I figured." There was no trace of the demon down here, though charred spots on the concrete floor indicated that maybe it had consumed someone here, maybe a vagrant, a blanket and an empty peaches can against a wall suggested someone had stayed here. Maybe Yaqrun had torched a security guard.

She took a step up, looked down. "Ijul, protect Otter, remember. Always protect Otter."

Otter opened his mouth to say something, but apparently thought better of it.

Bridget climbed higher. "You coming?"

"You talking to me? Or you talking to your invisible demonic buddy?"

"Yes," Bridget said. "Let's get this over with."

She guessed it was about ninety feet up to the top level. And with every other rung she climbed she said "Yaqrun." Saying its name would hold it in place. That, and its arrogance and lack of fear. Hilimaz said Aldî-nîfaeti feared only the gods—*some* of the gods—and that for the most part they were unaware Enlil had learned how to capture them and passed that knowledge to his chosen people.

"Yaqrun," she said.

"Please do not do this thing, Bridget," Ijul grumbled.

"What did I tell you," she shot back.

"To protect Otter. To not feast on human hearts."

She should have worn gloves. Bridget cradled the box to her with one hand and kept her other hand on the railing. Not that she needed help in climbing, but she worried that the steps were so rusted one might give way and she wanted something to cling to. She hadn't given a thought to what would happen to her if she plummeted dozens of feet and hit the concrete below; her concern was for the bowls she'd crafted and inscribed.

The higher she went, the colder the railing became. It wasn't her imagination. It was bone-numbing cold of the sort that no matter how many blankets you piled on or how close to a fire you sat you could not feel any warmth.

Some Aldî-nîfaeti exude cold, Hilimaz had told her one summer day, particularly if they are happy. "I do not know why," the old potter said, "only that they do it. Some say hell is cold, and my husband's mother—who spoke directly to Enlil, who had been banished there for a time—claimed that hell freezes your eyes open and your throat shut. That Aldî-nîfaeti would be pleased if the world became so cold like unto hell, like their home."

"Yaqrun," Bridget said again. "Yaqrun. Yaqrun. Yaqrun."

"Please do not do this thing. With Yaqrun we can claim this city."

"Yaqrun." Bridget stepped off the ladder and opened the box, reached inside and gingerly withdrew the top bowl. She sat the box down at her feet away from the stairwell. Running her fingers around the letters she'd carved, she took a look around and shivered from more than the cold.

Bringing Otter had been a very bad idea.

Light streamed in through broken windows and the dust and ash particles in the air were suspended like snowflakes that refused to fall. She counted at least a dozen piles of ashes with charred bones and bits of the dead owners' possessions. Here a blackened boot, there a gun, a still-smoldering blanket, a polished white human skull that looked incongruous with all the other dark matter, the singed carcasses of a few rats, syringes, a ball cap with the brim burned off. There was a bite to the air, an acridness that clings to burned-out buildings mixed with the touch of roasted flesh. Bridget heard Otter gag; she'd gotten so used to foul-smelling things that she could handle it.

"You don't have to come all the way up," she told him. "In fact, you might want to go back down. This was a bad idea, Otter. I'm sorry I said okay."

He ignored her and clambered up the rest of the way. "Holy shit! Those were people."

Vagrants, urban explorers, security guards, maybe people on the docks the Aldî-nîfaeti had found and brought up here to devour leisurely. Remembering how the museum guards died, Bridget knew all of these had suffered horribly.

Their deaths—whoever they were—rested squarely on her. She'd let the damn demon out of the bowl. She'd not considered the repercussions.

"Yaqrun."

The top floor was one big circular room with rusted steel girders holding up a cement roof and rusted steel braces on the side wearing the graffiti of gangers and lovers. Sarah & Pedro were inside a lavender heart. Jander & Joe inside another. Posters for bands called THE HAPPY PROBLEM, STREETS OF LAREDO, and SISTER SPARROW were affixed above a table made of boards and plastic milk crates—the only objects not incinerated by the demonic occupant.

"Yaqrun. Yaqrun. Yaqrun."

"Bridget, please do not—"

A glare cut her demon off. It squatted next to Otter, breath puffing away like noxious little clouds through a slit in its bulbous lips and through gills in its thick neck. She'd not noticed the gills before.

"Yaqrun, I call the slayer of farmers, burner of children, destroyer of—"

"Civilizations. Yaqrun the mighty, the supreme, the pillager." The Aldî-nîfaeti had somehow merged with the concrete, but now pulled itself out. It had grown since Bridget last saw it at her brownstone, and its appearance had changed.

"Oh my God!" Otter shouted. "Holy fuck!"

"Get out of here, Otter. I said this was a bad idea." She heard him clamber back down the stairs, clumsy in his haste.

"Protect Otter," Ijul said as it lumbered after the boy, breath still puffing away in the cold.

The first time she'd seen the tentacle monstrosity, she likened its height to an NBA center. Now it was easily a dozen feet tall, and the octopus-like appendages at its base were swollen, twitching against the marble floor, steam rising from their ends. Its cylindrical body that rose like a column was no longer smooth. It had the appearance of blackened tree bark, and the whorls looked like carved faces. Each face was different, one a young man, one an old woman, one a stern-faced person of indeterminate sex, another had a long nose and prominent cheekbones. Maybe they were the faces of the Aldî-nîfaeti's victims. One near the base of its body had a mouth open as if caught in a scream. Its two mannish arms had thickened and lengthened, and the lobster-shaped claws they ended in glowed red like hot coals. Its simian head had more detail to it ... or maybe the improved light allowed her to see it better.

The face was truly hideous, eyes limned with rivulets of lava, nose upturned and showing the flicker of flames in its wide nostrils. The cheeks were overly exaggerated and the skin cracked across them, embers burning in the crevices. What initially had looked like crabgrass going on top of its head now appeared as the talons of large birds, and they flexed and quivered as she watched in horror. It opened its mouth and a frigid blast of air rushed out. Despite its penchant for burning, it radiated a cold more intense than the winter outside. The cold of hell maybe, Bridget mused, as she stepped to the wall, recited the spell and placed the bowl down against it.

"I Bridget the strong-willed call Yaqrun, Aldî-nîfaeti, slayer of farmers, destroyer of children. I take her by the tentacles. I pierce her dark and evil eyes that she may no longer look upon the people of New York. Sahtiel help me in this catching. Aid me that I might grab Yaqrun by her many limbs and by her thick neck and say 'remove the curses and the pain from the hearts of those you have raged against.' I adjure you in the name of Ruphael and Sathietl and in the name of Prael the great and under the eyes of Inanna of the morning and evening. Bother no more the people of New York City. They must be teased no longer, teased nevermore, cursed no more, Aldî-nîfaeti-vexed no more. I am Bridget the strong-willed, the binder and the cleanser. I turn away all things fetid and foul. I protect the people of New York City. I bind. I bind in clay and powerful words. I heal and annul. With these words I catch I bind. Weapon of clay, mother wet-earth, in the names of angels Sariel and Barakiel and Prael the great. Under the gaze of Inanna of the morning and evening, I Bridget the strong-willed shackle the Aldî-nîfaeti named Yaqrun, slayer of farm-ers. In so doing I free the hearts of the people of New York City. I ease their troubles. I Bridget the strong-willed protect this city from all vileness. Bind and seal and capture forevermore the Aldî-nîfaeti named Yaqrun."

She knew she'd recited it perfectly. Had memorized it and repeated it in her mind again and again. The beast should be pulled toward it and under it. Hilimaz, now dust, had taught her and pronounced her an apt student.

But Yaqrun only looked at her and made a painful noise that stabbed into her head.

"Christ!" Bridget hollered. "Bind and seal and capture forevermore the Aldî-nîfaeti named Yaqrun."

Its voice came deep and musical and sickly beautiful. "Yaqrun, slayer of farmers, burner of children, destroyer of civilizations. Yaqrun the mighty, the supreme, the pillager." The lava that had limned its eyes spilled down over its cheeks. More lava spread from its swollen tentacles and oozed toward her.

"Shit. Shit. Shit." Bridget plucked the bowl up, leaped over a trail of lava, and rushed to the stairs. She'd barely managed to grab up the box with the other bowl when the lava flow increased. "Run, Otter!" she hollered as she thundered down the steps, cradling the box and the bowl to her chest. "Shit. Shit. Shit."

She'd done everything Hilimaz had taught her. The old potter wouldn't have tricked her. Hilimaz had wanted Yaqrun snared. Had done everything perfect, except ...

"Shit and two is four and four is eight," she spat as she cleared the last few steps and landed in a crouch on the level below. Bridget heard metal groan and saw the rusted iron steps behind her melt.

"Run Otter!" Bridget hurried down to the next level, the stairs giving way underneath her. She jumped a span equal to her height and landed in a crouch, nearly dropping the box and bowl. "Run baby!"

Down another flight, faster this time. She sensed the silo shift around her. Could lava melt concrete? Was the whole damn place coming down? The girders! The feckin' demon was taking out the steel girders.

She'd done everything right ... except the crucial thing. On the bottom floor, she spied it. Though the silo was round, there were two cement walls at right angles on this level, probably at one time marking off a storage room. It would work.

Lava dripped down the open stairwell, and when she glanced behind her, she saw tentacles coming down with it. The Aldî-nîfaeti was lowering itself like some octopus creature in a SyFy channel schlockfest.

Bridget spun and ran toward the wall, then fell to her knees when fiery agony lanced into her back. All efforts on keeping the bowls from breaking, she ground her teeth together to fight the agony from a glob of lava that had been hurled at her back and burned through her coat to her skin. She screamed in pain as she glanced behind her. That glance that cost her a moment was nearly her undoing. A tentacle lashed out and struck her face, the heat so unbearable she feared her flesh was melting. The icy wave that radiated from the creature threatening to put her in shock.

"Yaqrun the mighty, the supreme, the pillager, slayer of farmers, burner of children, destroyer of civilizations."

If not for the demon's arrogance, at blathering on about the armies it had bested, she'd be done, so much slag like Yaqrun's other victims. Holding the box and bowl to her chest, she crawled the last few feet to where the ninety-degree cement wall joined the building's exterior. It was the thing she hadn't gotten right on her first attempt. Always Hillimaz had placed her bowls where walls joined, that was part of the magic.

Bridget fought against the pain and recited the spell as she went. Turned the bowl upside down, making sure the rim touched both walls. She finished: "Weapon of clay, mother wet-earth, in the names of angels Sariel and Barakiel and Prael the great. Under the gaze of Inanna of the morning and evening, I Bridget the strong-willed shackle the Aldî-nîfaeti named Yaqrun, slayer of farmers. In so doing I free the hearts of the people of New York City. I ease their troubles. I Bridget the strong-willed protect this city from all vileness. Bind and seal and capture forevermore the Aldî-nîfaeti named Yaqrun."

The demon shrieked, the sound like metal slicing across metal, but louder than anything she'd ever heard before. Through half-closed eyes she saw its shadow on the wall and watched its writhing tentacles flailing against the concrete in an effort to find purchase and stop itself from being dragged along the wall and into the clay.

As some point the noise stopped—or rather Bridget's ability to hear did. In utter silence, the massive now one-dimensional Aldînîfaeti was pulled to the bowl and sucked under it. Bridget sagged onto the freezing cement floor next to it, pressing her burned face against the cold in an effort to find some relief.

Otter nudged her shoulder. His mouth moved, but she couldn't hear him ... couldn't hear anything. He pulled her into a sitting position and propped her against the wall, pushed the box aside and fretted over her.

After a few minutes, her hearing started to return.

"I'm okay," she said. "I'm okay. Really. I'm okay."

"No, you're not." Otter looked from her to the overturned bowl to her again. "Is it in there? I thought I saw something slide under the rim, something black. That flaming demon that burned your house? Is it in there?"

She nodded.

"Holy fuck that thing was huge."

She nodded again.

"Wait'll I tell Lacy. She won't believe me."

"You shouldn't tell Lacy. You shouldn't tell anyone."

"Yeah, Mom, you're right. They'd think I was a nutter. We gotta get you to a hospital."

Bridget shook her head.

"Your face, Mom. It's all ... burned."

Part of it anyway, Bridget thought, *like Hilimaz had been burned by the same demon.* "I'm okay," she said again. "We've got another one to catch. I don't think Kaliv-re will be as difficult."

"Kaliv-re?"

"It looks like a big piece of Silly Putty."

289

I t wasn't as difficult.

They were back in Adiella's pit by noon, and Bridget placed the demon-filled bowls in their carefully-packed box inside the witch's trunk for safe-keeping. Bridget entertained renting out a safety-deposit box for them, but in the end thought this might be better.

"You need a hospital, boss," Rob said. "Me and Marsh'll—"

"I need to get to my bank," Bridget returned. She was out of money, and what she had to do next wouldn't be free.

"Get yourself to that spa, okay?" She put her hands on Otter's shoulders. "Get Rob and Marsh to take you shopping and get something nice to wear for the service." She looked to Rob. "Do you guys got any money to cover it? A credit card? I'll pay you back."

"Sure thing, boss. Take care of yourself. Okay? We'll get Otter and us cleaned up for the funeral."

There were questions ... from Quin about his brother, from Michael about what happened with the demons, from Adiella about how Bridget managed to catch demons when she wasn't a witch. Bridget left Otter to answer everything the best he could.

Bridget slipped out of the pit as a subway train trundled past.

37

On Utica Avenue, Carle-Rotzski's advertised itself as the largest funeral home in Brooklyn. Bridget had been to a service here last year, for one of the "Westies boys" she used to box with late at night in the closed gym. The man—Wesley O'Donahue—had still been in the life and had recently gotten caught up with a sour crowd that dealt drugs and firearms, was taken down in a drive-by. That visitation had been in one of the smaller rooms, and most of the people who attended were old friends and talked with Irish accents. Bridget had felt more comfortable there, and the display of pictures had been kept to one table.

Tavio's service was in the largest room. Good thing, Bridget realized. The place was packed. All ages and stripes were present, friends of Tavio—some of whom she recognized and steered clear of so she wouldn't have to talk about old times when the two of them were married, business associates she'd seen but had never met, a bevy of women in high-end clothes and somber shades of makeup, hair perfectly done up. Bridget wondered how many of them were Tavio's former lovers, maybe some of the well-groomed young men in turtle-necks, dabbing the corners of their eyes with tissues fit into that cate-

291

gory as well. Tavio had liked sex; Bridget believed he thought it passed for love.

Otter was at the front, next to Adiella, both dressed in black, standing next to one of the displays of pictures. Otter had to practically beg his grandmother to attend. Adiella had told him she preferred to grieve alone. In the end, Otter had won out; Bridget wasn't sure the witch's presence was a good thing. Bridget'd had more than enough of Adiella in the past week.

From a distance—Bridget stayed at the back of the room—she couldn't see all the details of the photographs arrayed on tables and on easels, but she spotted a couple of large framed pictures that had been taken at her and Tavio's wedding reception on the boat.

Marsh and Rob were seated toward the center of the room, in the middle of the rows of chairs. No sign of Quin or Michael. Rob had told her not to expect them, that both men relayed they were finished with her employ. She would find them later and send them some money for all the recent troubles they'd endured.

She'd cleaned up well. Bridget had treated herself at the Oasis Day Spay on Park Avenue, a massage and facial and steam bath. Though she was not as badly scarred as Hilimaz—she suspected the invincibility she seemed to enjoy because of her demon had helped—the left side of her face was still marred from Yaqrun's flaming tentacle. The skin looked wet and shiny, and the two thousand dollar wig she'd purchased at Disomone's helped cover some of it. The wig was not quite as red as her own hair, but it suited her nonetheless.

She was one of the few people in attendance who wasn't wearing black or gray or deep navy blue. Bridget had spotted a brown cashmere sweater dress in the window of a designer resale shop on Eighty-first. A Bluefly calf-length design, it was beautiful and yet simple. She'd bought a few other pieces at the shop, a suitcase from a department store, and stashed all of it at the two-bedroom loft apartment. Not in the best of neighborhoods, Bridget hadn't the time to be picky and look around for a better place to temporarily live. She'd taken the first open thing she found and had the keys in under an hour. It was a short-term lease, and she signed it for the minimum—three months. But Bridget didn't intend to stay there that long.

She watched Otter greet people who passed by. The boy looked serious, but she hadn't seen him crying. He'd probably already done his grieving in the days while her mind was in Sumer, though she suspected the brunt of his sadness would sink in some time from now when things quieted down. The demon-snaring business done ... at least until she could figure out what to do with the gobshite of a beast that still clung to her ankles, oozing and belching and babbling in Sumerian about how tasty the hearts of these people might be ... she would settle Otter back into his routine of school.

But the routine wouldn't last long; Bridget was formulating another plan.

The boy was adamant that he was keeping Tavio's Italian restaurant, and that he was also keeping an after-school appoint-ment next week with his dad's investment counselor. Bridget would go along, wanting to make sure no one took advantage of Otter ... though she figured he'd be savvy enough without her guidance.

"Fifteen, not fifty," she whispered. She glanced down at the tri-fold memorial card. Tavio had claimed to be Catholic, but in the years she'd known him he hadn't put in many appearances in church. The front was a placid picture of Christ, the words "In Remembrance" beneath it. Inside: the Lord's Prayer and opposite it, Tavio Vren Vãduva-Madera; services in the Carle-Rotzski Serenity Chapel; officiating Father E.J. Larson. On the back, a quote from a James Montgomery hymn: "There is a world above, where parting is unknown, a whole eternity of love, form'd for the good alone; and faith beholds the dying here, translated to that happier sphere."

Was there a heaven?

Bridget knew there was a hell. It was where Yaqrun and Kaliv-re had come from, and Ijul at her side. It was where Enlil had been banished for a time, and where she was likely to end up. She'd done little good in her life ... theft, fraud, murder if you stacked on what the demons did after she'd freed them. Had she done *any* good?

Saving Otter.

293

Now maybe she could work on saving herself.

Sergeant McGinty, dressed in a dark pinstriped suit, came through the rear chapel doors and headed straight toward her.

"Christ on a—"

"Bridget, that man's heart will taste—"

"No eating hearts, Ijul, not ever again. Remember?"

"As you command, Bridget." The demon glowered. "No more hearts."

"Miss O'Shea." McGinty stuck out his hand, but Bridget didn't take it. She kept her fingers wrapped around the edges of a clutch purse she'd picked up in the same resale shop. "Sorry for your loss." The cop drew in his lower lip, nodded toward the front, and then gave her a steely look. "Is there somewhere we can go to talk ... after this."

Bridget had guessed this was coming, but she thought they'd have the decency to wait until tomorrow, though maybe they figured this was best, as they were certain to find her here. With her properties burned to the ground, she might otherwise be difficult to locate.

"There's a reception at Tavio's ... at my son's ... restaurant after this. So no. Talk here, but keep it short." She moved against the back wall, next to a table overflowing with flower arrangements. The smell from the blooms was so strong it covered the stench of her demon.

"Your ex-husband dead." McGinty gave a respectful nod. "Your home burned. Your antique business and a warehouse you owned, all burned. Some other properties that might have belonged to you, gone, and—"

"Am I a suspect, Sergeant?" Bridget dug her manicured nail extensions into the clutch.

"Oddly, no, Miss O'Shea. We don't think you did any of it. But you are most certainly at the heart of all of it. So we're looking into your involvement in various activities, nothing concrete yet. Seeing who you might have riled."

Concrete. Bridget shuddered, recalling her morning excursion to the Red Hook concrete silo.

"Gang involvement maybe," he said. "Or one of the mobs. I'm here out of courtesy, Miss O'Shea, as I don't believe you're quite the devil my lieutenant thinks."

"And what do *you* think?"

McGinty scratched his head. "I think you're the victim of something unfortunate. Caught up in a wave of ugliness. Someone is definitely out to get you and your business ... put you out of business ... whatever that business really is. I don't think you're squeaky clean, Miss O'Shea. You're too young to have so much. Uh, to have had so much. Can't see where you inherited it. Can't seem to trace your family."

"My mother went back to Ireland a lot of years ago," Bridget said. "I've been on my own since I was a teenager. I earned my own way, sergeant. And I don't think there'll be any more trouble aimed at me. I think it's done."

He shifted back and forth, his leather soles making a creaking sound. New shoes, Bridget guessed by the look, probably uncomfortable, not yet broken in. "Well, Miss O'Shea, expect some scrutiny into your finances. The paperwork's already running on that. Too many burned buildings, a dead husband—"

"—ex-husband."

"Too much unfortunate activity. Too many flaming red flags. Spotlight's on you and your son. Stay in town, Miss O'Shea." He looked to the front of the room. "Again, my condolences."

Bridget had spent her entire adult life in this city, had never planned to go anywhere else. The subway took her close enough to all the places she needed to be. Everything was here.

But she wasn't going to stay in her beloved city, despite the sergeant's admonition. At least not stay long. She'd break the news to Otter later tonight. No, she'd tell him maybe first thing in the morning. Or maybe when he came back in the afternoon from school. She'd get him settled into the rental, buy a few changes of clothes for him, a suitcase. Then after the appointment with Otter's financial advisor, she'd visit a friend who was good at documents. She'd need passports and paperwork for both of them. Hell, if it didn't take too many days, she'd go the legit route and get the real stuff.

Otter had inherited half of a restaurant in Italy. She'd take him out of school on the pretext of going to Italy to look it over, hire a tutor so he could finish out the academic year. Then over the summer think. Think and think and think.

What would come next?

Maybe come back here. Otter would probably want that, finish up his junior and senior high school years. She couldn't imagine staying away from her beloved city too long.

But she had to get out for a time. Put some months between all of this. Get out from under the hairy eyeballs of the New York City police.

Buy her a few months. Some time to think.

Decide if she should rebuild her operation; her property was burned and her inventory slagged, but she still had contacts, investments, and the ability to put it all back together. She was a smuggler and a broker and a thief. She was good at all those things. It made sense that she would return to that, and keep Rob and Marsh and any of the others who wanted to stay in the fold.

But did she want to?

Father E.J. Larson stepped up to the podium and people gravitated to the seats.

"This is a house," Larson said, pointing to his chest. "And when this house is gone, we move to another, to a room in our Father's house. Tavio left his house and has moved into another room." He continued for several minutes. Then a woman stood and began singing, her voice piercing and clear, a professional singer Otter had arranged through Carle-Rotzski's.

Tears slipped down Bridget's cheeks, for Tavio and Otter, Dustin and Jimmy, the museum guards and all the people she did not know and that her demon had slain. Maybe a few of the tears were for her.

38

Bridget sat on the stoop in the alley, outside the restaurant's back door. Otter's restaurant now. The yellow light that hung crooked above her made the buckle in her fingers gleam darkly. Ijul squatted across from her between a Dumpster and a garbage can. The demon had snared a large rat under a taloned claw, and it dribbled blobs of acidic goo on the helpless creature. Ijul looked up, maybe expecting Bridget to tell it not to play with the thing. But she didn't react. The demon grinned and thrust a talon into the rat; it squirmed and squealed and fell silent.

"You killed it, you eat it," Bridget said in Sumerian.

"As you command."

She closed her eyes and focused on the buckle. The metal was faintly warm against her skin. Bridget was cold everywhere else. The temperature was in the low teens, snow was falling and had been since the funeral. The forecast suggested the city would get ten to twelve inches over the next two days. Despite the weather, more than two hundred had showed up for the reception in the restaurant. Perhaps they came for the free food—good Italian food that Otter had requested. Certainly some had shown up simply out of respect for Otter. His girlfriend and her parents were inside. Lacy, right? A pretty girl. Bridget had only briefly talked to them before she came out here. Even Adiella was inside. Bridget saw the witch inspect the kitchen before sitting at a table to eat.

"Tell me a little," she coaxed the buckle, dipping her senses inside. She was prepared for it to wholly sap her, as it had before. The effort tugged considerable energy from her, but it was not as taxing as her first foray.

Perhaps because she wasn't trying to go as far back.

Bridget watched Elijah Stone take the briefcase from a man who appeared unaware during a high spell in pedestrian traffic outside of Grand Central Station. Stone's steps were light as he hurried away, giddy at his acquisition. In less than a day he saw the demon.

"Command me, master," Ijul had said in Sumerian.

Stone, unable to understand it, looked horrified.

"Command me, master," Ijul repeated.

Bridget saw the demon's eyes glimmer, perhaps with the realization that Stone could not understand it.

"As my master before me," Ijul continued, "you ignore me. I will rip out the hearts of your loved ones, master. I detest you. Free me, master. Free all the Aldî-nîfaeti in this world. Command me, no? Then I am free to act."

And so the slaying of Stone's loved ones began, and the beast's babbling became threatening. "I will rip out the heart of your mother unless you free the Aldî-nîfaeti, master. I will—"

Bridget nudged her mind farther back, saw the man Stone had stolen the briefcase from, saw the man who had owned it before that. Earlier a disheveled woman had it, though it was affixed to a worn purse then. The woman had found the buckle near a railroad track in a southern state—cannas and butterfly lilies were thick along road, and Bridget caught a whiff of fragrance. Before that woman, another man owned it; he'd carried the buckle in his pocket and had committed suicide on the track when he couldn't bear to have another of his loved ones slaughtered. Back and back, Bridget sent her senses, the faces of the previous owners flashing in a corner of her mind.

Usually the buckle passed from hand to hand by thievery;

someone coveting the shiny trinket, but sometimes a misfortunate soul simply came upon it because the owner could not live with the demon and so killed him or herself and left the buckle abandoned. The owners' faces were careworn, beautiful, young, old, black, white, Hispanic, Asian, male, female. One had been a boy of eight or ten.

Always death was linked. Although Ijul's penchant for eating the hearts of loved ones was not as pronounced or frequent the farther back she looked. Perhaps the demon discovered through the decades that if its owner would not issue commands, it was free to wreck havoc, to threaten and demand the release of its hellish brethren. Perhaps it simply got more brutal and hungry through the years.

"Farther," Bridget coaxed. Her face felt numb from the cold, and she briefly thought about retreating inside to the kitchen, where it was warm and the smell of the Italian food would combat the stench of Ijul and the foulness of the alley. But she needed to be alone for this.

Cars passed by out on the street, their tires slushing up snow, rap music spilling from the open window where one driver didn't seem to mind the bone-numbing chill. A siren wailed, crescendoed, and then cut to nothing; probably a simple traffic stop. Laughter came from out on the sidewalk, people leaving the restaurant.

Bridget let it all drift to the background and thrust her concentration farther into the buckle and felt her throat go dry and a familiar headache sprout behind her eyes. It had never been a buckle, that's just what she called it because it looked like a buckle on a briefcase. She discovered it had originally been a decoration on some burial effigy, discovered in Iran before oil and religion turned the land into a warzone—touched by gloved hands, never human skin. That had been the trigger, the touch of skin. The effigy also had been in a museum, not a big one, a small building in a small city where children and their mothers came to look at artifacts that had been dug up locally. Bridget watched Ijul sleeping at the base of the exhibit, bound to the buckle, eyelids twitching as if caught in some malevolent dream.

The effigy was stolen—finally touched by human hands, sold but continued to come back to the thief until someone in turn stole it

299

from him. Later it ended up in a British museum, stolen again, finding its way to California, where its owner died and a relative pulled the buckle off the effigy and added it to other belongings. With each owner, Ijul had tried to communicate without success.

"Farther." Bridget wanted to go back to the beginning, where she'd watched the woman forge the metal into its odd shape. She'd had to back off when she'd done this before, the effort too taxing when she'd already been so tired.

The cold of the alley was keeping her awake, and her deter-mination was riding out the pain caused by the mental link. In her mind's eye she was back in the ancient metallurgist's workshop, at the woman's shoulder.

Was this in Hilimaz's day?

Didn't have the same feel, and so Bridget guessed it was farther back in time than when she'd stayed with Hilimaz, judging by the home's construction and the tools. Though just how long in the past she couldn't tell.

"Ninlil, I have done as you said." The woman bowed before a figure in the doorway. The woman had the voice of someone who drank and smoke, rough and interesting. Bridget watched the scene play out. "Ninlil, I have followed your perfect instructions." Flames from her fireplace stretched out to show the figure the woman addressed. It was only vaguely human-looking, and Bridget guessed it was the mysterious figure she had half-glimpsed on her first foray. "Praise to Ninlil," the woman continued.

Ninlil stepped into the fireplace light. She was tall and thin, skin a glistening pale blue with darker blue veins visible behind it. She had three fingers on each hand, long and slender like bird talons. Her head was bird-shaped, too, with a small beak for a mouth and white feathers for hair.

Ninlil.

Bridget had heard the name before. Ninlil ... she had read it when she'd searched the Internet for Enlil, the Sumerian god who taught his chosen how to capture demons. Ninlil was the goddess he'd raped and so

300

found himself banished to hell for a time. Ninlil was inhumanly beautiful. But Bridget doubted she was a god. A creature, yes, Bridget would believe that, maybe a demon. Certainly something with magic. Maybe a witch.

Ninlil stretched out a talon and touched the buckle, made a chirping sound like a bird. The buckle glowed bright blue with motes of light dancing around it.

Finally the bird-woman spoke. "My brother Enlil teaches his followers how to banish demons. Se-Kol-trem, I teach you how to harness them. Bind one to your soul and take its power. Become invincible and strong. Command it and nurture it. This city will be yours."

The metallurgist bowed deeper, brought the glowing buckle to her lips and kissed it.

"You can give this to no one," Ninlil continued. "Do you understand? It can never be given away."

"No, I would never give it away," Se-Kol-trem returned. "I understand."

Hence why the owner was stuck with it, Bridget surmised. Part of the magic was that it could not be *given* away. But apparently Ninlil hadn't thought of theft. Maybe thievery was not such a consideration then.

"I will call a demon tonight," Se-Kol-trem said. "I will become invincible. I will take this city."

Ninlil's beak worked into what Bridget guessed was a smile. Her eyes sparkled with bright motes. Then she vanished.

Bridget watched the metallurgist summon one demon after the next, using spells similar to what Hillimaz had used, dismissing each one except Ijul, the smallest of the lot, who she bound to the buckle. She'd seemed to find Ijul acceptable. Se-Kol trem bent over and patted Ijul's warty head, and the two plotted late into the evening about how they would crush her enemies.

"Free the Aldî-nîfaeti," Ijul begged her. "As Enlil has taught others to catch them, Ninlil wants them released. Together, we will take this country. Free the Aldî-nîfaeti."

"We will free all the Aldî-nîfaeti," Se-Kol trem purred. "The ones caught, and the ones others are catching now. We will free them all."

Bridget felt sick to her stomach, sensed the evil swirl around the woman and her pet demon. She fast-forwarded the image and witnessed Se-Kol trem and Ijul lead a dozen of the vile Aldî-nîfaeti against the city's primitive guards. Blood and fire rushed across the streets, and everywhere there was death.

Even Se-Kol trem died, not as invincible as she'd believed. It took a strong force of men armed with spears to finally bring her down. Her body was a pincushion, and yet still she thrashed, Ijul ripping out the hearts of her attackers. One strong man thrust his spear through her forehead, ending the woman's plans. The freed demons continued the slaughter and Bridget pushed time forward to get past the slaughter.

Se-Kol trem was buried with others in a mass grave, the buckle on a leather strap around her neck buried with her. No one had thought to take it … and thereby unwittingly take on Ijul.

Centuries passed in the blink of Bridget's eye, and the archaeologists came and uncovered Se-Kol-trem's skeleton and the buckle. A gloved hand reached in and took it, and later affixed it to an effigy they'd acquired from another dig and that seemed to be missing its ornamentation.

"And eventually you ended up with me," Bridget said. She disconnected her senses from the buckle and put it in her pocket. "So what the hell do I do with you?" Bridget looked next to the Dumpster, where Ijul was eating another rat.

"Free the Aldî-nîfaeti," Ijul said.

"You know that ain't feckin' happening." Bridget stood and worked a kink out of her neck.

"Where are we going, master?"

"Inside," she told the demon. "I'm hungry."

"Mmmmmmmmmmmm."

"I'll see that you get a heaping plate of Rigatoni con la Pajata." She looked down at the disgusting beast. "Then I guess you're going to Italy with us."

"It-tal-ee." The demon tried out the word then belched a cloud of noxiousness.

Bridget glanced out at the street as a taxi sloshed by. Streetlights made the pavement shiny, but snow was building up along the curbs.

There was more laughter, and a muted conversation, people out on the sidewalk beyond her line of sight. She heard another siren—always there were sirens in this city. It sounded desperate.

And then there was another and another, all muffled by the canyon of buildings.

OTHER BOOKS BY JEAN RABE PUBLISHED BY BOONE STREET PRESS

The Dead of Winter: A Piper Blackwell Mystery

The Dead of Night: A Piper Blackwell Mystery

The Dead of Summer: A Piper Blackwell Mystery

The Dead of Jerusalem Ridge: A Piper Blackwell Mystery

The Bone Shroud

Fenzig's Fortune

The Finest Creation

The Finest Choice

The Finest Challenge

ABOUT THE AUTHOR

I write...a lot.

And I write with dogs wrapped around my feet. I get to wear sandals or bedroom slippers to work, and old, comfortable clothes. When the weather is fine I get to write on my back porch. I love summer. I started getting published when I was twelve, studied journalism at Northern Illinois University, and then went to work as a news reporter...eventually for Scripps Howard, where I managed their Western Kentucky bureau. Getting itchy feet, I moved to Wisconsin and went to work for TSR, Inc., the then-producers of the Dungeons & Dragons game. I wrote Dragonlance tales for several years and reached the *USA Today's* Bestseller list with a few of them.

I've written more than forty novels (along with a couple of ghosted projects), more than a hundred short stories, and I've edited more magazines and anthologies than I care to count. I was honored to receive the Faust Award in 2020, the Grand Master award of the International Association of Media Tie-In Writers. My novel, *The Bone Shroud*, won the 2019 Soon To Be Famous Illinois Author Project competition, voted on by librarian judges across the state. I was presented the award in the adult fiction category at the Illinois Library Association annual conference.

Consider signing up for my monthly newsletter at my website: jeanrabe.com. Friend or follow me on Facebook and Twitter. I try to answer all the emails I receive.

Visit me at jeanrabe.com or at these other awesome places
Amazon – https://www.amazon.com/Jean-Rabe
Bookbub - https://www.bookbub.com/authors/jean-rabe
Facebook – https://www.facebook.com/jeanrabeauthor/
Twitter – https://twitter.com/jeanerabe

OTHER BOOKS BY JEAN RABE PUBLISHED BY BOONE STREET PRESS

The Dead of Winter

The Dead of Night

The Dead of Summer

The Dead of Jerusalem Ridge

The Bone Shroud

Fenzig's Fortune

The Finest Creation

The Finest Choice

The Finest Challenge